GRAND CENTRAL
PUBLISHING

LARGE
PRINT

# WHITE FIRE

DOUGLAS PRESTON
& LINCOLN CHILD

GRAND CENTRAL
PUBLISHING

## LARGE PRINT

Copyright © 2013 by Splendide Mendax, Inc. and Lincoln Child
All rights reserved. In accordance with the U.S. Copyright Act of 1976, the scanning, uploading, and electronic sharing of any part of this book without the permission of the publisher is unlawful piracy and theft of the authors' intellectual property. If you would like to use material from the book (other than for review purposes), prior written permission must be obtained by contacting the publisher at permissions@hbgusa.com. Thank you for your support of the authors' rights.

Grand Central Publishing
Hachette Book Group
237 Park Avenue
New York, NY 10017

HachetteBookGroup.com

Printed in the United States of America

RRD-C

First Edition: November 2013
10 9 8 7 6 5 4 3 2 1

Grand Central Publishing is a division of Hachette Book Group, Inc.
The Grand Central Publishing name and logo is a trademark of Hachette Book Group, Inc.

The Hachette Speakers Bureau provides a wide range of authors for speaking events. To find out more, go to www.hachettespeakersbureau.com or call (866) 376-6591.

The publisher is not responsible for websites (or their content) that are not owned by the publisher.

Library of Congress Cataloging-in-Publication Data
Preston, Douglas J.
   White fire / Douglas Preston & Lincoln Child. — First edition.
      pages cm
   ISBN 978-1-4555-2583-6 (hardcover) — ISBN 978-1-4555-7623-4 (large print hardcover) — ISBN 978-1-61969-461-3 (audio download) — ISBN 978-1-4555-2585-0 (ebook)
   1. Pendergast, Aloysius (Fictitious character)—Fiction. I. Child, Lincoln, author. II. Title.
PS3566.R3982W45 2013
813'.54—dc23

2013005680

ISBN 978-1-4555-5363-1 (international paperback)

*Grateful acknowledgment to Conan Doyle Estate Ltd.*
*for permission to use the Sherlock Holmes characters*
*created by the late*
*Sir Arthur Conan Doyle.*

*Lincoln Child dedicates this book to his daughter,*
VERONICA

*Douglas Preston dedicates this book to*
DAVID MORRELL

# WHITE
# FIRE

# PROLOGUE:
## A TRUE STORY

*August 30, 1889*

The young doctor bid his wife good-bye on the Southsea platform, boarded the 4:15 express for London, and arrived three hours later at Victoria Station. Threading his way through the noise and bustle, he exited the station and flagged down a hansom cab.

"The Langham Hotel, if you please," he told the driver as he stepped up into the compartment, flushed with a feeling of anticipation.

He sat back in the worn leather seat as the cabbie started down Grosvenor Place. It was a fine late-summer evening, the rarest kind in London, with a dying light falling through the carriage-choked streets and sooty buildings, enchanting everything with a golden radiance. At half past seven the lamps were only just starting to be lit.

The doctor did not often get the chance to come up to London, and he looked out the window of the hansom cab with interest. As the driver turned right onto Piccadilly, he took in St. James's Palace and the Royal Academy, bathed in the afterglow of sunset. The crowds, noise, and stench of the city, so different from his home countryside, filled him with energy. Countless horseshoes rang out against the cobbles, and the sidewalks thronged with people from all walks of life: clerks, barristers, and swells rubbed shoulders with chimneysweeps, costermongers, and cat's-meat dealers.

At Piccadilly Circus, the cab took a sharp left onto Regent Street, passing Carnaby and the Oxford Circus before pulling up beneath the porte cochere of the Langham. It had been the first grand hotel erected in London, and it remained by far the most stylish. As he paid off the cabbie, the doctor glanced up at the ornate sandstone façade, with its French windows and balconies of wrought iron, its high gables and balustrades. He had a small interest in architecture, and he guessed the façade was a mixture of Beaux-Arts and North German Renaissance Revival.

As he entered the great portal, the sound of music reached him: a string quartet, hidden behind a screen of hothouse lilies, playing Schubert. He paused to take in the magnificent lobby, crowded with men seated in tall-backed chairs, reading freshly ironed copies of *The Times* and drinking port or sherry. Expensive cigar smoke hung in the air, mingling with the scent of flowers and ladies' perfume.

At the entrance to the dining room, he was met by a small, rather portly man in a broadcloth frock coat and dun-colored trousers, who approached him with brisk steps. "You must be Doyle," he said, taking his hand. He had a bright smile and a broad American accent. "I'm Joe Stoddart. So glad you could make it. Come in—the others just arrived."

The doctor followed Stoddart as the man made his way among linen-covered tables to a far corner of the room. The restaurant was even more opulent than the lobby, with wainscoting of olive-stained oak, a cream-colored frieze, and an ornate ceiling of raised plasterwork. Stoddart stopped beside a sumptuous table at which two men were already seated.

"Mr. William Gill, Mr. Oscar Wilde," Stoddart said. "Allow me to introduce Dr. A. Conan Doyle."

Gill—whom Doyle recognized as a well-known Irish MP—stood and bowed with good-humored gravitas. A heavy gold Albert watch chain swayed across his ample waistcoat. Wilde, who was in the midst of taking a glass of wine, dabbed at his rather full lips with a damask napkin and motioned Conan Doyle toward the empty chair beside him.

"Mr. Wilde was just entertaining us with the story of a tea party he attended this afternoon," Stoddart said as they took their seats.

"At Lady Featherstone's," Wilde said. "She was recently widowed. Poor dear—her hair has gone quite gold from grief."

"Oscar," Gill said with a laugh, "you really are wicked. Talking about a lady in such a manner."

Wilde waved his hand dismissively. "My lady would thank me. There is only one thing in the world worse than being talked about, and that is not being talked about." He spoke rapidly, in a low, mannered voice.

Doyle examined Wilde with a covert look. The man was striking. Almost gigantic in stature, he had unfashionably long hair parted in the middle and carelessly thrown back, his facial features heavy. His choice of clothing was of an eccentricity bordering on madness. He wore a suit of black velvet that fitted tightly to his large frame, the sleeves embroidered in flowery designs and puffed at the shoulders. Around his neck he had donned a narrow, three-rowed frill of the same brocaded material as the sleeves. He had the sartorial audacity to sport knee breeches, equally tight fitting, with stockings of black silk and slippers with grosgrain bows. A *boutonnière* of an immense white orchid drooped pendulously from his fawn-colored vest, looking as if it might dribble nectar at any moment. Heavy gold rings glittered on the fingers of his indolent hands. Despite the idiosyncrasy of his clothing, the expression on his face was mild, balancing the keen quality of his eager brown eyes. And for all this the man displayed a remarkable delicacy of feeling and tact. He spoke in a curious precision of statement, with a unique trick of small gestures to illustrate his meaning.

"You're most kind to be treating us out like this, Stoddart," Wilde was saying. "At the Langham, no less. I'd have been left to my own devices otherwise. It's not that I want for supper money, of course. It is only people who pay their bills who lack money, you see, and I never pay mine."

"I fear you'll find my motives are completely mercenary," Stoddart replied. "You might as well know that I'm over here to establish a British edition of *Lippincott's Monthly*."

"Philadelphia not large enough for you, then?" Gill asked.

Stoddart chuckled, then looked at Wilde and Doyle in turn. "It is my intention, before this meal is complete, to secure a new novel from each of you."

Hearing this, a current of excitement coursed through Doyle. In his telegram, Stoddart had been vague about the reasons for asking him to come to London for dinner, but the man was a well-known American publisher and this was exactly what Doyle had been hoping to hear. His medical practice had had a slower start than he would have liked. To fill the time, he'd taken to scribbling novels while waiting for patients. His last few had met with a small success. Stoddart was precisely the man he needed to further his progress. Doyle found him pleasant, even charming—for an American.

The dinner was proving delightful.

Gill was an amusing fellow, but Oscar Wilde was nothing short of remarkable. Doyle was captivated by the graceful wave of his hands; the languid expression that became quite animated when he delivered his peculiar anecdotes or amusing *bons mots*. It was almost magical, Doyle considered, that—thanks to modern technology—he'd been transported in a few short hours from a sleepy seacoast town to this elegant place, surrounded by an eminent editor, a member of Parliament, and the famous champion of aestheticism.

The dishes came thick and fast: potted shrimps, galantine of chicken, tripe fried in batter, *bisque de homard*. Red and yellow wine had appeared at the beginning of the evening, and the generous flow never ceased. It was astonishing how much money the Americans had; Stoddart was spending a fortune.

The timing was excellent. Doyle had just begun a new novel that Stoddart would surely like. His penultimate story, *Micah Clarke*, had been favorably reviewed, although his most recent novel, about a detective, based in part on his old university professor Joseph Bell, had been rather disappointingly received after appearing in *Beeton's Christmas Annual*...He forced himself back to the conversation at hand. Gill, the Irish MP, was questioning the veracity of the maxim that the good fortune of one's friends made one discontented.

Hearing this, a gleam appeared in Wilde's eyes. "The devil," he replied, "was once crossing the desert, and he came upon a spot where a number of fiends were tormenting a holy hermit. The man easily shook off their evil suggestions. The devil watched their failure and then stepped forward to give them a lesson. 'What you do is too crude,' said he. 'Permit me for one moment.' With that he whispered to the holy man, 'Your brother has just been made bishop of Alexandria.' A scowl of malignant jealousy at once clouded the serene face of the hermit. 'That,' said the devil to his imps, 'is the sort of thing which I should recommend.'"

Stoddart and Gill laughed heartily, then began to fall into an argument about politics. Wilde turned to Doyle. "You must tell me," he said. "Will you do a book for Stoddart?"

"I was rather thinking I would. The fact is, I've started work on a new novel already. I was thinking of calling it *A Tangled Skein*, or perhaps *The Sign of the Four*."

Wilde pressed his hands together in delight. "My dear fellow, that's wonderful news. I certainly hope it will be another Holmes story."

Doyle looked at him in surprise. "You mean to say you've read *A Study in Scarlet*?"

"I didn't read it, dear boy. I *devoured* it." Reaching into his vest, Wilde pulled out a copy of the Ward Lock & Co. edition of the book, with its vaguely Oriental lettering so in vogue. "I even looked through it again when I heard you would be dining with us this evening."

"You're very kind," Conan Doyle said, at a loss for a better reply. He found himself surprised and gratified that the prince of English decadence would enjoy a humble detective novel.

"I feel you have the makings of a great character in Holmes. But..." And here Wilde stopped.

"Yes?" Doyle said.

"What I found most remarkable was the *credibility* of the thing. The details of the police work, Holmes's inquiries, were enlightening. I have much to learn from you in this way. You see, between me and life there is a mist of words always. I throw probability out of the window for the sake of a phrase, and the chance of an epigram makes me desert truth. You don't share that failing. And yet...and yet I believe you could do more with this Holmes of yours."

"I would be much obliged if you'd explain," Doyle said.

Wilde took a sip of wine. "If he's to be a truly great detective, a great *persona*, he should be more eccentric. The world doesn't need another Sergeant Cuff or Inspector Dupin. No—make his humanity aspire to the greatness of his art." He paused a moment, thinking, idly stroking the orchid that drooped from his buttonhole. "In *Scarlet*, you call Watson 'extremely lazy.' In my opinion, you should allow the virtues of dissipation and idleness to be bestowed on your hero, not his errand boy. And make Holmes more reserved. Don't have *delight shining on his features*, or have him *barking with laughter*."

Doyle colored, recognizing the infelicitous phraseology.

"You must confer on him a vice," Wilde went on. "Virtuous people are so banal; I simply cannot bear them." He paused again. "Not just a vice, Doyle—give him a *weakness*. Let me think—ah, yes! I recall." He opened his copy of *A Study in*

*Scarlet*, leafed quickly through the pages, found a passage, and began to quote Dr. Watson: "'I might have suspected him of being addicted to the use of some narcotic, had not the temperance and cleanliness of his whole life forbidden such a notion.'" He returned the book to his vest pocket. "There—you had the perfect weakness in your hands, but you let it go. Pluck it up again! Deliver Holmes into the clutches of some addiction. Opium, say. But no: opium is so dreadfully common these days, it's become quite overrun by the lower classes." Suddenly Wilde snapped his fingers. "I have it! Cocaine hydrochloride. There's a novel and elegant vice for you."

"Cocaine," Doyle repeated a little uncertainly. As a doctor, he had sometimes prescribed a seven percent solution to patients suffering from exhaustion or depression, but the idea of making Holmes an addict was, on the face of it, quite absurd. Although Doyle had asked for Wilde's opinion, he found himself slightly put out at actually receiving criticism from the man. Across the table, the good-humored argument between Stoddart and Gill continued.

The aesthete took another sip of wine and tossed his hair back.

"And what about you?" Doyle asked. "Will you do a book for Stoddart?"

"I shall. And it shall be under your influence—or rather, Holmes's influence—that I will proceed. Do you know, I've always believed there's no such thing as a moral or immoral book. Books are well written or badly written—that's all. But I find myself taken with the idea of writing a book about both art *and* morals. I'm planning to call it *The Picture of Dorian Gray*. And do you know, I believe it will be rather a ghastly story. Not a ghost story, exactly, but one in which the protagonist comes to a beastly end. The kind of story one wishes to read by daylight—not lamplight."

"Such a story doesn't seem to be exactly in your line."

Wilde looked at Doyle with something like amusement. "Indeed? Did you think that—as one who would happily sacrifice himself on the pyre of aestheticism—I do not recognize the face of horror when I stare into it? Let me tell you: the shudder of fear is as sensual as the shudder of pleasure, if not more so." He underscored this with another wave of his hand. "Besides, I was once told a story so dreadful, so distressing in its particulars and in the extent of its evil, that now I truly believe nothing I hear could ever frighten me again."

"How interesting," Doyle replied a little absently, still mulling over the criticism of Holmes.

Wilde regarded him, a small smile forming on

his large, pale features. "Would you care to hear it? It is not for the faint of heart."

The way Wilde phrased this, it sounded like a challenge. "By all means."

"It was told to me during my lecture tour of America a few years back. On my way to San Francisco, I stopped at a rather squalid yet picturesque mining camp known as Roaring Fork. I gave my lecture at the bottom of their mine, and it was frightfully well received by the good gentlemen of the camp. After my lecture, one of the miners approached me, an elderly chap somewhat the worse—or, perhaps, the better—for drink. He took me aside, said he'd enjoyed my story so much that he had one of his own to share with me."

Wilde paused, wetting his thick, red lips with a delicate sip of wine. "Here, lean in a little closer, that's a good fellow, and I'll tell it you exactly as it was told to me..."

Ten minutes later, a diner at the restaurant in the Langham Hotel would have been surprised to note—amid the susurrus of genteel conversation and the tinkle of cutlery—a young man in the dress of a country doctor abruptly rise from his table, very pale. Knocking over his chair in his agitation, one hand to his forehead, the man staggered from the room, nearly upsetting a waiter's tray of delicacies. And as he vanished in the direction of the gentlemen's toilet area, his face displayed a perfect expression of revulsion and horror.

# I

*Present Day*

Corrie Swanson stepped into the ladies' room for the third time to check how she looked. A lot had changed with her since she'd transferred to the John Jay College of Criminal Justice at the beginning of her sophomore year. John Jay was a buttoned-down place. She had resisted it for a while, but finally realized she needed to grow up and play the game of life instead of acting the rebel forever. Gone were the purple hair, the piercings, the black leather jacket, the dark eye shadow and other Goth accoutrements. There was nothing she could do about the Möbius strip tattoo on the nape of her neck, beyond combing her hair back and wearing high collars. But someday, she realized, that would have to go as well.

If she was going to play the game, she was going to play it well.

Unfortunately, her personal transformation had taken place too late for her advisor, a former NYPD cop who had gone back to school and turned professor. She got the feeling his first impression of her had been that of a perp, and nothing she'd done in the year since she'd first met him had erased that. Clearly, he had it in for her. He had already rejected her first proposal for the Rosewell thesis, which involved a trip to Chile to do a perimortem analysis on skeletal remains discovered in a mass grave of Communist peasants murdered by the Pinochet regime back in the 1970s. Too far away, he said, too expensive for a research project, and besides it was old history. When Corrie replied that this was the point—these were old graves, requiring specialized forensic techniques—he said something about not involving herself in foreign political controversies, especially Communist ones.

Now she had another idea for her thesis, an even better one, and she was willing to do almost anything to see it happen.

Examining herself in the mirror, she rearranged a few strands of hair, touched up her conservative lipstick, adjusted her gray worsted suit jacket, and gave her nose a quick powdering. She hardly recognized herself; God, she might even be mistaken for a Young Republican. So much the better.

She exited the ladies' room and walked briskly down the hall, her conservative pumps clicking professionally against the hard linoleum. Her advisor's door was shut, as usual, and she gave it a brisk, self-confident rap. A voice inside said, "Come in."

She entered. The office was, as always, neat as a pin, the books and journals all lined up flush with the edges of the bookshelves, the comfortable, masculine leather furniture providing a cozy air. Professor Greg Carbone sat behind his large desk, its acreage of burnished mahogany unbroken by books, papers, family photographs, or knickknacks.

"Good morning, Corrie," Carbone said, rising and buttoning his blue serge suit. "Please sit down."

"Thank you, Professor." She knew he liked to be called that. Woe to the student who called him Mister or, worse, Greg.

He settled back down as she did. Carbone was a strikingly handsome man with salt-and-pepper hair, wonderful teeth, trim and fit, a good dresser, articulate, soft-spoken, intelligent, and successful. Everything he did, he did well, and as a result he was an accomplished asshole indeed.

"Well, Corrie," Carbone began, "you are looking well today."

"Thank you, Dr. Carbone."

"I'm excited to hear about your new idea."

"Thanks." Corrie opened her briefcase (no backpacks at John Jay) and took out a manila file folder, placing it on her knee. "I'm sure you've been reading about the archaeological investigation going on down in City Hall Park. Next to the location of the old prison known as the Tombs."

"Tell me about it."

"The parks department has been excavating a small cemetery of executed criminals to make way for a new subway entrance."

"Ah yes, I did read about that," said Carbone.

"The cemetery was operational from 1858 to 1865. After 1865, all execution burials were moved to Hart Island and remain unavailable."

A slow nod from Carbone. He looked interested; she felt encouraged.

"I think this would make for a great opportunity to do an osteological study of those skeletons—to see if severe childhood malnourishment, which as you know leaves osteological markers, might correlate with later criminal behavior."

Another nod from Carbone.

"I've got it all outlined here." She laid a proposal

on the table. "Hypotheses, methodology, control group, observations, and analysis."

Carbone laid a hand on the document, drew it toward himself, opened it, and began perusing.

"There are a number of reasons why this is a great opportunity," she went on. "First, the city has good records on most of these executed criminals—names, rap sheets, and trial records. Those who were orphans raised in the Five Points House of Industry—about half a dozen—also have some childhood records. They were all executed in the same way—hanging—so the cause of death is identical. And the cemetery was used for only seven years, so all the remains come from roughly the same time period."

She paused. Carbone was slowly turning over the pages, one after another, apparently reading. There was no way to tell what he was thinking; his face was a blank.

"I made a few inquiries, and it seems the parks department would be open to having a John Jay student examine the remains."

The slow turning of the pages paused. "You already contacted them?"

"Yes. Just a feeler—"

"A feeler…You contacted another city agency without seeking prior permission?"

*Uh-oh.* "Obviously I didn't want to bring you a

project that might get shot down later by outside authorities. Um, was that wrong?"

A long silence, and then: "Did you not read your undergraduate handbook?"

Corrie was seized with apprehension. She had in fact read it—when she'd been admitted. But that was over a year ago. "Not recently."

"The handbook is quite clear. Undergraduate students are not to engage other city departments except through official channels. This is because we're a city institution, as you know, a senior college of the City University of New York." He said this mildly, almost kindly.

"I...Well, I'm sorry, I didn't recall that from the handbook." She swallowed, feeling a rising panic—and anger. This was such unbelievable bullshit. But she forced herself to keep her cool. "It was just a couple of phone calls, nothing official."

A nod. "I'm sure you didn't *deliberately* violate university regulations." He began turning the pages again, slowly, one after the other, not looking up at her. "But in any case I find other problems with this thesis proposal of yours."

"Yes?" Corrie felt sick.

"This idea that malnourishment leads to a life of crime...It's an old idea—and an unconvincing one."

"Well, it seems to me worth testing."

"Back then, almost everyone was malnourished. But not everyone became a criminal. And the idea is redolent of...how shall I put it?...of a certain philosophy that crime in general can be traced to unfortunate experiences in a person's childhood."

"But malnourishment—severe malnourishment—might cause neurological changes, actual damage. That isn't philosophy; that's science."

Carbone held up her proposal. "I can already predict the outcome: you'll discover that these executed criminals *were* malnourished as children. The *real* question is why, of all those hungry children, only a small percentage went on to commit capital crimes. And your research plan does not address that. I'm sorry, this won't fly. Not at all."

And, opening his fingers, he let her document drop gently to his desk.

## 2

The famous—some might say infamous—"Red Museum" at the John Jay College of Criminal Justice had started as a simple collection of old investigative files, physical evidence, prisoners' property, and memorabilia that, almost a hundred years ago, had been put into a display case in a hall at the old police academy. Since then, it had grown into one of the country's largest and best collections of criminal memorabilia. The crème de la crème of the collection was on display in a sleek new exhibition hall in the college's Skidmore, Owings & Merrill building on Tenth Avenue. The rest of the collection—vast rotting archives and moldering evidence from long-ago crimes—remained squirreled away in the hideous basement of the old police academy building on East Twentieth Street.

Early on at John Jay, Corrie had discovered this archive. It was pure gold—once she'd made friends with the archivist and figured out her way around the disorganized drawers and heaping shelves of stuff. She had been to the Red Museum archives many times in search of topics for papers and projects, most recently in her hunt for a topic for her Rosewell thesis. She had spent a great deal of time in the old unsolved-case files—those cold cases so ancient that all involved (including the possible perps) had definitely and positively died.

Corrie Swanson found herself in a creaking elevator, descending into the basement, one day after the meeting with her advisor. She was on a desperate mission to find a new thesis topic before it became too late to complete the approval process. It was mid-November already, and she was hoping to spend the winter break researching and writing up the thesis. She was on a partial scholarship, but Agent Pendergast had been making up the difference in tuition, and she was absolutely determined not to take one penny more from him than necessary. If her thesis won the Rosewell Prize, with its twenty-thousand-dollar grant, she wouldn't have to.

The elevator doors opened to a familiar smell: a mixture of dust and acidifying paper, underlain by an odor of rodent urine. She crossed the hall to a pair of dented metal doors, graced with a sign that said RED MUSEUM ARCHIVES, and pressed the bell.

An unintelligible rasp came out of the antiquated speaker; she gave her name, and a buzzer sounded to let her in.

"Corrie Swanson? How good to see you again!" came the hoarse voice of the archivist, Willard Bloom, as he rose from a desk in a pool of light, guarding the recesses of the storage room stretching off into the blackness behind him. He presented a rather cadaverous figure, stick-thin, with longish gray hair, yet underneath was charming and grandfatherly. She didn't mind the fact that his eyes often wandered over various parts of her anatomy when he thought she wasn't paying attention.

Bloom came around with a veined hand extended, which she took. The hand was surprisingly hot, and it gave her a bit of a start.

"Come, sit down. Have some tea."

Some chairs had been set around the front of his desk, with a coffee table and, to the side, a battered cabinet with a hot plate, kettle, and teapot, an informal seating area in the midst of dust and darkness. Corrie flopped into a chair, setting her briefcase down with a thump next to her. "Ugh," she said.

Bloom raised his eyebrows in mute inquiry.

"It's Carbone. Once again he rejected my thesis idea. Now I have to start all over again."

"Carbone," Bloom said in his high-pitched voice, "is a well-known ass."

This piqued her interest. "You know him?"

"I know everyone who comes down here. Carbone! Always fussing about getting dust on his Ralph Lauren suits, wanting me to play step-n-fetchit. As a result, I can never find anything for him, poor man...You know the real reason he keeps rejecting your thesis ideas, right?"

"I figure it's because I'm a junior."

Bloom put a finger to his nose and gave her a knowing nod. "Exactly. And Carbone is old school, a stickler for protocol."

Corrie had been afraid of this. The Rosewell Prize for the year's outstanding thesis was hugely coveted at John Jay. Its winners were often senior valedictorians, who went on to highly successful law enforcement careers. As far as she knew, it had never been won by a junior—in fact, juniors were quietly discouraged from submitting theses. But there was no rule against it, and Corrie refused to be deterred by such bureaucratic baggage.

Bloom held up the pot with a yellow-toothed smile. "Tea?"

She looked at the revolting teapot, which did not appear to have been washed in a decade. "That's a teapot? I thought it was a murder weapon. You know, loaded with arsenic and ready to go."

"Always ready with a riposte. But surely you know most poisoners are women? If I were a murderer, I'd want to see my victim's blood." He poured out the tea. "So Carbone rejected your idea. Surprise, surprise. What's plan B?"

"That *was* my plan B. I was hoping you might be able to give me some fresh ideas."

Bloom sat back in his chair and sipped noisily from his cup. "Let's see. As I recall, you're majoring in forensic osteology, are you not? What, exactly, are you looking for?"

"I need to examine some human skeletons that show antemortem or perimortem damage. Got any case files that might point to something like that?"

"Hmm." His battered face screwed up in concentration.

"The problem is, it's hard to come by accessible human remains. Unless I go prehistoric. But that opens up a whole other can of worms with Native American sensitivities. And I want remains for which there are good written records. *Historic* remains."

Bloom sucked down another goodly portion of tea, a thoughtful expression on his face. "Bones. Ante- or perimortem damage. Historic. Good records. Accessible." He closed his eyes, the lids so dark and veiny they looked like he might have been punched. Corrie waited, listening to the ticking sounds in the archives, the faint sound of forced air, and a pattering noise she feared was probably rats.

The eyes sprang open again. "Just thought of something. Ever heard of the Baker Street Irregulars?"

"No."

"It's a very exclusive club of Sherlock Holmes devotees. They have a dinner in New York every year, and they publish all sorts of Holmesian scholarship, all the while pretending that Holmes was a real person. Well, one of these fellows died a few years back, and his widow, not knowing what else to do, shipped his entire collection of Sherlockiana to us. Perhaps she didn't know that Holmes was a *fictional* detective, and we only deal in *nonfiction* here. At any rate, I've been dipping into it now and then. Lot of rubbish, mostly. But there was a copy in there of Doyle's diary—just a photocopy, unfortunately—and it made entertaining reading for an old man stuck in a thankless job in a dusty archive."

"And what did you find, exactly?"

"There was something in there about a man-eating bear."

Corrie frowned. "A man-eating bear? I'm not sure—"

"Come with me."

Bloom went to a bank of switches and struck them all with the flat of his palm, turning the archives into a flickering sea of fluorescent light. Corrie fancied she could hear the rats scurrying and squealing away as the tubes blinked on, one aisle after another.

She followed the archivist as he made his way down the long rows between dusty shelving and wooden cabinets with yellowed, handwritten labels, finally reaching an area in the back where library tables were piled with cardboard boxes. Three large boxes sat together, labeled BSI. Bloom went to one box, rummaged through it, hauled out an expandable folder, blew off the dust, and began sorting through the papers.

"Here we are." He held up an old photocopy. "Doyle's diary. Properly, of course, the man should be referred to as 'Conan Doyle,' but that's such a mouthful, isn't it?" In the dim light, he flipped through the pages, then began to read aloud:

...I was in London on literary business. Stoddart, the American, proved to be an excellent fellow, and had two others to dinner. They were Gill, a very entertaining Irish MP, and Oscar Wilde…

He paused, his voice dying into a mumble as he passed over some material, then rising again as he reached a passage he deemed important.

…The highlight of the evening, if I may call it that, was Wilde's account of his lecture tour in America. Hard to believe, perhaps, but the famed champion of aestheticism attracted huge interest in America, especially in the West, where in one place a group of uncouth miners gave him a standing ovation…

Corrie began to fidget. She had so little time to waste. She cleared her throat. "I'm not sure Oscar Wilde and Sherlock Holmes are quite what I'm looking for," she said politely. But Bloom continued to read, holding up his finger for attention, his reedy voice riding over her objections.

…Towards the close of the evening, Wilde, who had indulged a great deal in Stoddart's excellent claret, told me, sotto voce, a story of such singular horror, of such grotesque hideousness, that I had to excuse myself from the table. The story involved the killing and eating of eleven miners some years previous, purportedly by a monstrous "grizzled bear" in a mining camp called Roaring Fork. The actual details are so abhorrent I cannot bring myself to commit them to paper at this time, although the impression left on my mind was indelible and one that will, unfortunately, follow me to the grave.

He paused, taking a breath. "And there you have it. Eleven corpses, eaten by a grizzly bear. In Roaring Fork, no less."

"Roaring Fork? You mean the glitzy ski resort in Colorado?"

"The very one. It started life as a silver boomtown."

"When was this?"

"Wilde was there in 1881. So this business with the man-eating bear probably took place in the 1870s."

She shook her head. "And how am I supposed to turn this into a thesis?"

"Nearly a dozen skeletons, eaten by a bear? Surely they will display exquisite perimortem damage—tooth and claw marks, gnawing, crunching, biting, scraping, worrying." Bloom spoke these words with a kind of relish.

"I'm studying forensic criminology, not forensic bearology."

"Ah, but you know from your studies that many, if not most, skeletal remains from murder victims show animal damage. You should see the files we have on that. It can be very difficult to tell the difference between animal marks and those left by the murderer. As far as I can recall, no one has done a comprehensive study of perimortem bone damage of this kind. It would be a most original contribution to forensic science."

*Very true*, Corrie thought, surprised at Bloom's insight. *And come to think of it, what a fabulous and original subject for a thesis.*

Bloom went on. "I have little doubt at least some of the poor miners were buried in the historic Roaring Fork cemetery."

"See, that's a problem. I can't go digging up some historic cemetery looking for bear victims."

A yellow smile appeared on Bloom's face. "My dear Corrie, the only reason I brought this up at all was because of the fascinating little article in the *Times* this very morning! Didn't you see it?"

"No."

"The original 'boot hill' of Roaring Fork is now a stack of coffins in a ski equipment warehouse. You see, they're relocating the cemetery on account of development." He looked at her and winked, his smile broadening.

# 3

Along the Cote d'Azur in the South of France, on a bluff atop Cap Ferrat, a man in a black suit, surrounded by bougainvillea, rested on a stone balcony in the afternoon sun. It was warm for the time of year, and the sunlight gilded the lemon trees that crowded the balcony and descended the steep hill to the Mediterranean, ending in a strip of deserted white beach. Beyond could be seen a field of yachts at anchor, the rocky terminus of the cape topped by an ancient castle, behind which ran the blue horizon.

The man reclined in a chaise longue covered with silk damask, beside a small table on which sat a salver. His silvery eyes were half closed. Four items sat on the tray: a copy of Spenser's *Faerie Queene*; a small glass of pastis; a beaker of water; and a single unopened letter. The salver had been brought out two hours ago by a manservant, who now awaited further orders in the shade of the portico. The man who had rented the villa rarely received mail. A few letters bore the return address of one Miss Constance Greene in New York; the rest came from what appeared to be an exclusive boarding school in Switzerland.

As time passed, the manservant began to wonder whether the sickly gentleman who had hired him at excessively high wages might have suffered a heart attack—so motionless had he been these past few hours. But no—a languid hand now moved, reaching for the beaker of water. It poured a small measure into the glass of pastis, turning the yellow liquid a cloudy yellowish green. The man then raised the glass and took a long, slow drink before replacing it on the tray.

Stillness returned, and the shadows of afternoon grew longer. More time passed. The hand moved again, as if in slow motion, again raising the cut-crystal glass to pale lips, taking another long, lingering sip of the liqueur. He then picked up the book of poetry. More silence as the man appeared to read, turning the pages at long intervals, one after another. The afternoon light blazed its last glory on the façade of the villa. From below, the sounds of life filtered upward: a distant clash of voices raised in argument, the throbbing of a yacht as it moved in the bay, birds chattering among the trees, the faint sound of a piano playing Hanon.

And now the man in the black suit closed the book of poetry, laid it upon the salver, and turned his attention to the letter. Still moving as if underwater, he plucked it up and, with a long, polished nail, slit it open, unfolded it, and began to read.

*Nov. 27*

*Dear Aloysius,*

*I'm mailing this to you c/o Proctor, in hopes he'll pass it along. I know you're still traveling and probably don't want to be bothered, but you've been gone almost a year and I figured maybe you were about ready to come home. Aren't you itching by now to end your leave of absence from the FBI and start solving murders again? And anyway, I just had to tell you about my thesis project. Believe it or not, I'm off to Roaring Fork, Colorado!*

*I got the most amazing idea for a thesis. I'll try to be brief because I know how impatient you are, but to explain I do have to go into a little history. In 1873, silver was discovered in the mountains over the Continental Divide from Leadville, Colorado. A mining camp sprang up in the valley, called Roaring Fork after the river flowing through* it, and the surrounding mountains became dotted with claims. In May of 1876, a rogue grizzly bear killed and ate a miner at a remote claim in the mountains—and for the rest of the summer the bear totally terrorized the area. The town sent out a number of hunting teams to track and kill it, to no avail, as the mountains were extremely rugged and remote. By the time the rampage stopped, eleven miners had been mauled and horribly eaten. It was a big deal at the time, with a lot of local newspaper articles (that's how I learned these details), sheriff's reports, and such. But Roaring Fork was remote and the story died pretty quickly once the killings stopped.

The miners were buried in the Roaring Fork cemetery, and their fate was pretty much forgotten. The mines closed up, Roaring Fork dwindled in population, and in time it almost became a ghost town. Then, in 1946, it was bought up by investors and turned into a ski resort—and now of course it's one of the fanciest resorts in the world—average home price over four million!

So that's the history. This fall, the original Roaring Fork cemetery was dug up to make way for development. All the remains are *now stacked in an old equipment shed high up on the ski slopes while everyone argues about what to do with them. A hundred and thirty coffins—of which eight are the remains of miners killed by the grizzly. (The other three were either lost or never recovered.)*

*Which brings me to my thesis topic:*

## *A Comprehensive Analysis of Perimortem Trauma in the Skeletons of Eight Miners Killed by a Grizzly Bear, from a Historic Colorado Cemetery*

*There has never been a large-scale study of perimortem trauma on human bones inflicted by a large carnivore. Ever! You see, it isn't often that people are eaten by animals. Mine will be the first!!*

*My thesis advisor, Prof. Greg Carbone, rejected my two earlier topics, and I'm glad the bastard did, if you'll excuse my language. He would have rejected this one, too, for reasons I won't bore you with, but I decided to take a page out of your book. I got my sweaty hands on Carbone's personnel file. I knew the man was too perfect to be real. Some years back, he'd been boning an undergraduate student in one of his classes—and then was dumb enough to flunk her when she broke it off. So she complained, not about the sex, but the bad grade. No laws were broken (the girl was twenty), but the scumbag gave her an F when she deserved an A. It was all hushed up, the girl got her A and had her tuition "refunded" for the year—a way of paying her off without calling it that, no doubt.*

*You can find anybody these days, so I tracked her down and gave her a call. Her name's Molly Denton and she's now a cop in Worcester, Mass.—a decorated lieutenant in the homicide department, no less. Boy, did she give me the lowdown on my advisor! So I went into the meeting with Carbone armed with a couple of nukes, just in case.*

*I wish you'd been there. It was beautiful. Before I even got into my new thesis idea, I mentioned all nice and polite that we had a mutual acquaintance: Molly Denton. And I gave him a big fat smirk, just to make sure he got the message. He went all pale. He couldn't wait to change the subject back to my thesis, wanted to hear about it, listened attentively, instantly agreed it was the most marvelous thesis proposal he'd heard in years, and promised he would personally shepherd it through the faculty committee.*

*And then—this is the best part—he sug-
gested I leave "as soon as possible" for Roaring Fork. The guy was butter in my hands.*

*Winter break just started, and so I'm off
to Roaring Fork in two days! Wish me well.
And if you feel like it, write me back c/o your
pal Proctor, who will have my forwarding address as soon as I know it.*

*Love,*

*Corrie*

*P.S. I almost forgot to tell you one of the
best things about my thesis idea. Believe it
or not, I first learned about the grizzly bear
killings from the diary of Arthur Conan
Doyle! Doyle heard it himself from no less
than Oscar Wilde at a dinner party in London in 1889. It seems Wilde was a collector
of horrible stories, and he'd picked up this one
on a lecture tour of the American West.*

The manservant, standing in the shadows,
watched his peculiar employer finish reading the
letter. The long, white fingers seemed to droop,
and the letter slid to the table, as if discarded. As
the hand moved to pick up the glass of pastis, the
evening breeze gently lofted the papers and wafted
them over the railing of the balcony, over the tops
of the lemon trees; then they went gliding off into

blue space, fluttering and turning aimlessly until they had vanished from view, unseen, unnoticed, and completely disregarded by the pale man in the black suit, sitting on a lonely balcony high above the sea.

# 4

The Roaring Fork Police Department was located in a classic, Old West–style Victorian red-brick building, impossibly picturesque, that stood in a green park against a backdrop of magnificent snowy peaks. In front of it was a twelve-foot statue of Lady Justice, covered with snow, and—rather oddly—not wearing the traditional blindfold.

Corrie Swanson had loaded up with books about Roaring Fork and she had read all about this courthouse, which was noted for the number of famous defendants who had passed through its doors, from Hunter S. Thompson to serial killer Ted Bundy. Roaring Fork, she knew, was quite a resort. It had the most expensive real estate in the country. This proved to be annoying in the extreme, as she found herself forced to stay in a town called Basalt, eighteen winding miles down Route 82, in a crappy Cloud Nine Motel, with cardboard walls and an itchy bed, at the stunning price of $109 a night. It was the first day of December, and ski season was really ramping up. From her work-study jobs at John Jay—and money left over from the wad Agent Pendergast had pressed on her a year back, when he'd sent her away to stay with her father during a bad time—she had saved up almost four thousand dollars. But at a hundred and nine dollars a night, plus meals, plus the ridiculous thirty-nine bucks a day she was paying for a Rent-a-Junker, she was going to burn through that pretty fast.

In short, she had no time to waste.

The problem was, in her eagerness to get her thesis approved, she had told a little lie. Well, maybe it wasn't such a little lie. She had told Carbone and the faculty committee that she'd gotten permission to examine the remains: carte blanche access. The truth was, her several emails to the chief of the Roaring Fork Police Department, whom she determined had the power to grant her access, had gone unanswered, and her phone calls had not been returned. Not that anyone had been rude to her—it was just a sort of benign neglect.

By marching into the police station herself the day before, she'd finally finagled an appointment with Chief Stanley Morris. Now she entered the building and approached the front desk. To her surprise it was manned, not by a burly cop, but by a girl who looked to be even younger than Corrie herself. She was quite pretty, with a creamy complexion, dark eyes, and shoulder-length blond hair.

Corrie walked up to her, and the girl smiled.

"Are you, uh, a policeman?" Corrie asked.

The girl laughed and shook her head. "Not yet."

"What, then—the receptionist?"

The girl shook her head again. "I'm interning at the station over the winter vacation. Today just happens to be my day to man the reception desk." She paused. "I would like to get into law enforcement someday."

"That makes two of us. I'm a student at John Jay."

The girl's eyes widened. "No kidding!"

Corrie extended her hand. "Corrie Swanson."

The girl shook it. "Jenny Baker."

"I have an appointment with Chief Morris."

"Oh, yes." Jenny consulted an appointment book. "He's expecting you. Go right in."

"Thanks." This was a good beginning. Corrie tried to get her nervousness under control and not think about what would happen if the chief denied her access to the remains. At the very least, her thesis depended on it. And she had already spent a fortune getting here, nonrefundable airplane tickets and all.

The door to the chief's office was open, and as she entered the man rose from behind his desk and came around it, extending a hand. She was startled by his appearance: a small, rotund, cheerful-looking man with a beaming face, bald pate, and rumpled uniform. The office reflected the impression of informality, with its arrangement of old, comfortable leather furniture and a desk pleasantly disheveled with papers, books, and family photographs.

The chief ushered her over to a little sitting area in one corner, where an elderly secretary brought in a tray with paper coffee cups, sugar, and cream. Corrie, who had arrived the day before yesterday and was still feeling a bit jet-lagged, helped herself, refraining from her usual four teaspoons of sugar only to see Chief Morris put no less than five into his own cup.

"Well," Morris said, leaning back, "sounds like you've got a very interesting project going here."

"Thank you," Corrie said. "And thanks for meeting me on such short notice."

"I've always been fascinated with Roaring Fork's past. The grizzly bear killings are part of local lore, at least for those of us who know the history. So few do these days."

"This research project presents an almost perfect opportunity," Corrie said, launching into her carefully memorized talking points. "It's a real chance to advance the science of forensic criminology." She waxed enthusiastic as Chief Morris listened attentively, his chin resting pensively on one soft hand. Corrie touched on all the salient points: how her project would surely garner national press attention and reflect well on the Roaring Fork Police Department; how much John Jay—the nation's premier law enforcement college—would appreciate his cooperation; how she would of course work closely with him and follow whatever rules were laid down. She went into a revisionist version of her own story: how she'd wanted to be a cop all her life; how she'd won a scholarship to John Jay; how hard she'd worked—and then she concluded by enthusing over how much she admired his own position, how ideal it was having the opportunity to work in such an interesting and beautiful community. She laid it on as thick as she dared, and she could see, with satisfaction, that he was responding with nods, smiles, and various noises of approval.

When she was done, she gave as natural a laugh as she could muster, and said she'd been talking way too much and would love to hear his thoughts.

At this Chief Morris took another sip of coffee, cleared his throat, praised her for her hard work and enterprise, told her how much he appreciated her coming in, and—again—how interesting her project sounded. Yes, indeed. He would have to think about it, of course, and consult with the local coroner's office, and with the historical society, and a few others, to get their views, and then the town attorney should probably be brought into the loop...And he finished off his coffee and put his hands on the arm of his chair, looking as if he was getting ready to stand up and end the meeting.

*A disaster.* Corrie took a deep breath. "Can I be totally frank with you?"

"Why, yes." He settled back in his chair.

"It took me ages to scrape together the money for this project. I had to work two jobs in addition to my scholarship. Roaring Fork is one of the most expensive places in the country, and just being here is costing me a fortune. I'll go broke waiting for permission."

She paused, took a breath.

"Honestly, Chief Morris, if you consult with all those people, it's going to take a long time. Maybe weeks. Everyone's going to have a different opinion. And then, no matter what decision you make, someone will feel as if they were overridden. It could become controversial."

"Controversial," the chief echoed, alarm and distaste in his voice.

"May I make an alternative suggestion?"

The chief looked a bit surprised but not altogether put out by this. "Certainly."

"As I understand it, you have the full authority to give me permission. So…" She paused and then decided to just lay it out, completely unvarnished. "I'd be incredibly grateful if you'd please just give me permission right now, so I can do my research as quickly as possible. I only need a couple of days with the remains, plus the option to take away a few bones for further analysis. That's all. The quicker this happens, the better for everyone. The bones are just sitting there. I could get my work done with barely anyone noticing. Don't give people time to make objections. Please, Chief Morris—it's *so* important to me!"

This ended on more of a desperate note than she intended, but she could see that, once again, she had made an impression.

"Well, well," the chief said, with more throat clearings and hemmings and hawings. "I see your point. Hmmm. We don't want controversy."

He leaned over the edge of his chair, craned his neck toward the door. "Shirley? More coffee!"

The secretary came back in with two more paper cups. The chief proceeded once again to heap an astonishing amount of sugar into the cup, fussing with the spoon, the cream, stirring the cup endlessly while his brow remained furrowed. He finally laid down the plastic spoon and took a good long sip.

"I'm very much leaning toward your proposal," he said. "Very much. I'll tell you what. It's only noon. If you like I'll take you over now, show you the coffins. Of course you can't actually handle the remains, but you'll get an idea of what's there. And I'll have an answer for you tomorrow morning. How's that?"

"That would be great! Thank you!"

Chief Morris beamed. "And just between you and me, I think you can depend on that answer being positive."

And as they stood up, Corrie had to actually restrain herself from hugging the man.

# 5

Corrie slid into the passenger seat of the squad car, next to the chief, who apparently eschewed a driver and drove himself about. Instead of the usual Crown Vic, the vehicle was a Jeep Cherokee, done up in the traditional cop-car two-tone, with the city symbol of Roaring Fork—an aspen leaf—painted on the side, surrounded by a six-pointed sheriff's star.

Corrie realized she had lucked out, big-time. The chief appeared to be a decent, well-meaning man, and although he seemed to lack spine he was both reasonable and intelligent.

"Have you been to Roaring Fork before?" Morris asked as he turned the key, the vehicle roaring to life.

"Never. Don't even ski."

"Good gracious. You need to learn. We're in

the high season here—Christmas approaching and all—so you're seeing it at its finest."

The Jeep eased down East Main Street and the chief began pointing out some of the historic sights—City Hall, the historic Hotel Sebastian, various famous Victorian mansions. Everything was done up in festive lights and garlands of fir, the snow lying on the roofs, frosting the windows, and hanging on the boughs of the trees. It was like something out of a Currier & Ives print. They passed through a shopping district, the streets thicker with upscale boutiques than even the gold mile of Fifth Avenue. It was amazing, the sidewalks thronging with shoppers decked out in furs and diamonds or sleek ski outfits, packing shopping bags. The traffic moved at a glacial pace, and they found themselves creeping down the street sandwiched among stretch Hummers, Mercedes Geländewagens, Range Rovers, Porsche Cayennes—and snowmobiles.

"Sorry about the traffic," the chief said.

"Are you kidding? This is amazing," Corrie said, almost hanging out the window as she watched the parade of stores slide by: Ralph Lauren, Tiffany, Dior, Louis Vuitton, Prada, Gucci, Rolex, Fendi, Bulgari, Burberry, Brioni, the windows stuffed with expensive merchandise. They never seemed to end.

"The amount of money in this town is off the charts," said the chief. "And frankly, from a law enforcement point of view, that can be a problem. A lot of these people think the rules don't apply to them. But in the Roaring Fork Police Department, we treat everyone—and I mean *everyone*—the same."

"Good policy."

"It's the only policy in a town like this," he said, not without a touch of pomposity, "where just about everyone is a celebrity, a billionaire, or both."

"Must be a magnet for thieves," Corrie said, still staring at the expensive stores.

"Oh, no. The crime rate here is almost nil. We're so isolated, you see. There's only one road in—Route 82, which can be an obstacle course in the winter and is frequently closed due to snow—and our airport is only used by private jets. Then there's the cost of actually staying here—well beyond the means of any petty thief. We're too expensive for thieves!" He laughed merrily.

*Tell me about it*, Corrie thought.

They were now passing a few blocks of what looked like a re-creation of a western boomtown: bars with swinging doors, assay offices, general goods stores, even a few apparent bordellos with gaudily painted windows. Everything was spotlessly neat and clean, from the gleaming cuspidors on the raised wooden sidewalks to the tall false fronts of the buildings.

"What's all that?" Corrie asked, pointing at a family getting their picture taken in front of the Ideal Saloon.

"That's Old Town," the chief replied. "What remains of the earliest part of Roaring Fork. For years, those buildings just sat around, decaying. Then, when the resort business picked up, there was a move to clear it all away. But somebody had the idea to restore the old ghost town, make it into a kind of museum for Roaring Fork's past."

*Disneyland meets ski resort*, Corrie thought, marveling at the anachronism of this scattering of old relics amid such a hotbed of conspicuous consumption.

As she stared at the well-maintained structures, a brace of snowmobiles roared past, throwing up billows of powder in their wakes.

"What's with all the snowmobiles?" she asked.

"Roaring Fork has an avid snowmobile culture," the chief told her. "The town's famous not only for its ski runs, but also for its snowmobile trails. There are miles and miles of them—mostly utilizing the maze of old mining roads that still exist in the mountains above the town."

They finally cleared the shopping district and,

after a few turns, passed a little park full of snow-covered boulders.

"Centennial State Park," the chief explained. "Those rocks are part of the John Denver Sanctuary."

"John Denver?" Corrie shuddered.

"Every year, fans gather on the anniversary of his death. It's a really moving experience. What a genius he was—and what a loss."

"Yes, absolutely," Corrie said quickly. "I love his work. 'Rocky Mountain High'—my favorite song of all time."

"Still brings tears to my eyes."

"Right. Me, too."

They left the tight grid of downtown streets behind and continued up through a gorgeous stand of giant fir trees heavy with snow.

"Why was the cemetery dug up?" Corrie asked. She knew the answer, of course, but she wanted to see what fresh light the chief could shed on things.

"There's a very exclusive development up ahead called The Heights—ten-million-dollar homes, big acreages, private access to the mountain, exclusive club. It's the most upscale development in town, and it carries a great deal of cachet. Old money and all that. Back in the late '70s, during the initial stage of its development, The Heights acquired 'Boot Hill'—the hill with the town's original cemetery—and got a variance to move it. That was in the days when you could still do that sort of thing. Anyway, a couple of years ago, they exercised that right so they could build a private spa and new clubhouse on that hill. There was an uproar, of course, and the town took them to court. But they had some pretty slick lawyers, and also that 1978 agreement, signed and sworn, with ironclad provisions in perpetuity. So they won, the cemetery ultimately got dug up, and here we are. For now, the remains are being stored in a warehouse up on the mountain. There's nothing left but buttons, boots, and bones."

"So where are they being moved to?"

"The development plans to rebury them in a nearby site as soon as spring comes."

"Is there still controversy?"

The chief waved his hand. "Once it was dug up, the furor died down. It wasn't about the remains, anyway—it was about preserving the historic cemetery. Once that was gone, people lost interest."

The fir trees gave way to a broad, attractive valley, glittering in the noontime light. At the near end stood a plain, hand-carved sign, of surprisingly modest dimensions, which read:

**THE HEIGHTS**

MEMBERS ONLY

PLEASE CHECK IN AT GUARD STATION

Behind was a massive wall of river stones set with wrought-iron gates, beside which stood a fairy-tale guard house with a pointed cedar-shake roof and shingled sides. The valley floor was dotted with gigantic mansions, hidden among the trees, and the walls of the valley rose up behind, rooflines peeking above the firs—many with stone chimneys trailing smoke. Beyond that rose the ski area, a braid of trails winding up to the peaks of several mountains, and a high ridge sporting yet more mansions, all framed against a brilliant blue Rocky Mountain sky sprinkled with clouds.

"We're going in?" Corrie asked.

"The warehouse is to one side of the development, on the edge of the slopes."

The chief was waved through by a security guard, and they headed along a winding, cobblestone drive, beautifully plowed and cleared. No, not cleared. The road was strangely free of ice and utterly dry, while the verges showed no signs of piled or plowed snow.

"Heated road?" asked Corrie as they passed what appeared to be the clubhouse.

"Not so uncommon around here. The ultimate

in snow clearance—the flakes evaporate as soon as they touch down."

Climbing now, the road crossed a stone bridge over a frozen stream—which the chief labeled Silver Queen Creek—then passed through a service gate. Beyond, screened by a tall fence, up hard against a ski run, stood several large equipment sheds built of Pro-Panel on a leveled area of ground. Ten-foot icicles hung down their sides, glittering in the light.

The chief pulled up into a plowed area before the largest shed, parked, and got out. Corrie followed. It was a cold day but not desperately so, twenty or twenty-five perhaps, and windless. The great door to the shed had a smaller one set to the side of it, which Chief Morris unlocked. Corrie followed him into the dark space, and the smell hit her right away. And yet it was not an unpleasant odor, no scent of rot. Just rich earth.

The chief palmed a bank of switches and sodium lamps in the roof turned on, casting a yellow glow over all. If anything, it was colder inside the shed than outside, and she drew her coat more closely around her, shivering. In the front section of the shed, practically in the shadow of the large door, sat a line of six snowmobiles, almost all of identical make. Beyond, a row of old snowcats, some nearly antique looking, with huge treads and rounded cabs, blocked their view toward the back. They threaded their way among the cats and came to an open area. Here was the makeshift cemetery, laid out on tarps: neat rows of baby-blue plastic coffins of the kind used by medical examiners to remove remains from a crime scene.

They walked over to the nearest row, and Corrie looked at the first box. Taped to the lid was a large card of printed information. Corrie knelt to read it. The card indicated where the remains had been found in the cemetery, with a photo of the grave in situ; there was space to record whether or not there had been a tombstone and, if so, room for the information printed on it, along with another photo. Everything was numbered, cataloged, and arranged. Corrie felt relief: there would be no problems with documentation here.

"The tombstones are over there," said Chief Morris. He pointed to a far wall, against which was arrayed a motley collection of tombstones—a few fancy ones in slate or marble, but mostly boulders or slabs with lettering carved into them. They, too, had been cataloged and carded.

"We've got about a hundred and thirty human remains," said the chief. "And close to a hundred tombstones. The rest...we don't know who they are. They may have had wooden markers, or perhaps some tombstones were lost or stolen."

"Did any identify bear victims?"

"None. They're traditional—names, dates, and sometimes a phrase from the Bible or a standard religious epitaph. The cause of death isn't normally put on tombstones. And being eaten by a grizzly would not be something you'd want memorialized."

Corrie nodded. It didn't really matter—she had already put together a list of the victims from researching old local newspaper reports.

"Would it be possible to open one of these lids?" she asked.

"I don't see why not." The chief grasped a handle on the nearest box.

"Wait, I've got a list." Corrie fumbled in her briefcase and withdrew the folder. "Let's look for one of the victims."

"Fine."

They spent a few minutes wandering among the coffins, until Corrie found one that matched a name on her list: Emmett Bowdree. "This one, please," she said.

Morris grabbed the handle and eased the lid off.

Inside were the remains of a rotten pine coffin that held a skeleton. The lid had disintegrated and was lying in pieces around and on top of the skeleton. Corrie stared at it eagerly. The bones of both arms and a leg lay to one side; the skull was crushed; the rib cage had been ripped open; and both femurs had been broken into pieces, crunched up by powerful jaws to obtain the marrow, no doubt. In her studies at John Jay, Corrie had examined many skeletons displaying perimortem violence, but nothing—*nothing*—quite like this.

"Jesus, the bear really did a number on him," murmured Morris.

"You're not kidding."

As she examined the bones, Corrie noticed something: some faint marks on the broken rib cage. She knelt, looking closer, trying to make them out. Christ, what she needed was a magnifying glass. Her eyes darted about, and—on the crushed femur—she noticed another, similar mark. She reached out to pick up the bone.

"Whoa, there, no touching!"

"I need to just examine this a little closer."

"No," said the chief. "Really, that's enough."

"Just give me a moment," Corrie pleaded.

"Sorry." He slid the lid back on. "You'll have plenty of time later."

Corrie rose, perplexed, not at all sure about what she'd seen. It might have been her imagination. Anyway, the marks surely must be antemortem: no mystery there. Roaring Fork was a rough place back in those days. Maybe the fellow had survived a knife fight. She shook her head.

"We'd better get going," the chief said.

They emerged into the brilliant light, the blaze off the glittering blanket of snow almost blinding. But try as she might, Corrie couldn't quite rid herself of the strangest feeling of disquiet.

# 6

The call came the following morning. Corrie was seated in the Roaring Fork Library, reading up on the history of the town. It was an excellent library, housed in a modern building designed in an updated Victorian style. The interior was gorgeous, with acres of polished oak, arched windows, thick carpeting, and an indirect lighting system that bathed everything in a warm glow.

The library's historical section was state of the art. The section librarian, Ted Roman, had been very helpful. He turned out to be a cute guy in his midtwenties, lithe and fit, who had recently graduated from the University of Utah and was taking a couple of years off to be a ski bum. She had told him about her research project and her meeting with Chief Morris. Ted had listened attentively, asked intelligent questions, and showed her how to use the history archives. To top it off, he had asked her out for a beer tomorrow night. And she'd accepted.

The library's albums of old newspapers, broadsheets, and public notices from the silver boom days had been beautifully digitized in searchable PDF form. She'd been able, in a matter of hours, to pull up dozens of articles on the history of Roaring Fork and on the grizzly killings, obituary notices, and all kinds of related memorabilia—far more than she'd obtained in New York.

The town had a fascinating history. In the summer of 1873, a doughty band of prospectors from Leadville braved the threat of Ute Indians and crossed the Continental Divide, penetrating unexplored territory westward. There, they and others who followed made one of the biggest silver strikes in U.S. history. A silver rush ensued, with hordes of prospectors staking claims all through the mountains lining the Roaring Fork River. A town sprang up, along with stamp mills for crushing ore and a hastily built smelter for separating silver and gold from ore. Soon the hills were crawling with prospectors, dotted with mines and remote camps, while the town itself teemed with mining engineers, assayists, charcoal burners, sawmill workers, blacksmiths, saloonkeepers, merchants, teamsters, whores, laborers, piano players, faro dealers, con men, and thieves.

The first killing took place in the spring of 1876. At a remote claim high on Smuggler Mountain, a lone miner was killed and eaten. It took weeks for the man to be missed, and as a consequence his body wasn't discovered immediately, but the high mountain air kept it fresh enough to tell the gruesome tale. The body had been ripped open, obviously by a bear, then gutted, the limbs torn off. It appeared the bear had returned over the course of a week to continue feasting, with most of the bones stripped of their flesh, the tongue and liver eaten, the entrails and organs spread about and more or less consumed.

It was a pattern that would be repeated ten more times over the course of the summer.

From the beginning, Roaring Fork—and indeed much of Colorado Territory—had been plagued by aggressive grizzlies who were being driven to higher altitudes by settlements in the lower valleys. The grizzly bear—it was noted with relish in almost every newspaper report—was one of the few animals known to hunt and kill a human being for food.

During the course of that long summer, eleven miners and prospectors were killed and eaten by the rogue grizzly at a variety of remote claims. The animal had a large territory that, unfortunately, encompassed much of the upper range of the silver district.

The killings caused widespread panic. But federal law required miners to "work a claim" in order to maintain rights to it, so even at the height of the terror most miners refused to abandon their sites.

Hunting posses were formed several times to chase the grizzly, but it was hard to track the animal in the absence of snow, amid the rocky upper reaches of the mountains above the tree line. Still, the real problem, it seemed to Corrie, was that the hunting posses were none too eager to find the bear. They seemed to spend more time organizing in the saloons and making speeches than actually out in the field tracking the bear.

The killings stopped in the fall of 1876, just before the first snow. Over time, people began to think the bear had moved on, died, or perhaps gone into hibernation. There was some apprehension the following spring, but when the killings did not resume...

Corrie felt her phone vibrate, plucked it out of her handbag, and saw it was a call from the police station. Glancing around and noting the library was empty—save for the ski bum librarian, sitting at his desk reading Jack Kerouac—she figured it was okay to answer.

But it wasn't the chief. It was his secretary. Before Corrie could even get through the usual niceties, the lady was talking fast and breathily.

"The chief is so sorry, so very sorry, but it turns out he can't give you permission to examine the remains."

Corrie's mouth went dry. "What?" she croaked. "Wait a minute—"

"He's tied up all day in meetings so he asked me to call you. You see—"

"But he said—"

"It's just not going to be possible. He feels very sorry he can't help you."

"But *why*?" she managed to break in.

"I don't have the specifics, I'm sorry—"

"Can't I speak to him?"

"He's caught up in meetings all day and, um, for the rest of the week."

"For the rest of the *week*? But just yesterday he said—"

"I'm sorry, I told you I'm not privy to his reasons."

"Look," said Corrie, trying to control her voice without much success, "just a day ago he told me there wouldn't be any problems. That he'd approve it. And now he changes his mind, refuses to say why, and…and then dumps on you the job of giving me the bum's rush! It isn't fair!"

Corrie got a final, frosty *I wish I could help you, but the decision is final*, followed by a decisive click. The line went dead.

Corrie sat down and, banging her palm on the table, cried: "Damn, damn, *damn!*"

Then she looked up. Ted was looking over at her, his eyes wide.

"Oh, no," Corrie said, covering her mouth. "I've disturbed the whole library."

He held up his hand with a smile. "As you can see, there's nobody here right now." He hesitated, then came around his desk and walked over. He spoke again, his voice having dropped to a whisper. "I think I understand what's going on here."

"You do? I'd wish you'd explain it to me, then."

Even though there was nobody around, he lowered his voice still further. "*Mrs. Kermode.*"

"Who?"

"Mrs. Betty Brown Kermode got to the chief of police."

"Who is Betty Brown Kermode?"

He rolled his eyes and looked around furtively. "Where to begin? First, she owns Town and Mount Real Estate, which is *the* real estate agency in town. She's the head of the Heights Neighborhood Association, and was the force behind getting the cemetery moved. She's basically one of those self-righteous people who run everything and everybody and brook no dissent. Fact is, she's the real power in this town."

"A woman like that's got influence over the chief of police?"

Ted laughed. "You met Morris, right? Nice guy. *Everyone* has influence over him. But especially her. I'm telling you, she's fearsome—even more so than that brother-in-law of hers, Montebello. I'm sure Morris had every intention of giving you permission—until he called Kermode."

"But why would she want to stop me? What harm would it do?"

"That," said Ted, "is what you're going to have to find out."

# 7

At nine the next morning, Corrie pulled her Rent-a-Junker up to the gates of The Heights. There the guard—not nearly as friendly as the last time she'd passed through, with the chief of police—spent a long, insolent amount of time checking her ID and calling to verify her appointment, all the while casting disdainful looks at her car.

Corrie was careful to remain polite, and at length she was driving along the road toward the clubhouse and development offices. A cluster of buildings on the valley floor soon came into view: picturesque, snowcapped and icicled, their stone chimneys smoking. Beyond, well up on the far side of the snow-blanketed valley, Corrie could see a massive dirt scar of ongoing construction—no doubt the new clubhouse and spa. She watched backhoes and loaders busily at work digging footings. She couldn't help but wonder why they needed a new clubhouse when the old one looked pretty amazing.

She parked in the visitor's lot and entered the clubhouse, where the secretary pointed her toward the offices of Town & Mount Real Estate.

The reception area of Town & Mount was sumptuous—all wood and stone, with Navajo rugs on the walls, a spectacular chandelier made of deer antlers, cowboy-style leather-and-wood furniture, and a stone fireplace in which a real log fire burned. Corrie took a seat and settled in to wait.

An hour later, she was finally ushered into the office of Mrs. Kermode, president of Town & Mount and director of the Heights Association. Corrie had dressed in her most corporate mode, a gray suit with a white blouse and low pumps. She was absolutely determined to keep her cool and win Mrs. Kermode over with flattery, charm, and persuasion.

The previous afternoon, she had done her damnedest to dig up dirt on Kermode, heeding the Pendergastian dictum that if you want something from somebody, always have something "ugly" to trade. But Kermode seemed to be a woman above reproach: a generous donor to local charities, an elder in the Presbyterian church, a volunteer at the local soup kitchen (it surprised Corrie that a town like Roaring Fork would even have a soup kitchen), and a businesswoman of acknowledged integrity. While she was not exactly loved, and was in fact heartily disliked by many, she was respected—and feared—by all.

Mrs. Kermode surprised Corrie. Far from being the dowdy woman conjured up by the name Betty Brown Kermode, she was an extremely well-put-to-gether woman in her early sixties, slender and fit, with beautifully coiffed platinum hair and under-stated makeup. She was dressed in high cowboy style with a beaded Indian vest, white shirt, tight jeans, and cowboy boots. A Navajo squash blossom necklace completed the ensemble. The walls of her office were covered with photographs of her riding a stunning paint horse in the mountains and compet-ing in an arena, charging through a herd of cows. A water cooler stood in one corner. Another corner of the office was dominated by a magnificent western saddle, tooled all over and trimmed in silver.

In an easy, friendly way, Mrs. Kermode came forward and shook Corrie's hand, inviting her to sit down. Corrie's irritation at being kept waiting for an hour began to dissipate in the warm welcome.

"Now, Corrie," she began, speaking with a pro-nounced Texas accent, "I want to thank you for coming in. It gives me a chance to explain to you, in person, why Chief Morris and I unfortunately can't grant your request."

"Well, I was hoping to explain—"

But Kermode was in a hurry and overrode Corrie's attempt to present her talking points. "Corrie, I'm going to be frank. The scientific examination of those mortal remains for a…college thesis is, in our view, disrespectful of the dead."

This was not what Corrie expected. "In what way?"

Kermode gave a poisonous little laugh. "My dear Miss Swanson, how can you ask such a question? Would you want some student pawing through your grandfather's remains?"

"Um, I would be fine with it."

"Come, now. Of course you wouldn't. At least where I come from, we treat our dead with respect. These are *sacred* human remains."

Corrie tried desperately to get back to her talking points. "But this is a unique opportunity for forensic science. This is going to help law enforcement—"

"A college thesis? Contribute to forensic science? Aren't you exaggerating the importance of this project just a *teensy* little bit now, Miss Swanson?"

Corrie took a deep breath. "Not at all. This could be a very important study and data collection of perimortem trauma caused by a large carnivore. When a skeleton of a murder victim is found, forensic pathologists have to distinguish animal tooth marks and other postmortem damage from the marks on the bones left by the perpetrator. It's a serious issue and this study—"

"So much Greek to me!" Mrs. Kermode gave a laugh and waved her hand, as if she understood nothing.

Corrie decided to shift tack. "It's important for me personally, Mrs. Kermode—but it could be important for Roaring Fork, as well. It's doing something constructive, something positive with these human remains. It would reflect well on the community and the chief—"

"It's just not respectful," said Kermode firmly. "It's not *Christian*. There are many in this town who would find it deeply offensive. We are the guardians of those remains, and we take our responsibility seriously. I just can't under any circumstances allow it."

"But..." Corrie could feel her temper rising despite her best efforts to keep it down. "But...you dug them up to begin with."

A silence, and then Kermode spoke softly. "The decision was made long ago. Back in 1978, in fact. The town signed off on it. Here at The Heights we've been planning this new clubhouse and spa for almost a decade."

"Why do you need it when you've already got a beautiful clubhouse?"

"We'll need a larger one to serve Phase Three, as we open up West Mountain to a select number of custom home lots. Again, as I've repeatedly said to you, this has been in planning for years. We are responsible to our owners and investors."

*Our owners and investors.* "All I want to do is examine the bones—with the utmost respect—for valid and important scientific purposes. There's no disrespect in that, surely?"

Mrs. Kermode rose, a bright fake smile plastered on her face. "Miss Swanson, the decision has been made, it is final, and I am a very busy woman. It is now time for you to leave."

Corrie rose. She could feel that old, horrible, blood-boiling sensation inside her. "You dig up an entire cemetery so you can make money on a real estate development, you dump the bodies in plastic boxes and store them in a ski warehouse—and then you tell me *I'll* be disrespecting the dead by studying the bones? You're a hypocrite—plain and simple!"

Kermode's face grew pale. Corrie could see a vein in her powdered neck throbbing. Her voice became very low, almost masculine. "You little bitch," she said. "I'll give you five minutes to vacate the premises. If you ever—*ever*—come back, I'll have you arrested for trespassing. Now get out."

Corrie suddenly felt very calm. This was the end. It was over. But she wasn't going to let anyone call her a bitch. She stared back at Mrs. Kermode with narrowed eyes. "You call yourself an elder in the church? You're no Christian. You're a goddamn phony. A fake, grasping, deceitful *phony*."

On the way back to Basalt, it began to snow. As she crawled along at ten miles an hour in her car, windshield wipers slapping back and forth ineffectually, an idea came to her. Those anomalous marks she'd noticed on the bones...with a flash of insight, she realized there was possibly another way to skin this particular cat.

## 8

Lying on the bed of her room at the Cloud Nine Motel in Basalt, Colorado, Corrie made her decision. If those marks on the bones were what she thought they might be, her problems would be solved. There wouldn't be any choice: the remains would have to be examined. Even Kermode couldn't stop it. That would be her trump card.

But only if she could prove it.

And to do that, she needed access to the bones one more time. Five minutes, tops—just long enough to photograph them with the powerful macro lens on her camera.

But how?

Even before she asked herself the question, she knew the answer: she would have to break in.

All the arguments against such an action lined themselves up before her: that B&E was a felony;

that it was ethically wrong; that if she got caught, her entire law enforcement career would be flushed down the toilet. On the other hand, it wouldn't be all that difficult. During their visit two days before, the chief hadn't turned off any alarm systems or other security devices; he'd simply unlocked a padlock on the door and they had walked in. The shed was isolated from the rest of the development, surrounded by a tall wooden fence and screened by trees. It was partly open to one of the ski slopes, but nobody would be skiing at night. The shed was marked on trail maps of the area, and they showed a service road leading to it from the equipment yard of the ski area itself, bypassing The Heights entirely.

As she weighed the pros and cons, she found herself asking the question: what would Pendergast do? He never let legal niceties stand in the way of truth and justice. Surely he would break in and get the information he needed. While it was too late to achieve justice for Emmett Bowdree, it was never too late for the truth.

The snow had stopped at midnight, leaving a brilliantly clear night sky with a three-quarter moon. It was extremely cold—according to the WeatherBug app on her iPad, it was five degrees. Outside, it felt a lot colder than that. The service road turned out to be snowmobile-only, covered with hard-packed snow but still walkable.

Leaving her car at the very base of the road, by a tall stand of trees and as inconspicuous as possible, Corrie labored uphill, her knapsack heavy with gear: the Canon with tripod and macro, a portable light and battery pack, loupes, flashlight, bolt cutter, ziplock bags, and her iPad loaded with textbooks and monographs on the subject of osteological trauma analysis. The thin mountain air left her gasping, the smoke of her condensing breath blossoming in the moonlight as she hiked, her feet squeaking in the layer of fluff atop the hard-packed snow. Below, the lights of the town spread out in a magical carpet; above, she could see the warehouse, illuminated by lights on poles and casting a yellow glow through the fir trees. It was two o'clock in the morning and all was quiet. The only activity was some headlights high on the mountain, where the grooming equipment was being operated.

Again and again, she had choreographed in her head the exact series of steps she'd need to take, rearranging and refining them to ensure that she would spend as little time in the shed as possible. Five minutes, ten at most—and she'd be gone.

Approaching the shed, she did a careful recon to assure herself that she was alone. Then she stepped up to the fence gate and peered over it. To the left was the side door that she and the chief had used, illuminated in a pool of light, the snow well beaten down before it. The door was securely padlocked. By habit, she carried a set of lock picks. In high school, she had practically memorized the underground manual known as the *MIT Guide to Lockpicking*, and she took great pride in her skills. The padlock was a ten-dollar, hardware-store variety—no problem there. But she would have to cross the lighted area in order to reach the door. And then she'd have to stand in the light while dealing with the lock. This was one of two elements of unavoidable danger in her plan.

She waited, listening, but all was quiet. The grooming machines were high up on the mountain and didn't look like they'd be passing by anytime soon.

Taking a deep breath, she vaulted the fence and darted across the lighted area. She had her set of lock picks ready. The lock itself was freezing, and her fingers quickly grew stupid in the cold. Nevertheless it took only twenty seconds for the padlock to spring open. She pulled the door ajar, ducked inside, and gently closed it behind her.

Inside the shed it was very cold. Fumbling a small LED light out of her backpack, she flicked it on and quickly moved past the rows of snowmobiles and antique snowcats to the rear of the structure. The coffins, laid out in neat rows, gleamed dully in her light. It only took a moment to find Emmett Bowdree's coffin. She removed the lid with care, trying to keep the noise to a minimum, then knelt, playing the light over the bones. Her heart was pounding in her chest, and her hands were shaking. Once again, a voice inside her pointed out that this was one of the dumbest things she'd ever done, and once again another voice responded that it was the only thing she could do.

*Get a grip*, she whispered to herself. *Focus.*

Following her mental script, Corrie pulled off her gloves again, laid her backpack on the ground, and unzipped it. She quickly inserted a loupe to her eye, tugged the gloves back on, pulled out the broken femur she'd noticed before, and peered at it under the light. The bone showed several long, parallel scrapes in the cortical surface. She examined them carefully for any sign of healing, bone remodeling or periosteal uplifting, but there was none. The longitudinal marks were clean, fresh, and showed no sign of an osseous reaction. That meant the scraping had occurred perimortem: at the time of death.

No bear could have made a mark like this. It had been done with a crude tool, perhaps the blade of a dull knife, and—clearly—it had been done to strip the flesh from the bones.

But could she be sure? Her field experience was so limited. Removing her gloves again, she fumbled out her iPad and called up one of her school e-textbooks, *Trauma Analysis*. She looked through the illustrations of antemortem, perimortem, and postmortem injuries, including some with scrapes similar to these, and compared the illustrations with the bone in her hand. They confirmed her initial impression. She tried to warm her frozen fingers by breathing on them, but that didn't work and so she pulled her gloves back on and beat her hands together as quietly as she could. That brought back a little sensation.

Now she had to photograph the damaged bone. Once again the gloves had to come off. She hauled out the portable light, battery pack, and small tripod from her backpack. Next came her digital camera, with the massive macro lens attachment that had cost her a fortune. She screwed the camera into the mount and set it up. Placing the bone on the floor, she arranged things as best she could in the dark, then flicked on the light.

This was the second danger point—the light would be visible from outside. But it was absolutely indispensable. She had arranged things so that it would be on for the shortest possible amount of time, without a red flag of turning it off and on—and so that right afterward she could pack up and leave.

God, it was bright, casting a glow over everything. She quickly positioned the camera and focused. She took a dozen photos as quickly as she could, moving the bone a little bit each time and adjusting the light for a raking effect. As she did this, she noticed, under the strong glare, something else on the bone: apparent tooth marks. She stopped just a moment to examine them with the loupe. They were indeed tooth marks, but not those of a grizzly: they were far too feeble, too close together, and with too flat a crown. She photographed them from several angles.

She hurriedly put the bone back in the coffin, and moved on to the next anomalous mark she'd noticed on her first visit—the broken skull. The cranium showed massive trauma, the skull and face literally crushed. The biggest and, it seemed, first blow had occurred to the right of the parietal bone, shattering the skull in a star pattern and separating it along the sutures. These, too, were clearly perimortem injuries, for the simple reason that survival was impossible after such a violent blow. The green-bone nature of the fractures indicated they had occurred when the bone was still fresh.

The anomaly here was a mark at the point of the blow. She examined the point of fracture. A bear could certainly shatter a skull with the strike of a paw, or crush it with its jaws and teeth. But this mark did not look like either teeth or claws. It was irregular, with multiple indents.

Under the loupe, her suspicions were confirmed. It had been made by a rough, heavy object—almost certainly a rock.

Working even more quickly now, she took a series of photographs of the skull fragments with her macro. This was proof enough. Or was it? She vacillated a moment, then on impulse took out a couple of ziplock bags and slipped the fragment of femur and one of the damaged skull fragments into them. *That* was proof.

*Done.* She snapped off the light. Now she had incontrovertible evidence that Emmett Bowdree had not been killed and eaten by a bear. Instead, he had been killed and eaten by a human. In fact, judging from the extensive nature of the injuries, there might have been two or three, maybe more, who participated in the killing. They had first disabled him with a blow to the head, crushed his skull, smashed his bones, and literally ripped him apart with their bare hands. Then they had stripped the meat from the bones with a crude knife or piece of metal. Finally, they had eaten him raw—attested by the tooth marks and the absence of bone scorching and other evidence of cooking.

Horrible. Unbelievable. She had discovered a hundred-and-fifty-year-old murder. Which begged the next question: *Were the other ten miners killed in the same way, by humans?*

She glanced at her watch: eleven minutes. She felt a sudden shiver of fear: time to get the hell out. Quickly she began packing up her stuff, preparing to exit the shed.

Suddenly she thought she heard a noise. She flicked off the LED and listened. Silence. Then she heard it again: the faintest crunching sound of snow outside the door.

Jesus, someone was coming. Paralyzed with fear, her heart pounding, she continued to listen. A definite *crunch, crunch, crunch.* And then— across the warehouse, in a window high up in the eaves—she saw a beam of light flash quickly across the glass. More silence. And then the muf- fled sound of talk and the hiss of a two-way radio.

There were people outside. With a radio.

Heights security? Cops?

She zipped up her backpack with infinite care. The coffin lid was still off. Should she slide it back on? She began to move it back into place, but it made such a loud scraping noise that she stopped.

She had to get it back on, though, so in one hasty movement she shoved it back in place.

Outside she could hear more activity: crunching, whispers. There were several people outside and they were trying, not very successfully, to be quiet.

She slid the knapsack over her shoulder and moved away from the coffins. Was there an exit door in the rear? She couldn't tell now—it was too dark—but she didn't recall seeing one. What she needed to do was find a secure hiding place and wait this out.

Tiptoeing across the floor, she headed for the rear of the warehouse, where the giant pieces of an old ski lift had been stored—pylons, chairs, and wheels. Even as she moved across the floor she heard the door open, and she ran the last few yards. Now hushed voices could be heard in the shed. More radio noise.

Reaching the stacks of old equipment, she burrowed her way in, getting down on her hands and knees and crawling as far back as she could, twisting and turning among the giant pieces of metal.

A sudden snapping noise, and then the fluorescent tubes came popping and clinking on, bathing the warehouse in brilliant light. Corrie crawled faster, throwing herself behind a huge coil of steel cable and balling herself up, hugging her backpack to her chest, making herself as small as possible. She waited, hardly daring to breathe. Maybe they thought the padlock had been accidentally left open. Maybe they hadn't noticed her car. Maybe they wouldn't find her...

Footsteps crossed the cement floor. And then Corrie heard a burst of whispering. Now she could distinguish individual voices and catch snatches of phrases. With a thrill of absolute horror she heard her own name spoken—in the Texas drawl of Kermode: querulous, inciting.

She buried her head in her gloved hands, reeling from the nightmare. She could feel her heart almost bursting with anxiety and dismay. Why had she done this? *Why?*

She heard a voice speak, loud and clear: the harsh twang of Kermode. "Corrie Swanson?"

It echoed dreadfully in the cavernous room.

"Corrie Swanson, we know you're in here. We *know* it. You're in a world of trouble. If you come out and show yourself now, that would be the smart thing to do. If you force these policemen to have to find you, that won't be smart. Do you understand?"

Corrie was choking with fear. More sounds: additional people were arriving. She couldn't move.

"All right," she heard the chief's unhappy voice say. "You, Joe, start in the back. Fred, stay by the door. Sterling, you poke around those cats and snowmobiles."

Still Corrie couldn't move. The game was up. She should show herself. But some crazy, desperate hope kept her hidden.

Burying her head deeper into her gloves, like a child hiding under the covers, she waited. She heard the tap of footsteps, the scrape and clank of equipment being moved, the hiss and crackle of radios. A few minutes passed. And then, almost directly above her, she heard, loudly: "Here she is!" And then, aimed at her: "This is the police. Stand up slowly and keep your hands in sight."

She simply could not move.

"Stand up slowly, hands in sight. *Now.*"

She managed to raise her head and saw a cop standing just a few feet away, service revolver drawn and pointed. Two other cops were just arriving.

Corrie rose stiffly, her hands out. The cop came over, grasped her wrist, spun her around, pulled her arms behind her, and slapped on a pair of handcuffs.

"You have the right to remain silent," she heard him say, as if from a great distance. "Anything you say may be used against you in court..."

Corrie couldn't believe this was happening to her.

"...You have the right to consult with an attorney, and to have that attorney present during questioning. If you are indigent, an attorney will be provided at no cost to you. Do you understand?"

She couldn't speak.

"Do you understand? Please speak or nod your answer."

Corrie managed to nod.

The cop said loudly: "I make note of the fact the prisoner has acknowledged understanding her rights."

Holding her by the arm, the cop led her out of the stacks of equipment and into the open. She blinked in the bright light. Another cop had unzipped her backpack and was looking through it. He soon extracted the two ziplock bags containing the bones.

Chief Morris watched him, looking exceedingly unhappy. Standing beside him and surrounded by several security officers of The Heights was Mrs. Kermode, dressed in a slim, zebra-striped winter outfit trimmed in fur—with a look on her face of malice triumphant.

"Well, well," she said, breathing steam like a dragon. "The girl studying law enforcement is actually a criminal. I had you pegged the moment I saw you. I knew you'd try something like this—and here you are, predictable as clockwork.

Trespassing, vandalism, larceny, resisting arrest." She reached out and took a ziplock bag from the cop and waved it in Corrie's face. "And *grave robbing.*"

"That's enough," the chief said to Kermode. "Please give that evidence back to the officer and let's go." He took Corrie gently by the arm. "And you, young lady—I'm afraid you're under arrest."

# 9

Five long days later, Corrie remained locked up in the Roaring Fork County Jail. Bail had been set at fifty thousand dollars, which she didn't have—not even the five-thousand-dollar surety—and the local bail bondsman declined to take her as a client because she was from out of state, with no assets to pledge and no relatives to vouch for her. She had been too ashamed to call her father, and anyway he sure didn't have the money. There was no one else in her life—except Pendergast. And even if she could reach him, she'd die before she took any more money from him—especially bond money.

Nevertheless, she'd had to write him a letter. She had no idea where he was or what he was doing. She hadn't heard from him in nearly a year. But he, or someone acting for him, had continued paying her tuition. And the day after her arrest, with the story plastered all over the front page of the *Roaring Fork Times*, she realized she had to write. Because if she didn't, and he heard about her arrest from someone else, saw those head-lines...She owed it to him to tell him first.

So she had written a letter to his Dakota ad-dress, care of Proctor. In it she told the whole story, unvarnished. The only thing she left out was the bail situation. Writing everything down had really impressed on her what a brainless, overconfident, and self-destructive thing she had done. She con-cluded by telling him his obligation to her was over and that no reply was expected or wanted. He was no longer to concern himself with her. She would take care of herself from now on. Except that someday, as soon as she was able, she would pay him back for all the tuition he had wasted sending her to John Jay.

Writing that letter had been the hardest thing she had ever done. Pendergast had saved her life; plucked her out of Medicine Creek, Kansas; freed her from a drunken, abusive mother; paid for her to go to boarding school—and then financed her education at John Jay. And...for what?

But that was all over now.

The fact that the jail was relatively posh only made her feel worse. The cells had big, sunny win-dows looking out over the mountains, carpeted floors, and nice furniture. She was allowed out of her cell from eight in the morning until lockdown at 10:30 PM. During free time, the prisoners were allowed to hang around the dayroom and read, watch TV, and chat with the other inmates. There was even an adjacent workout room with an elliptical trainer, weights, and treadmills.

At that moment, Corrie was sitting in the dayroom, staring at the black-and-white checkered carpet. Doing nothing. For the past five days she had been so depressed that she couldn't seem to do anything—read, eat, or even sleep. She just sat there, all day, every day, staring into space, and then spent each night in her cell, lying on her back in her cot, staring into darkness.

"Corrine Swanson?"

She roused herself and looked up. A detention guard was standing in the door of the room, holding a clipboard.

"Here," she said.

"Your attorney has arrived for your appointment."

She'd forgotten. She hauled herself to her feet and followed the guard to a separate room. She felt as if the air around her were thick, granular. Her eyes wouldn't stop leaking water. But she wasn't crying, exactly; it seemed like a physiological reaction.

She went into a small conference room to find

the public defender waiting at the table, briefcase open, manila folders spread out in a neat fan. His name was George Smith and she had already met with him a few times. He was a middle-aged, slight, sandy-haired, balding man with a perpetually apologetic look on his face. He was nice enough, and he meant well, but he wasn't exactly Perry Mason.

"Hello, Corrie," he said.

She eased down in a chair, saying nothing.

"I've had several meetings with the DA," Smith began, "and, well, I've made some progress on the plea deal."

Corrie nodded apathetically.

"Here's where we stand. You plead to breaking and entering, trespassing, and desecration of a human corpse, and they'll drop the petty larceny charge. You'll be looking at ten years, max."

"Ten years?"

"I know. It's not what I'd hoped. There's a lot of pressure being brought to bear to throw the book at you. I don't quite understand it, but it may have something to do with all the publicity this case has generated and the ongoing controversy about the cemetery. They're making an example of you."

"Ten *years?*" Corrie repeated.

"With good behavior, you could be out in eight."

"And if we go to trial?"

The lawyer's face clouded. "Out of the question. The evidence against you is overwhelming. There's a string of felonies here, starting with the B and E and going all the way to the desecration of a human corpse. That latter crime alone carries a sentence of up to thirty years in prison."

"You're kidding—thirty years?"

"It's a particularly nasty statute here in Colorado because of a long history of grave robbing." He paused. "Look, if you don't plead, the DA will be pissed and he could very well ask for that maximum sentence. He's threatened as much to me already."

Corrie stared at the scarred table.

"You've *got* to plead out, Corrie. It's your only choice."

"But...I can't believe it. Ten years, just for what I did? That's more than some murderers get."

A long silence. "I can always go back to the DA. The problem is, they've got you cold. You don't have anything to trade."

"But I *didn't* desecrate a human corpse."

"Well, according to the way those statutes are written, you did. You opened the coffin, you handled the bones, you photographed them, and you took two of them. That's what they'll argue, and I'd be hard-pressed to counter. It's not worth the risk. The jury pool here is drawn from the entire county, not just Roaring Fork, and there are a lot of conservative ranchers and farmers out there, religious folk, who would not look kindly on what you did."

"But I was just trying to prove that the marks on the bones..." She couldn't finish.

The attorney spread his thin hands, a pained look pinching his narrow face. "It's the best I can do."

"How long do I have to think about it?"

"Not long. They can withdraw the offer at any moment. If you could decide right now, that would be best."

"I've *got* to think about it."

"You have my number."

Corrie rose and shook his limp, sweaty hand, walked out. The guard, who had been waiting outside the door, led her back to the dayroom. She sat down and stared at the black-and-white carpet and thought about what her life would look like in ten years, after she got back out. Her eyes began leaking again, and she wiped at them furiously, to no avail.

# 10

Jenny Baker arrived at the Roaring Fork City Hall lugging Chief Stanley Morris's second briefcase in both hands. The chief carried two bulging briefcases to every meeting he attended, it seemed, so as to be prepared to answer any question that might come up. Jenny had tried to persuade him to get a tablet computer, but he was a confirmed Luddite and refused even to use the desktop computer in his office.

Jenny rather liked that, despite the inconvenience of having to lug around two briefcases. So far, the chief had proven a pleasant man to work for, rarely made demands, and was always agreeable. In the two weeks she had interned in the police station, she'd seen him flustered and worried but never angry. Now he walked alongside her, chatting about town business, as they entered the meeting room. Big town meetings were sometimes held in the Opera House, but this one—on December thirteenth, less than two weeks from Christmas—was not expected to be well attended.

She took a seat just behind the chief in the town-official seating area. They were early—the chief was always early—and she watched as the mayor came in, followed by the Planning Board, the town attorney, and other officials whose names she did not know. Hard on their heels came a contingent from The Heights, led by Mrs. Kermode, her coiffed, layered helmet of blond hair utterly perfect. She was followed by her brother-in-law, Henry Montebello, and several anonymous-looking men in suits.

The main item of the meeting—the agenda was routinely published in the paper—involved a proposal from The Heights regarding where the Boot Hill remains were to be reinterred. As the meeting opened, with the usual pledge of allegiance and the reading of minutes, Jenny's thoughts drifted to the woman she had met—Corrie—and what had happened to her. It sort of freaked her out. She had seemed so nice, so professional—and then to be caught breaking into a warehouse, desecrating a coffin, and stealing bones. You never could tell what some people were capable of doing. And a student at John Jay, too. Nothing like that had ever happened in The Heights, and the neighborhood was still up in arms about it. It was all her parents talked about at breakfast every morning, even now, ten days after the event.

As the preliminaries went on, Jenny was surprised to see just how many people were filing into the public seating area. It was already packed, and now the standing-room area in the back was filling up. Maybe the cemetery thing was going to erupt into controversy again. She hoped this wasn't going to make the meeting run late—she had a dinner date later that evening.

The meeting moved to the first item on the agenda. The attorney for The Heights rose and gave his presentation in a nasal drone. The Heights, he said, proposed to rebury the disinterred remains in a field they had purchased for just such a purpose on a hillside about five miles down Route 82. This surprised Jenny; she had always assumed the remains would be reburied within the town limits. Now she understood why so many people were there.

The attorney went through some legal gobbledygook about how this was all perfectly legal, reasonable, proper, preferable, and indeed, unavoidable for various reasons she didn't understand. As he continued, Jenny heard a slow rising of disapproving sounds, murmurings—even a few hisses—from the public area. She glanced in the direction of the noise. The proposal was, it seemed, not being greeted with favor.

Just as she was about to turn her attention back to the stage, she noted a striking figure in a black suit appear in the very rear of the public area. There was something about the man that gave her pause. Was it his sculpted, alabaster face? Or his hair, so blond it was almost white? Or his eyes of such pale gray-blue that, even across the room, he looked almost like an alien. Was he a celebrity? If not, Jenny decided, he should be.

Now a landscape designer was on his feet and giving his spiel, complete with slide show, images on the portable screen displaying a plat of the proposed burial area, followed by three-dimensional views of the future cemetery, with stone walls, a quaint wrought-iron archway leading in, cobbled paths among the graves. Next came slides of the actual site: a lovely green meadow partway up a mountain. It was pretty—but it wasn't in Roaring Fork.

As he spoke, the murmurings of disapproval, the restlessness, of the gathered public grew in suppressed intensity. Jenny recognized a reporter from the *Roaring Fork Times* sitting in the front row of the public area, and the look of anticipatory delight on his face signaled that he expected fireworks.

And now, at last, Mrs. Betty Brown Kermode

rose to speak. At this, a hush fell. She was a commanding presence in town—even Jenny's father seemed intimidated by her—and those who had gathered to express their opinions were temporarily muted.

She began by mentioning the exceedingly unfortunate break-in of ten days earlier, the shocking violation of a corpse, and how this demonstrated the need to get those human remains back in the ground as soon as possible. She mentioned in passing the seriousness of the crime—so serious that the perpetrator had accepted a plea bargain that would result in ten years' incarceration.

The Heights, she went on, had been taking care of these remains with the utmost attention, deeply aware of their sacred duty to see that these rough miners, these pioneers of Roaring Fork, were given a burial site suitable to their sacrifice, their spirit, and their contribution to the opening of the American West. They had, she said, found the perfect resting place: on the slopes of the Catamount, with heartbreaking views of the Continental Divide. Surrounding the graveyard, they had purchased over a hundred acres of open space, which would remain forever wild. This is what these Colorado pioneers deserved—not being jammed into some town lot, surrounded by the hustle and bustle of commerce, traffic, shopping, and sport.

It was an effective presentation. Even Jenny found herself agreeing with Mrs. Kermode. The grumbling was no longer audible when she returned to her seat.

Next to stand was Henry Montebello, who had married into Kermode's family and, as a result, gained instant power and respectability in the town. He was an older man, gaunt, reserved, and weathered looking. Jenny did not like him and was, in fact, afraid of him. He had a laconic mid-Atlantic accent that somehow caused every observation he made to sound cynical. Although he had been the master architect for The Heights way back when, unlike Kermode he did not live within the development, but rather had his home and office in a large mansion on the other side of town.

He cleared his throat. No expense had been spared, he told the gathered crowd, in developing The Heights—and not that alone, but also in ensuring that it conformed, not only with the spirit and aesthetic of Roaring Fork, but to the local ecology and environment, as well. He could say this, Montebello continued, because he had personally supervised the preparation of the site, the design of the mansions and clubhouse, and the construction of the development. He would, he said, oversee the creation of the new cemetery with the same close, hands-on attention he had given to The Heights.

The implication seemed to be that the long-dead occupants of Boot Hill should be grateful to Montebello for his personal ministrations on their behalf. Montebello spoke with quiet dignity, and with aristocratic gravitas—and yet there was a steely undertone to his words, subtle but unmistakable, that seemed to dare anyone to challenge a single syllable of what he'd uttered. No one did, and he once again took his seat.

And now the mayor rose, thanked Mrs. Kermode and Mr. Montebello, and called for public comment. A number of hands went up, and the mayor pointed at someone. But as that person rose to speak, the man in the black suit—who had somehow slipped all the way to the front—held up his hand for silence.

"You are out of turn, sir," said the mayor, sternly, rapping his gavel.

"That remains to be seen," came the reply. The voice was as smooth as honey, an unusual Deep South accent Jenny could not place, but something about it gave the mayor just enough pause to allow the man to continue.

"Mrs. Kermode," the man said, turning to her, "as you well know, permission from a qualified descendant is required to exhume human remains. In the case of historic burials, both Colorado and federal law state that a 'good-faith effort' must be

made to locate such descendants before any remains can be exhumed. I assume that The Heights
made such an effort?"

The mayor rapped his gavel. "I repeat, you are
out of turn, sir!"

"I'm happy to answer the question," Mrs. Kermode said smoothly. "We did indeed make a
diligent search for descendants. None could be
found. These miners were mostly transients
without families, who died a century and a half
ago, leaving no issue. It's all in the public documentation."

"Very good," said the mayor. "Thank you, sir,
for your opinion. We have many other people who
wish to speak. Mr. Jackson?"

But the man went on. "That is strange," he said.
"Because in just fifteen minutes of idle, ah, *surfing*
on the Internet, I was able to locate a direct descendant of one of the miners."

A silence, and then the mayor spoke. "Just who
are you, sir?"

"I'll get to that in a moment." The man raised
a piece of paper. "I have here a letter from Captain
Stacy Bowdree, USAF, just back from a tour in
Afghanistan. When Captain Bowdree heard that
you people had dug up her great-great-grandfather
Emmett Bowdree, dumped his remains in a box,
and stored them in a filthy equipment shed on a ski

slope, she was exceedingly upset. In fact, she plans to press charges."

This was greeted by silence.

The man held up another piece of paper. "Colorado statute is very strict on the desecration of cemeteries and human remains. Allow me to read from Section Ninety-Seven of the Colorado Criminal Codes and Statutes: *Desecration of a Cemetery.*" And he began to quote aloud.

(2) (a) Every person who shall knowingly and willfully dig up, except as otherwise provided by law with the permission of an authorized descendant, any corpse or remains of any human being, or cause through word, deed or action the same to happen, shall upon conviction be guilty of a Class A felony and shall be imprisoned for not more than thirty (30) years or fined not more than Fifty Thousand Dollars ($50,000.00), or both, in the discretion of the court.

Now the mayor rose in a fury, hammering his gavel. "This is not a court of law!" *Bang!* "I will not have these proceedings co-opted. If you, sir, have legal questions, take them up with the town attorney instead of wasting our time in a public meeting!"

But the man in the black suit would not be silenced. "Mayor, may I direct your attention to the language? *Or cause through word, deed or action the same to happen.* That seems to apply to *you* quite specifically, as well as to Mrs. Kermode and the chief of police. All three of you were responsible in *word, deed or action* for the illegal exhumation of Emmett Bowdree—were you not?"

"Enough! Security, remove this man from the premises!"

Even as two cops struggled to make their way to the man, he spoke again, his voice cutting the air like a razor. "*And are you not about to sentence someone to ten years in prison for violating this very statute that you, yourselves, have already so clearly violated?*"

Now the public was aroused, both pro and con. There were some murmurings and scattered shouts: "Is it true?" and "What goes?" along with "Get rid of him!" and "Who the hell is this guy?"

The two cops, pushing their way through the now-standing public crowd, reached the man. One took his arm.

"Don't give us any trouble, sir."

The man freed himself from the cop's grasp. "I would advise you not to touch me."

"Arrest him for disturbing the peace!" the mayor cried.

"*Let him speak!*" someone shouted.

"Sir," Jenny heard the cop say, "if you won't co-operate, we'll have to arrest you."

The man's response was drowned out by the hubbub. The mayor rapped his gavel repeatedly, calling for order.

"You're under arrest," said the cop. "Place your hands behind your back."

Instead of obeying the order, Jenny saw the man remove his wallet with a single, smooth motion and flip it open. There was a flash of gold, and the two officers froze.

The hubbub began to die down.

"In response to your earlier question," the man told the mayor in his dulcet southern voice, "I am Special Agent Pendergast of the Federal Bureau of Investigation."

Now the entire room went deathly silent. Jenny had never before seen the look she now saw on Mrs. Kermode's face: shock and fury. Henry Montebello's face betrayed nothing at all. Chief Morris, for his part, looked paralyzed. *Paralyzed* wasn't the word—he looked wilted. Slumped. As if he wanted to melt into his chair and disappear. The mayor looked merely undone.

"Emmett Bowdree," the man named Pendergast continued, "is just one of a hundred and thirty human remains that the four of you—Mrs. Kermode, the mayor, Mr. Montebello, and the chief of police who signed the actual order—are responsible for desecrating, according to Colorado statute. The criminal and civil liability is staggering."

Mrs. Kermode recovered first. "Is this how the FBI operates? You come in here, interrupt our public meeting, and make threats? Are you even a real agent? Come down here and present your credentials to the mayor in the proper fashion!"

"Gladly." The pale man slipped through the gate separating the public area from the official one and strolled down the aisle with a sort of insolent casualness. He arrived in front of the mayor and laid the shield down on the podium. The man examined it, his face reflecting growing consternation.

With a sudden, lithe movement, Agent Pendergast plucked the mayor's microphone out of its mount. Only then did Jenny realize that inviting the stranger to the front had probably not been the best idea. She could see the reporter from the *Roaring Fork Times* scribbling madly, a look of pure joy on his face.

Now the mayor spoke, raising his voice on account of having lost his amplification. "Agent Pendergast, are you here in an official capacity?"

"Not yet," came the answer.

"Then I move we adjourn this meeting so that our attorneys, the attorneys from The Heights, and you can address these issues in private." A bang of the gavel sealed this statement.

Agent Pendergast's black-clad arm snaked out, took the gavel, and moved it out of reach of the mayor's hand. "Enough of that uncivilized pounding."

This brought a laugh from the public section.

"I am not yet finished." Pendergast's voice, now amplified by the sound system, filled the hall. "Captain Bowdree wrote me that, since her great-great-grandfather's remains have been so rudely disinterred, and nothing can remedy the insult to his memory, she believes that they should at least be examined for cause of death—for historical purposes, of course. Therefore, she has given permission for a certain Ms. Corrine Swanson to examine those remains before they are reburied. In their *original* resting place, by the way."

"What?" Kermode rose in a fury. "Did that girl send you? Is *she* behind this?"

"She has no idea I'm even here," the man said smoothly. "However, it would seem that the most serious charge against her is now moot—but has instead redounded to the four of you. *You* are now the ones facing thirty years in prison—not on one count, but on one hundred and thirty." He paused. "Imagine if your sentences were to be served sequentially."

"These accusations are outrageous!" the mayor cried. "I hereby adjourn this meeting. Will security immediately clear the room!"

Chaos ensued. But Pendergast did nothing to prevent it, and the meeting room was finally cleared, leaving him alone with the town fathers, The Heights attorneys, Kermode, Montebello, Chief Morris, and a few other officials. Jenny waited in her seat beside the chief, breathless. What would happen now? For the first time, Kermode looked defeated—haggard, her platinum hair undone. The chief was bathed in sweat, the mayor pale.

"It looks like there's going to be quite a story in the *Roaring Fork Times* tomorrow," said Pendergast.

Everyone seemed to stagger at the thought. The mayor wiped his brow.

"In addition to that story," said Pendergast, "I'd like to see another one appear."

There was a long silence. Montebello was the first to speak. "And what might that be?"

"A story stating that you—" Agent Pendergast turned to Chief Morris— "have dropped all charges against Corrine Swanson and released her from jail."

He let that sink in.

"As I said before, the most serious charge is now moot. Ms. Swanson has permission to examine the remains of Emmett Bowdree. The other charges—trespassing and B and E—are less grave and could be dismissed with relative ease. Everything can, in fact, be chalked up to an unfortunate miscommunication between Chief Morris here and Ms. Swanson."

"This is blackmail," said Kermode.

Pendergast turned to her. "I might point out it wasn't actually a miscommunication. My understanding is that Chief Morris indicated she would have access to the remains. He then withdrew that assurance, due to your own gross interference. It was unfair. I am merely rectifying a wrong."

There was a pause while the others digested this. "And what," asked Kermode, "will you do for us in return? That is, if the chief releases this lady friend of yours."

"I'll persuade Captain Bowdree not to take her complaint *officially* to the FBI," Pendergast said smoothly.

"I see," said Kermode. "It all depends on this Captain Bowdree. Provided, of course, this person even exists."

"How unfortunate for you that Bowdree was an unusual name. It made my task so much easier. A phone call established that she was well aware of her Colorado roots and, in fact, quite proud of them. Mrs. Kermode, you claimed The Heights made a good-faith effort to locate descendants. That is clearly a falsehood. Naturally, this is something the FBI would have to look into."

Jenny noticed that under her makeup, Mrs. Kermode's face was very pale. "Let's get this straight. This Swanson girl—she's what, your girlfriend? A relative?"

"She's no relation to me." Agent Pendergast narrowed his silvery eyes and looked at Kermode in a most unsettling way. "I will, however, be remaining in Roaring Fork to take in the Christmas season—and to make sure you don't interfere with her again."

As Jenny watched, Pendergast turned to the chief. "I suggest you call the newspaper right away—I imagine their deadline is looming. I've already booked a room for Ms. Swanson at the Hotel Sebastian, and I hope that—for your sake—she does not spend another night in your jail."

# 11

It was a few minutes before midnight when the silver Porsche 911 Turbo S Cabriolet pulled up to the elegant front door of 3 Quaking Aspen Drive. It did not stop there, however, but continued on into the shadow of the four-car garage beyond.

The young man at the wheel put the vehicle into park. "Home," he said. "As you requested." He leaned over the gear lever to nuzzle the girl in the passenger seat.

"Stop it," she said, pushing him away.

The young man pretended to look hurt. "I'm a friend, aren't I?"

"Yes."

"Then bring on the benefits." Another attempt at nuzzling.

"What a dork." The girl got out of the car with a laugh. "Thanks for dinner."

"*And* the movie."

"And the movie." Jenny Baker slammed the door, then watched the car move off down the long, curving driveway until it reached the road leading to the gatehouse of The Heights, down in the valley half a mile away. For a lot of her girlfriends back at Hollywood High, losing one's virginity seemed like a badge of honor: the sooner the better. But Jenny didn't feel that way. Not on a first date, and certainly not with a dweeb like Kevin Traherne. Like so many of the male youth in Roaring Fork, he seemed to think that his father's dough was the only excuse he needed to get into a girl's pants.

She stepped up to the closest garage door, punched a code into the panel, and waited for the door to ascend. Then she walked past the row of gleaming, expensive cars, pressed the button to close the garage, and opened the door to the house. The security alarm was, as usual, off—there were few burglaries in Roaring Fork, and never a one in The Heights...unless you counted Corrie Swanson's breaking into the warehouse, of course. Her thoughts returned to the town meeting earlier in the day, and to the intimidating FBI agent in the black suit who'd descended on it like an avenging angel. She felt sorry for the chief: he was a decent guy, but he had a real problem with letting other people—like that witch Kermode—walk all over him. Nevertheless, she was glad the agent—Pendergast was his name, she remembered—had gotten Corrie out of jail. She hoped to run into her again, ask her about John Jay, maybe...as long as the chief wasn't around.

Jenny walked through the mudroom, through the pantry, and into the expansive kitchen of the vacation home. Through glass doors she could see the Christmas tree, all decked out and blinking. Her parents and her younger sister, Sarah, would be upstairs asleep.

She snapped on a bank of lights. They illuminated the long granite countertops; the Wolf oven and dual Sub-Zero refrigerator and freezer units; the three doors leading, respectively, into the laundry, the second kitchen, and the dining room.

She suddenly realized there had been no patter of nails on the floor, no shaggy, friendly dog wagging his misshapen tail in greeting. "Rex?" she called out.

Nothing.

With a shrug, she got a glass from one of the cabinets, walked over to the fridge—decorated, as usual, with Sarah's stupid Nicki Minaj photos—poured herself a glass of milk, then took a seat at the table in the breakfast nook. There was a stack of books and magazines in the window seat, and she pushed a few aside—noting as she did so that

Sarah had finally taken her advice and begun reading *Watership Down*—and plucked out her copy of Schmalleger's *Criminal Justice Today*. As she did so, she noticed that one of the chairs of the kitchen table had been knocked over.

Sloppy.

She found her page in the book and began to read, sipping her milk as she did so. It drove her father—a high-profile Hollywood lawyer—crazy that she wanted to go into law enforcement. He tended to look down on cops and prosecutors as lower forms of life. But in point of fact he was partly responsible for her interest. All the cop action movie premieres she'd attended—produced or directed by her father's clients—had left her fascinated with the job from an early age. And starting next fall, she'd be studying the subject full-time, as a freshman at Northeastern University.

Finishing her milk, she closed the book again, put her glass in the sink, and walked out of the kitchen, heading for the stairs up to her room. Her father had the connections to keep her from getting summer jobs with the California police, but there was nothing he could do to prevent her winter break internship here in Roaring Fork. The very idea of it made him nuts.

Which, of course, was part of the fun.

The huge, rambling house was very still. She ascended the curving staircase to the second floor, the landing above dark and silent. As she climbed, she thought once again about the mysterious FBI agent. *FBI*, she thought. *Maybe I should look into an internship in Quantico next summer...*

At the top of the stairs, she stopped. Something was wrong. For a moment, she wasn't sure what it was. And then she realized: Sarah's door was wide open, faint light streaming out into the dim hall.

At sixteen, Sarah had reached the age where adolescent privacy was all-important. These days her door was closed at all times. Jenny sniffed the air, but there was no smell of weed. She smiled: her sister must have fallen asleep over a magazine or something. She'd take the opportunity to sneak in and rearrange her sister's stuff. That was sure to get a rise out of her.

Quietly, she crept down the hallway, approaching her sister's room on silent feet. She came up to the door frame, placed one hand upon it, then slowly leaned her head in.

At first, she could not quite process what she saw. Sarah lay on her bed, tied fast with wound wire, a dirty rag stuffed into her mouth, a billiard ball at its center—Jenny noticed a number, seven, engraved into its yellow-and-white surface—and secured behind her head with a bungee cord. In the faint blue light, Jenny saw that her sister's knees were bleeding profusely, staining the bedcovers black. As she gasped in horror and shock, Jenny saw Sarah's eyes staring back at her: wide, terrified, pleading.

Then Jenny registered something in her peripheral vision. She turned in mid-gasp to see a fearful apparition in the hall beside her: wearing black jeans and a tight-fitting jacket of dark leather. The figure was silent and utterly motionless. Its hands were gloved and gripped a baseball bat. Worst of all was the clown mask—white, huge red lips smiling maniacally, bright red circles on each cheek. Jenny stumbled backward, her legs going weak beneath her. Through the eyeholes on each side of the long pointed nose, she could see two dark eyes staring back at her, dreadful in their lack of expression, in awful counterpoint to the leering mask.

Jenny opened her mouth to scream, but the figure—springing into sudden, violent motion—reached forward and quickly stuffed an awful-smelling cloth over her mouth and nose. As her senses went black and she sank to the floor, she could just hear—as the darkness rushed over her—a faint, high-pitched keening coming through Sarah's gag...

Slowly, slowly, she regained her senses. Everything was fuzzy and vague. For a moment, she didn't know where she was. She was lying on something hard and smooth and that seemed to encircle her. Then, looking around in the darkness, she understood: she was in the tub of her private bathroom. What was she doing here? It felt as if she'd been asleep for hours. But no—the wall clock above her sink read ten minutes to one. She'd only been out for a couple of minutes. She tried to move—and realized she had been bound, hand and foot.

That was when the memory of what had happened came rushing back, falling upon her like a dead weight.

Instantly her heart accelerated, pounding hard in her chest. The rag was still in her mouth. She tried to spit it out, found she could not. The tight rope chafed at her wrists and ankles. Crime-scene photos she'd seen came into her mind, flashing quickly by in a terrible parade.

*I'm going to be raped*, she thought, shuddering at the recollection of that leering clown mask. But no—if rape was what he was after, he wouldn't have tied her up the way he did. This was a home invasion—and she'd walked right into the middle of it.

A home invasion.

*Maybe he only wants money*, she thought. *Maybe he only wants jewelry. He'll take what he can get, then leave, and then...*

But it was all so horribly stealthy—so diabolically calculating. First Sarah, now her...

...*What about Mom and Dad?*

At this thought, stark panic bubbled to the surface.

She struggled violently, jaw working, tongue pushing against the cloth wedged into her mouth. She tried to rise up, and an agonizing pain that almost caused her to faint lanced through her legs. She saw that her kneecaps had been beaten like her sister's, white edges of broken bone jutting up through torn, bloody flesh. She remembered the baseball bat clutched in one black-gloved hand, and she moaned in fresh panic, thrashing against the bottom of the tub despite the awful pain in her knees.

All of a sudden, sounds of fighting erupted from down the hall: her father yelling, her mother crying out in fear. Jenny listened in unspeakable horror. Furniture was overturned; there was the sound of breaking glass. Her mother's screams spiked in volume. A heavy thud. Abruptly, her father's shouts of anger and alarm changed to cries of pain. There was an ugly crack of what sounded like wood on bone, and his voice was abruptly cut off.

Jenny listened to the dreadful silence, whimpering under the gag, her heart beating even faster.

And then, a moment later, came another sound: sobs, running feet. It was her mother, racing down the hall, trying to escape. Jenny heard her mother go into Sarah's room; heard her scream. And now a heavier tread came down the hall. It was not her father's.

Another cry of fear from her mother; the sound of feet pattering down the stairs. *She'll get away now*, Jenny thought, hope suddenly rising within her like white light. *She'll hit the alarm, she'll run out, call the neighbors, call the cops...*

The unfamiliar tread, faster now, went stomping down the steps.

Heart in her throat, Jenny listened as the sounds grew fainter. She heard her mother's step, running toward the kitchen and the master alarm panel. There was a cry as she was apparently cut off. The thunk of an overturned chair; the sound of glassware and dishes crashing to the floor. Jenny, struggling against her bonds, could hear it all, could follow the chase with dreadful articulation. She heard her mother's footsteps, running through the den, the living room, the library. A moment of silence. And then came a low, cautious sliding sound: it was her mother, quietly opening the door to the indoor pool. *She's going out the back*, Jenny thought. *Out the back, so she can get to the MacArthurs' house...*

All of a sudden there was a series of brutal

crashes—her mother gave out a single, sharp scream—and then silence.

No…not quite silence. As Jenny listened, wide-eyed, whimpering, the blood rushing in her ears, she could make out the unfamiliar tread again. It was moving slowly now, deliberately. And it was getting closer. It was crossing the front hall. Now it was coming back up the stairs: she heard the squeak of the tread her father kept saying he'd get fixed.

Closer. Closer. The steps were coming down the hall. They were in her bedroom. And now a dark figure appeared in the doorway of her bath. It was silent, save for labored breathing. The clown mask leered down at her. There was no longer a baseball bat in one of the hands. It had been re-placed by a plastic squeeze bottle, glowing pale gold in the faint light.

The figure stepped into the bathroom.

As it came closer, Jenny writhed in the tub, heedless of the pain in her knees. Now the invader was hovering over her. The hand holding the squeeze bottle came forward in her direction. As the figure began silently squeezing the liquid over her in long, arc-like jets, a powerful stench rose up: gasoline.

Jenny's struggles became frantic.

Painstakingly, Clown Mask sent the looping

squirts of gasoline over and around her, missing nothing, dousing her clothes; her hair; the surrounding porcelain. Then—as her struggles grew ever more violent—the invader put down the bottle and took a step back. A hand reached into the pocket of the leather jacket, withdrew a safety match. Holding the match carefully by its end, the figure struck it against the rough surface of the bathroom wall. The head of the match flared into yellow life. It hovered over her, dangling, for an endless, agonizing second.

And then, with the parting of a thumb and index finger, it dropped.

...And Jenny's world dissolved into a roar of flame.

# 12

Corrie Swanson entered the dining room of the Hotel Sebastian and found herself dazzled by its elegance. It was done up in Gay Nineties style, with red velvet flocked wallpaper, polished-brass and cut-glass fixtures, a pressed-tin ceiling, and Victorian-era mahogany tables and chairs trimmed in silk and gold. A wall of windowpanes looked across the glittering Christmas lights of Main Street to the spruce-clad foothills, ski slopes, and mountain peaks beyond.

Even though it was close to midnight, the dining room was crowded, the convivial murmur of voices mingling with the clink of glassware and the bustle of waiters. The light was dim, and it took her a moment to spy the solitary figure of Pendergast, seated at an unobtrusive table by one of the windows.

She brushed off the maître d's pointed inquiries

as to how he could help her—she was still dressed from jail—and made her way to Pendergast's table. He rose, extending his hand. She was startled by his appearance: he seemed to be even paler, leaner, more ascetic—the word *purified* seemed somehow to apply.

"Corrie, I am glad to see you." He took her hand in his, cool as marble, then held out her seat for her. She sat down.

She'd been rehearsing what she would say, but now it all came out in a confused rush. "I can't believe I'm free—how can I ever thank you? I was toast, I mean, I was up shit creek, you know they'd already forced me to accept ten years—I really thought my life was over—thank you, *thank you* for everything, for saving my ass, for rescuing me from my incredible, unbelievable *stupidity*, and I'm so sorry, really, *really* sorry—!"

A raised hand stopped the flow of words. "Will you have a drink? Wine, perhaps?"

"Um, I'm only twenty."

"Ah. Of course. I shall order a bottle for myself, then." He picked up a leather-bound wine list that was so massive, it could have been a murder weapon.

"This sure beats jail," said Corrie, looking around, drinking in the ambience, the aroma of food. It was hard to believe that, just a few hours ago, she'd been behind bars, her life utterly ruined. But once again Agent Pendergast had swooped in, like a guardian angel, and changed everything.

"It took them rather longer than I'd hoped to complete the paperwork," said Pendergast, perusing the list. "Fortunately, the Sebastian's dining room is open late. I think the Château Pichon-Longueville 2000 will do nicely—don't you?"

"I don't know jack about wine, sorry."

"You should learn. It is one of the true and ancient pleasures that make human existence tolerable."

"Um, I know this may not be the time…But I just have to ask you…" She found herself coloring. "*Why* did you rescue me like this? And why do you go to all this trouble for me? I mean, you got me out of Medicine Creek, you paid for my boarding school, you're helping pay my tuition at John Jay—why? I'm just a screwup."

He looked at her with an inscrutable gaze. "The Colorado rack of lamb for two would go well with the wine. I understand it's excellent."

She glanced at the menu. She was, it had to be admitted, starving. "Sounds good to me."

Pendergast waved over the waiter and placed the order.

"Anyway, getting back to what I was talking about…I would really like to know, once and for all, why you've helped me all these years. Especially when I keep, you know, effing up."

Again that impenetrable gaze met hers. "*Effing?* I see your penchant for charming euphemisms has not abated."

"You know what I mean."

The gaze seemed to go on forever, and then Pendergast said: "Someday, perhaps, you may make a good law enforcement officer or criminalist. That is why. No other reason."

She felt herself coloring again. She wasn't quite sure she liked the answer. Now she wished she hadn't asked the question.

Pendergast picked up the wine list again. "Remarkable how many bottles of excellent French wine in rare vintages have found their way into this small town in the middle of the mountains. I certainly hope they are drunk soon; the altitude here is most unhealthy for Bordeaux." He laid down the list. "And now, Corrie, please tell me in detail what you noticed about the bones of Mr. Emmett Bowdree."

She swallowed. Pendergast was so damn... *closed*. "I only had a few minutes to examine the bones. But I'm sure the guy was not killed by a grizzly bear."

"Your evidence?"

"I took some photographs, but they confiscated

the memory chip. I can tell you what I saw—or at least *think* I saw."

"Excellent."

"First of all, the skull showed signs of having been bashed in by a rock. And the right femur had scrape marks made by some blunt tool, with no signs that I could see of an osseous reaction or infectious response."

A slow nod.

She went on with growing confidence. "It looked to me like there were faint human tooth marks in some of the cancellous bone. They were pretty feeble and blunt, not sharp like a bear's. I think the corpse was cannibalized."

In her zeal she'd raised her voice, and now she realized it had carried farther than she'd intended. The diners closest to them were staring at her.

"Oops," she said, looking down at her place setting.

"Have you told anyone of this?" Pendergast asked.

"Not yet."

"Very good. Keep it quiet. It will only create trouble."

"But I need access to more remains."

"I'm working on that. Of the other miners in question, I'm hoping we might find descendants in at least a few cases. And then, naturally, we'd have to get permission."

"Oh. Thanks, but, you know, I could really do those things myself." She paused. "Um, how long do you plan to stay? A few days?"

"Such a lovely, self-indulgent, *rich* little town. I don't believe I've seen anything quite like it. And so charming at Christmastime."

"So you're going to stay...a long time?"

"Ah, here's the wine."

It had arrived, along with two big glasses. Corrie watched as Pendergast went through the whole routine of swirling the wine around in the glass, smelling it, tasting it, tasting it again.

"Corked, I'm afraid," he told the waiter. "Please bring another bottle. Make it an '01, to be on the safe side."

With profuse apologies, the waiter hurried off with the bottle and glass.

"Corked?" Corrie asked. "What's that?"

"It's a contaminant of wine, giving it a taste redolent of, some say, a wet dog."

The new bottle came out and Pendergast went through the routine again, this time nodding his approval. The waiter filled his glass, motioned the bottle toward Corrie. She shrugged and the man filled her glass as well.

Corrie sipped it. It tasted like wine to her—no

more, no less. She said, "This is almost as good as the Mateus we all used to drink back in Medicine Creek."

"I see you still enjoy provoking me."

She took another sip. It was amazing, how quickly the memory of jail was fading. "Getting back to my release," she said. "How did you do it?"

"As it happens, I was already on my way back to New York when I received your second letter."

"You finally got sick of traveling the world?"

"It was your first letter, in part, that prompted my return."

"Oh? Why's that?"

Instead of answering, Pendergast peered into the dark ruby of his wineglass. "I was fortunate in locating Captain Bowdree so quickly. I explained everything to her frankly—how her ancestor had been rudely exhumed from his historic resting place to make way for a spa. I explained who you were, what your background was, how the chief promised you access and then withdrew it. I told her about your foolish break-in, how you got caught. And then I mentioned you were facing a ten-year prison sentence."

He sipped his wine. "The captain understood the situation immediately. She was most unwilling for you to be, as she put it, *fucked over* like that. She repeated that phrase several times with remarkable emphasis, and it led me to believe she may have had some experience in that line—perhaps in the military. At any rate, together we composed a rather effective letter, which on the one hand threatened to complain to the FBI and, on the other, gave you permission to study the remains of her ancestor."

"Oh," said Corrie. "And that's how you got me out?"

"There was a rather boisterous town meeting this afternoon, at which I discussed the captain's letter." Pendergast allowed himself the faintest of smiles. "My presentation was singularly effective. You'll read all about it in tomorrow's paper."

"Well, you saved my butt. I can't thank you enough. And please thank Captain Bowdree for me."

"I shall."

There was a sharp murmur in the dining room; a stir. Several patrons had begun looking toward the wall of windows, and some had stood up from their tables and were pointing. Corrie followed their gaze and saw a small, flickering yellow light on the side of a nearby ridge. As she watched, it rapidly grew in brightness and size. Now more restaurant patrons were standing, and some were walking toward the windows. The hubbub increased.

"Oh, my God, that's a house on fire!" Corrie said, standing up herself to get a better view.

"So it would seem."

The fire blossomed with shocking rapidity. It appeared to be a huge house and the flames engulfed it with increasing violence, leaping into the night air, sending up columns of sparks and smoke. A fire siren began to go off in the town somewhere, followed by another. And now the entire dining room was on its feet, eyes glued to the mountain. A sense of horror had fallen on the diners, a hush—and then a voice rang out.

"That's the Baker house, up in The Heights!"

## 13

Larry Chivers had seen many scenes of destruction in his career as a fire investigator, but he had never seen anything like this. The house had been gigantic—fifteen-thousand-plus square feet—and built with massive timbers, beams, log walls, and soaring, cedar-shake roofs. It had burned with a ferocity that left puddles of glass where the windows had been and even warped the steel I-beam stringers. The snow had completely vanished from within a five-hundred-yard perimeter of the house, and the ruin still radiated heat and plumes of foul steam.

Chivers, who ran a fire investigation consulting firm out of Grand Junction, had been called in at seven that morning. Most of his work was for insurance companies looking to prove arson so they didn't have to pay claims. But once in a while he got called in by the police to determine if a fire was an accident or a crime. This was one of those times.

It was a two-hour drive from Grand Junction, but he'd made it in ninety minutes, driving like hell in his Dodge pickup. Chivers liked traveling with the lightbar and siren going full blast, whipping past the poor speed-limit-bound schmucks on the interstate. Adding to the appeal of this case, the Roaring Fork Police Department paid well and didn't nickel-and-dime him to death like some of the other PDs he worked for.

But his exhilaration had been dampened by this scene of horror. Even Morris, the chief of police, seemed undone by it: stammering, inarticulate, unable to take charge. Chivers did his best to shake the feeling. The fact is, these were rich Hollywood types who used this colossal house as a second home—second home!—only a few weeks out of the year. It was hard to gin up a lot of sympathy for people like that. No doubt the homeowner could build five more just like it and barely dent his wallet. The man who owned this house, a fellow named Jordan Baker, hadn't been heard from, and nobody had been able to reach him yet to inform him of the fire. He and his family were probably off at some posh resort. Or maybe they had a *third* home. It wouldn't surprise Chivers.

He began preparing himself for the walk-through, checking and organizing his equipment, testing his digital recorder, putting on latex gloves. One good thing about the chief's apparent paralysis was that the fire scene hadn't been trampled over and messed up by all the forensic specialists who were still gathering around, waiting to do their thing. Morris had pretty much kept everyone out, waiting for his arrival, and for that he was grateful. Although, as usual, there was considerable disturbance from firefighter activity—chopped-through floors and walls, shoveled and turned debris, everything soaked with water. The fire department had done a cursory structural integrity survey and had identified the areas that were unstable, taping them off.

Chivers shouldered his bag and nodded to Chief Morris. "Ready."

"Good," the chief said absently. "Fine. Rudy will take you through."

The fireman named Rudy lifted the tape for him, and he followed the man down the brick walkway and through where the front door had been. The fire scene stank heavily of burnt and soggy plastic, wood, and polyurethane. There was still some residual heat—despite the freezing temperature the house itself was still sending plumes of steam into the cold blue sky. While he was required to wear a hard hat, he did not wear a respirator: Chivers saw himself as an old-fashioned fire-scene investigator, tough, no-nonsense, who relied more on intuition and left the science to the lab rats. He was used to the stench—and he needed his nose to sniff out any residual accelerants.

Inside the door, in what had been the entryway, he paused. The second floor had collapsed into the first, creating a crazy mess. A staircase ended in the sky. Puddles of glass and metal lay in the low spots, along with heaps of fire-shattered porcelain.

He walked from the entryway into what had obviously been the kitchen, observing the burn patterns. The first order of business was to determine if this was arson—if a crime had been committed. And Chivers was already sure one had. Only accelerants could have caused a fire to burn so hot and fast. This was confirmed as he looked around the kitchen, where he could see faint pour patterns on the remains of the slate floor. He knelt, removed a portable hydrocarbon sniffer from his bag, and took some air samples, moving it about. Moderate.

Still kneeling, he jammed a knife into the burnt, flaking floor and pried up a couple of small pieces, placing them in nylon evidence bags.

The kitchen was a mess, everything fused, scorched, melted. A second-floor bathroom had fallen into the middle of it, with the remains of a porcelain-covered iron claw-foot tub and bits of the sink, toilet, tiled floor, and walls all heaped and scattered about.

Using the sniffer, he got a big positive hit from the remains of the second-floor bathroom. Moving forward on hands and knees, keeping the sniffer low to the ground, Chivers swept it about, looking for a source. The hydrocarbon signature appeared to increase as he approached the tub itself. He rose, peered inside. There was a lot of stuff in the tub—and at the bottom, a layer of thick, black muck in which debris was embedded.

He sampled the muck, giving it a little stir with a gloved finger. The sniffer went off the charts. And then Chivers stopped cold. Among the muck and debris he could see the fragments of bones poking up—and in the area he had stirred up, some teeth. Human teeth. He carefully probed with his gloved finger, exposing a small piece of a skull, a fragment of jaw, and the rim of an orbit.

Chivers steadied himself, lowered the sniffer. The needle shot up again.

He took out his digital recorder and began murmuring into it. The house had not been empty, after all. Clearly, a body had been placed in the bathtub and burned with accelerant. Putting aside the recorder, he removed another nylon evidence bag and took samples of the debris and muck, in-

cluding a few small bone fragments. As he poked
about in the black paste he saw the gleam of something—a lump of gold, no doubt once a piece of
jewelry. He left that, but took samples from the
grit and muck around it, including a charred pha-
lange.

He stood up, breathing heavily, feeling a faint
wave of nausea. This was a bit more than he was
used to. But then again, this was clearly going to
be a big case. A very big case. *Focus on that*, he told
himself, taking another deep breath.

Chivers nodded to Rudy and continued to follow the fireman through the rest of the house,
working the sniffer, taking samples, and speaking
his observations into the handheld digital recorder.
The charred corpse of what had once been a dog
was fused to the stone floor at the back door of
the house. Next to it lay two long, disordered piles
of gritty ashes, which Chivers recognized as the
much-burnt remains of two more victims, both
adults judging by the length of the piles, lying side
by side. More puddles of gold and silver.

Jesus. He took a sniffer reading but didn't come
up with anything significant. Christ, no one had
told him—and now he realized they probably
didn't know—that the fire had claimed human victims.

Another couple of deep breaths, and Chivers

moved on. And then, in what had been the living room, he came upon something else. Debris from the collapsed floor above lay in sodden heaps, and sitting in the center was a set of partly melted bedsprings. As he moved toward the twisted springs, he noted loops of baling wire affixed to them, as if something had been tied to the bed. Four loops—approximately where the ankles and hands would have been. And in one of those loops, he spied a fragment of a small, juvenile tibia.

*Oh, Jesus and Mary.* Chivers moved the sniffer to it, and again the needle pinned. It was all too clear what had happened. A kid had been wired to the bed, doused with accelerant, and set on fire.

"I need some air," he said abruptly, rising and staggering. "Air."

The fireman grabbed his arm. "Let me help you out, sir."

As Chivers exited the fire scene and reeled down the walkway, he saw—out of the corner of his eye—a pale man, dressed in black, no doubt the local coroner, standing beyond the edge of the crowd, staring at him. He made a huge effort to pull himself together.

"I'm all right, thanks," he said to the firefighter, shedding the embarrassing arm. He looked around, located Chief Morris at the makeshift command center, surrounded by the gathering forensic teams—photographers, hair and fiber, latent, ballistics, DNA. They were suiting up, preparing to go in.

*Take it easy*, he said to himself. But he could not take it easy. His legs felt like rubber, and it was hard to walk straight.

He approached the chief. Morris was sweating, despite the cold. "What did you find?" he asked, his voice quiet.

"It's a crime scene," said Chivers, trying to control the quaver in his voice. Faint lights were dancing in front of his eyes now. "Four victims. At least, four so far."

"Four? Oh, my God. So they were in there. The whole family…" The chief wiped his brow with a shaking hand.

Chivers swallowed. "One of the remains is of a…a juvenile who was…tied to a bed, doused with accelerant…and set on fire. Another was burned in…in…"

As Chivers tried to get out the words, the chief's face went slack. But Chivers barely noticed. His own world was getting darker and darker.

And then, as he was still trying to finish his sentence, Chivers folded to the ground, collapsing in a dead faint.

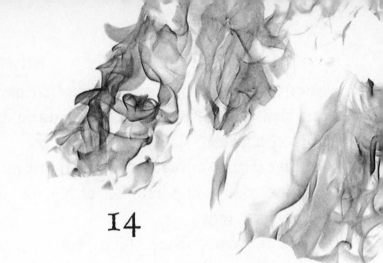

# 14

Corrie had risen before dawn, gathered her equipment, and headed up to Roaring Fork. Now, as noon approached, she was ensconced in the warehouse at The Heights and well into her work. The remains of Emmett Bowdree were carefully arranged on a plastic folding table Corrie had bought at Walmart, under a set of strong studio lights. She had her stereo zoom in place, hooked to her laptop, the screen displaying the view from the microscope. Her Nikon stood on its tripod. It was like a little piece of heaven, being able to work carefully and thoroughly, without being half scared out of her wits and worrying about detection at any moment.

The only problem was, she was freezing her ass off. It had been below zero when she began the long drive from Basalt—having refused the free room at the Hotel Sebastian, courtesy of Pendergast. She had skipped breakfast to save money, and now she was starving as well as cold. She'd set up a cheap electric heater at her feet, but it was rattling and humming and the stream of warm air seemed to dissipate within inches of its grille. It was doing a good job of warming her shins, but that was about it.

Still, not even the cold and hunger could dampen her growing excitement at what she was finding. Almost all the bones showed trauma in the form of scrape marks, blunt cuts, and gouges. None of the marks showed signs of an osseous reaction, inflammation, or granulation—which meant the damage had been inflicted at the actual time of death. The soft, cancellous or spongy bone tissue showed unmistakable tooth marks—not bear but human, judging from the radius of the bite and the tooth profile. There were, in fact, no bear tooth or claw marks at all.

Inside the broken femur and inside the skull, she had discovered additional scraping and gouging marks, indicating that the marrow and brains had been reamed out by a metal tool. Under the stereo zoom, these defleshing marks disclosed some very faint parallel lines, close together, and what looked like iron oxide deposits—which suggested the tool was iron and, quite possibly, a worn file.

The initial blow to the cranium had definitely been inflicted by a rock. Under the microscope, she had been able to extract a few tiny fragments of it, which a cursory examination showed to be quartz.

The rib cage had been split open—also with a rock—and pulled apart, as if to get at the heart. The bones showed little evidence of trauma inflicted by a sharp edge—such as an ax or knife—nor were there any injuries consistent with a gunshot wound. This puzzled her, as most miners of the time would no doubt have been armed with either a knife or a pistol.

The contemporary newspaper account of the discovery of Emmett Bowdree's body indicated that his bones had been found scattered on the ground a hundred yards beyond the door of a cabin; he had been "almost entirely eaten" by the so-called bear. The newspaper article, perhaps for reasons of delicacy, didn't go into much detail on exactly what had been eaten or how the bones were disarticulated, except to note that "pieces of the heart and other viscera were discovered at a distance from the body, partially consumed." The article made no mention of a fire or cooking, and her examination of the remains showed no evidence of heat.

Emmett Bowdree had been eaten raw.

As she worked, she began to see, in her mind's eye, the sequence of injuries that had been inflicted on the body of Bowdree. He had been set upon by a group—no single person could have pulled a human body apart with such an extremity of violence. They struck him on the back of the head with a rock, causing a severe depressed fracture. While it may not have killed him instantly, it almost certainly rendered him unconscious. They gave the body a savage beating that broke almost every bone, and then proceeded to chop and pound at the body's major articulations—there was evidence of disorganized, haphazard hacking with broken rocks, followed by separation via a strong lateral force. After breaking the joints, they pulled the arms and legs from the torso, separated the legs at the knees, broke open the skull and removed the brains, stripped the flesh from the bones, broke up the larger bones and reamed out the marrow, and removed most of the organs. The killers appeared to have only one tool, a worn-out file, which they supplemented with sharp pieces of quartz rock, their hands, and their teeth.

Corrie surmised that the killing started out as a product of fury and anger, then evolved into—essentially—a cannibal feast. She stepped back from the remains for a moment, thinking. Who was the gang who did this? Why? Again, it seemed exceedingly strange to her that a gang of murderers would be roaming the mountains in the 1870s without guns or knives. And why didn't they cook the meat? It was almost as if they were a tribe of Stone Age killers, merciless and savage.

*Merciless and savage.* As she warmed herself in front of the heater, rubbing her hands together, Corrie's mind wandered once again to the terrible fire that had taken place the evening before—and the death of the girl, Jenny Baker. It was beyond horrible, the entire family perishing in the fire like that. A maintenance worker had stopped by the warehouse an hour earlier and given her the news. No wonder she'd managed to breeze through The Heights security at ten that morning with barely a nod, left to her own devices without a minder.

The horror of it, and the face of Jenny Baker—so earnest and pretty—haunted her. *Focus on your work*, she told herself, straightening up and preparing to place another bone on the stage for examination.

What she really needed was to get her hands on more sets of remains for comparison. Pendergast had said he was going to help her track down more descendants. She paused for a moment in her work, trying to figure out what it was about this that annoyed her. The force of his personality was such that he dominated any situation he was in.

But this was *her* project—and she wanted to do it on her own. She didn't want to have people back at John Jay, especially her advisor, dismissing her work because of the help of a big-time FBI agent. Even the smallest amount of assistance from him might contaminate her achievement, giving them an opening to dismiss it all.

Then Corrie shook this thought away as well. The guy had just saved her career and maybe even her life. To get so possessive, so proprietary, was churlish. Besides, Pendergast always shunned credit or publicity.

She pulled off her gloves to position a tibia on the stereo zoom stage, moving it around until the light raked over it at just the right angle. It showed the same signs as the other bones: fracture damage with plastic response, no evidence of healing, scrape marks, and the clearest set of tooth marks yet. The people who had done this were freaks. Or had they just been really, really angry?

Her hands just about froze, but she managed to get a set of photographs before she had to stop and warm herself again at the heater.

Of course, it was possible this was an isolated case. The other victims might have indeed been killed by a rogue grizzly. The news reports quoted witnesses who had seen the animal, and in one instance a miner had been found in the process of being eaten—or, at least, his bones gnawed upon. Corrie was sorely tempted to check one of the other coffins, but resisted the impulse. From now on, she was going to do everything absolutely and totally by the book.

Able to feel her hands once again, she straightened up. If the other remains did prove to be the work of a gang of killers, her thesis would have to change. She would have a hundred-and-fifty-year-old serial killing on her hands to document. And it would be very cool—and a huge boost to her nascent career—if she could actually manage to solve it.

# 15

Larry Chivers stood beside his truck, sealing the nylon evidence bags with a heat sealer and finishing up his notes and observations. He had recovered from his fainting spell, but not from his sense of furious embarrassment. Such a thing had never happened to him—ever. He imagined that everyone was looking at him, whispering about him.

With a grimace, he finished working on the final evidence bag, careful to make the seal complete. Already, he'd narrated the rest of his observations into the digital recorder while they were still fresh. He had to make absolutely sure he did everything just right. This was going to be a huge case—probably even national.

There was a sound behind him, and he turned to see Chief Morris approaching. The man looked utterly undone.

"Sorry about my reaction back there," Chivers muttered.

"I knew the family," the chief told him. "One of the girls worked as an intern in my office."

Chivers shook his head. "I'm sorry."

"I'd like to hear your reconstruction of the fire."

"I can give you my first impressions. The lab results may take a few days."

"Go ahead."

Chivers took a deep breath. "Point of origin of the fire, in my view, would be either the second-floor bath or the bedroom above the living room. Both areas were doused heavily with accelerant—so much so that the perp would have had to leave the house fairly quickly. Both areas contained human remains."

"You mean, the Bakers...the victims...were burned with accelerant?"

"Two of them, yes."

"Alive?"

*What a question.* "That'll have to wait for the M.E. But I doubt it."

"Thank God."

"Two more victims were found by the back door—probably where the perp made his exit. There was the body of a dog there, too."

"Rex," said the chief to himself, wiping his brow with a trembling hand.

Chivers noted the same man in the black suit he'd seen before, floating in the background, eyes on them. He frowned. Why was the undertaker allowed inside the cordon?

"Motive?" asked the chief.

"Now I'm guessing," Chivers continued, "but from thirty years of experience I'd say pretty definitely we're looking at a home invasion and robbery, combined with possible sex crimes. The fact that the entire family was subdued and controlled suggests to me there might have been more than one perp."

"This was no robbery," came a soft, drawling voice.

Chivers jerked his head around to find that the man in the black suit had somehow managed to approach without being noticed and was now standing behind them.

Chivers's scowl deepened. "I'm talking to the chief. Do you mind?"

"Not at all. But if I may, I would like to offer a few observations for the benefit of the investigation. A mere robber would not have gone to the trouble to tie up his victims and then burn them alive."

"*Alive?*" the chief said. "How do you know?"

"The sadism and rage evident in the arc of this crime are palpable. A sadist wishes to see his victims suffer. That is how he derives his gratification. To tie someone to a bed, douse that person with gasoline, and light them on fire—where's the gratification in that, if the person is already dead?"

The chief's face went as gray as putty. His mouth moved but no sound came out.

"Bullshit," said Chivers fiercely. "This was a home invasion and robbery. I've seen it before. The perps break in, find a couple of pretty girls, have their way with them, load up on jewelry, and then burn down the place thinking they'll destroy the evidence—particularly the DNA inside the girls."

"Yet they didn't take the jewelry, as you yourself noted in your taped observations a few minutes ago, regarding some lumps of gold you discovered."

"Hold on, here. You were *listening* to me? Who the hell are you?" Chivers turned to the chief. "Is this guy official?"

The chief passed a sopping handkerchief across his brow. He looked indecisive and frightened. "Please. Enough."

The man in the black suit regarded him a moment with his silver eyes, and then shrugged nonchalantly. "I have no official role here. I am merely a bystander offering his impressions. I shall leave you gentlemen to your work."

With that he turned and began to leave. Then

he paused to speak over his shoulder. "I should mention, however: there may well be...*more.*"

And with that he walked off, slipping under the tape and disappearing into the crowd of rubber-neckers.

## 16

Horace P. Fine III stopped, swiveled on his instep, and looked Corrie up and down, as if he had just thought of something.

"Do you have any experience house-sitting?" he asked.

"Yes, absolutely," Corrie replied immediately. It was sort of true: she'd watched their trailer home overnight more than once when her mother went on an all-night bender. And then there was the time she'd stayed at her father's apartment six months before, when he'd gone to that job fair in Pittsburgh.

"Never anyplace this big, though," she added, looking around.

Fine looked at her suspiciously—but then again, maybe it was just the way his face was put to- gether. It seemed that every syllable she'd uttered had been greeted by distrust.

"Well, I don't have time to check your references," he replied. "The person I'd arranged to take the position backed out at the last minute, and I'm overdue in New York." His eyes narrowed slightly. "But I'll be keeping an eye on you. Come on, I'll show you to your rooms."

Corrie, following the man down the long, echoing first-floor hallway, wondered just how Horace P. Fine planned to keep an eye on her from two thousand miles away.

At first it had seemed almost like a miracle. She'd learned of the opening by coincidence: a conversation, overheard at a coffee shop, about a house that needed looking after. A few phone calls led her to the mansion's owner. It would be an ideal situation—in Roaring Fork no less. No more driving eighteen miles each way to her fleabag motel room. She could even move in that very day. Now she'd be earning money instead of spending it—and doing so in style.

But when she'd dropped by the mansion to meet with the owner, her enthusiasm dimmed. Although the house was technically in Roaring Fork, it was way up in the foothills, completely isolated, at the end of a narrow, winding, mile-long private road. It was huge, to be sure, but of a dreary postmodern design of glass, steel, and slate that was more reminiscent of an upscale dentist's office than a home. Unlike most of the big houses she'd seen, which were perched on hillsides offering fantastic views, this house was built in a declivity, practically a bowl in the mountains, surrounded on three sides by tall fir trees that seemed to throw the place into perpetual gloom. On the fourth side was a deep, icy ravine that ended in a rockfall of snow-covered boulders. Ironically, most of the vast plate-glass windows of the house overlooked this "feature." The decor was so aggressively contemporary as to be almost prison-like in austerity, all chrome and glass and marble—not a straight edge to be found anywhere save the doorways—and the walls were covered with grinning masks, hairy weavings, and other creepy-looking African art. And the place was cold, too—almost as cold as the ski warehouse where she did her work. Corrie had kept her coat on during the entire walk-through.

"This leads down to the second basement," Fine said, pausing to point at a closed door. "The older furnace is down there. It heats the eastern quarter of the house."

*Heats. Yeah, right.* "Second basement?" Corrie asked aloud.

"It's the only part of the original house that still exists. When they demolished the lodge, the developer retained the basement for retrofitting into the new house."

"There was a lodge here?"

Fine scoffed. "It was called Ravens Ravine Lodge, but it was just an old log cabin. A photographer used it for a home base when he went out into the mountains to take pictures. Adams, the name was. They tell me he was famous."

*Adams. Ansel Adams?* Corrie could just picture it. There had probably been a cozy, rustic little cabin here once, nestled in among the pines—until it got razed for this monstrosity. She wasn't surprised that Fine was not familiar with Adams—only a Philistine, or his soon-to-be ex-wife, could have bought all this freaky art.

Horace Fine himself was almost as cold as the house. He ran a hedge fund back in Manhattan. Or maybe it was the U.S. branch of some foreign investment bank; Corrie hadn't really been listening when he told her. Hedge, branch—it was all so much shrubbery to her. Luckily, he seemed not to have heard of her or her recent stay in the local jail. He'd made it quite clear that he detested Roaring Fork; he hated the house; and he loathed the woman who had forced him to buy it and who was now making its disposal as difficult as she possibly could. "The virago" was the way he had named her to Corrie over the last twenty minutes. All he wanted to do was get someone in the house and get the hell back to New York, the sooner the better.

He led the way down the corridor. The house was as strangely laid out as it was ugly. It seemed to be made up of a single endless hallway, which veered at an angle now and then to conform with the topography. All the important rooms were on the left, facing the ravine. Everything else—the bathrooms, closets, utility rooms—was on the right, like carbuncles on a limb. From what she could tell, the second floor featured a similar layout.

"What's in here?" she asked, stopping before a partially open door on the right. There were no overhead lights on inside, but the room was nevertheless lit up with a ghostly gleam from dozens of points of green, red, and amber.

Fine stopped again. "That's the tech space. You might as well see it, too."

He opened the door wide and snapped on the light. Corrie looked around at a dizzying array of panels, screens, and instrumentation.

"This is a 'smart' house, of course," Fine said. "Everything's automated, and you can monitor it all from here: the generator status, the power grid, the security layout, the surveillance system. Cost a fortune, but it ultimately saved me a lot in insurance charges. And it's all networked and Internet-accessible, too. I can run the whole system from my computers in New York."

*So that's what he meant by keeping an eye on me,*

Corrie thought. "How does the surveillance system work?"

Fine pointed to a large flat panel, with a small all-in-one computer to one side and a device below that looked like a DVD player on steroids. "There are a total of twenty-four cameras." He pressed a button and the flat panel sprang to life, showing a picture of the living room. There was a number in the upper left-hand corner of the image, and time and date stamps running along the bottom. "These twenty-four buttons, here, are each dedicated to one of the cameras." He pressed the button marked DRIVEWAY and the image changed, showing a picture of, what else, the driveway, with her Rent-a-Junker front and center.

"Can you manipulate the cameras?" Corrie asked.

"No. But any motion picked up by the sensors activates the camera and is recorded on a hard disk. There—take a look." Fine pointed to the screen, where a deer was now passing across the driveway. As it moved, it became surrounded by a small cloud of black squares—almost like the framing windows of a digital camera—that followed the animal. At the same time, a large red $M$ inside a circle appeared on the screen.

"$M$ for 'movement,'" Fine said.

The deer had moved off the screen, but the red

letter remained. "Why is the M still showing?" Corrie asked.

"Because when one of the cameras detects movement, a recording of that video feed is saved to the hard disk, starting a minute before movement begins and continuing one minute past when it stops. Then—if there's no more movement—the M goes away."

*Movement.* "And you can monitor all this over the Internet?" Corrie asked. She didn't like the idea of being the subject of a long-distance voyeur.

"No. That part of the smart system was never connected to the Internet. We stopped the work on the security system when we decided to sell the house. Let the new owner pick up the cost. But it works just fine from in here." Fine pointed to another button. "You can also split the screen by repeatedly pressing this button." For the first time, Fine seemed engaged. He demonstrated, and the image split in two: the left half of the monitor showing the original image of the driveway, with the right showing a view looking over the ravine. Repeated pressings of the button split the screen into four, then nine, then sixteen increasingly smaller images, each from a different camera.

Corrie's curiosity was quickly waning. "And how do I operate the security alarm?" she asked.

"That was never installed, either. That's why I

need someone to keep an eye on the place."

He snapped off the light and led the way out of the room, down the hallway, and through a door at its end. Suddenly the house became different. Gone was the expensive artwork, the ultramodern furniture, the gleaming professional-grade appliances. Ahead lay a short, narrow hall with two doors on each side, ending in another door leading into a small bathroom with cheap fixtures. The floor was of linoleum, and the pasteboard walls were devoid of pictures. All the surfaces were painted dead white.

"The maid's quarters," Fine said proudly. "Where you'll be staying."

Corrie stepped forward, peering into the open doors. The two on the left opened into bedrooms of almost monastic size and asceticism. One of the doors on the right led into a kitchen with a dorm-style refrigerator and a cheap stove; the other room appeared to be a minuscule den. It was barely a cut above her motel room in Basalt.

"As I said, I'm leaving almost immediately," Fine said. "Come back to the den and I'll give you the key. Any questions?"

"Where's the thermostat?" Corrie asked, hugging herself to keep from shivering.

"Down here." Fine stepped out of the maid's quarters and went back down the hall, turning in to the sitting room. There was a thermostat on the wall, all right—covered in a clear plastic box with a lock on it.

"Fifty degrees," Fine said.

Corrie looked at him. "I'm sorry?"

"Fifty degrees. That's what I've set the house at and that's where it's going to stay. I'm not going to spend a penny more on this goddamn house than I have to. Let the virago pay the utilities if she wants to. And that's another thing—keep electricity use to a minimum. Just a couple of lights, as absolutely necessary." A thought seemed to strike the man. "And by the way, the thermostat settings and the kilowatt usage *have* been wired into the Internet. I'll be able to monitor them from my iPhone."

Corrie looked at the locked thermostat with a sinking heart. *Great. So now I'm going to be freezing my rear off by night as well as by day.* She began to understand why the original applicant had decided against the job.

Fine was glancing at her with a look that meant the interview was over. That left just one question.

"How much does the house-sitting job pay?" she asked.

Fine's eyes widened in surprise. "Pay? You're getting to stay, free, in a big, beautiful house, right here in Roaring Fork—and you expect a *salary*? You're lucky I'm not charging you rent."

And he led the way back toward the den.

# 17

Arnaz Johnson, hairdresser to the stars, had seen a lot of unusual people in his day hanging out at the famous Big Pine Lodge on the very top of Roaring Fork Mountain—movie starlets decked out as if for the Oscars; billionaires squiring about their trophy girlfriends in minks and sables; wannabe Indians in ten-thousand-dollar designer buckskins; pseudo-cowboys in Stetson hats, boots, and spurs. Arnaz called it the Parade of the Narcissists. Very few of them could even ski. The Parade was the reason Arnaz bought a season pass and took the gondola to the lodge once or twice a week: that, and the atmosphere of this most famous ski lodge in the West, with its timbered walls hung with antique Navajo rugs, the massive wrought-iron chandeliers, the roaring fireplace so large you could barbecue a bull in it. Not to mention the walls of glass that looked out over a three-hundred-sixty-degree ocean of mountains, currently gray and brooding under a darkening sky.

But Arnaz had never seen anyone quite like the gentleman who sat at a small table by himself before the vast window, a silver flask of some unknown beverage in front of him, gazing out in the direction of snowbound Smuggler's Cirque, with its complex of ancient, long-abandoned mining structures huddled like acolytes around the vast rickety wooden building that housed the famous Ireland Pump Engine: a magnificent example of nineteenth-century engineering, once the largest pump in the world, now just a rusted hulk.

Arnaz had been observing the ghostly man with fascination for upward of thirty minutes, during which time the man had not moved so much as a pinkie. Arnaz was a fashionista, and he knew his clothes. The man wore a black vicuña overcoat of the finest quality, cut, and style, but of a make that Arnaz did not recognize. The coat was unbuttoned, revealing a bespoke tailored black suit of an English cut, a Zegna tie, and a gorgeous cream-colored silk scarf, loosely draped. To top off the ensemble—literally—the man wore an incongruous, sable-colored trilby hat of 1960s vintage on his pale, skull-like head. Even though it was warm in the great room of the lodge, the man looked as cold as ice.

He wasn't an actor; Arnaz, a movie buff, knew he had never seen him on the silver screen, even in a bit part. He surely wasn't a banker, hedge fund manager, CEO, lawyer, or other business or financial wizard; that getup would be entirely unacceptable in such a crowd. He wasn't a poseur, either; the man wore his clothes casually, nonchalantly, as if he'd been born in them. And he was far too elegant to be in the dot-com business. So what the heck was he?

A gangster.

Now, that made sense. He was a criminal. A very, very successful criminal. Russian, perhaps—he did have a slightly foreign look about him, in those pale eyes and high cheekbones. A Russian oligarch. But no…where were his women? The Russian billionaires that came to Roaring Fork—and there were quite a few—always went about with a passel of spangled, buxom whores.

Arnaz was stumped.

Pendergast heard himself being addressed and turned, slowly, to see Chief Stanley Morris approaching him from across the vast room.

"May I?"

Pendergast opened his hand in a slow invitation to sit.

"Thank you. I heard you were up here."

"And how did you hear that?"

"Well…You're not exactly inconspicuous, Agent Pendergast."

A silence. And then Pendergast removed a small silver cup from his overcoat, and placed it on the table. "Sherry? This is a rather indifferent Amontillado, but nevertheless palatable."

"Ah, no thanks." The chief looked restless, shifting his soft body in the chair once, twice. "Look, I realize I messed up with your, um, protégée, Miss Swanson, and I'm sorry. I daresay I had it coming there at the town meeting. You don't know what it's like being chief of police in a town like this, where they're always pulling you in five different directions at once."

"I am indeed sorry to say this, but I fear your microscopic problems do not interest me." Pendergast poured himself a small tot of sherry and tossed it back in one feral motion.

"Listen," said the chief, shifting about again, "I came to ask your help. We've got this horrific quadruple murder, a one-acre crime scene of unbelievable complexity. All my forensic people are arguing with each other and that fire expert, they're paralyzed, they've never seen anything like this before…" His voice cracked, then trailed off. "Look, the girl—Jenny, the older daughter—was my intern. She was a *good* kid…" He managed to pull himself together. "I need help. Informally. Advice, that's all I'm asking. Nothing official. I looked into your background—very impressive."

The pale hand snaked out again, poured another tot; it was tossed off in turn. There was silence. Finally, Pendergast spoke. "I came here to rescue my protégée—your term, not mine—from your incompetency. My goal—my *only* goal—is to see Miss Swanson finish her work without further meddling from Mrs. Kermode or anyone else. And then I shall leave this perverse town and fly home to New York with all possible alacrity."

"Yet you were up at the scene of the fire this morning. You showed your badge to get inside the tape."

Pendergast waved away these words as one might brush off a fly.

"You were there. Why?"

"I saw the fire. I was ever so faintly intrigued."

"You said there would be more. Why did you say that?"

Another casual wave-off.

"Damn it! *What made you say that?*"

No answer.

The chief rose. "You said there would be more murders. I looked into your background and I realized that you, of all people, would know. I'm telling you, if there are more—and you refuse to help—then those murders will be on your head. I swear to God."

This was answered by a shrug.

"Don't you shrug at me, you son of a bitch!" the chief shouted, losing his temper at last. "You saw what they did to that family. How can you just sit there, drinking your sherry?" He gripped the side of the table and leaned forward. "I have just one thing to say to you, Pendergast—fuck you, and thanks for nothing!"

At this, the smallest hint of a smile crossed the thin lips. "Now, that is more like it."

"More like what?" Morris roared.

"An old friend of mine in the NYPD has a colorful expression that is appropriate for this situation. What was it again? Ah, yes." Pendergast glanced up at the chief. "I will help you, but only on the condition that you—as I believe he would put it—*grow a pair.*"

# 18

Chief Stanley Morris stared at the ruined house. The residual heat from the previous day's fire was now gone and a light snow had fallen the night before, covering the scene of horror with a soft white blanket. Plastic tarps had been spread over the main areas of evidence, and now his men were carefully removing them and shaking off the snow in preparation for the walk-through. It was eight o'clock in the morning, sunny, and fifteen degrees above zero. At least there was no wind.

Nothing like this had ever happened to Morris, on either a personal or a professional level, and he steeled himself for the ordeal that lay ahead. He'd hardly slept the night before, and when he finally did a dreadful nightmare had immediately awakened him again. He felt like hell and still hadn't been able to fully process the depravity and horror of the crime.

He took a deep breath and looked around. To his left stood Chivers, the fire specialist; to his right, the figure of Pendergast, in his vicuña overcoat, incongruously pulled over an electric-blue down jacket. Puffy mittens and a hideous wool hat completed the picture. The man was so pallid he looked like he'd already been stricken by hypothermia. And yet his eyes were very much alive, moving restlessly about the scene.

Morris cleared his throat and made an effort to project the image of a chief of police firmly in control. "Ready, gentlemen?"

"You bet," said Chivers, with a distinct lack of enthusiasm. He was clearly unhappy about the presence of the FBI agent. *Tough shit*, thought Morris. He was getting fed up with the disagreements, turf squabbles, and departmental infighting this case was generating.

Pendergast inclined his head.

The chief ducked under the tape, the others following. The fresh snow covered everything save where the tarps had been laid down, and those areas were now large dark squares in an otherwise white landscape. The M.E. had not yet removed the human remains. Forensic flags of various colors dotted the ruins, giving the scene an incongruously festive air. The stench of smoke, burnt electrical wiring, rubber, and plastic still hung heavy and foul.

Now Pendergast took the lead, moving lightly despite the bulky clothing. He darted forward, knelt, and with a small brush whisked away a patch of snow, examining the burnt slate floor. He did this at several apparently random spots as they continued moving through. At one point a glass tube made an appearance from under his coat, into which he put some microscopic sample with tweezers.

Chivers hung back, saying nothing, a frown of displeasure gathering on his thick face.

They finally reached the gruesome bathtub. Morris could hardly look at it. But Pendergast went right over and knelt beside it, bowing over it almost as if he were praying. Removing one glove, he poked around with his white fingers and the pair of long tweezers, putting more samples into tubes. At last he rose and they continued making their way through the ruined house.

They came to the burnt mattress with its loops of wire and bone fragments. Here Pendergast stopped again, gazing at it for the longest time. Morris began to shiver as the inactivity, cold, and a clammy sick feeling all began to penetrate. The agent removed a document from his coat and opened it, revealing a detailed plat of the house—where had he gotten that?—which he consulted at length before folding it up and putting it away. Then he knelt and examined with a magnifying glass the charred remains of the skeleton tied to the mattress, really just bone fragments, and various other things as well. Morris could feel the cold creeping deeper into his clothing. Chivers was becoming restless, moving back and forth and sometimes slapping his gloves together in an effort to keep warm—broadcasting through his body language that he considered this a waste of time.

Pendergast finally straightened up. "Shall we move on?"

"Great idea," said Chivers.

They continued through the burnt landscape: the ghostly standing sticks covered with hoarfrost, the scorched walls, the heaps of frozen ashes, the glistering puddles of glass and metal. Now the corpse of the dog could be seen to one side, along with the two parallel, crumbled piles of ash and bone representing Jenny Baker's mother and father.

Morris had to look away. It was too much.

Pendergast knelt and examined everything with the utmost care, taking more samples, maintaining his silence. He seemed particularly interested in the charcoaled fragments of the dog, carefully probing with his long-stemmed tweezers and a tool that looked like a dental pick. They moved into the ruins of the garage, where the burnt and fused hulks of three cars rested. The FBI agent gave them a cursory look.

And then they were done. Beyond the perimeter tape, Pendergast turned. His eyes startled Morris—they glittered so sharply in the bright winter sun.

"It is as I feared," he said.

Morris waited for more but was greeted only with silence.

"Well," said Chivers loudly, "this just reinforces what I reported to you earlier, Stanley. All the evidence points toward a botched robbery with at least two perps, maybe more. With a possible sex-crime component."

"Agent Pendergast?" Morris finally said.

"I'm sorry to say that an accurate reconstruction of the sequence of the crime may be impossible. So much information was taken by the fire. But I am able to salvage a few salient details, if you wish to hear them."

"I do. Please."

"There was a single perpetrator. He entered through an unlocked back door. Three members of the family were at home, all upstairs and probably sleeping. The perpetrator immediately killed the dog who came to investigate. Then he—or she—ascended the front staircase to the second floor, surprised a juvenile female in her bedroom, incapacitated and gagged her before she could make significant noise, and wired her to the bed, still alive. He may have been on his way to the parents' room when the second juvenile female arrived home."

He turned to Morris. "This would be your intern, Jenny. She came in through the garage and went upstairs. There she was ambushed by the perpetrator, incapacitated, gagged, and placed in the bathtub. This was accomplished with utmost efficiency, but nevertheless this second assault appears to have awakened the parents. There was a short fight, which began upstairs and ended downstairs. I suspect one of the parents was killed there, on the spot, while the other was dragged down later. They may have been beaten."

"How can you know all this?" said Chivers. "This is sheer speculation!"

Pendergast went on, ignoring this outburst. "The perpetrator returned upstairs, doused both juvenile victims with gasoline, and set them on fire. He then made a—by necessity—rapid exit from the premises, dragging the other parent down the stairs and spreading additional accelerant on his way out. He left on foot—not by car. A pity the snowy woods around the house were trampled by neighbors and firefighters."

"No way," said Chivers, shaking his head. "No

way can you draw all those conclusions from the information we have—and the conclusions you've drawn, well, with all due respect, most of them are wrong."

"I must say I share Mr. Chivers's, ah, skepticism as to how you can learn all this from a mere walk-through," said Morris.

Pendergast replied in the tone of someone explaining to a child. "It's the only logical sequence that fits the facts. And the facts are these: When Jenny Baker returned home, the perpetrator was already in the house. She came in through the garage—the boyfriend confirmed that—and if the parents had already been killed she would have seen their bodies at the back door. She didn't see the dog's body because it was behind a counter that once existed, here." He pulled out the plat.

"But how do you know he was already upstairs when Jenny arrived home?"

"Because Jenny was ambushed upstairs."

"She could have been attacked in the garage and forced upstairs."

"If she was the first victim, and was attacked in the garage, the dog would be alive and would have barked, awakening the parents. No—the very first victim was the dog, killed at the back door, probably with a blow to the head by something like a baseball bat."

"A *bat*?" Chivers said in disbelief. "How do you know he didn't use a knife? Or gun?"

"The neighbors heard no shots. Have you ever tried to kill a German shepherd with a knife? And finally, the dog's burnt cranium showed green-bone fracture patterns." He paused. "One needn't be Sherlock Holmes to analyze a few simple details like these, Mr. Chivers."

Chivers fell silent.

"Therefore, when Jenny arrived home, the perpetrator was already upstairs and had already incapacitated the sister, as he would not have been able to subdue two at once."

"Unless there were two perps," said Chivers.

"Go on," Morris told Pendergast.

"Using the bat or some other method, he immediately subdued Jenny."

"Which is exactly why there must have been two perps!" said Chivers. "It was a robbery gone bad. They broke into the house, but things spiraled out of control before they could commence the robbery. Happens all the time."

"No. The sequence was well planned and the perpetrator had everything under control at all times. The psychological hallmarks of the crime—the savagery of it—suggests a lone perpetrator who had a motive other than robbery."

Chivers rolled his eyes at Morris.

"And as for your theory about a burglary gone wrong, the perpetrator was well aware there were at least three people at home. An organized burglar doesn't break into an occupied house."

"Unless there are a couple of girls they might want to..." Chivers swallowed, glanced at the chief.

"The girls were not molested. If he intended to rape the girls he would have removed the threat of the parents by killing them first. And a rape fits neither the time line nor the sequence. I might point out that the elapsed time between the boyfriend dropping Jenny off and the fire appearing on the mountain was ten minutes or less."

"And how do you know one of the parents was killed downstairs and the other dragged down later?"

"That is, admittedly, an assumption. But it is the only one that matches the evidence. We are dealing with a lone killer, and it seems unlikely he would have fought both parents, downstairs, simultaneously. This arranging of the parents is another staged element of the attack—a grisly detail, intended to sow additional fear and unrest."

Chivers shook his head in disgust and disbelief.

"So." The chief could hardly bring himself to ask the question he knew he had to. "What makes you think there might be more killings like this?"

"This was a crime of hatred, sadism, and brutality, committed by a person who, while probably insane, was still in possession of his faculties. Fire is often the weapon of choice for the insane."

"A revenge killing?"

"Doubtful. The Baker family was not well known in Roaring Fork. You yourself told me they appear to have no enemies in town and only spend a couple of weeks here a year. So if not revenge, what is the motive? Hard to say definitively, but it may not be one directed at this family specifically—but rather, *at what this family represents.*"

A silence. "And what does this family represent?" Morris asked.

"Perhaps what this entire town represents."

"Which is?"

Pendergast paused, and then said: "Money."

# 19

Corrie entered the history section of the Roaring Fork Library. The beautiful, wood-paneled space was once again empty save for Ted Roman, who was reading a book at his desk. He looked up as Corrie entered, his lean face lighting up.

"Well, well!" he said, rising. "Roaring Fork's most infamous girl returns in triumph!"

"Jeez. What kind of a welcome is that?"

"A sincere one. I mean it. You and that FBI agent really nailed Kermode. God, it was one of the best things I've ever seen in this town."

"You were at the town meeting?"

"Sure as hell was. It's about time someone took down that…well, I hope you won't be offended if I use the word, but here goes: that *bitch*."

"No offense here."

"And not only did the man in black cut Kermode off at the knees, but he took on that cozy little triumvirate, her, the police chief, and the mayor. Your friend just about had the three of them soiling their drawers—Montebello, too!" He almost cackled with glee, and his laugh was so infectious Corrie had to join in.

"I have to admit, it was satisfying to hear the story," Corrie said. "Especially after spending ten days in jail because of them."

"I knew as soon as I read you'd been arrested that it was bullshit..." Ted tried to smooth down the cowlick that projected from his forehead. "So. What are you working on today?"

"I want to find out all I can about the life of Emmett Bowdree—and his death."

"The miner you've been analyzing? Let's see what we can find."

"Is the library always this empty?" she asked as they walked over to the computer area.

"Yeah. Crazy, huh? The prettiest library in the West and nobody comes. It's the people in this town—they're too busy parading down Main Street in their minks and diamonds." He aped a movie star, sashaying as if on a fashion runway, making faces.

Corrie laughed. Ted had a funny way about him.

He sat down at a computer terminal and logged on. He began various searches, explaining what he was doing while she peered over his shoulder.

"Okay," he said, "I've got some decent hits on your Mr. Bowdree." She heard a printer fire up behind her. "You take a look at the list and tell me what you want to see."

He fetched the printed sheets and she scanned them quickly, pleased—in fact, almost intimidated—by the number of references. It seemed that there was quite a lot on Emmett Bowdree: mentions in newspaper articles, employment and assay records, mining documents and claims, and other miscellanea.

"Say…" Ted began, then stopped.

"What?"

"Um, you know, considering how you stood me up for that beer last time…"

"Sorry. I was busy getting myself arrested."

He laughed. "Well, you still owe me one. Tonight?"

Corrie looked at him, suddenly blushing and awkward and hopeful. "I'd love to," she heard herself say.

# 20

The chief had held press conferences before, usually when some bad-boy celebrity got in trouble. But this was different—and worse. As he observed the audience from the wings, he felt a rising apprehension. These people were seething, demanding answers. Because the old police station building only had a small conference room, they were back in the City Hall meeting room—site of his recent humiliation—and the reminder was not a pleasant one.

On the other hand, he had Pendergast on his side. The man who had started out as his nemesis was now—he might as well admit it—his crutch. Chivers was furious, and half his own department was in revolt, but Morris didn't care. The man was brilliant, even if he was a bit strange, and he was damn grateful to have him in his corner. But Pendergast wasn't going to be able to help him with this crowd. This was something he had to do on his own. He had to go in there looking like the Man in Charge.

He glanced at his watch. Five minutes to two—the hubbub of voices was like an ominous growl. *Grow a pair*. Fair enough: he would try his best.

Reviewing his notes one last time, he stepped out on stage, walking briskly to the podium. As the sound of voices dropped, he took another moment to observe the audience. The room was packed, standing-room only, and it looked like more were outside. The press gallery, too, was crammed. His eye easily picked out the black blot of Pendergast, sitting anonymously in the public area in front. And in the reserved section, he could see the ranks of officials, the mayor, fire chief, senior members of his department, the M.E., Chivers, and the town attorney. Conspicuously absent was Mrs. Kermode. Thank God.

He leaned over, tapped the microphone. "Ladies and gentlemen."

The room fell silent.

"For those who may not know me," he said, "I'm Chief Stanley Morris of the Roaring Fork Police Department. I'm going to read a statement, and then I will take questions from the press and the public."

He squared his papers and began to read, keeping his voice stern and neutral. It was a short statement that confined itself to the indisputable facts: the time of the fire, the number and identity of the victims, the determination it was a homicide, the status of the investigation. No speculation. He ended with an appeal for all persons to come forward with any information they might have, no matter how trivial. He of course did not mention Pendergast's suggestion that there might be more such events; that would be far too incendiary. Besides, there was no evidence for it—as Chivers had said, it was mere speculation.

He looked up. "Questions?"

An immediate tumult from the press gallery. Morris had already decided whom he was going to call on and in what order, and he now pointed to his number one journalist, an old pal from the *Roaring Fork Times*.

"Chief Morris, thank you for your statement. Do you have any suspects?"

"We have some important leads we're following up," Morris replied. "I can't say more than that." *Because we don't have shit*, he thought grimly.

"Any idea if the perp is local?"

"We don't know," said Morris. "We've gotten guest lists from all the hotels and rentals, we've got lift ticket sales, and we've enlisted the help of the National Center for the Analysis of Violent Crime, which is currently searching their databases for previous arson convictions."

"Any possible motive?"

"Nothing concrete. We're looking into various possibilities."

"Such as?"

"Burglary, revenge, perverted kicks."

"Wasn't it true that one of the victims worked in your office?"

God, he had hoped to avoid that line of questioning. "Jenny Baker was an intern in my office, working over her winter break." He swallowed, tried to go on despite the sudden fuzziness in his voice. "She was a wonderful girl who had aspirations to a career in law enforcement. It was...a devastating loss."

"There's a rumor that one of the victims was tied to a bed and doused with gasoline," another reporter interjected.

*Son of a bitch. Did Chivers leak that?* "That is true," said the chief, after a hesitation.

This caused a sensation.

"And another victim was found burned to death in a bathtub?"

"Yes," said the chief, without elaborating.

More uproar. This was getting ugly.

"Were the girls molested?"

The press would ask anything; they had no shame. "The M.E. hasn't concluded his examination. But it may not be possible to know, given the state of the remains."

"Was anything taken?"

"We don't know."

"Were they burned alive?"

Rising furor.

"It'll be at least a week before most of the evidence has been analyzed. All right—please—enough questions from the press—we'll move on to the public." The chief dearly hoped this would be easier.

The entire section was on its feet, hands waving. Not a good sign. He pointed to someone he didn't know, a meek-looking elderly woman, but a person in front of her misunderstood—deliberately or not—and immediately responded in a booming voice. Christ, it was Sonja Marie Dutoit, the semi-retired actress, infamous in Roaring Fork for her obnoxious behavior in shops and restaurants and for her face, which had been lifted and Botoxed so many times it bore a perpetual grin.

"Thank you for choosing me," she said in a smoke-cured voice. "I'm sure I speak for everyone when I say how shocked and horrified I am about this crime."

"Yes, indeed," said Morris. "Your question, please?"

"It's been thirty-six hours since this terrible, horrible, frightening fire. We all saw it. And judging from what you just said, you haven't made much progress—if any."

Chief Morris said, calmly, "Do you have a question, Ms. Dutoit?"

"I certainly do. Why haven't you caught the killer yet? This isn't New York City: we've only got two thousand people in this town. There's only one road in and out. So what's the problem?"

"As I said, we've brought tremendous resources to bear, bringing in specialists from as far away as Grand Junction, as well as the involvement of the NCAVC. Now, I'm sure other people have questions—"

"I'm not done," Dutoit went on. "When's the next house going to get burned down?"

This led to a susurrus of muttering. Some people were rolling their eyes in reaction to Dutoit's questions; others were beginning to look ever so slightly nervous.

"There's not a shred of evidence that we're dealing with a serial arsonist," the chief said, eager to cut off this avenue of speculation.

But Dutoit, it seemed, was not yet through. "Which one of us is going to wake up in flames in their own bed tonight? *And what in the name of God are you doing about it?*"

# 21

It was hard to believe the Mineshaft Tavern was part of Roaring Fork, with the sawdust on the floor, the basement rock walls hung with rusty old mining tools, the smell of beer and Texas barbecue, the scruffy working-class clientele—and above all, the talentless stoner at the mike strumming some tune of his own composition, his face contorted with excessive pathos.

As she walked in, Corrie was pleasantly surprised. This was much more her kind of place than the restaurant of the Hotel Sebastian.

She found Ted at "his" table in the back, just where he'd said he would be, with an imperial pint in front of him. He stood up—she liked that—and helped her into her seat before sitting down again.

"What'd you like?"

"What are you drinking?"

"Maroon Bells Stout, made right down the road. Fantastic stuff."

The waiter came over and she ordered a pint, hoping she wouldn't get carded. That would be embarrassing. But there were no problems.

"I didn't know a place like this could exist in Roaring Fork," said Corrie.

"There are still plenty of real people in this town—ski lift attendants, waiters, dishwashers, handymen...*librarians*." He winked. "We need our cheap, low-down places of entertainment."

Her beer arrived, and they clinked glasses. Corrie took a sip. "Wow. Good."

"Better than Guinness. Cheaper, too."

"So who's the guy on stage?" Corrie kept her voice neutral in case he was a friend of Ted's.

Ted snickered. "Open-mike night. Don't know him, poor fellow. Let's hope he hasn't quit his day job." He picked up his menu. "Hungry?"

She thought for a moment: could she spare the money? But the menu wasn't too expensive. If she didn't eat, she might get drunk and do something stupid. She smiled, nodded.

"So," said Ted. "How are things going in the charnel house up on the mountain?"

"Good." Corrie contemplated telling him about what she'd discovered but decided against it. She didn't know Ted well enough. "The remains of

Emmett Bowdree have a lot to say. I hope to get permission to work on a few more skeletons soon."

"I'm glad it's working out for you. I love to think of Kermode getting her knickers in a twist while you're up there doing your thing."

"I don't know," Corrie said. "She's got worse things to worry about now. You know—the fire."

"I'll say. Jesus, how awful was that?" He paused. "You know, I grew up there. In The Heights."

"Really?" Corrie couldn't hide her surprise. "I never would have guessed that."

"Thank you, I'll take that as a compliment. My dad was a television producer—sitcoms and the like. He palled around with a lot of Hollywood people. My mother slept with most of them." He shook his head, sipped his beer. "I had a kind of messed-up childhood."

"Sorry to hear that." In no way was Corrie ready to talk to Ted about her own childhood, however.

"No big deal. They got divorced and my dad raised me. With all the sitcom residuals, he never had to work again. When I came back from college I got my butt out of The Heights and found an apartment in town, down on East Cowper. It's tiny, but I feel better about breathing its air."

"Does he still live up there in The Heights?"

"Nah, he sold the house a few years back, died of cancer last year—only sixty years old, too."

"I'm really sorry."

He waved his hand. "I know. But I was glad to get rid of the connection to The Heights. It really frosts me the way they handled that Boot Hill thing—digging up one of the most historic cemeteries in Colorado to build a spa for rich assholes."

"Yeah. Pretty ugly."

Then Ted shrugged, laughed lightly. "Well, stuff happens. What are you going to do? If I hated the place so much, I wouldn't still be here—right?"

Corrie nodded. "So what did you major in at the University of Utah?"

"Sustainability studies. I wasn't much of a student—I wasted too much time skiing and snowmobiling. I love snowmobiling almost as much as I do skiing. Oh, and mountain climbing, too."

"Mountain climbing?"

"Yeah. I've climbed forty-one Fourteeners."

"What's a Fourteener?"

Ted chuckled. "Man, you really are an eastern girl. Colorado has fifty-five mountains over fourteen thousand feet—we call them Fourteeners. To climb them all is the holy grail of mountaineering in the U.S.—at least, in the lower forty-eight."

"Impressive."

Their food arrived: shepherd's pie for Corrie, a burger for Ted, with another pint for him. Corrie declined a refill, thinking about the scary mountain road up to her dentist's-office-on-the-hill.

"So what about you?" Ted asked. "I'm curious about how you know the man in black."

"Pendergast? He's my..." *God, how to put it?* "He's sort of my guardian."

"Yeah? Like your godfather or something?"

"Something like that. I helped him on a case a few years ago, and ever since he's kind of taken an interest in me."

"He's one cool dude—no kidding. Is he really an FBI agent?"

"One of the best."

A new singer took over the mike—much better than the previous one—and they listened for a while, talking and finishing their meal. Ted tried to pay but Corrie was ready for him and insisted on splitting the check.

As they got up to leave, Ted said, his voice dropping low: "Want to see my tiny apartment?"

Corrie hesitated. She was tempted—very tempted. Ted looked like he was all sinew and muscle, lean and hard, and yet charming and goofy, with the nicest brown eyes. But she had never quite been able to feel good about a relationship if she slept with the guy on the first date.

"Not tonight, thanks. I've got to get home, get my sleep," she said, but added a smile to let him know it wasn't absolute.

"No problem. We'll have to do this again—soon."

"I'd like that."

As she drove away from the restaurant, heading toward the dark woods and thinking about crawling into a freezing bed, Corrie started to regret her decision not to "see" Ted's tiny apartment.

# 22

In his suite of rooms on the top floor of the Hotel Sebastian, Agent Pendergast laid aside the book he was reading, drained the small cup of espresso that sat on the side table, and then—standing up—walked over to the picture window on the far side of the sitting room. The suite was perfectly silent: Pendergast disliked the clamor of anonymous neighbors and had reserved the rooms on both sides of his own to ensure he would remain undisturbed. He stood at the window, absolutely still, looking down over East Main Street and the light snow that was falling onto the sidewalks, buildings, and passersby, softening the evening scene and bestowing a muted, dream-like quality on the millions of Christmas lights stretching many blocks. He remained there for perhaps ten minutes, gazing out into the night. Then, turning away again, he walked over to the desk, where a FedEx envelope lay, unopened. It was from his factotum in New York, Proctor, addressed to him in care of the Hotel Sebastian.

Pendergast picked up the envelope, slit it open with a smooth motion, and let the contents slip onto the desk. Several sealed envelopes of various sizes fell out, along with an oversize card—embossed and engraved—and a brief note in Proctor's handwriting. The note said merely that Pendergast's ward, Constance Greene, had left for Dharamsala, India, where she planned to spend two weeks visiting the nineteenth rinpoche. The fancy card was an invitation to the wedding of Lieutenant Vincent D'Agosta and Captain Laura Hayward, which was scheduled for May twenty-ninth of the following spring.

Pendergast's gaze moved to the sealed envelopes. He glanced over them for a moment without touching any. Then he picked up an airmail envelope and turned it over thoughtfully in his hands. Leaving the others, he walked back to his sitting room chair, sat down, and opened the letter. A single sheet of thin paper lay inside, a letter in a childish hand, written in the old-fashioned German script known as Sütterlin. He began to read.

*December 6*
*École Mère-Église*
*St. Moritz, Switzerland*
*Dear Father,*

*It seems a long time since you last visited. I have been counting the days. They number one hundred and twelve. I hope you will again soon come.*

*I am treated well. The food here is very good. On Saturday suppers we have Linzer Torte for desert. Have you ever eaten Linzer Torte? It is good.*

*A lot of the teachers here speak German but I try always to use my English. They say my English is getting better. The teachers are very nice except for Madame Montaine who always smells of rose water. I like History and Science but not Mathematiks. I am not good at Mathematiks.*

*In the autumn I enjoyed walking on the hill sides after classes but now there is too much snow. They tell me that over the Christmas holidays I will be taught how to ski. I think I will like that.*

*Thank you for your letter. Please send me another. I hope we shall meet again soon.*

*Love,*
*Your son,*
*Tristram*

Pendergast read the letter a second time. Then, very slowly, he refolded it and placed it back into its envelope. Turning off the reading lamp, he sat in the dark, lost in thought, book forgotten, as the minutes ticked by. Finally he stirred again, pulled a cell phone from his suit pocket, and dialed a number with a northern Virginia area code.

"Central Monitoring," came the crisp, accentless voice.

"This is S. A. Pendergast. Please transfer me to South American Operations, Desk 14-C."

"Very good." There was a brief silence, a click, and then another voice came on the line. "Agent Wilkins."

"Pendergast speaking."

The voice stiffened slightly. "Yes, sir."

"What's the status of Wildfire?"

"Stable but negative. No hits."

"Your monitoring efforts?"

"All listening posts are active. We're monitoring national and local police reports and news media twenty-four seven, and we're electronically combing the daily NSA feeds as well. In addition, we continue to interface with CIA field agents in Brazil and the surrounding countries in search of any...anomalous activity."

"You have my updated location?"

"In Colorado? Yes."

"Very good, Agent Wilkins. As always, please inform me immediately if the status of Wildfire changes."

"We'll do that, sir."

Pendergast ended the call. Picking up the house phone, he ordered another espresso from room service. Then he used his cell phone to make another call: this one to a suburb of Cleveland called River Pointe.

The call was answered on the second ring. There was no voice; just the sound of a connection being made.

"Mime?" Pendergast said into the silence.

For a moment, nothing. Then a high, thin voice wheezed: "Is that my main man? My main Secret Agent Man?"

"I'd like an update, please, Mime."

"All quiet on the Western Front."

"Nothing?"

"Not a peep."

"One moment." Pendergast paused as a room service attendant brought in the espresso. He tipped the man, then waited until he was once again alone. "And you're confident that you've cast your net widely, and finely, enough to spot the...target if he surfaces?"

"Secret Agent Man, I've got a series of AI algorithms and heuristic search patterns online that would make you stain your government-issue BVDs. I'm monitoring all official, and a goodly amount of unofficial, web traffic in and out of the target area. You can't imagine the bandwidth I'm burning through. Why, I've had to siphon off server farms from at least half a dozen—"

"I can't imagine. Nor do I want to."

"Anyway, the objective's totally offline, no Facebook updates for this dude. But if the guy's as sick as you say, then the moment he surfaces—hoo, boy!" A sudden silence. "Um, oops. I keep forgetting Alban's your son."

"Just keep up the monitoring operations, please, Mime. And let me know the instant you note anything."

"You got it." The phone went dead.

And Pendergast sat in the darkened room, unmoving, for a long time.

# 23

Corrie parked her Rent-a-Junker Ford Focus in the sprawling driveway of 1 Ravens Ravine Road—aka, the Fine mansion—and got out. It was almost midnight, and a huge pale moon, hanging low in the sky, turned the pine trees blue against a creamy bed of white snow, striped with shadows. A light snow was falling, and here, in this bowl-like vale at the edge of a ravine, she felt like she was inside some child's overturned snow globe. Ahead, the row of six garage doors stood against the cement drive like big gray teeth. She killed the engine—for some obscure reason, Fine didn't want her to use the garage—and got out of the car. She walked up to the closest door, plucked off her glove, punched in the code. Then, as it rose on its metal rails, she turned suddenly, with a sharp intake of breath.

There, in the shadow of the side of the garage,

was a shape. At first, Corrie couldn't make out what it was. But as the light from the garage door motor provided a faint illumination, she made out a small dog, shivering in the darkness.

"Well!" Corrie said, kneeling beside it. "What are you doing out here?"

The dog came over, whining, and licked her hand. It was a mutt, looking like a cross between a small hound dog and a spaniel, with droopy ears, big sad brown eyes, and brown and white splotches of fur. It was not wearing a collar.

"You can't stay out here," she said. "Come on in."

The dog followed her eagerly into the garage. Walking up to a bank of buttons, she pressed the one for the bay she'd entered. The garage was empty—a ludicrous expanse of concrete. Outside, she could hear the moaning of the wind as it shook the trees. Why on earth couldn't she park in here?

She glanced down at the dog, which was looking up at her and wagging its tail, a desperately hopeful look in its eyes. Screw Mr. Fine—the pooch would stay.

Corrie waited until the garage door had closed completely before unlocking the door and stepping into the house. Inside, it was almost as cold as outdoors. She walked through a laundry room with machines big enough to service a battalion, past a pantry larger than her father's entire apartment, and then into the hallway that ran the length of the mansion. She continued on, dog at her heels, along the corridor as it bent once, then twice, following the contours of the ravine, past room after huge room filled with uncomfortable-looking avant-garde furniture. The corridor itself was filled with that African statuary, all big bellies and long angry faces and carven eyes that seemed to follow her as she passed by. The tall picture windows of the various rooms to her left had no curtains, and the bright moonlight threw skeletal shadows against the pallid walls.

The night before—her first night in the place—Corrie had checked out both the second floor and the basement, familiarizing herself with the rest of the layout. The upstairs consisted of a huge master bedroom, with dual bathrooms and walk-in closets, six other unfurnished bedrooms, and numerous guest bathrooms. In the main basement was a gym, a two-lane bowling alley, a mechanical room, a swimming flume—empty—and several storage areas. It seemed obscene that any house should be this big—or this empty.

She finally reached the end of the hallway and the door leading into her own small suite of rooms. She entered, closed the door behind her, and switched on the small space heater in the room she'd chosen as her own. Pulling a couple of bowls from the cabinet, she set out water and an improvised dinner of crackers and cereal for the dog—tomorrow, if she couldn't find the owner, she'd pick up some kibble.

She watched the little brown-and-white animal as it ate ravenously. The poor thing was starving. While a mutt, it was an endearing one, with a big shock of unruly hair that fell over its eyes. It reminded her of Jack Corbett, a kid she'd known in seventh grade back in Medicine Creek. His hair had flopped down over his face in just the same way.

"Your name is Jack," she said to the dog, while it looked up at her, wagging its tail.

She thought for a moment about fixing a cup of herbal tea for herself, but she felt too tired to make the effort and instead washed up, changed quickly into her nightwear, then slipped between the chilly sheets. She heard the tick of claws as the dog came in and settled down on the floor at the foot of the bed.

Gradually, her body heat and the little space heater—cranked to maximum—blunted the worst of the cold. She decided against doing any reading, preferring to use the electricity for heat instead of light. She'd gradually increase the amount of juice she used, and see if Fine complained.

Her thoughts drifted back to the date she'd had with Ted. He was earnest, and funny, and nice, if a bit goofy—but then, ski bums were supposed to be goofy. Handsome and goofy and carefree. He was no lightweight, though—he had principles. Idealistic, too. She admired his independence in leaving his parents' grand house for a small apartment downtown.

She turned in the bed, slowly becoming drowsy. He was hot, and on top of it a nice guy, but she wanted to get to know him just a little better before…

…Somewhere, from the distant spaces of the house overhead, came a loud bump.

She sat up in bed, instantly wide awake. What the hell was that?

She remained motionless. The only light in the room came from the bright orange coils of the space heater. As she sat, listening intently, she could hear, faintly, the mournful call of the wind as it coursed through the narrow valley.

There was nothing else. It must have been a dead branch, broken loose by the wind and knocked against the roof.

Slowly, she settled back down into the bed. Now that she was aware of the wind, she listened to its faint muttering and groaning as she lay in the darkness. As the minutes passed, drowsiness began to return. Her thoughts drifted toward her plans for the next day. Her analysis of the Bowdree skeleton was just about complete, and if she was going to make any progress on her theory she'd need to get permission to examine some of the other remains. Of course, Pendergast had offered to do just that, and she knew enough of his meddling ways to believe that he would—

*Meddling.* Now, why had she used that word?

And come to think of it, why did the mere thought of Pendergast—for the first time ever, since she'd known him—cause an upwelling of annoyance? After all, the man had rescued her from a ten-year prison sentence. He'd saved her career. He'd paid for her education, basically put her life on track.

If she was honest with herself, she had to admit it had nothing to do with Pendergast—and everything with herself. This cache of skeletons was a big project, and an incredible opportunity. She was wary at the thought of anyone else stepping in and stealing some of the limelight. And Pendergast—unintentionally—was capable of doing just that. If even a whiff got out that he'd helped her, everyone would assume that he'd done the real work and discount her own contribution.

Her mother had taken great relish in pointing out, again and again, what a loser she was. Her classmates back in Medicine Creek had called her a freak, a waste of space. She'd never realized, until now, just how much it meant to her to accomplish something important…

*There it was*: another sound. But this was no bump of a tree branch hitting the roof. This was a low scratching sound, coming from some spot not all that far away from her own bedroom: soft, even stealthy.

Corrie listened. Maybe it was the wind again, rubbing a pine branch back and forth against the house. But if it was the wind, it sounded awfully regular.

She pushed back the covers, got out of bed, and—heedless of the cold—stood in her darkened bedroom, listening.

Scratch. Scratch. Scratch. Scratch. Scratch.

At her feet, Jack whined.

She stepped out into the little hallway, turned on the light, opened the door into the mansion proper, and paused again to listen. The sound seemed to have stopped. No: there it was again. It seemed to be coming from the ravine side of the house, maybe the living room.

Corrie walked quickly down the corridor, shadow-striped and echoing, and ducked into the security room. The various devices were on, humming and clicking, but the central flat panel was off. She turned it on. An image swam into view: camera one, the default, showing the front drive, currently empty.

She pushed the button that toggled the screen into a checkerboard of smaller images, looking at the feeds from various cameras. Two, four, nine, sixteen…and there, in the window of camera nine, she saw it: a red *M*, with a circle around it.

*M for "movement."*

Quickly she pressed the button dedicated to camera nine. Now its image filled the screen: it was the view out the back door, leading from the kitchen onto the vast deck overlooking the ravine. The *M* was much bigger now. But there was no movement, nothing she could see. She squinted at the pixelated image. Nothing.

What the hell had Fine said? When a camera registered movement, it recorded the video feed to hard disk: one minute prior to detecting the movement, and continuing for another minute after the movement ceased.

So what movement had triggered camera nine?

It couldn't be the wind, shaking the tree limbs: there were no trees in view. Even as Corrie watched, the *M* disappeared from the screen. Now she saw only the back of the house, with the date and time stamps imprinted across the bottom of the feed.

She toggled it back to the checkerboard of cameras and looked at the computer, hoping to get a playback of camera nine. The machine was turned on, but when she moved the mouse a window popped open, demanding a password.

*Shit.* Now she cursed herself for not asking more questions.

Something red flashed in her peripheral vision. Quickly she turned back to the screen. There it was, in camera eight: something large and dark, creeping around the side of the house. Black rectangles hovered around it, tracking its progress. The *M* was once again flashing on the screen.

Maybe she should call 911. But she'd left her mobile in her car, and the cheap bastard Fine had of course disconnected the house phones.

Corrie looked closer, heart starting to pound. That section of the back deck was in shadow, the moonlight obscured by the house, and she couldn't make out exactly what she was seeing. Was it an animal? A coyote, maybe? No: it was too big to be a coyote. Something about the stealthy, deliberate way in which it moved sent a thrill of fear coursing through her.

Now it was off the screen. No alerts came up on the other images. But Corrie was not reassured. Whatever she'd seen, it had been coming around the side of the house. Her side of the house.

She turned suddenly. What was that noise? The squeaking of a mouse? Or—maybe, just maybe— the soft protesting squeal of a window, being gingerly tried?

Heart in her mouth, she ran out of the security room and across the corridor into the den. The tall windows yawned dark before her.

"Get the fuck away from here!" she yelled at them. "I've got a gun—and I'm not afraid to use it! Any closer, and I'm calling the cops!"

Nothing. Utter silence.

Corrie stood in the darkness, breathing hard. Still nothing.

At length she returned to the security room. The video feeds were quiet; no movement registered on any of them.

She stayed before the monitor, eyes glued to the various feeds, for fifteen minutes. Then she went through the entire house, dog at her heels, checking all the doors and windows to make sure they were locked. Finally she returned to her bedroom, lay down in the dark, and gathered the covers around her. But she did not fall asleep.

# 24

The following morning was, if possible, even colder than it had been the day before. But for the time being, as she bustled around the ski shed, Corrie barely noticed. After a breakfast spent convincing herself she'd been imagining things the night before, she bundled up and went outside—only to find out there were very real, very human footprints in the snow all around the house. Someone apparently had been wandering around out there for a long time, perhaps hours.

It scared the hell out of her, but she couldn't follow the confused welter of tracks or figure out where they'd come from.

Getting into her car and checking her cell phone, she played back a message from Pendergast announcing that he'd arranged the necessary permissions for her to examine three more skeletons from among the coffins in the shed. She drove down to the Hotel Sebastian to collect the necessary paperwork and thank Pendergast—only to learn that he was out, but had left everything for her at the front desk.

She almost forgot the cold as she tracked down the first of the three skeletons—Asa Cobb—carefully removed the remains from the rude coffin, and placed them on the examination table. Arranging her tools, she took a deep breath, then began a methodical analysis of the bones.

It was as she suspected. Many of the bones displayed damage from a tool: scrapes, gouges, cuts. Again, there were tooth marks: clearly human, not bear. And again, there was no sign of pot polishing, burning, or cooking of any kind—this man, too, had been eaten raw. Nor were there signs of bullet or knife wounds—death had been caused by a massive blow to the head with a rock, followed by the same brutal beating and dismemberment evidenced by the bones of Bowdree. The old brown bones told a graphic, violent tale of a man who was set upon, torn to pieces, and consumed raw.

She straightened up. There was no longer any doubt: these miners had fallen victim to a gang of serial killers.

"Is it as you expected?" came the honeyed drawl from behind her.

Corrie whirled around, heart suddenly pounding like mad in her chest. There was Pendergast, dressed in a black overcoat, a silk scarf around his neck. His face and hair were almost as white as the snow that clung to his shoes. The guy had the damnedest ability to sneak up on a person.

"I see you got my message," Pendergast said. "I had tried calling you last night, as well, but you didn't pick up your phone."

"Sorry." As her heart returned to normal, she felt herself flushing. "I was on a date."

One eyebrow went up. "Indeed? May I inquire as to whom with?"

"Ted Roman. A librarian here in Roaring Fork. Grew up in town. Nice guy, ex–ski bum, snowmobile addict. Good researcher, too. He's helped me quite a bit."

Pendergast nodded, then turned—significantly—toward the examination table.

"I've only had a chance to examine one of the skeletons," she said, "but it seems to have all the earmarks of the Bowdree killing."

"So it's your opinion we're dealing with, how shall we call it, a *group* engaged in serial killing."

"Exactly. I would think at least three or four, possibly more."

"Interesting." Pendergast picked up one of the bones and turned it over in his hands, giving it a perfunctory examination. "Two murderers work-ing together is uncommon, but not unheard of. Three or more, however, acting in concert, is a *rara avis* indeed." He put the bone back on the table. "Technically, three separate killings are necessary to establish a serial killer."

"Eleven miners died. Isn't that enough to qual-ify?"

"Almost assuredly. I shall look forward to receiv-ing your detailed reports on the other two miners, as well."

Corrie nodded.

Hands in his pockets, Pendergast looked around the equipment shed before finally returning his pale gaze to her. "When was the last time you read *The Hound of the Baskervilles*?"

This question was so unexpected, Corrie was certain she'd misheard. "What?"

"*The Hound of the Baskervilles*. When did you last read it?"

"The Sherlock Holmes story? Ninth grade. Maybe eighth. Why?"

"Do you recall the initial letter you sent me re-garding your thesis? In a postscript, you made ref-erence to a meeting between Arthur Conan Doyle and Oscar Wilde. During that meeting, Wilde told Conan Doyle a rather dreadful story he'd heard on his American lecture tour."

"Right." Corrie stole a glance at the table. She was eager to get back to work.

"Would you find it interesting to know that one of the stops Oscar Wilde made on his lecture tour was right here in Roaring Fork?"

"I know all about that. It was in Doyle's diary. One of the Roaring Fork miners told Wilde the story of the man-eating grizzly, and Wilde passed on the story to Doyle. That's what gave me the idea for my thesis in the first place."

"Excellent. My question to you is this: Do you believe Wilde's story might have inspired Doyle to write *The Hound of the Baskervilles*?"

Corrie hopped from one cold foot to the other. "It's possible. Likely, even. But I'm not sure I see the relevance."

"Just this: if you were to take a look through *The Hound*, there's a chance you might come across some clues as to what actually happened."

"What actually happened? But...I'm sure Wilde heard the false story and told it to Doyle. Neither one could possibly have known the truth—that these miners weren't killed by a bear."

"Are you sure?"

"Doyle wrote about the 'grizzled bear' in his diary. He didn't mention a cannibalistic gang."

"Consider for a moment: what if Wilde heard the *real* story and told it to Doyle? And what if

Doyle found it too disturbing to put in his diary? What if Doyle instead concealed some of that information in *The Hound*?"

Corrie had to stop herself from scoffing. Was it possible Pendergast was serious? "I'm sorry, but that's pretty far-fetched. Are you really suggesting that a Sherlock Holmes story could possibly shed light on my project?"

Pendergast did not reply. He simply stood there in his black overcoat, returning her gaze.

She shivered. "Look, I hope you don't mind, but I'd really like to get back to my examination, if it's okay with you."

Still Pendergast said nothing; he merely regarded her with those pale eyes of his. For some reason, Corrie got the distinct feeling that she had just failed some kind of test. But she couldn't help that; the answer lay not in fictional stories but right here, in the bones themselves.

After a long moment, Pendergast gave the slightest of bows. "Of course, Miss Swanson," he said coolly. Then he turned and left the equipment shed as silently as he had come.

Corrie watched until she heard the faint clunk of the door shutting. Then—with a mixture of eagerness and relief—she returned to the earthly remains of Asa Cobb.

# 25

Chief Stanley Morris had shut his office door and given his secretary orders not to disturb him for any reason whatsoever while he updated his corkboard case-line. It was how the chief managed complex cases: reducing everything to color-coded three-by-five cards, each with a single fact, a piece of evidence, a photograph, or a witness. These he would organize chronologically, pin to a corkboard, and then—with string—connect the cards, looking for patterns, clues, and relationships.

It was a standard approach and it had worked well for him before. But as he surveyed the chaos on his desk, the corkboard overflowing with a rainbow of cards, the strings going in every direction, he began to wonder if he needed a different system. He felt himself growing more frustrated by the minute.

The phone buzzed and he picked it up. "For heaven's sake, Shirley, I asked not to be disturbed!"

"Sorry, Chief," said the voice, "but there's someone here you really must see—"

"I don't care if it's the pope. I'm busy!"

"It's Captain Stacy Bowdree."

It took a minute for the ramifications of this to sink in. Then he felt himself go cold. *This is all I need.* "Oh. Jesus...All right, send her in."

Before he could even prepare himself, the door opened and a striking woman strode in. Captain Bowdree had short auburn hair, a handsome face, and a pair of intense, dark brown eyes. She was all of six feet tall and somewhere in her midthirties.

He rose and held out his hand. "Chief Stanley Morris. This is quite a surprise."

"Stacy Bowdree." She gave his hand a firm shake. Even though she was dressed in casual clothes—jeans, a white shirt, and a leather vest— her bearing was unmistakably military. He offered her a seat, and she took it.

"First," said the chief, "I want to apologize for the problems with the exhumation of your, ah, ancestor. I know how upsetting it must be. We here at the Roaring Fork PD believed the developers had done a thorough search, and I was dismayed, *truly* dismayed, when your letter was brought to my attention—"

Bowdree flashed the chief a warm smile and waved her hand. "Don't worry about it. I'm not upset. Truly."

"Well, thank you for your understanding. I...We'll make it right, I promise you." The chief realized he was almost babbling.

"It's not a problem," she said. "Here's the thing. I've decided to take the remains back for reburial in our old family plot in Kentucky once the research is complete. That's why I'm here. So you see, given the circumstances there's no longer any reason to rebury Emmett in the original location, as I originally requested."

"Well, I'd be lying if I said I wasn't relieved. It makes things simpler."

"Say...is that coffee I smell?"

"Would you like a cup?"

"Thank you. Black, no sugar."

The chief buzzed Shirley and put in the order, with a second for himself. There was a brief, awkward silence. "So..." he said. "How long have you been in town?"

"Not long, a few days. I wanted to get the lay of the land, so to speak, before making my presence known. I realize my letter made quite a stir, and I didn't want to freak everyone out by storming into town like the Lone Ranger. You're the first person, in fact, that I've introduced myself to."

"Let me then welcome you most warmly to Roaring Fork." The chief felt hugely relieved by all she was saying—and also by her friendly, easygoing manner. "We're glad to have you. Where are you staying?"

"I was in Woody Creek, but I'm looking for a place in town. Having a little trouble finding something I can afford."

"I'm afraid we're in the high season. I wish I could give you some advice, but I think the town is pretty much full up." He recalled the tumultuous, acrimonious press conference and wondered if things would stay that way.

The coffee arrived and Bowdree accepted it eagerly, took a sip. "Not your usual police station coffee, I must say."

"I'm a bit of a coffee aficionado. We've got a coffee roaster in town who does a mean French roast."

She took another big sip, then another. "I don't want to keep you—I can see you're busy. I just wanted to drop in to introduce myself and tell you about my plans for the remains." She set down the cup. "And I also wondered if you could help me. Where exactly are the remains now, and how do I get there? I wanted to see them and meet the woman who's doing the research."

The chief explained, drawing her a little map of

The Heights. "I'll call Heights security," he said. "Tell them you're coming."

"Thanks." Captain Bowdree rose, once again impressing the chief with her stature. She was a damn fine-looking woman, supple and strong. "You've been really helpful."

Morris rose again hastily and took her hand. "If there's anything I can do, anything at all, please let me know."

He watched her leave, feeling like the week from hell might finally be ending on a positive note. But then his gaze drifted to the corkboard, and the chaos of cards and strings on his desk, and the old feeling of dread returned. The week from hell, he realized, was far from over.

# 26

Corrie heard the clang of the ski shed door and paused in her work, wondering if Pendergast had returned. But instead of a dark-suited figure, a tall woman strode into view wearing fleece winter warm-ups and a big knitted woolen hat with dangling pom-poms.

"Corrie Swanson?" she said as she approached.

"That's me."

"Stacy Bowdree. I'd shake your hand, but I've got these coffees." She handed Corrie a tall Starbucks cup. "Venti skinny latte with four shots, extra sugar. I had to guess."

"Wow. You guessed right." Corrie accepted the cup gratefully. "I had no idea you were coming to Roaring Fork. This is quite a surprise."

"Well, here I am."

"God, Stacy—can I call you that?—do I *owe* you.

You saved my butt with that letter. I was looking at ten years in prison, I can't thank you enough—"

"Don't embarrass me!" Bowdree laughed, uncovered her own coffee, and took a generous swig. "If you want to thank someone, you can thank your friend Pendergast. He explained the whole situation to me, and what they'd done to you. I was only too happy to help." She looked around. "Look at all these coffins. Which one's Great-Great-Granddad Emmett?"

"Right over here." Corrie led her to the man's remains, spread out on an adjacent table. If she'd known the woman was coming, she could have tried to put them in some modicum of order. She hoped Emmett's descendant would understand.

Corrie sipped her coffee a little nervously as Bowdree walked over, reached out, and gently picked up a piece of skull. "Jeez, that bear really did a number on him."

Corrie started to say something, then stopped herself. Pendergast, with excellent reason, had advised her against telling anyone—anyone—of the real cause of death until she had finished her work.

"I think this work is fascinating," said Bowdree, gently putting down the piece of skull. "So you really want to be a cop?"

Corrie laughed. She liked Bowdree immediately. "Well, I think I'd like to become an FBI agent, actually, with a specialty in forensic anthropology. Not a lab rat, but a field agent with special skills."

"That's great. I've sort of been thinking about law enforcement myself...I mean, it's logical after a career in the military."

"Are you out, then? No longer a captain?"

She smiled. "I'll always be a captain, but yes, I've been discharged." She paused. "Well, I'd better get a move on. I've got to find a cheaper place to stay if I'm going to hang around here much longer—the hotel I'm in now is bankrupting me."

Corrie smiled. "I know the feeling."

"I just wanted to introduce myself and tell you that I think what you're doing here is great." Bowdree turned to go.

"Just a minute."

Bowdree turned back.

"Want to grab a coffee at Starbucks later?" She gestured with her cup. "I'd like to return the favor—if you don't mind it being on the late side. I plan to make a long day of it—assuming I don't freeze first."

Bowdree's face brightened. "That would be great. How does nine o'clock sound?"

"See you then."

## 27

Mrs. Betty B. Kermode sipped a cup of Earl Grey tea and looked from the picture window of her living room over the Silver Queen Valley. Her house on the top of the ridge—the best lot in the entire development of The Heights—commanded a spectacular view, with the surrounding mountains rising up and up toward the Continental Divide and the towering peaks of Mount Elbert and Mount Massive, the highest and second highest peaks in Colorado, which were mere shadows at this hour of the night. The house itself was quite modest—despite what people assumed, she was not by nature a showy woman—one of the smallest in the development, in fact. It was more traditional than the others, as well, built in stone and cedar on a relatively intimate scale: none of this ultra-contemporary, postmodern style for her.

The window also afforded an excellent view of

the equipment shed. It had been from this same window that, not quite two weeks before, Mrs. Kermode had seen the telltale light go on in the shed, very late at night. She immediately knew who was inside and had taken action.

The cup rattled in its saucer as she put it down and she poured herself another. It was difficult to make a decent cup of tea at eight thousand five hundred feet, where water boiled at one hundred ninety-six degrees, and she could never get used to the insipid flavor, no matter what kind of mineral water she used, how long she steeped it, or how many bags she put in. She pursed her lips tightly as she added milk and a touch of honey, stirred, and sipped. Mrs. Kermode was a lifelong teetotaler—not for religious reasons, but because her father had been an abusive alcoholic and she associated drinking with ugliness and, even worse, a lack of control. Mrs. Kermode had made control the centerpiece of her life.

And now she was angry, quietly but furiously angry, at the humiliating disruption of her control by that girl and her FBI friend. Nothing like that had ever happened to her, and she would never forget, let alone forgive, it.

She took another swallow of tea. The Heights was the most sought-after enclave in Roaring Fork. In a town filled with vulgar new money, it was one of the oldest developments. It represented taste, Brahmin stability, and a whiff of aristocratic superiority. She and her partners had never allowed it to grow shabby, as other 1970s-era ski developments tended to do. The new spa and clubhouse would be a vital part of keeping the development fresh, and the opening of Phase III—thirty-five two-acre lots, priced at $7.3 million and up—promised to bring a stupendous financial windfall to the original investors. If only this cemetery business could be resolved. The *New York Times* article had been an annoyance, but it was nothing compared with the bull-in-a-china-shop antics of Corrie Swanson.

That bitch. It was her fault. And she would pay.

Kermode finished her cup, put it down, took a deep breath, then picked up the phone. It was late in New York City, but Daniel Stafford was a night owl and this was usually the best time to reach him.

He picked up on the second ring, his smooth patrician voice coming down the line. "Hello, Betty. How's the skiing?"

A wave of irritation. He knew perfectly well she didn't ski. "They tell me it's excellent, Daniel. But I'm not calling to bandy civilities."

"Pity."

"We've got a problem."

"The fire? It's only a problem if they don't catch

the fellow—which they will. Trust me, by the time Phase Three comes online he'll be heading to the electric chair."

"The fire isn't what I'm calling about. It's that girl. And the meddling FBI agent. I hear he's managed to dig up three more descendants who've given permission to look at their ancestors' bones."

"And the problem?"

"What do you mean, *and the problem*? It's bad enough that this Captain Bowdree has shown up in person—at least she wants to bury her ancestor's bones somewhere else. Daniel, what if those other descendants demand reburial in the original cemetery? We're five million dollars into construction!"

"Now, now, Betty, calm down. Please. That's never going to happen. If any so-called descendants take legal action—which they haven't yet—our attorneys will tie them up in knots for years. We've got the money and legal power to keep a case like this going forever."

"It's not just that. I'm worried about where it could lead—if you know what I mean."

"That girl's just looking at the bones, and when she's done, it ends. It isn't going to lead where you're worried it might lead. How could it? And if it does, trust me, we'll take care of it. Your problem, Betty, is that you're like your mother: you worry too much and you cherish your anger. Mix yourself a martini and let it go."

"You're disgusting."

"Thank you." A chuckle. "I'll tell you what. To ease your mind, I'll get my people to dig into their background, find some dirt. The girl, the FBI agent…anyone else?"

"Captain Bowdree. Just in case."

"Fine. Remember, I'm only doing this to keep our powder dry. We probably won't have to use it."

"Thank you, Daniel."

"Anything for you, my dear cousin Betty."

# 28

They sat in comfortable chairs in the all-but-empty Starbucks. Corrie cradled her cup, grateful for the warmth. Across the small table, Stacy Bowdree stared into her own coffee. She seemed quieter, less effusive, than she had that morning.

"So why did you leave the air force?" Corrie asked.

"At first I wanted to make a career of it. After 9/11. I was in college, both my parents were dead, and I was looking for direction, so I transferred to the academy. I was really gung-ho, totally idealistic. But two tours in Iraq, and then two more in Afghanistan, cured me of that. I realized I wasn't cut out to be a lifer. It's still a man's game, no matter what they say, especially in the air force."

"Four tours? Wow."

Bowdree shrugged. "Not uncommon. They need a lot of people on the ground over there."

"What did you do?"

"On the last tour, I was the commanding officer of the 382nd Expeditionary EOD Bunker. Explosive Ordnance Disposal. We were stationed at FOB Gardez, Paktia Province."

"You defused bombs?"

"Sometimes. Most of the time, we'd clear areas of the base or take munitions to the range and get rid of them. Basically, any time they wanted to put a shovel in the ground, we had to clear the area first. Once in a while, we had to go beyond the wire and clear IEDs."

"You mean, with those big bomb suits?"

"Yeah, like in that film *The Hurt Locker.* Although mostly we used robots. Anyway, that's all in the past. I got my discharge a few months ago. I've sort of been drifting, wondering what to do with my life—and then Pendergast's bit of news came along."

"And so you're here in Roaring Fork."

"Yes, and you're probably wondering why."

"Well, I am, a little." Corrie laughed, still a little nervous. She had been afraid to ask the question.

"When you're done with him, I'm taking Great-Great-Granddad back to Kentucky and I'm going to bury him in the family plot."

Corrie nodded. "That's cool."

"My parents are gone, I don't have any brothers

or sisters. I've been getting interested in my family's past. The Bowdrees go back a long way. We've got Colorado pioneers like Emmett, we've got military officers going back to the Revolution, and then there's my favorite, Captain Thomas Bowdree Hicks, who fought for the South in the Army of Northern Virginia—a real war hero and a captain, just like me." Her face glowed with pride.

"I think it's great."

"I'm glad you think so. Because I'm not here to rush your work along. I don't have any burning agenda—I just want to reconnect with my past, with my roots, to make a personal journey of sorts, and in the end bring my ancestor back to Kentucky. Maybe by then I'll have a better idea of what to do next."

Corrie simply nodded.

Bowdree finished her coffee. "What a bizarre thing, getting eaten by a bear."

Corrie hesitated. She'd been thinking about it all afternoon, and had decided she really couldn't in good conscience keep back the truth. "Um, I think there's something you should know about your ancestor."

Bowdree looked up.

"This has to remain confidential—at least until I've finished my work."

"It will."

"Emmett Bowdree wasn't killed and eaten by a grizzly bear."

"No?"

"Nor were the other remains—at least the ones I've looked at." She took a deep breath. "They were murdered. By a gang of serial killers, it seems. Murdered and..." She couldn't quite say it.

"Murdered and...?"

"Eaten."

"You've got to be kidding me."

Corrie shook her head.

"And nobody knows this?"

"Only Pendergast."

"What are you going to do about it?"

Corrie paused. "Well, I'd like to stay here and solve the crime."

Bowdree whistled. "Good God. Any idea of who? Or why?"

"Not yet."

A long silence ensued. "You need any help?"

"No. Well, maybe. I've got a whole lot of old newspapers to comb through—I guess I could use a hand with that. But I need to do all the forensic analysis on my own. It's my first real thesis and...well, I want it to be my own work. Pendergast thinks I'm crazy and wants me to finish up and go back to New York with what I've got, but I'm not ready for that yet."

Bowdree gave a big smile. "I get it totally. You're just like me. I like doing things on my own."

Corrie sipped her drink. "Any luck finding a place to stay?"

"Nada. I've never seen such a gold-plated town."

"Why don't you stay with me? I'm house-sitting an empty mansion on Ravens Ravine Road, just me and a stray dog, and to be honest the place is creeping me out. I'd love to have someone keep me company." *Especially ex-military.* She'd been thinking about those footprints all afternoon, thinking how much better she'd feel with a room-mate. "All you'll have to do is avoid a few security cameras—the nonresident owner is a bit of a busy-body. But I'd love to have you."

"Are you serious? Really?" Bowdree's smile widened. "That would be fantastic! Thank you so much."

Corrie drained her drink and stood up. "If you're ready, you can follow me up there now."

"I was born ready." And with that, Bowdree grabbed her gear and followed Corrie out into the freezing night.

29

At five minutes to four in the morning, London time, Roger Kleefisch stepped into the large sitting room of his town house on Marylebone High Street and surveyed the dim surroundings with satisfaction. Everything was in its precise position: the velvet-lined easy chairs on each side of the fireplace; the bearskin hearth rug on the floor; the long row of reference works on the polished mantelpiece, a letter jammed into the wood directly below them by a jackknife; the scientific charts on the wall; the bench of chemicals heavily scarred with acid; the letters *V.R.* tattooed into the far wall with bullet holes—simulated bullet holes, of course. There was even a worn violin sitting in a corner—Kleefisch had been trying to learn how to play, but of course even discordant scrapings would have been sufficient. As he looked around, a smile formed on his face. Perfect—as close as he could possibly make it to the descriptions in the stories themselves. The only thing he'd left out had been the solution of cocaine hydrochloride and hypodermic needle.

He pressed a button beside the door, and the lights came up—gas, of course, specially installed at great expense. He walked thoughtfully over to a large mahogany bookcase and peered through the glass doors. Everything within was devoted to a single subject—*the* subject. The top three shelves were taken up with various copies of The Canon—of course he wasn't able to purchase the very first editions, even on his barrister's salary, but he nevertheless had some extremely choice copies, especially the 1917 George Bell edition of *His Last Bow*, with dust wrapper intact, and the 1894 George Newnes printing of *The Memoirs of Sherlock Holmes*, the spine still quite bright, with just the smallest amount of wear and foxing. The lower shelves of the bookcase were taken up by various volumes of scholarship and back issues of the *Baker Street Journal*. This last was a periodical issued by the Baker Street Irregulars, a group devoted to the study and perpetuation of Sherlockiana. Kleefisch had himself published several articles in the *Journal*, one of which—an exceedingly detailed work devoted to Holmes's study of poisons—had prompted the Irregulars to offer him a membership in the organization and present him with an "Irregular Shilling." One did not apply for membership in the Irregulars; one had to be asked. And becoming an Investiture was, without doubt, the proudest achievement of Kleefisch's life.

Opening the cabinet doors, he hunted around the lower shelves for a periodical he wanted to re-read, located it, closed the doors again, then walked over to the closest armchair and sat down with a sigh of contentment. The gaslights threw a warm, mellow light over everything. Even this town house, in the Lisson Grove section, had been chosen for its proximity to Baker Street. If it had not been for the infrequent sound of traffic from beyond the bow window, Kleefisch could almost have imagined himself back in 1880s London.

The phone rang, an antique "Coffin" dating to 1879, of wood and hard rubber with a receiver shaped like an oversize drawer handle. The smile fading from his face, he glanced at his watch and picked up the receiver. "Hallo."

"Roger Kleefisch?" The voice was American—southern, Kleefisch noticed—coming in from a long distance, it seemed. He vaguely recognized it.

"Speaking."

"This is Pendergast. Aloysius Pendergast."

"Pendergast." Kleefisch repeated the name, as if tasting it.

"Do you remember me?"

"Yes. Yes, of course." He had known Pendergast at Oxford, when he had been studying law and Pendergast had been reading philosophy at the Graduate Centre of Balliol College. Pendergast had been a rather strange fellow—reserved and exceedingly private—and yet a kind of intellectual bond had formed between them that Kleefisch still remembered with fondness. Pendergast, he recalled, had seemed to be nursing some private sorrow, but Kleefisch's tactful attempts to draw him out on the subject had met with no success.

"I apologize for the lateness of the call. But I remembered your keeping, shall we say, unusual hours and hoped that the habit had not deserted you."

Kleefisch laughed. "True, I rarely go to bed before five in the morning. When I'm not in court, I prefer to sleep while the rabble are out and about. To what do I owe this call?"

"I understand you are a member of the Baker Street Irregulars."

"I have that honor, yes."

"In that case, perhaps you can assist me."

Kleefisch settled back in the chair. "Why? Are you working on some academic project regarding Sherlock Holmes?"

"No. I am a special agent with the FBI, and I'm investigating a series of murders."

There was a brief silence while Kleefisch digested this. "In that case, I can't imagine what possible service I could be to you."

"Let me summarize as briefly as I can. An arsonist has burned down a house and its inhabitants at the ski resort of Roaring Fork, Colorado. Do you know of Roaring Fork?"

Naturally, Kleefisch had heard of Roaring Fork.

"In the late nineteenth century, Roaring Fork was a mining community. Interestingly, it is one of the places where Oscar Wilde stopped on his lecture tour of America. While he was there, he was told a rather colorful tale by one of the miners. The tale centered on a man-eating grizzly bear."

"Please continue," Kleefisch said, wondering just where this strange story was going.

"Wilde told this story, in turn, to Conan Doyle during their 1889 dinner at the Langham Hotel. It seemed to have had a powerful effect on Conan Doyle—powerful, unpleasant, and lasting."

Kleefisch said nothing. He knew, of course, about the legendary dinner. He would have to take another look at the Conan Doyle diary entry about that.

"I believe that what Conan Doyle heard so affected him that he wove it—suitably fictionalized, of course—into his work, as an attempt at catharsis. I'm speaking in particular about *The Hound of the Baskervilles*."

"Interesting," Kleefisch said. To the best of his knowledge, this was a new line of critical thinking. If it proved promising, it might even lead to a scholarly monograph for the Irregulars. To be written by himself, of course: of late he had been searching for a new subject on which to focus. "But I confess I still don't see how I can be of help. And I certainly don't understand what all this has to do with the arson case you're investigating."

"On the latter point, I'd prefer to keep my own counsel. On the former point, I am becoming increasingly convinced that Conan Doyle knew more than he let on."

"You mean, more than he alluded to in *The Hound of the Baskervilles*?"

"Precisely."

Kleefisch sat up. This was more than interesting—this was downright exciting. His mind began to race. "How do you mean?"

"Just that Conan Doyle might have written more about this man-eating bear, somewhere else—perhaps in his letters or unpublished works. Which is why I'm consulting you."

"You know, Pendergast, there might actually be something in your speculations."

"Pray explain."

"Late in life, Conan Doyle supposedly wrote one last Holmes story. Nothing about it is known—not its subject, not even its name. The story goes that Conan Doyle submitted it for publication, but it was returned to him because its subject was too strong for the general public. What happened to it then is unknown. Most suspect it was destroyed. Ever since, this lost Holmes story has been the stuff of legends, endlessly speculated upon by members of the Irregulars."

There was silence on the other end of the line.

"To tell you the truth, Pendergast, I'd rather suspected it of being just another Holmesian tall tale. They are legion, you know. Or, perhaps, a shaggy dog story perpetuated by Ellery Queen. But given what you've said, I find myself wondering if the story might actually exist, after all. And if it does, that it might..." His voice trailed off.

"That it might tell the rest of the story that always haunted Conan Doyle," Pendergast finished for him.

"Exactly."

"Do you have any idea how one might go about searching for such a story?"

"Not off the top of my head. But as an Irregular, and a Holmes scholar, there are various resources at my disposal. This could be an extraordinary new avenue of research." Kleefisch's brain was working even faster now. To uncover a lost Sherlock Holmes story, after all these years…

"What's your address in London?" Pendergast asked.

"Five-Seventy-Two, Marylebone High Street."

"I hope you don't mind if I call on you in the near future?"

"How near?"

"Two days, perhaps. As soon as I can break away from this arson investigation. I'll be staying at the Connaught Hotel."

"Excellent. It will be a pleasure to see you again. In the meantime, I'll make some initial inquiries, and we'll be able to—"

"Yes," Pendergast interrupted. His voice had changed abruptly; a sudden urgency had come into it. "Yes, thank you, I'll do my best to see you then. But now, Kleefisch, I have to go; you'll excuse me, please."

"Is something wrong?"

"There appears to be another house on fire." And with that, Pendergast abruptly hung up and the line went dead.

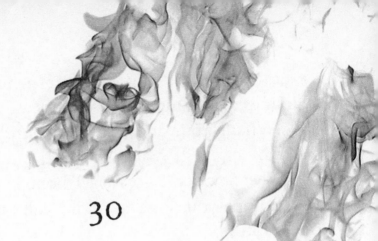

# 30

Even with liberal goosing of the siren and repeated yelling through the squad car's external megaphone, Chief Morris couldn't get closer than a block to the station, so thick was the press of cars, media, and people. And it wasn't even eight o'clock in the morning. With this second arson, the story had gone national—no surprise, given the identity of the victims—and the crime feeders were all there, along with the network news shows, CNN, and God only knew who else.

The chief now regretted he'd driven himself; he had no one to run interference, and his only option was to get out of the car and scrimmage his way through these jokers. They had surrounded his squad car, cameras rolling, microphones waving at him like clubs. He'd spent all night at the scene of the fire, which had started at eight in the evening, and he was now filthy, stinking of smoke, exhausted, coughing, and hardly able to think. What a state to face the cameras.

The chief's car was jostled and rocked by the unruly crowd of reporters. They were calling out questions, hollering at him, jockeying with each other for position. He realized he'd better think of something to say.

He took a deep breath, collected himself, and forced open the door. The reaction was instant, the crowd pushing forward, the cameras and mikes swinging dangerously, one even knocking his hat off. He stood up, dusted off his hat, replaced it, and held up his hands. "All right. All right! Please. I can't make a statement if you keep this up. Give me some room, *please!*"

The crowd backed off a little. The chief looked around, acutely aware that his image was going to be broadcast on every nightly news show in the country.

"I will make a brief statement. There will be no questions afterward." He took a breath. "I've just come from the crime scene. I can assure you we are doing everything humanly possible to solve these vicious crimes and bring the perpetrators to justice. We have the finest forensic and crime-scene investigators in the state on this case. All our resources and those of the surrounding communities have been brought to bear. On top of that, we have brought in as a consultant one of the FBI's top agents specializing in serial killings and deviant psychology, as it appears we may be dealing with a serial arsonist."

He cleared his throat. "Now to the crime itself. The scene is of course still being analyzed. Two bodies have been recovered. They have been tentatively identified as the actress Sonja Dutoit and her child. Our thoughts and prayers are with the victims, their families, and all of you who have been touched by this horrible event. This is a huge tragedy for our town and, truthfully, I can't find the words to express the depth of my shock and sorrow..." He found himself temporarily unable to continue, but quickly mastered the constriction in his throat and wrapped things up. "We will have more information for you at a press conference later today. That is all I have to say for the moment. Thank you."

He barreled forward, ignoring the shouted questions and the forest of microphones, and within five minutes managed to stagger into his office. There was Pendergast, sitting in the outer office, dressed in his usual impeccable style, sipping tea. The television was on.

Pendergast rose. "Allow me to congratulate you on a most effective appearance."

"What?" Morris turned to Shirley. "I was on the tube already?"

"It was live, Chief," she said. "And you handled it very well. You looked like a hero, with that determined voice...and those streaks of soot on your face."

"Soot? On my face?" Damn, he should have washed up.

"A Hollywood makeup artist couldn't have done a finer job," said Pendergast. "That, combined with the disheveled uniform, the windswept hair, and the evident emotion, made for a singular impression."

The chief threw himself down in a chair. "I couldn't care less what they think. My God, I've never seen anything like this. Agent Pendergast, if you heard what I said on television, then you know I just elevated you to official consulting status."

Pendergast inclined his head.

"So I hope to God in heaven you will accept. I need your help more than ever. How about it?"

The man responded by removing a slim envelope from his suit and dangling it in front of Morris by his fingertips. "I'm afraid I beat you to it. I'm not just consulting—now I'm official."

## 31

As Corrie entered the empty library, it seemed less cheerful than before, more foreboding. Maybe it was because an atmosphere of doom seemed to have descended on the town—or perhaps it was simply due to the dark storm clouds that were gathering over the mountains, promising snow.

Stacy Bowdree, following her into the history section, whistled softly. "Does this town have money, or what?"

"Yeah, but nobody ever comes in here."

"Too busy shopping."

She saw Ted, at his desk across the room, rising from his book to greet them. He was wearing a tight T-shirt and looking exceptionally good, and Corrie felt her heart flutter unexpectedly. She took a breath and introduced Stacy.

"What's on the program today, ladies?" Ted asked, giving Stacy an appreciative once-over. Corrie had to admit Stacy was striking and that any man would enjoy looking at her, but his attentive eye still concerned her.

"Murder and mayhem," Corrie said. "We want all the articles you've got on murders, hangings, robberies, vigilantism, shootings, feuds—in short, everything bad—for the period of the grizzly killings."

At this Ted laughed. "Just about every issue of the old *Roaring Fork Courier* is going to have some kind of crime story. It was a hot town in those days—a real place, unlike now. What issues do you want to start with?"

"The first grizzly killing was in May 1876, so let's start with, say, April first, 1876, and go six months out from that."

"Very good," Ted replied.

Corrie noticed that his eyes were still straying regularly to Stacy—and not just to her face. But the captain seemed oblivious—or perhaps she was just used to it from her years in the military.

"The old newspapers are all digitized. I'll set you up at some terminals and show you what to do." He paused. "Sure is crazy in town today."

"Yeah," said Corrie. The truth was, aside from all the traffic she hadn't paid much attention.

"It's like *Jaws*."

"What do you mean?"

"What was the name of that town—Amity? You know, the tourists leaving in droves. Well, that's what's happening here. Haven't you noticed? All of a sudden the ski slopes are deserted, the hotels are emptying out. Even the second-homers are making preparations to leave. In a day or two, the only people who'll still be here are the press. It's nuts." He typed away at two side-by-side terminals, then straightened. "Okay, they're all set up for you." He showed them how to work the equipment. He paused. "So, Stacy, when did you get here?"

"Four days ago. But I've been lying low, didn't want to cause a ruckus."

"Four days. The day before the first fire?"

"I guess it must have been. I heard about it the following morning."

"I hope you enjoy our little town. It's a fun place—if you're rich." He laughed, winked, and, to Corrie's relief, went back to his desk. Was she jealous? She didn't have a lock on him—she'd even declined his offer to see his apartment.

They divided up the searching by date, Corrie taking the first three months while Stacy took the next three. Silence descended, broken only by the soft rapping of keys.

And then Stacy whistled softly. "Listen to this."

## THEY WANTED THE SAME GIRL
### And They Fought a Duel by Lantern Light on Her Account
## BOTH MEN LITERALLY CUT TO RIBBONS

Two Ohio swains meet at midnight and, by the aid of a lantern, proceed to hack each other with swords and pocket knives until both are unconscious. One of the rivals, rousing himself, runs his adversary through with his sword, causing a fatal injury. The lady, Miss Williams, is prostrate with grief over the terrible affray.

"That's pretty bizarre," said Corrie, hoping that Stacy wasn't going to read aloud every silly story she came across. It was only with a degree of soul searching that she'd accepted Stacy's offer of assistance.

"I like that. *Prostrate with grief.* I'll bet she just soaked her bloomers over the *affray*."

The crudity of the comment shocked Corrie. But maybe that was the way women talked in the military.

As Corrie paged through the headlines, she realized Ted was right: Roaring Fork, at least in the summer of 1876, was a bloody town. There was practically a murder a week, along with daily stab-bings and shootings. There were stagecoach rob-beries on Independence Pass, mining claim dis-putes, the frequent murder of prostitutes, stealing of horses, and vigilante hangings. The town was overrun with card sharps, shysters, thieves, and murderers. There was also a huge economic di-vide. Some few struck it rich and built palatial mansions on Main Street, while most lived in teem-ing boardinghouses, four or five to a room, and tent encampments overrun with filth, rats, and mosquitoes. A casual and pervasive racism infected everything. One end of town, called "China Camp," was populated with so-called coolies who were horribly discriminated against. There was also a "Negro Town." And the newspaper noted a squalid camp in a nearby canyon that was occupied by "assorted drunken, miserable specimens of the Red Race, the sad remnants of the Utes of yore."

In 1876, law had barely come to Roaring Fork. Most "justice" was administered by shadowy vig-ilantes. If a drunken shooting or knifing occurred in a saloon the night before, the perpetrator would often be found the next morning hanging from a large cottonwood tree at the far end of town. The corpses were left up for days to greet newcomers. In a busy week there might be two, three, or even four bodies hanging on the tree, with "the maggots dropping out of them," as one reporter wrote with relish. The papers were full of colorful and outrageous stories: of a feud between two families that ended with the complete extermination of all but one man; of an obese horse thief whose weight was such that his hanging decapitated him; of a man who went berserk from what the newspaper called a "Brain Storm," thought he was Jesus, barricaded himself in a whorehouse, and proceeded to kill most of the ladies in order to rid the town of sin.

Work in the mines was dreadful, the miners descending before daybreak and coming up after sunset, six days a week, only seeing the light of day on Sundays. Accidents, cave-ins, and explosions were common. But it was even worse in the stamp mills and the smelter. There, in a large industrial operation, the silver ore was pulverized by gigantic metal "stamps" weighing many tons. These literally smashed the ore, pounding day and night, producing a ceaseless din that shook the entire town. The resulting grit was dumped into immense iron tanks with mechanical agitators and grinding plates to further reduce it to a mush-like paste; then mercury, salt, and copper sulfate were added. The resulting witches' brew was cooked and stirred for days, heated by enormous coal-fired boilers that belched smoke. Because the town was in a valley surrounded by mountains, the coal smoke created a choking, London-style fog that blocked the sun for days on end. Those who worked in the mill and smelter had it worse than the miners, as they were often scalded to death by burst steam pipes and boilers, suffocated by noxious fumes, or horribly maimed by heavy equipment. There were no safety laws, no regulation of hours or pay, and no unions. If a man was crippled by machinery, he was immediately dismissed without even an extra day's wage, cast off to fend for himself. The worst and most dangerous jobs were given to the Chinese "coolies," whose frequent deaths were reported in the back of the paper in the same offhand tone one might use to describe the death of a dog.

Corrie found herself becoming increasingly indignant as she read about the injustice, the exploitation, and the casual cruelty in pursuit of profit perpetrated by the mining companies. What surprised her most, however, was to learn that it was the Staffords—one of the most respected philanthropist families in New York City, famous for the Stafford Museum of Art and the wealthy Stafford Fund—who had initially established their fortune during the Colorado silver boom as the financiers behind the mill and smelter in Roaring Fork. The Stafford family, she knew, had done a lot of good with their money over the years—which made the unsavory origin of their fortune all the more surprising.

"What a place," said Stacy, interrupting Corrie's train of thought. "I had no idea Roaring Fork was such a hellhole. And now look at it: the richest town in America!"

Corrie shook her head. "Ironic, isn't it?"

"So much violence and misery."

"True," said Corrie, adding in a low voice: "though I'm not finding anything that might point to a gang of cannibalistic serial killers."

"Me neither."

"But the clues are there, somewhere. They *have* to be. We just have to find them."

Stacy shrugged. "You think it might be those Ute Indians up in the canyon? They had a good motive: their land was stolen by the miners."

Corrie considered this. Around that time, she'd read, the White River and Uncompahgre Utes had been fighting back against the whites who were pushing them westward through the Rocky Mountains. The conflict culminated in the White River War of 1879, when the Utes were finally expelled from Colorado. It was possible that some Indians in the conflict had worked their way southward and taken revenge on the miners of Roaring Fork.

"I thought of that," she said at length. "But the

miners weren't scalped—scalping leaves distinctive markings. And I learned that the Utes had a huge taboo against cannibalism."

"So did whites. And maybe they didn't scalp them so as to conceal their identity."

"Possible. But the killings were high-quality. What I mean is," Corrie hastily added, "they were not sloppy and disorganized. It can't be easy to ambush a wily, hardened Colorado miner guarding his claim. I don't think a sad camp of Utes could have perpetrated these killings."

"What about the Chinese? I can't believe how terribly they were treated—it was as if they were considered subhuman."

"I thought about that, too. But if the motive was revenge, why *eat* them?"

"Maybe they just faked the eating thing, to make it look like a bear."

Corrie shook her head. "My analysis shows they really did consume the flesh—raw. And another question: why did they suddenly stop? What goal had they accomplished, if any?"

"That's a really good question. But it's one o'clock, and I don't know about you, but I'm so hungry I could eat a couple of miners myself."

"Let's get lunch."

As they got up to leave, Ted came over. "Say, Corrie," he began. "I meant to ask you. How about dinner tonight? Won't be any problems getting a reservation." He ran his fingers through his curly brown hair and looked at her, smiling.

"I'd love to," she said, gratified that Ted, despite his attention to Stacy, still was interested. "But I'm supposed to have dinner with Pendergast."

"Oh. Well. Some other time, then." He smiled, but Corrie noticed he wasn't quite able to fully conceal a look of hurt. It reminded her of a puppy dog, and she felt a stab of guilt. Nevertheless, he turned gamely toward Stacy and gave her a wink. "Good to meet you."

As they bundled up in their coats and walked out into the winter air, Corrie wondered where another date with Ted might lead. The fact was, it seemed like a long time since she'd had a boyfriend, and her bed in the mansion up Ravens Ravine was so very, very cold.

# 32

It was like a persistent nightmare, which terrifies you one night, then returns the next in an even more malevolent form. At least, so it seemed to Chief Morris as he walked through what was left of the Dutoit house. The smoldering ruins stood on the shoulder of a hill, with sweeping views of the town below and the surrounding ring of snowy mountains. He could hardly bear it: walking along the same corridors of plastic tape; smelling the same stench of burnt wood, plastic, and rubber; seeing the charred walls and melted puddles of glass, the scorched beds and heat-shattered toilets and sinks. And then there were the little things that had weirdly survived: a drinking glass, a bottle of perfume, a sodden teddy bear, and a poster of the movie *Marching Band*, Dutoit's most famous film, still pinned to a gutted wall.

It had taken most of the night to extinguish

the fire and beat it down to this damp, steaming pile. The forensic specialists and the M.E. had gone in at dawn, and had identified the victims as best they could. They hadn't been burned quite as badly as the Baker family—which only added to the horror. At least, the chief thought, he didn't have to deal with Chivers this time, who had already been through the crime scene and was now off preparing his report—a report that Chief Morris was doubtful of. Chivers was clearly in over his head.

He was, however, grateful for Pendergast's presence. The man was strangely reassuring to the chief, despite his eccentricities—and despite the fact that everyone else was put out by his presence. Pendergast wandered ahead of Morris, dressed in his inappropriate formal black coat and white silk scarf, with that same strange hat on his head, silent as the grave. The sun was obscured by heavy winter clouds, and the temperature outside the ruin was hovering in the low teens. Inside, though, the residual heat and plumes of steam created a humid, stinking microclimate.

They finally reached the first victim, which the M.E. had tentatively identified as Dutoit herself. The remains looked more or less like an oversize, blackened fetus nestled in a pile of springs, metal plates, screws, carpet tacks, and burnt layers of cotton batting, with bits of melted plastic and wire here and there. The skull was whole, the jaws gaping in a frozen scream, the arms burned to the bone, the finger bones clenched, the body curled in upon itself by the heat.

Pendergast halted and spent a long time just looking at the victim. He did not pull out test tubes and tweezers and take samples. All he did was look. Then, slowly, he circled the hideous thing. A hand lens came out, and he used it to peer at traces of melted plastic and other, obscure points of interest. While he was doing this, the wind shifted and the chief got a noseful of roasted meat, causing an instant gagging sensation. God, he wished Pendergast would hurry it up.

Finally the FBI agent rose and they continued their perambulation of the gigantic ruin, heading inexorably toward the second victim—the young girl. This was even worse. The chief had deliberately skipped breakfast in preparation, and there was nothing in his stomach to lose, but nevertheless he could feel the dry heaves coming on.

The victim, Dutoit's daughter, Sallie, had been ten years old. She went to school with the chief's own daughter. The two children had not been friends—Sallie had been a withdrawn child, and no wonder, with a mother like that. Now, as they approached the corpse, the chief ventured a glance.

The girl's body was in a sitting position, burned only on one side. She had been handcuffed to the pipes under a sink.

He felt the first dry heave, which came like a hiccup, then another, and quickly looked away.

Again, Pendergast spent what seemed a lifetime examining the remains. The chief didn't even begin to understand how he could do it. Another heave came, and he tried to think of something else—*anything* else—to get himself under control.

"It's so perplexing," Morris said, more to distract himself than for any other reason. "I just don't understand."

"In what way?"

"How…well, how the perp selects his victims. I mean, what do the victims have in common? It all seems so random."

Pendergast rose. "The crime scene is indeed challenging. You are correct that the victims are random. However, the *attacks* are not."

"How so?"

"The killer did not choose victims. He—or she, as the etiology of the attacks does not yet indicate gender—chose houses."

The chief frowned. "Houses?"

"Yes. Both houses share one trait: they are spectacularly visible from town. The next house will no doubt be equally conspicuous."

"You mean, they were selected for show? In God's name, why?"

"To send a message, perhaps." Pendergast turned away. "Now back to the matter at hand. This crime scene is primarily interesting for the light it sheds on the mind of the killer." Pendergast spoke slowly as he peered around. "The perpetrator would appear to meet the Millon definition of a sadistic personality of the 'explosive' subtype. He seeks extreme measures of control; he takes pleasure—perhaps sexual pleasure—in the intense suffering of others. This disorder presents violently in an individual who would otherwise seem normal. In other words, the person we seek might appear to be an ordinary, productive member of the community."

"How can you know that?"

"It is based on my reconstruction of the crime."

"Which is?"

Pendergast looked around the ruins again before letting his eyes settle on the chief. "First, the perpetrator entered through an upstairs window."

The chief refrained from asking how Pendergast could determine this, especially since there was no second floor left.

"We know this because the house doors were massive and the locks were all engaged. To be expected, given the fear recently generated by the first fire and, perhaps, by the relative isolation of the structure. In addition, the first-floor windows are of massive, multi-light construction, glazed with expensive, high-R-value triple-paned glass with anodized aluminum cladding over oak. The ones I examined were all locked, and we can assume the rest were shut and locked as well, given the low temperatures and, as I said, the fear generated by the first attack. Such a window is extremely hard to break, and any attempt would be noisy and time consuming. It would alarm the house. Someone would have called nine-one-one or hit a panic button, with which this house was equipped. But the two victims were caught unawares—upstairs, probably while sleeping. The upstairs windows were less robust, double-paned, and furthermore not all locked—as is evident from this one, here." Pendergast pointed at a tracery of ash and metal at his feet. "Thus, I conclude that the killer came and left by an upstairs window. The two victims were subdued, then brought downstairs for the, ah, *denouement.*"

The chief found it hard to concentrate on what Pendergast was saying. The wind had shifted again, and he was breathing assiduously through his mouth.

"This tells us not only the killer's state of mind, but also some of his physical characteristics. He or she is certainly an athletic individual, perhaps with some rock climbing or other strenuous field experience."

"Rock climbing experience?"

"My dear Chief, it follows directly from the fact there is no evidence of a ladder or rope."

Chief Morris swallowed. "And the, ah, 'explosive' sadism?"

"The woman, Dutoit, was duct-taped to the downstairs sofa. The tape was wrapped all the way around the sofa—quite a job—rendering her immobile. She appears to have been doused with gasoline and burned alive. Most significantly, this occurred without the victim being gagged."

"Which means?"

"The perpetrator wanted to talk to her, to hear her plead for her life, and then, after the fire began...to hear her scream."

"Oh, dear Lord." Morris remembered Dutoit's strident voice at the press conference. He felt another dry heave.

"But the sadism evident here—" Pendergast made a gentle gesture in the direction of the remains of the dead girl— "is even more extreme."

Morris didn't want to know more, but Pendergast went on. "This girl was not doused with gasoline. That would have been too quick for our perpetrator. Instead, he started a fire to the right of her, there, and let it burn toward her. Now, if you will examine the pipes that the victim was hand-cuffed to, you will notice that they are bent. She was pulling on them with all her might in an effort to escape."

"I see." But the chief didn't even make a pre-tense of looking.

"But note the *direction* in which they are bent."

"Tell me," said Chief Morris, covering his face, no longer able to take it.

"They are bent in the direction of the fire."

A silence fell. "I'm sorry," the chief said. "I don't understand."

"Whatever she was trying to get away from—it was even worse than the fire."

# 33

The last time Corrie was in the old Victorian police station, she'd been in handcuffs. The memory was fresh enough that she felt a twinge upon entering. But Iris, the lady at the reception desk, was almost too nice and happily directed her to Pendergast's temporary office in the basement.

She descended the stuffy staircase, walked past a dim, rumbling furnace, and came to a narrow corridor. The office at the end had no name on it, just a number; she knocked and Pendergast's voice invited her in.

The special agent stood behind an ancient metal desk covered by racks of test tubes, along with a chemistry setup of unknown function that was bubbling away. The office had no windows, and the air was stifling.

"Is this what they gave you?" Corrie asked. "It's a dungeon!"

"It is what I requested. I did not wish to be disturbed, and this office is in a location where that is assured. No one comes to bother me here—no one."

"It's hot as Hades in here."

"It's no worse than a New Orleans spring. As you know, I am averse to cold."

"Shall we go to dinner?"

"So as not to blight our meal with talk of corpses and cannibalism, perhaps we could spend a few moments catching up with your research first. Please sit down."

"Sure thing, but can we please keep it short? *I'm* averse to heatstroke." She took a seat and Pendergast did likewise.

"How are you progressing?"

"Great. I've finished examining four sets of remains, and they tell the same story: all victims of a gang of cannibalistic serial killers."

Pendergast inclined his head.

"It's unbelievable, really. But there's no question. I did find something interesting in the last skeleton I looked at. The guy with the weird name, Isham Tyng. He was one of the first to be killed, and his bones do show extensive signs of perimortem damage from a large, powerful animal, no doubt a grizzly bear—along with the usual signs of beating, dismemberment, and cannibalism performed by human beings. I looked up the newspaper accounts of the killing, and in this case a bear was scared off the remains by the arrival of Tyng's partners. No doubt the bear was scavenging the victim *after* he'd been killed by the cannibal gang. But this sighting is clearly what cemented the idea in everyone's mind that the killer was a grizzly. A reasonable assumption—but also, sheer coincidence."

"Excellent. The story is now complete. I assume you don't need to examine any more remains?"

"No, four is plenty. I've got all the data I need."

"Very good," murmured Pendergast. "And when will you be returning to New York?"

Corrie took a deep breath. "I'm not going back yet."

"And why is that?"

"I've…decided to expand the scope of my thesis."

She waited, but Pendergast did not react.

"Because, I'm sorry, but the fact is the story *isn't* complete. Now that we know these miners were murdered…" She hesitated. "Well, I'm going to do my damnedest to *solve* the murders."

Another dead silence. Pendergast's silver eyes narrowed ever so slightly.

"Look, it's a fascinating case. Why not pursue it to its end? Why were these miners killed? Who did it? And why did the killings stop so abruptly? There are tons of questions, and I want to find the answers. This is my chance to turn a good thesis into a really great one."

"If you survive," said Pendergast.

"I don't think I'm in any danger. In fact, since the fires I've been ignored. And nobody knows about my most important discovery—everyone still believes a grizzly did it."

"Nevertheless, I am uneasy."

"Why? I mean, if you're worried about where I'm house-sitting, it's miles away from the houses that were burned. And I've got a new room-mate—Captain Bowdree, as it happens. You couldn't ask for better protection than that. Let me tell you something: she's got a .45 and, believe me, she knows how to use it." She didn't mention the footsteps she'd found circling the mansion.

"I have no doubt. But the fact is, I must leave Roaring Fork for several days, perhaps longer, and as a result I'll be unable to give you the benefit of my protection. I fear that your looking into this case may awaken the proverbial sleeping dog. And there is an ugly dog sleeping in this rich little town, of that I am sure."

"Surely you don't believe the arson attacks are somehow linked to the miner killings? They were a hundred and fifty years ago."

"I don't *believe* anything—yet. But I sense deep, strong water. I'm not in favor of your remaining in Roaring Fork any longer than necessary. I advise you to leave on the first plane out."

Corrie stared at him "I'm twenty, and this is *my* life. Not yours. I'm really thankful for all your help, but…you're not my father. I'm staying."

"I will discourage it by withdrawing my financial support."

"Fine!" Corrie's pent-up anger came bursting out. "You've been interfering with my thesis from the beginning. You can't help interfering—it's the way you are—but I don't appreciate it. Can't you see how important this is to me? I'm getting tired of you telling me what to do."

Something flashed across Pendergast's face—something that, had she not been so angry, she would have recognized as dangerous. "My only concern in the matter is your safety. And I must add that the risks you face are greatly augmented by your unfortunate tendency toward impetuousness and imprudence."

"If you say so. But I'm done talking. And I'm staying in Roaring Fork whether you like it or not."

As Pendergast began to speak again, she got up so abruptly she knocked over her chair and left the room without waiting to hear him out.

# 34

It was one of the most prominent Victorian mansions on the main drag. Ted, who was a fountain of information on Roaring Fork, had told Corrie its story. The house had been built by Harold Griswell, known as the Silver King of Roaring Fork, who made a fortune and was then bankrupted by the Panic of 1893. He committed suicide by leaping into the main shaft of the Matchless Mine, leaving behind a young widow—a former saloon dancer named Rosie Ann. Rosie Ann spent the next three decades hiring and firing lawyers and bringing countless lawsuits, trying tirelessly to recover the repossessed mines and properties; eventually, when all her legal options ran out, she boarded over the windows of the Griswell Mansion and became a recluse, refusing even to shop for basic provisions and subsisting on the kindness of neighbors, who took it upon themselves to leave food at her door. In 1955, the neighbors complained of a bad smell coming from the house. When the police entered, they found an incredible scene: the entire house was packed floor-to-ceiling with tottering stacks of documents and other bric-a-brac, much of it amassed during the woman's endless lawsuits. There were bundles of newspapers, canvas bags full of ore samples, theater bills, broadsheets, ledgers, assay reports, mining certificates, depositions, trial transcripts, payroll records, bank statements, maps, mine surveys, and the like. They had found Rosie Ann's wizened body buried under a ton of paper; an entire wall of documents, undermined by gnawing mice, had toppled over and pinned her to the floor. Rosie Ann Griswell had starved to death.

She died intestate with no heirs, and the town acquired the building. The hoarded documents proved a historical treasure trove of unruly proportions. Over half a century later, the sorting and cataloging process was still going on, fitfully, whenever the impecunious Roaring Fork Historical Society could scrape together a grant.

Ted had warned Corrie about the state of the collection, which was very unlike the sleek, digitized newspaper archive that he ran. But after combing through the papers for evidence of a cannibalistic gang of killers and coming up empty-handed, Corrie decided to look into the Griswell Archive.

The archivist, it seemed, came in only two days a week. Ted had warned Corrie that he was an unqualified asshole. When Corrie arrived that gray December morning, with a few flakes drifting down from a zinc sky, she found the archivist in the mansion's parlor, sitting behind a desk, messing around with his iPad. While the parlor was free of paper, she could see, through the open doors leading off it, floor-to-ceiling metal shelves and filing cabinets packed with stuff.

The archivist rose and held out his hand. "Wynn Marple," he said. He was a prematurely balding, ponytailed man in his late thirties, with an incipient potbelly but retaining the confident, winking air of an aging Lothario.

She introduced herself and explained her mission—that she was looking for information on the year 1876, the grizzly killings, and also on crime and possible gang activity in Roaring Fork.

Marple responded at length, quickly segueing to what was evidently his favorite subject: himself. Corrie learned that he, Marple, had once been on the Olympic Ski Team that trained in Roaring Fork, which is why he had fallen in love with the town; that he was still a rad skier and a hot dude off piste as well; and that there was no way he could allow her into the archives without the proper paperwork and approvals, not to mention a much more specific and narrower scope of work.

"You see," he said, "fishing expeditions aren't permitted. A lot of these documents are private and of a confidential, controversial, or—" and here came another wink— "scandalous nature."

This speech was accompanied by several lickings of the lips and rovings of the eyes over Corrie's body.

She took a deep breath and reminded herself not to be her own worst enemy for once. A lot of guys just couldn't help being jerks. And she needed these archives. If the answer to the killings wasn't here, then it had probably been lost to history.

"You were an Olympic skier?" she asked, larding her voice with phony admiration.

That produced another gust of braggadocio, including the information that he would have won a bronze but for the course conditions, the temperature, the judges... Corrie stopped listening but kept nodding and smiling.

"That's really cool," she said when she realized he was finished. "I've never met an Olympic athlete before."

Wynn Marple had a lot more to say on that point. After five or ten minutes, Corrie, in desperation, had agreed to a date with Wynn for Saturday night—and, in return, gained complete and unrestricted access to the archive.

Wynn tagged along after her as she made her way into the elegant yet decayed rooms, packed with paper. Adding to her woes, the papers had only been roughly sorted chronologically, with no effort made to arrange them by subject.

With the now-eager Wynn fetching files, Corrie sat down at a long baize-covered table and began to sort through them. They were all mixed up and confused, full of extraneous and misfiled material, and it became obvious that whoever had done the filing was either negligent or an idiot. As she sorted through one bundle after another, the smell of decaying paper and old wax filled the room.

The minutes turned into hours. The room was overheated, the light was dim, and her eyes started to itch. Even Wynn finally got tired of talking about himself. The papers were dry, and dust seemed to float off the pages with every shuffle. There were reams of impenetrable legal documents, filings, depositions, notices and interrogatories, trial transcripts, hearings, grand jury proceedings, commingled with plats, surveys, assay results, mining partnership agreements, payrolls, inventories, work orders, worthless stock certificates, invoices, and completely irrelevant posters and broadsides. Once in a while the tide of documents yielded a colorful playbill announcing the arrival of a busty burlesque queen or slapstick comedy troupe.

Infrequently, Corrie would turn up a document of faint interest—a criminal complaint, the transcript of a murder trial, WANTED posters, police records pertaining to undesirables and transients who were suspected of or charged with crimes. But there was nothing that stood out, no gang of crazies, no one with a motive to murder and consume eleven miners.

The name of Stafford turned up regularly, especially with respect to the smelting and refining personnel records. Those records were particularly odious, with ledger pages that listed killed workers like so much damaged equipment, next to sums paid to their widows or orphans, never amounting to more than five dollars, with the majority of the sums listed as $0.00 along with the notation "no payment/worker error." There were records of workers crippled, poisoned, or injured on the job who were then summarily dismissed with no compensation or recourse whatsoever.

"What a bunch of scumbags," Corrie muttered to herself, handing over another batch of papers to Wynn.

At one point a handbill turned up that stopped Corrie.

**THE AESTHETIC THEORY**

*A lecture by*
Mr. Oscar Wilde of London, England
*The practical application of the principles*
*of the aesthetic theory, with observations*
*upon the fine arts, personal adornment,*
*and house decoration*
To Be Given at The Grand Gallery
of the
Sally Goodin Mine
Sunday Afternoon, June 2$^{\text{d}}$
At Half-Past Two O'Clock
Tickets Seventy-Five Cents

Corrie almost had to laugh at the odd quaintness of it. This had to be the lecture where Wilde heard the story of the grizzly killings. And clipped to the handbill was a sheaf of news items, letters, and notes about the lecture appearance. It seemed ludicrous that the rough miners of Roaring Fork would have had any interest whatsoever in the aesthetic theory, let alone personal adornment or house decoration. But by all accounts the lecture had been a great success, resulting in a standing ovation. Perhaps it was the figure Wilde cut, with his outré dress and foppish mannerisms, or his preternatural wit. The poor miners of Roaring Fork had precious little entertainment beyond whoring and drinking.

She quickly leafed through the attached documents and came across an amusing handwritten note, apparently a letter by a miner to his wife back east. It was entirely without punctuation.

*My Deere Wife Sun Day there was a Lektior by Mister Oscor Wild of London After the Lektior which was veery well Reseeved Mister Wild enjoyt talking to the Miners and Roufh Necks he was veery gray sheous while I was wating to speek to him that old drunk cogger Swinton button holt him pulld him asite and told him a storey that turnt the pore Man as Pail as a Gost I thot he wud drop and fent...*

Wynn, reading over her shoulder, made a snorting laugh. "Illiterate bastard." He tapped the lecture handbill. "You know, I'll bet this is worth money."

"I'm sure it is," she said, hesitating, and then clipping it all back together. As charming as the miner's letter was, it was too far afield to merit inclusion in her thesis.

She shuffled the papers aside and moved on to the next file. She noted that when Wynn carried the bundle back to the shelf, he slipped out the handbill and tucked it in another place. The guy was probably going to sell it on eBay or something.

She told herself what he did was none of her business. The next big bundle arrived, and then the next. Most of the papers dealt with milling and refining, and this time almost everything related to the Stafford family, which, by all indications, became more oppressive as their wealth and power increased. They seemed to have survived the silver panic of 1893 nicely, and even used the opportunity to pick up mines and claims at pennies on the dollar. There were plenty of faded maps of the mining districts, as well, with each mine, shaft, and tunnel carefully marked and identified. Strangely, though, there were precious few records of the smelting operations.

And then a document stopped her cold. It was a postcard dated 1933, from a family member named Howland Stafford to a woman named Dora Tiffany Kermode. It opened *Dear Cousin*.

*Kermode. Cousin.*

"Jesus!" Corrie blurted out. "That bitch Kermode is *related* to the family who squeezed this town dry."

"Who are you talking about?" Wynn asked.

She slapped the document with the back of her hand. "Betty Kermode. That horrible woman who runs The Heights. She's related to the Staffords—you know, the ones who owned the smelter back in Roaring Fork's mining days. Unbelievable."

It was only then that Corrie realized her mistake. Wynn Marple was drawing himself up. He spoke in a reproving, almost schoolmarmish tone. "Mrs. Kermode is one of the finest, most *gracious* people in this entire town."

Corrie hastily backtracked. "I'm sorry. I was just...I mean, she's responsible for putting me in jail...I didn't realize she was a friend of yours."

Her stammered apology seemed to work. "Well, I can appreciate how you might be upset with her for that, but I can vouch for her, I really can. She's *good people.*" Another wink.

*Bully for you.* In five hours, Corrie hadn't found anything, and now she was saddled with going on a date with this buffoon for nothing. She hoped it could be made short and in a place where Ted would never, ever see them. Or maybe she could beg off sick at the last moment. That's what she'd do.

She glanced at her watch. There was no way she was going to find what she needed in this hellhole of paper. For the first time, she began to feel that maybe she was overreaching. Perhaps Pendergast was right. She had enough for an excellent thesis already.

She got up. "Look, this isn't working. I'd better be going."

Wynn followed her to the front parlor. "I'm sorry you weren't more successful. But at least..." He winked again. "It resulted in our getting together."

She would definitely have to call in sick.

She swallowed. "Thanks for your help, Wynn."

He leaned toward her, way too close. "My pleasure."

She suddenly paused. What was that she felt on her ass? His hand. She took a half step back and turned, but the hand followed like an octopus's sucker, this time giving her butt cheek a little squeeze.

"Do you *mind?*" she said acidly, brushing it away.

"Well...we *do* have a date coming up."

"And that *justifies* you *groping* my *ass?*"

Wynn looked confused. "But...I was just being friendly. I figured you'd like it. I mean, it isn't every day you get to go out with an Olympic skier, and I figured...?"

It was the final leering wink that did it. Corrie rounded on him. "Olympic skier? When was the last time you looked at yourself in the mirror? Here's what you'll see—a balding, potbellied, mouth-breathing loser. I wouldn't go on a date with you if you were the last man alive."

With that she turned, grabbed her coat, and left, the cold air hitting her like a wall as she stepped outside.

Wynn Marple sat down at his desk. Both his hands were trembling and his breath was coming shallow and fast. He could hardly believe how that bitch had treated him, after all the help he'd given her. One of those feminazi types, objecting to a little innocent, friendly pat.

Wynn was so furious, so outraged, he felt the blood pounding in his head like a tom-tom. It took a few minutes, but then finally he was able to pick up the phone and dial.

# 35

Betty Brown Stafford Kermode, sitting in the living room of her house at the top of The Heights, a piñon fire roaring in the fireplace, hung up the princess phone. She sat very still for some minutes, staring out the picture window at the mountains, considering the problem. Her brother-in-law, Henry Montebello, sat in a wing chair on the opposite side of the fire. He was dressed in a three-piece suit, a hand-knotted bow tie of dark paisley setting off a crisp white shirt. He was examining his nails with an air of patrician boredom. A weak winter sun filtered in.

Kermode considered the problem for another minute. And then she picked up the phone again and dialed Daniel Stafford.

"Hello again, my dear," came the dry, sardonic voice. Kermode did not particularly enjoy talking to her cousin Daniel, but "liking" and "caring" did not figure in the bonds that held the Stafford family together. Those bonds were made of money, and all family relationships were defined by it. As Daniel was not only the head of the Stafford Family Trusts, with assets of two billion dollars, but also one of two managing partners of the family investment company, with assets under management of sixteen billion dollars, she considered him close to her. Very close. It never occurred to her to wonder whether she actually liked the man or not.

"Am I on speakerphone?" Stafford asked.

"Henry is here with me," Kermode replied. She paused. "We have a problem."

"If you're referring to the new fire, thank heaven it didn't occur in The Heights. This is wonderful, in fact—the impact on The Heights is now much diluted. What we need is a third fire even farther afield." A dry chuckle followed.

"That's not amusing. In any case, I'm not calling about that. I'm calling because that girl—Corrie Swanson—made the connection between the Kermodes and the Staffords."

"That's not exactly a state secret."

"Daniel, she got into the Griswell Archive and hit a trove of documents related to the mines, mills, and smelter operations going way back. *All the way back.*"

A silence. And then she heard her cousin swear

genteelly on the other end of the line. "Anything, ah, *more* than that?" His voice was suddenly less flippant.

"No. At least, not yet."

More silence. "How good a researcher is she?"

"She's like a damn terrier, sinks her sharp little teeth in and never lets go. She doesn't seem to have made the connection yet, but if she keeps digging, she will."

Another long silence. "I was under the impression that the germane documents had been removed."

"A mighty effort was made, but the archives are a complete mess. Anything might have slipped through."

"I see. Well now, this *is* a problem."

"Did you dig up any dirt on her and the others, as you promised?"

"I did. This fellow Pendergast has a checkered history, but he's untouchable. Bowdree's something of a war hero, with a raft of citations and medals, which makes her a tricky target. Except that she got a medical discharge from the air force."

"Was she wounded?" Kermode asked. "She looked healthy enough to me."

"She spent a couple of months at the U.S. military hospital in Landstuhl, Germany. Her actual medical records are sealed, and the air force protects those files like the dickens."

"And the girl, Swanson?"

"She's a little hellion. Grew up in a trailer park in a dreadful little town in Kansas. Parents were low, *low* working-class, split up after she was born. Mother's a raging alcoholic, father a ne'er-do-well, once accused of robbing a bank. She herself has a juvenile record as long as your arm. The only reason she got as far as she did is because this Pendergast fellow took her under his wing and financed her schooling. No doubt there's a quid pro quo there. The problem is, as long as Pendergast is around she'll be hard to get at."

"The chief of police tells me he left for London last night."

"That's lucky news. You'd better act fast."

"And do what, exactly?"

"You're perfectly capable, my dear, of taking care of this problem before that FBI agent returns. I might just remind you what is at stake here. So don't play games. Hit hard. And if you decide to hire out, only hire the best. Whatever you do, I don't want to know about it."

"What a coward you are."

"Thank you. I'm quite willing to concede that you're the one in this family with the high testosterone, dear cousin."

Kermode pressed the SPEAKERPHONE button with an angry jab, ending the phone call.

Montebello had remained silent throughout the conversation, his attention seemingly focused on his well-manicured nails. Now, however, he looked up. "Leave this to me," he said. "I know just the person for the job."

# 36

Espelette, the upscale brasserie off the lobby of the Connaught Hotel, was a cream-and-white confection of tall windows and crisp linen tablecloths. The climatic change from Roaring Fork was most welcome. London had so far been blessed with a mild winter, and mellow afternoon sunlight flooded the gently curving space. Special Agent Pendergast, seated at a large table overlooking Mount Street, rose to his feet as Roger Kleefisch entered the restaurant. The figure was, Pendergast noted, a trifle stouter, his face seamed and leathery. Kleefisch had been practically bald even as a student at Oxford, so the shiny pate was no surprise. The man still walked with a brisk step, moving with his body thrust forward, nose cutting the air with the anxious curiosity of a bloodhound on a scent. It was these qualities—as much as the man's credentials as a Baker Street

Irregular—that had given Pendergast confidence in his choice of partner for this particular adventure.

"Pendergast!" Kleefisch said, extending his hand with a broad smile. "You look exactly the same. Well, almost the same."

"My dear Kleefisch," Pendergast replied, shaking the proffered hand. They had both fallen easily into the Oxbridge convention of referring to each other by their last names.

"Look at you: back at Oxford, I'd always assumed you'd been in mourning. But I see that was a misapprehension. Black suits you." Kleefisch sat down. "Can you believe this weather? I don't think Mayfair has ever looked so beautiful."

"Indeed," said Pendergast. "And I noted this morning, with no little satisfaction, that the temperature in Roaring Fork had dropped below zero."

"How dreadful." Kleefisch shivered.

A waiter approached the table, laid out menus before them, and withdrew.

"I'm so glad you were able to catch the morning flight," Kleefisch said, rubbing his hands as he looked over the menu. "The 'chic and shock' afternoon tea here is especially delightful. And they serve the best Kir Royale in London."

"It is good to be back in civilization. Roaring

Fork, for all its money—or perhaps because of it—is a boorish, uncouth town."

"You mentioned something about a fire." The smile faded from Kleefisch's face. "The arsonist you spoke of struck again?"

Pendergast nodded.

"Oh, dear...On a brighter note, I think you'll be pleased with a discovery I've made. I'm hopeful your trip across the pond won't prove entirely in vain."

The waiter returned. Pendergast ordered a glass of Laurent-Perrier champagne and a ginger scone with clotted cream, and Kleefisch a variety of finger sandwiches. The Irregular watched the waiter move away, then reached into his fat lawyer's briefcase, withdrew a slender book, and slid it across the table.

Pendergast picked it up. It was by Ellery Queen, and was titled *Queen's Quorum: A History of the Detective Crime Short Story As Revealed in the 106 Most Important Books Published in This Field Since 1845.*

"*Queen's Quorum,*" Pendergast murmured, gazing over the cover. "I recall you mentioning Ellery Queen in our phone conversation."

"You've heard of him, of course."

"Yes. Them, to be more accurate."

"Precisely. Two cousins, working under a pseudonym. Perhaps the preeminent anthologizers of detective stories. Not to mention being authors in their own right." Kleefisch tapped the volume in Pendergast's hands. "And this book is probably the most famous critical work on crime fiction—a collection, and study, of the greatest works in the genre. That's a first edition, by the way. But here's the odd thing: despite its title, *Queen's Quorum* has 107 entries—not 106. Have a look at *this*." And taking the book back, he opened it, turned to the contents page, and indicated an entry with his finger:

74. Anthony Wynne – *Sinner Go Secretly* – 1927
75. Susan Glaspell – *A Jury of Her Peers* – 1927
76. Dorothy L. Sayers – *Lord Peter Views the Body* – 1928
77. G.D.H. & M. Cole – *Superintendent Wilson's Holiday* – 1928
78. W. Somerset Maugham – *Ashenden* – 1928
78A. Arthur Conan Doyle – *The Adventure of* (?) – 1928 (?)
79. Percival Wilde – *Rogues in Clover* – 1929

"Do you see that?" Kleefisch said with something like triumph in his voice. "*Queen's Quorum* number seventy-eight A. Title uncertain. Date of composition uncertain. Even the existence uncertain: hence the *A*. And no entry in the main text—just

286 OF 586 LINCOLN CHILD

a mention in the contents. But clearly, Queen had—most likely due to his preeminence in the field—heard enough about its rarity, secondhand, to believe it worth inclusion in his book. Or then again, maybe not. Because when the book was later revised in 1967, bringing the list up to one hundred twenty-five books, *seventy-eight A was left out.*"

"And you think this is our missing Holmes story."

Kleefisch nodded.

Their tea arrived. "Uniquely, Conan Doyle has a prior entry in the book," Kleefisch said, taking a bite of a smoked salmon and wasabi cream sandwich. "*The Adventures of Sherlock Holmes. Queen's Quorum* number sixteen."

"Then it would seem that the obvious next step should be to determine just what Ellery Queen knew about this Holmes story, and where he—they—learned it from."

"Unfortunately, no. Believe me, the Irregulars have been down that path countless times. As you might imagine, *Queen's Quorum* seventy-eight A is one of the seminal bugbears of our organization. A special title has been created and is waiting to be conferred on the member who tracks down that story. The two cousins have been dead for decades and left behind no shred of evidence regarding either why seventy-eight A was in the first edition of *Queen's Quorum* or why it was later removed."

Pendergast took a sip of champagne. "This is encouraging."

"Indeed." Kleefisch put the book aside. "Long ago, the Irregulars amassed a large number of letters from Conan Doyle's later life. To date, we have not allowed outside scholars to examine the letters—we wish to mine them for our own scholarly publications in the *Journal* and elsewhere. However, the late-in-life letters have for the most part been ignored, since they deal with that time in Conan Doyle's life when he was heavily involved in spiritualism, writing such nonfiction works as *The Coming of the Fairies* and *The Edge of the Unknown* while Holmes was set aside."

Kleefisch picked up another finger sandwich, this one of teriyaki chicken and grilled aubergine. He took a bite, then another, closing his eyes as he chewed. He wiped his fingers daintily on a linen napkin, and then—with a mischievous twinkle in his eye—he reached into the pocket of his jacket and pulled out two worn, faded letters.

"I am hereby swearing you to secrecy," he told Pendergast. "I have, ah, temporarily borrowed these. You wouldn't want to see me blackballed."

"You have my assurance of silence."

"Very good. In that case, I don't mind telling

you that both of these letters were written by Conan Doyle in 1929—the year before his death. Each
is addressed to a Mr. Robert Creighton, a novelist
and fellow spiritualist that Conan Doyle befriended
in his last years." Kleefisch unfolded one. "This first
letter mentions, in passing: 'I expect any day to receive news of the Aspern Hall business, which has
been pressing on my mind rather severely of late.'"
He refolded the letter, returned it to his pocket,
and turned to the other. "The second letter mentions, also in passing: 'Have learned bad news
about Aspern Hall. I am now in a quandary about
how to proceed—or whether I should proceed at
all. And yet I cannot rest easy until I've seen the
matter through.'"

Kleefisch put the letter away. "Now, all the Irregulars who've read these letters—and there have
not been many—assumed that Conan Doyle was
involved in some sort of real estate speculation.
But I spent all of yesterday morning going over the
rolls of both England and Scotland...and there is
no record of any Aspern Hall on the register. *It does
not exist.*"

"So you're suggesting that Aspern Hall is not a
place—but a story title?"

Kleefisch smiled. "Maybe—just maybe—it's the
title of Conan Doyle's rejected tale: 'The Adventure of Aspern Hall.'"

"Where could the story be?"

"We know where it isn't. It's not in his house. After being bedridden for months with angina pectoris, Conan Doyle died in July 1930 at Windlesham, his home in Crowborough. In the years since, countless Irregulars and other Holmes scholars have traveled down to East Sussex and explored every inch of that house. Partial manuscripts, letters, other documents were found—but no missing Holmes story. That's why I can't help but fear that..." Kleefisch hesitated. "That the story's been destroyed."

Pendergast shook his head. "Recall what Conan Doyle said in that second letter: that he was in a quandary about how to proceed; that he couldn't rest until he'd *seen the matter through*. That doesn't sound like a man who would later destroy the story."

Kleefisch listened, nodding slowly.

"The same cathartic urge that prompted Conan Doyle to write the story in the first place would have prompted him to preserve it. If I had any doubts before, that entry in *Queen's Quorum* has silenced them. That story is out there—somewhere. And it may just contain the information I seek."

"Which is?" Kleefisch asked keenly.

"I can't speak of it yet. But I promise you that if

we find the story—you'll be the one to publish."

"Excellent!" He brought his hands together.

"And so the game—to coin a phrase—is afoot." With that, Pendergast drained his glass of champagne and signaled the waiter for another.

# 37

Stacy was proving to be a big-time sleeper, often not rising until ten or eleven, Corrie thought as she dragged herself out of bed in the dark and eyed with envy the form through the open door, sleeping in the other bedroom. She remembered being like that before figuring out what she wanted to do with her life.

Instead of making coffee in her tiny kitchen, Corrie decided to drive into town and splurge on a Starbucks. She hated the freezing house, and even with Stacy Bowdree in residence she spent as little time there as she could.

She glanced at the outdoor thermometer: two degrees below zero. The temperature just kept dropping. She bundled up in a hat, gloves, and down coat, and made her way out to the driveway where her car was parked. As she dusted it off—a very light snow had fallen the night before—she once again regretted her outburst at Wynn Marple. It had been stupid to burn that bridge. But it was vintage Corrie, with her temper and her long-standing inability to suffer jerks. That behavior might have worked in Medicine Creek, when she was still a rebellious high-school student. But there was no excusing it anymore—not here, and not now. She simply *had* to stop lashing out at people—especially when she knew all too well that it was counterproductive to her own best interests.

She started the car and eased down the steep driveway to Ravens Ravine Road. The sky was gray, and the snow had started falling yet again. The weather report said a lot more was on the way—which in a ski resort like Roaring Fork was greeted as a farmer greets rain, with celebration and chatter. Corrie for her part was sick to death of it. Maybe it really was time to cash in her chips and get out of town.

She drove slowly, as there were often patches of ice on the hairpin road going down the canyon and her rental car, with its crappy tires, had lousy traction.

So what now? She had at most a day or two more of work on the skeletons—crossing the T's forensically, so to speak. Then that would be that. Even though it seemed unlikely, she would see if Ted had any more ideas about where she might find clues to the identity of the killers—tactfully, since of course he didn't know the truth about how the miners had really died. He'd asked her out again, for dinner tomorrow; she made a mental note to talk to him about it then.

Six days before Christmas. Her father had been begging her to come to Pennsylvania and spend it with him. He would even send her the money for airfare. Perhaps it was a sign. Perhaps...

A loud noise, a shuddering *BANG!*, caused her to jam on the brakes and scream involuntarily. The car screeched and slid, but didn't quite go off the road, instead coming to a stop sideways.

"What the *hell?*" Corrie gripped the steering wheel. What had happened? Something had shattered her windshield, turning it into an opaque web of cracks.

And then she saw the small, perfectly round hole at their center.

With another scream she ducked down, scrunching herself below the door frame. All was silent as her mind raced a mile a minute. That was a bullet hole. Someone had tried to shoot her. Kill her.

*Shit, shit, shit...*

She had to get out of there. Taking a deep breath and tensing, she swung herself back up, punched at the sagging window with her gloved hand, ripped a hole big enough to see through, then grabbed the wheel again and jammed on the gas. The Focus skidded around and she managed to get it under control, expecting more shots at any moment. In her panic she accelerated too fast; the car hit a patch of ice and slid again, heading for the guardrail above the ravine. The car ricocheted off it, slid back onto the road with a screech of rubber, and turned around another hundred eighty degrees. Corrie was shaken but—after a brief, panicked moment—realized she was unhurt.

*"Shit!"* she screamed again. The shooter was still out there, might even be coming down the road after her. The car had stalled and the passenger side was all bashed up, but it didn't seem to be a total wreck; she turned the key and the engine came to life. She eased the Focus back around, forcing herself to do a careful three-point turn, and drove down the road. The car still ran, but it made a nasty noise—a fender seemed to be scraping one of the tires.

Slowly, carefully, hands trembling on the steering wheel, she guided the vehicle down the mountain and into town, heading straight for the police department.

After Corrie had filled out an incident report, the sergeant behind the desk promptly showed her into the chief's office. Apparently, she was now a person of importance. She found Chief Morris behind his desk, which was heaped with three-by-five cards, photographs, string, pins, and glue. On the wall behind him was an incomprehensible chart that was no doubt related to the arson killings.

The chief looked like death warmed over. His cheeks hung like slabs of suet on his face, his eyes were sunken coals, his hair was unkempt. At the same time, there was a severe cast to his eye that hadn't been there before. That, at least, was an improvement.

He took the report and gestured for her to sit. A few minutes went by while he read it, then read it again. And then he laid it on the table. "Is there any reason you can think of that someone might be unhappy with you?" he asked.

At this Corrie, shaken as she was, had to laugh. "Yeah. Like just about everyone in The Heights. The mayor. Kermode. Montebello. Not to mention you."

The chief managed a wan smile. "We're going to open an investigation, of course. But...listen, I hope you won't think I'm trying to brush this off if I tell you we've been looking for a poacher up in that area for several weeks now. He's been killing and butchering deer, no doubt selling the meat. One of his wild shots went through the window of a house just last week. So what happened to you might—*might*—have been a stray shot from his poaching activity. This happened early in the morning, which is when the deer—and our poacher—are active. Again, I'm not saying that's what happened. I'm just mentioning it as a possibility...to ease your mind more than anything."

"Thanks," said Corrie.

They rose, and the chief held out his hand. "I'm afraid I'll have to impound your car as evidence—do a ballistics analysis and see if we can recover the round."

"You're welcome to it."

"I'll have one of my officers drive you where you need to go."

"No, thanks, I'm just going around the corner for a Starbucks."

As Corrie sat sipping her coffee, she wondered if it really had been a poacher. It was true she had annoyed a lot of people early on, but that had blown over, especially with the start of the arson killings. Shooting at her car—that would be attempted murder. What kind of threat was she to merit that? Problem was, the chief was so overwhelmed—as was everyone else in the police department—that she had little faith he would be able to conduct an effective investigation. If the shooting was meant to intimidate her, it wasn't going to work. She might be frightened—but there was no way she'd be frightened out of town. If anything, it would make her want to stay longer.

Then again…it might be the poacher. Or it could be some other random crazy. It could even be the serial arsonist, switching M.O.'s. Her thoughts turned to Stacy up in the ravine, probably still asleep. She was eventually going to come into town, and she might also be in danger, get shot at, too.

She pulled out her cell phone and dialed Stacy. A sleepy voice answered. As soon as Corrie started telling her the story, she woke up fast.

"Somebody shot up your car? I'm going looking for the mother."

"Wait. Don't do that. That's crazy. Let the police handle it."

"His tracks will be out there, in the snow. I'll follow the fucker back to whatever spider hole he crawled out of."

"No, *please*." It took Corrie ten minutes to persuade Stacy not to do it. As Corrie was about to hang up, Stacy said: "I hope he shoots at *my* car. I've got a couple of Black Talon rounds just itching to explore his inner psyche."

Next, she called Rent-a-Junker. The agent went on and on about how the chief of police himself had just called, how awful being shot at must've been, was she all right, did she need a doctor…And would an upgrade—a Ford Explorer?—be accept-able, at no extra charge, of course?

Corrie smiled as she hung up. The chief seemed to be acquiring, at long last, a bit of backbone.

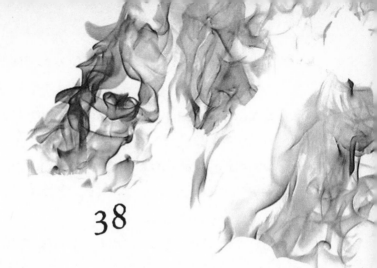

# 38

Roger Kleefisch sprawled in one of the two velvet-lined armchairs in the sitting room of his London town house, feet on the bearskin rug, his entire frame drinking in the welcome warmth from the crackling fire on the grate. Agent Pendergast sat in the other chair, motionless, his eyes gazing into the flames. When Kleefisch had let him in, the FBI agent had glanced around at the room, raising his eyebrows but making no other comment. And yet, somehow, Kleefisch felt that he approved.

He rarely let anyone into his sitting room, and he couldn't help but feel a little like Sherlock Holmes himself, here at home, partner in detection at his side. The thought managed to lift his spirits a little. Although, were he to be honest with himself, he should probably be assuming the role of Watson. After all, Pendergast was the professional detective here.

At last, Pendergast shifted, placed his whisky-and-soda on a side table. "So, Kleefisch. What have you uncovered so far?"

It was the question Kleefisch had been dreading. He swallowed, took a deep breath, and spoke. "Nothing, I'm afraid."

The pale eyes gazed at him intently. "Indeed?"

"I've tried everything over these last twenty-four hours," he replied. "I've looked back through old correspondence, read and re-read Conan Doyle's diary. I've examined every book, every treatise on the man's last years that I could find. I've even tried picking the brains—circumspectly—of several of our most brilliant Investitures. I've found nothing, not even a trace of evidence. And I must say, despite my initial enthusiasm, it doesn't come as a surprise. All this ground had been covered so thoroughly by Irregulars in the past. I was a fool to think there might be something new."

Pendergast did not speak. With the firelight flickering over his gaunt features, his head bowed, an expression of intense thought on his face, surrounded by Victorian trappings, he suddenly looked so much like Holmes himself that Kleefisch was taken aback.

"I'm truly sorry, Pendergast," Kleefisch said, averting his gaze to the bearskin rug. "I was so hopeful." He paused. "I fear you're on a wild goose chase—one that I may have encouraged. I apologize for that."

After a moment, Pendergast stirred. "On the contrary. You've already done a great deal. You confirmed my suspicions about the missing Holmes story. You showed me the evidence in *Queen's Quorum*. You made the connection, in Conan Doyle's letters, to Aspern Hall. Almost despite yourself, you've convinced me not only that 'The Adventure of Aspern Hall' existed—but that it still exists. I must locate it."

"For an Irregular like me, a Holmes scholar, that would be the coup of a lifetime. But again I have to ask—why is it so important to you?"

Pendergast hesitated a moment. "I have certain ideas, conjectures, that this story might confirm—or not."

"Conjectures about what?"

A small smile curled Pendergast's lip. "You—a Holmes scholar—encouraging an investigator to indulge in vulgar speculation? My dear Kleefisch!"

As this Kleefisch colored.

"While I normally despise those who claim a sixth sense," Pendergast said, "in this case I *feel* that the lost story is at the center of all mysteries here—past and present."

"In that case," Kleefisch finally said, "I'm sorry I've come up empty."

"Fear not," Pendergast replied. "I haven't."

Kleefisch raised his eyebrows.

Pendergast went on. "I proceeded on the assumption that the more I could learn about Conan Doyle's final years, the closer I'd come to finding the lost story. I focused my efforts on the circle of spiritualists he belonged to in the years before he died. I learned that this group frequently met at a small cottage named Covington Grange, on the edge of Hampstead Heath. The cottage was owned by a spiritualist by the name of Mary Wilkes. Conan Doyle had a small room at Covington Grange where he would sometimes write essays on spirituality, which he would read to the group of an evening."

"Fascinating," Kleefisch said.

"Allow me to pose this question: is it not likely that, while writing his late texts on spiritualism at Covington Grange, he also wrote his final Sherlock Holmes story, 'The Adventure of Aspern Hall'?"

Kleefisch felt a quickening of excitement. It made sense. And this was an avenue that had never, to his knowledge, been explored by a fellow Irregular.

"Given its incendiary nature, isn't it also possible that the author might not have hidden it somewhere in that little room he used for writing, or somewhere else in the Grange?"

"Might he not indeed!" Kleefisch rose from his chair. "My God. No wonder the manuscript was never found at Windlesham! So what's next, then?"

"What's next? I should have thought that obvious. Covington Grange is next."

# 39

Teacup in hand, Dorothea Pembroke stepped back into her tidy alcove at the Blackpool headquarters of the National Trust for Places of Historic Interest or Natural Beauty. It was past ten forty-five, and Miss Pembroke was almost as serious about her elevenses as she was about her position, about which she was very serious indeed. A cloth napkin, placed daintily upon the desktop; a cup of Harrisons & Crosfield jasmine tea, one lump; and a wheatmeal biscuit dipped twice—not once, not three times—into the cup before being nibbled.

In many ways, Ms. Pembroke felt, she *was* the National Trust. There were more important jobs than hers in the nonprofit association, of course, but nobody could boast a finer pedigree. Her grandfather, Sir Erskine Pembroke, had been master of Chiddingham Place, one of the more impressive stately homes in Cornwall. But his company had failed, and when the family realized they couldn't maintain either the taxes or the upkeep of the mansion, they entered into talks with the National Trust. The building's foundations and general fabric were restored, its gardens expanded, and ultimately Chiddingham Place was opened to visitors, while the family stayed on in modest rooms on the top floor. A few years later, her father had taken a position with the National Trust, as a development manager. As soon as she was out of school, Miss Pembroke had joined the Trust herself, rising over the past thirty-two years to the position of deputy administrator.

All in all, a most satisfactory rise.

As she put away the teacup and was folding the napkin, she became aware that a man was standing in the doorway. She was much too well bred to show surprise, but she paused just a moment before giving the napkin a final fold and placing it away in her desk. He was a rather striking-looking man—tall and pale, with white-blond hair and eyes the color of glacial ice, dressed in a well-cut black suit—but she did not recognize him, and visitors were usually announced.

"Forgive me," he said in an American accent—southern—accompanied by a charming smile. "I don't mean to intrude, Ms. Pembroke.

But the secretary in your outer office was away from her desk, and, well, we *did* have an appointment."

Dorothea Pembroke opened her book and glanced at the current day's page. Yes, indeed: she did have an eleven fifteen appointment with a Mr. Pendergast. She recalled that he had particularly asked to see her, as opposed to an administrator—most unusual. Still, he had not been announced, and she did not hold with such informality. But the man had a winning way about him, and she was prepared to overlook this breach of propriety.

"May I sit down?" he asked, with another smile.

Miss Pembroke nodded toward an empty seat before her desk. "What, may I inquire, do you wish to speak with me about?"

"I wish to visit one of your properties."

"Visit?" she said, allowing the faintest tinge of disapproval to color her voice. "We have volunteers out in front who can assist you with that." Really, it was too much, her being bothered with such a trivial request.

"I do apologize," the man replied. "I don't wish to take up your valuable time. I spoke about the matter with Visitor Services, and they referred me to you."

"I see." That did put another spin on things.

And, really, the man had the most courtly manners. Even his accent spoke of breeding—not one of those harsh, barbarous American drawls. "Before we get started, we have a little regulation here. We require visitor identification, if you please."

The man smiled again. He had beautifully white teeth. He reached into his black suit and removed a leather wallet, which he laid open upon the table, exposing a brilliance of gold on top with a photo ID card below. Miss Pembroke was startled.

"Oh! Goodness! The Federal Bureau of Investigation? Is this...a criminal matter?"

The man gave a most winning smile. "Oh, no, don't be the slightest bit alarmed. This is a personal matter, nothing official. I would have shown you my passport, but it's in the hotel safe."

Miss Pembroke allowed her fluttering heart to subside. She had never been involved in a criminal matter and looked on such a possibility with abhorrence.

"Well, then, Mr. Pendergast, that is reassuring, and I am at your service. Please tell me the property you'd like to visit?"

"A cottage named Covington Grange."

"Covington Grange. Covington Grange." Miss Pembroke was not familiar with the name. But then again, the Trust had hundreds of properties in its care—including many of England's greatest estates—and she could not be expected to remember all of them.

"Half a moment." She turned to her computer, moused through a few menus, and entered the name into the waiting field. Several photos and a long textual entry appeared on the screen. As she read the entry, she realized she did have a faint recollection of the site. No wonder the people at Visitor Services recommended the man speak to an administrator.

She turned back. "Covington Grange," she said again. "Formerly owned by Leticia Wilkes, who died in 1980, leaving it to the government."

The man named Pendergast nodded.

"I'm very sorry to tell you, Mr. Pendergast, that a visit to Covington Grange is out of the question."

At this news, a look of devastation crossed the man's face. He struggled to master himself. "The visit needn't be a long one, Ms. Pembroke."

"I'm sorry, it's quite impossible. According to the file, the cottage has been shut up for decades, closed to the public while the Trust decides what to do with it."

Poor man—he looked so desolated that even Dorothea Pembroke's hard and ever so correct heart began to soften. "It's suffered serious damage from the elements," she said, by way of explanation. "It is unsafe and requires extensive conservation before we could ever allow anyone inside. And at present, our funds—as you might imagine—are limited. There are numerous other properties, more important properties, that also need attention. And, to be frank, it is of marginal historical interest."

Mr. Pendergast looked down, clasping and unclasping his hands. Finally, he spoke. "I thank you for taking the time to explain the situation. It makes perfect sense. It's just—" And here, Mr. Pendergast looked up again, meeting her gaze— "It's just that I am Leticia Wilkes's last remaining descendant."

Miss Pembroke looked at him in surprise.

"She was my grandmother. Of the family line, only I remain. My mother died of cancer last year, and my father was killed in a train accident the year before. My…sister was killed just three weeks ago, in a robbery gone bad. So, you see…" Mr. Pendergast paused a moment to collect himself. "You see, Covington Grange is all I have left. It is where I spent my summers as a boy, before my mother took us to America. It contains all the happy memories I have of my lost family."

"Oh, I see." This was a heartbreaking story indeed.

"I just wanted to see the place one last time, just once, before the contents go to wrack and ruin.

And...in particular, there's an old family photo album I remember paging through as a boy, put up in a cupboard, which I'd like to take—if that's all right with you. I have nothing, *nothing*, of the family. We left everything behind when we went to America."

Miss Pembroke listened to this tragic story, pity welling up in her heart. After a moment she cleared her throat. Pity was one thing, *duty* quite another.

"As I've said, I'm very sorry," she said. "But for all the reasons I've told you, it's simply out of the question. And in any case all the contents belong to the Trust, even the photographs, which might hold historic interest."

"But they're just rotting away! It's been over thirty years and nothing's been done!" Pendergast's voice had taken on a wheedling tone. "Just ten minutes inside? Five? Nobody would have to know besides you and me."

This insinuation—that she might be privy to an underhanded scheme unbeknownst to the Trust—broke the spell. "That is out of the question. I am surprised you would make such an overture."

"And that's your final word?"

Miss Pembroke gave a curt nod.

"I see." The man's air changed. The forlorn expression, the faint tremor in the voice, vanished. He sat back in his chair and regarded her with quite a different expression than before. There was suddenly something in the expression—something Miss Pembroke could not quite put a finger on—that was ever so faintly alarming.

"This is of such importance to me," said the man, "that I will go to unreasonable lengths to achieve it."

"I'm not sure what that means, but my mind is made up," she said with absolute firmness.

"I greatly fear that your recalcitrance leaves me no choice." And, reaching into his pocket, the FBI agent pulled out a quire of papers and held them up.

"What is this?" she demanded.

"I have information here that might prove of interest to you." The man's tone of voice had changed, as well. "I understand your family used to reside at Chiddingham Place?"

"Not that it can be of any interest to you, but they still do."

"Yes. On the fourth floor. The material I think you'll find to be particularly interesting concerns your grandfather." He placed the papers on her desk with a courtly motion. "I have here information—*incontrovertible* information—that during the final months of his business, just before he went bankrupt, he borrowed against the value of the stocks of his own shareholders in a desperate attempt to keep the company alive. To do so, he not only committed serious financial fraud, but he also lied to the bank, claiming the securities as his own." He paused. "His criminal actions left many of his shareholders penniless, among whom were a number of widows and pensioners who, subsequently, died in abject penury. I fear the story makes highly unpleasant reading."

He paused.

"I'm sure, Ms. Pembroke, you would not wish the good name of your grandfather—and of the Pembroke family by extension—to be sullied." The man paused to display his white teeth. "So wouldn't it be in your best interests to give me temporary access to Covington Grange? A small thing. I think it would work out best for everyone—don't you?"

It was that final, cold smile—those small, even, perfect teeth—that did it. Miss Dorothea Pembroke went rigid. Then, slowly, she rose from her chair. Just as slowly, she picked up the papers the man Pendergast had left on her desk. And then, with a disdainful motion, she tossed them at his feet.

"You have the effrontery to come into my office and attempt to blackmail me?" Her voice remained remarkably calm, surprising her. "I have never in my life been subjected to such appalling behavior. You, sir, are nothing more than a confidence man. I wouldn't be surprised if that story you told me was as false as I suspect that badge is."

"True or false, the information I have on your grandfather is rock-solid. Give me what I want or I hand it over to the police. Think of your family."

"My duty is to my office and the truth. No less, no more. If you wish to destroy my family's name, if you wish to drag us through the muck, if you wish to take what little financial security we have—so be it. I shall live with that. What I shall *not* live with is a breach of my responsibility. And so I say to you, Mr. Pendergast—" she extended her arm, pointing a steady finger at the exit, her voice quiet yet unyielding— "leave this building at once, or I shall have you bodily ejected. Good day."

Standing on the front steps of the National Trust for Places of Historic Interest or Natural Beauty, Agent Pendergast glanced around for a moment, the look of exasperation slowly giving away to a very different expression: admiration. True courage sometimes revealed itself in the most unlikely places. Few could have resisted such a thorough assault; Miss Pembroke, who was, after all, just doing her job, was one in a thousand. His thin lips twitched in a smile. Then he tossed the papers into a nearby trash can. And—as he descended the steps, heading for the station and the train back to London—he quoted under his breath: "'To Sherlock Holmes she is always *the* woman. I have seldom heard him mention her under any other name. In his eyes she eclipses and predominates the whole of her sex...'"

# 40

Mockey Jones was smashed again and glad of it. Jones often thought of himself in the third person, and the little voice in his head was telling him that here was Mockey Jones, titubating down East Main Street, feeling no pain (or cold), with five expensive martinis and an eighty-dollar steak in his gut, his loins recently exercised, with a wallet full of cash and credit cards, no job, no work, and no worries.

Mockey Jones was one of the one percenters—actually one of the one-tenth of one-tenth of one percenters—and, while he hadn't actually earned a dime of his money, it didn't matter because money was money and it was better to have it than not have it, and better to have a lot of it than only some. And Mockey Jones had a lot of it.

Mockey Jones was forty-nine and had left three wives and as many children scattered in his wake—he gave a little bow as he proceeded down the street in homage to them—but now he was unattached and totally irresponsible, with nothing to do but ski, eat, drink, screw, and yell at his investment advisors. Mockey Jones was very happy to live in Roaring Fork. It was his kind of town. People didn't mind who you were or what you did as long as you were rich. And not just millionaire rich—that was bullshit. The country was lousy with cheap middle-class millionaires. Such people were despised in Roaring Fork. No—you had to be a billionaire, or at least a centimillionaire, to fit into the right circle of people. Jones was himself in the centi category, but while that was an embarrassment he had gotten used to, the two hundred million he had inherited from his jerk-off father—another bow to the memory—was adequate for his needs.

He stopped, looked around. Christ, he should have pissed back at the restaurant. This damn town had no public restrooms. And where the hell had he left his car? Didn't matter—he wasn't stupid enough to get behind the wheel in his condition. No way would there ever be the headline in the *Roaring Fork Times*: MOCKEY JONES ARRESTED FOR DUI. He would call one of the late-night drunk limo services, of which there were several, kept busy squiring home those like Mockey who had "dined too well." He pulled out his cell phone, but it slipped

out of his gloved hands and landed in a snowbank;
with an extravagant curse he bent down, picked
it up, brushed it off, and hit the appropriate speed
dial. In a moment he had arranged for the ride.
Those martinis back at Brierly's Steak House had
sure tasted good, and he was looking forward to
another when he got home.

Standing at the curb, swaying slightly, waiting
for the limo, Mockey Jones became vaguely aware
of something rapidly intruding on his right field of
vision. Something yellowish—and glowing unnat-
urally. He turned and saw, in the Mountain Lau-
rel neighborhood on the eastern hillside just at
the end of town, not even a quarter mile away,
a large house literally exploding in flames. Even
as he watched, he could feel the heat of it on his
cheek, see the flames leaping ever higher into the
air, the sparks rising like stars into the dark
sky...And—oh, dear God—was that someone in
an upstairs window, silhouetted by fire? Even as he
watched, the window exploded and the body came
tumbling out like a flaming comet, writhing, with
a hideous scream that cut like a knife through the
midnight air, echoing and re-echoing off the mountains as if it would never end, even after the burning body had disappeared below the fir trees. Almost immediately, within seconds it seemed, sirens
were going off; there were police cars and fire

trucks and bystanders in the streets; and—moments later—television vans with dishes on their roofs careening about. Last of all came the choppers, plastered with call signs, sweeping in low over the trees.

And then, with that hideous scream still echoing in his confused and petrified brain, Mockey Jones felt something first warm, then cool, between his legs. A moment later he realized he'd pissed his pants.

# 41

Corrie Swanson eased the rented Explorer into the driveway, and looked up at the cold, dark house. Not a light was on, even though Stacy's car was in the driveway. Where was she? For some reason, Corrie found herself worrying about Stacy, feeling oddly protective toward her, when in fact she had hoped the opposite would happen—that Stacy would make her feel safe.

Stacy had probably gone to bed, even though she seemed to be a late-to-bed, later-to-rise person. Or maybe a date had picked her up in his car and they were still out.

Corrie got out of the car, locked it, and went into the house. The kitchen light had been turned off. That settled it: Stacy was asleep.

A helicopter flew low overhead, then another. During her drive up the canyon, there had been a lot of chopper activity, accompanied by the faint sound of sirens coming from the town. She hoped it wasn't another house burning down.

Her date with Ted hadn't quite ended as she'd hoped. She wasn't sure why, but at the last minute she'd turned down his request to come back with her and warm her cold bed. She'd been tempted, exceedingly tempted, and she could still feel her lips tingling from his long kisses. Jesus, why had she said no?

It had been a wonderful evening. They'd eaten at a fancy restaurant in an old stone building that had been beautifully renovated, cozy and romantic, with candles and low lighting. The food had been excellent. Corrie, feeling famished, had consumed a gigantic porterhouse steak, rare, accompanied by a pint of ale, scalloped potatoes (her favorite), a romaine salad, and finished off with a brownie sundae that was positively obscene. They had talked and talked, especially about that jackass, Marple, and about Kermode. Ted had been fascinated—and shocked—to learn that Kermode was related to the infamous Stafford family. Having grown up in The Heights, he had known Kermode a long time and come to loathe her, but to learn she was part of the heartless family that had exploited and squeezed the town during the mining days really set him off. In turn, he told her an interesting fact: the Stafford family had originally owned the land The Heights had been built on—and their holding company still owned the development rights to the Phase III portion, slated to launch as soon as the new spa and clubhouse opened.

Putting away these thoughts, Corrie stepped out of the kitchen and into the central corridor. Something made her uneasy—there was a foreign feeling she couldn't quite pinpoint, a strange smell. She walked through the house and headed to their rooms to check on Stacy.

Her bed was empty.

"Stacy?"

No answer.

Suddenly she remembered the dog. "Jack?"

There hadn't been any barking, leaping, crazy little mutt to greet her. Now she was starting to freak out. She went down the little hall, calling the dog's name.

Still nothing.

She headed back into the main portion of the house. Maybe he was hiding somewhere, or had gotten lost. "Jack?"

Pausing to listen, she heard a muffled whine and a scratching sound. It came from the grand living room—a room that had been shut up and which she'd been strictly forbidden to enter. She went to the closed set of pocket doors. "Jack?"

Another whine and bark, accompanied by more scratching.

She felt her heart pounding. Something was very, very wrong.

She placed her hand on the doors, found them unlocked, and slowly pulled them apart. Immediately, Jack rushed out from the darkness beyond, crouching and whining and licking her, tail clamped between his legs.

"Who put you in here, Jack?"

She looked about the dark room. It seemed quiet, empty—and then she saw a dark outline of a figure on the sofa.

"Hey!" she cried in surprise.

Jack cowered behind her, whining.

The figure moved a little, very slowly.

"Who are you and what are you doing here?" Corrie demanded. This was stupid. She should get out, now.

"Oh," came a thick voice out of the blackness. "It's you."

"Stacy?"

No answer.

"Good God, are you all right?"

"Fine, no problem," came the slurred voice again.

Corrie turned on the lights. And there was Stacy, slumped on the sofa, a fifth of Jim Beam half empty in front of her. She was still bundled up in her winter clothes—scarf, hat, and all. A small puddle of water lay at her feet, and watery tracks led to the sofa.

"Oh, no. Stacy!"

Stacy waved her arm, before letting it fall to the sofa. "Sorry."

"What have you been doing? Were you outside?"

"Out for a walk. Looking for that mother who shot up your car."

"But I *told* you not to do that. You could have frozen to death out there!" Corrie noticed that Stacy was packing, a .45 holstered to her hip. Jesus, she would have to get that gun away.

"Don't worry about me."

"I do worry about you. I'm *totally* worried about you!"

"Come on, siddown, have a drink. Relax."

Corrie sat but ignored the offer of a drink. "Stacy, what's going on?"

At this Stacy hung her head. "I dunno. Nothing. My life sucks."

Corrie took her hand. No wonder the dog had been freaked out. "I'm sorry. I feel the same way myself sometimes. You want to talk about it?"

"My military career—shot. No family. No friends. Nothing. There's nothing in my life but a box of old bones to haul back to Kentucky. And for what purpose? What a fucked-up idea that was."

"But your military career. You're a captain. All those medals and citations—you can do any-thing..."

"My life's fucked. I was discharged."

"You mean...you didn't resign?"

Stacy shook her head. "Medical discharge."

"Wounded?"

"PTSD."

A silence. "Oh, Jesus. I'm sorry, I really am."

There was a long pause. Then Stacy spoke again. "You have *no* idea. I get these rages—no reason. Screaming like a fucking maniac. Or hy-perventilation: total panic attack. Christ, it's awful. And there's no warning. I feel so *down* sometimes, I can't get out of bed, sleep fourteen hours a day. And then I start doing this shit—drinking. Can't get a job. The medical discharge...they see that on a job application, it's like, oh, we can't hire her, she's fucking mental. They've all got yellow rib-bons on their cars, but when it comes to hiring a vet with posttraumatic stress disorder? Outta here, bitch."

She reached out to take up the bottle. Corrie intercepted her and gently grasped it at the same time. "Don't you think you've had enough?"

Stacy jerked the bottle out of her hand, went

to take a swig, and then, all of a sudden, threw it across the room, shattering it against the far wall. "Fuck, yeah. Enough."

"Let me help you get to bed." She took Stacy's arm. Stacy rose unsteadily to her feet while Corrie supported her. God, she stank of bourbon. Corrie felt so sorry for her. She wondered if she could slip the .45 out of its holster unnoticed, but decided that might not be a good idea, might set Stacy off. Just get her into bed and then deal with the gun.

"They catch the fuck shot your car?" Stacy slurred.

"No. They think it might have been a poacher."

"Poacher, my ass." She stumbled and Corrie helped right her. "Couldn't find the bastard's tracks. Too much fresh snow."

"Let's not worry about that now."

"I *am* worrying!" She clapped her hand to the sidearm and yanked it out, waving it about. "I'm gonna smoke that fucker!"

"You know you shouldn't handle a firearm when you've been drinking," Corrie said quietly and firmly, controlling her disquiet.

"Yeah. Right. Sorry." Stacy ejected the magazine, which she fumbled and dropped to the floor, scattering bullets. "You'd better take it."

She held it out, butt-first, and Corrie took it.

"Careful, there's still one in the chamber. Lemme eject it for you."

"I'll do it." Corrie racked the round out of the chamber, letting it fall to the floor.

"Hey. You know what you're doing, girl!"

"I'd better, since I'm studying law enforcement."

"Fuck, yeah, you're gonna make a good cop someday. You will. I *like* you, Corrie."

"Thanks." She helped Stacy along the hallway toward their rooms. Corrie could hear more choppers overhead, and, through a window, a spotlight from one of them trained on the ground, moving this way and that. Something was happening.

She finally got Stacy tucked under the covers, putting a plastic wastebasket next to the bed in case she puked. Stacy fell asleep instantly.

Corrie went back to the living room and started cleaning up, Jack trailing her. Stacy's drunkenness had freaked out the poor dog. It had freaked her out, as well. As she was straightening up she heard yet another chopper flying overhead. She went to the plate-glass windows and peered into the darkness. She could just see, over the ridge in the direction of town, an intense yellow glow.

# 42

Just when things couldn't possibly get worse, they did, thought Chief Morris as he looked at the two wrecked cars blocking Highway 82 and the furious, desperate traffic jam piling up behind. The medevac chopper was just lifting off, rotor wash blowing snow everywhere, as if there weren't enough of it in the air already, carrying away the two victims to the advanced trauma unit at Grand Junction, where at least one of them, shot through the head, was probably going to die. What really infuriated the chief was that no one had been hurt in the accident; instead, it had generated a road-rage incident in which the driver of a BMW X5 had pulled a gun and shot the two occupants of the Geländewagen that had rear-ended him. He could hear the perp now, handcuffed in the back of his cruiser while waiting for the snowcat to arrive, yelling at the top of his lungs about "self-defense" and "standing my ground." So if the victim died—and most people with a .38 round through the skull did—that would mean nine murders in little more than a week. All in a town that hadn't seen a murder in years.

What a nightmare—with no end in sight.

Four days before Christmas, and the snow was now falling heavily, with a prediction of twenty-four to thirty inches over the next three days, with accompanying high winds toward the tail end of the storm. Highway 82—the only way out of town—was gridlocked because of the accident; the snowplows couldn't operate; the blizzard was quickly getting ahead of them; and in an hour or less the road would have to be closed and all these people sitting furiously in their cars, yelling and honking and screeching like maniacs, would have to be rescued.

McMaster Field had seen nonstop flights out as all the Gulfstreams and other private jets and planes fled the town, but it, too, would soon be closing. And when that happened, Roaring Fork would be bottled up, no way in or out except by snowcat.

He glanced in the rearview mirror, back in the direction of town. The third arson attack had been the worst of all. Not in terms of numbers of deaths, but in terms of the psychological effect it had on

Roaring Fork. The burnt house stood just at the edge of town, on the first rise of the hill: a grand old Victorian belonging to Maurice Girault, the celebrity fund manager and New York socialite, number five on the Forbes list, a dashing older fellow with an ego as big as Mount Everest. The victims were himself and his fresh young wife, who looked as if she couldn't be a day over eighteen—and who had precipitated herself out an upper-story window while afire.

The entire town had seen it—and been traumatized. And this snarl of traffic, this road-rage shooting, this classic example of a FUBAR situation, was the result.

His thoughts returned, unwillingly, to Pendergast's now-prophetic words. *The next house will no doubt be equally conspicuous.* And his conclusion: *To send a message.*

But what message?

He returned his gaze to the mess. His idling squad car, with the shooter in the back, had its lights and sirens going—all for show. Idiots fleeing town had blocked both sides of the highway as well as the breakdown lanes, and high banks of snow on either side prevented cars from turning around—creating total gridlock. Even the chief was locked in; despite all his efforts to prevent cars from coming up behind and blocking him, they had.

At least they had managed to temporarily block the way out of town, preventing any more vehicles from adding to the mess. And, thank God, the RFPD had three snowcats, all of which were on their way. Even as he sat in his car, the wipers ineffectually swiping the snow back and forth, he heard the first one approaching. Immediately he grabbed his radio, directing the officer in the cat to get the perp out of there first. An angry crowd had started to gather around his squad car, yelling at the shooter, cursing and threatening him, offering to string him up on the nearest tree, while the perp, for his part, was yelling back, taunting them. It was amazing, just like the days of the vigilantes. The veneer of civilization was thin indeed.

And on top of everything else, Pendergast had vanished, split, gone off to London at the worst possible moment. Chivers, the fire investigator, was now openly at war with the police department, and his own investigators were demoralized, angry, and disagreeing with each other.

Now the second snowcat had arrived, delivering a CSI team and a couple of detectives to document the accident and crime scene and to interview witnesses. The snow was beginning to fall more heavily, big fat flakes coming down fast. Getting out of his squad car, the chief walked back to the cat and climbed aboard, along with some of his other men who needed to get back to town and work the new arson attack. A number of desperate motorists wanted a ride back to town as well, and the chief allowed a few of them—a couple with a baby—to get on board, causing a ruckus among those left behind.

As the vehicle headed back to town through the deep snow on the side of the highway, the chief turned his thoughts again, for the thousandth time, to the central mystery of the arson attacks: what was the message? Was he completely insane? But if that was the case, how could the crimes be so carefully planned and executed?

As they entered the town, the chief was struck—after the chaos down on the highway—by the eerie emptiness of it. It had practically returned to ghost-town status, the streets hung with Christmas decorations and the shop windows stuffed with glittering, expensive merchandise adding a Twilight Zone element. It felt like the day after Armageddon.

The chief wondered if Roaring Fork would ever be the same.

# 43

Later that afternoon, on her way back from the ski warehouse, Corrie decided to stop in town and warm up with a cup of hot chocolate while catching up on email. It was dark, the snow was falling, and she knew she should be getting home, but she did not want to face that horrible, cold mansion after spending most of the day freezing in the warehouse, which she had begun to refer to in her head as the "Siberian torture chamber."

The snow had lightened a bit as she parked her new Ford Explorer on the street. Since the arson attack of last evening, there was parking everywhere, when before you practically had to give up your firstborn to find a space. Despite the closing of the highway and the airport earlier in the day, an awful lot of people had managed to get out of town. She strolled into Ozymandias, one of the few ordinary, unpretentious cafés in town, with free Wi-Fi and a relaxed wait staff who didn't look down their noses at her.

The place was almost empty, but a friendly waitress came over and added a bit of cheer to Corrie's dreary mood. She ordered a hot chocolate and took out her iPad. There were quite a few emails, including one from her advisor asking for another update on her work, fishing for inside details on what was really going on in Roaring Fork, and complaining that she wasn't keeping him informed. It was true, she had been cagey in her reports; she didn't want him interfering or trying to shut her down, and she figured the less information he had to latch on to, the better. Once her thesis was completed and turned in, it would blow the committee away; her advisor would have no choice but to join in the general accolade; it would win the Rosewell Prize...or, at least, she hoped that's how it would happen. So to satisfy Carbone she composed a vague, ambiguous reply to his email, dressing it up as a report but saying essentially nothing, implying her work was getting off to a slow start and that she had little real information as yet. She hit the SEND button, hoping that would hold him for another few days.

Her hot chocolate arrived and she sipped it as she browsed through the last of the emails. Nothing from Pendergast—not that she'd expected it;

he wasn't, apparently, an emailer. Email complete, she checked the *New York Times*, the *Huff Post*, and a few other sites. The *Times* had a front-page story on the arson attacks, which she read with interest. The story had gone national after the second attack, but this third one elevated it to one of those horrific, sensationalistic stories that captured the attention of the country. Ironic: now it was big news, just as the storm was about to hit and no reporters could get in to cover it.

Chocolate finished, she figured she really had better get home. Pulling her scarf tight, she exited the café and was surprised to see, walking down the far side of the street, just passing under a streetlamp, a couple she recognized as Stacy and Ted. She stared. While they weren't exactly walking hand in hand, they seemed pretty friendly, talking and chatting together. As she watched, they disappeared into a restaurant.

Corrie experienced a sudden sick feeling. Earlier, Stacy had claimed she was going to spend the day back at the Fine house, on account of her hangover. But the hangover didn't seem so bad that she couldn't go to dinner with Ted. Were the two of them cheating on her behind her back? It seemed unthinkable—and yet, suddenly, quite possible. Maybe this was some sort of payback on Ted's part for her refusal to sleep with him the previous night. Was he taking up with Stacy on the rebound?

...And what about Stacy? Maybe she was messed up enough to do something like that. After all, she sure hadn't turned out to be the supremely confident air force captain that Corrie had initially thought, but rather a confused and lonely woman. She hated the idea that all this had changed her feelings toward Stacy, but she couldn't help but think of her now as a different person. She wondered what the PTSD meant and how it might manifest itself. And then there was the odd fact that Stacy had arrived in town several days before revealing herself to anyone. What had she been doing during that time? Had she really just been "getting a feel" for the place?

Corrie got into her car and started the engine. There was still some residual heat so it warmed up fast, which made her grateful. She drove out of town and headed up Ravens Ravine Road, taking the switchbacks very slow, the snow building up on her wipers. It was falling so thickly now that anyone waiting with a gun wouldn't even see her car on the road, let alone have a shot. So much the better. She thought ahead to her crappy meal of beans and rice—all she could afford—and another evening of freezing her ass in the house. The hell with it, she was going to pick the thermostat lock, turn up the heat, and let the owner howl. Ridiculous that a multimillionaire was so concerned about a few extra dollars.

The mansion emerged from the falling snow, dark and gloomy. Stacy's car was gone, as expected. Corrie hoped she wouldn't drink in the restaurant and try to drive home in this weather afterward.

She parked in the driveway. Her car would be plowed in the next morning, as it had been several times before, requiring her to shovel it out. All because the owner wouldn't let her use the garage. No wonder he was locked in a horrible divorce.

As she got out of the car, freezing already, it abruptly occurred to her that Pendergast was right. It was time to get out of Roaring Fork. Her basic research was complete, and it was all too clear she wasn't going to solve the hundred-fifty-year-old serial killings. She'd exhausted all avenues without coming up with so much as a clue. As soon as the highway was opened, she'd split.

Decision made.

She stuck her key into the door of the house and opened it, expecting the usual flurry of barks and yips to greet her—only to be met with silence.

She felt a welling of apprehension. It was like last night all over again. "Jack?" she called out.

No answer. Had Stacy brought the dog into town with her, in case he was lonely? But she hadn't shown much interest in Jack and professed to prefer cats.

"Jack? Here, *Jack!*"

Not even a whimper. Corrie tried once again to control her pounding heart. She flicked on all the lights—screw the electric bill—and called again and again. Making her way down the hall to her wing of the house, she found her bedroom door shut but unlocked. She pushed it open. "Jack?"

The room was dark. There was a form at the foot of the bed, and a very dark area around it. She turned on the lights, and saw Jack's body—minus the head—lying on top of the rug, surrounded by a huge crimson stain.

She didn't scream. She couldn't scream. She simply stared.

And then she saw the head, propped up on the dresser, eyes open and staring, a cascade of congealing blood dripping down the fake wood front. Stuck between the jaws was a piece of paper. In an almost dream-like state, disconnected, as if it was happening to someone else, Corrie managed to pick up a letter opener, pry open the jaws, take out the paper, and read the message.

*Swanson: Get out of town today or you're dead. A bullet through that sweet little head of yours.*

Corrie stared. It was like some sick take on *The Godfather*...And what made it totally ridiculous was that, even if she wanted to get out of town, she couldn't.

The note snapped her out of her fog. Amid a sick wash of fear and disgust, she also felt a groundswell of rage so powerful it frightened her: fury at the crude attempt at intimidation, fury for what had been done to poor, innocent Jack.

Leave? No way. She was staying right here.

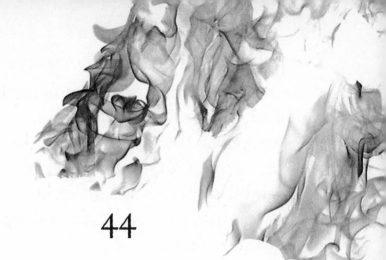

# 44

Hampstead Heath, Roger Kleefisch remarked to himself, had changed sadly since the days when Keats used to traverse it on his way from Clerkenwell to the cottage of Cowden Clarke, there to read his poetry and chat about literature; or since Walter Hartright, drawing teacher, had crossed it late at night, deep in thought, only to encounter the ghostly Woman in White on a distant byroad. These days it was hemmed in on all sides by Greater London, NW3, with bus stops and Underground stations dotted along its borders where once only groves of trees had stood.

Now, however, it was almost midnight; the weather had turned chilly, and the heath was relatively deserted. They had already left Parliament Hill and its marvelous panorama of the City and Canary Wharf behind and were making their way northwest. Hills, ponds, and clumps of woodlands were visible as mere shadows beneath the pale moon.

"I brought a dark lantern along," Kleefisch said, more to keep up his spirits than to be informative. He brandished the device, which he'd kept hidden beneath his heavy ulster. "It seemed appropriate to the occasion, somehow."

Pendergast glanced toward it. "Anachronistic, but potentially useful."

Earlier, from the comfort of his lodgings, planning this little escapade had filled Kleefisch with excitement. When Pendergast had been unable to secure permission to enter Covington Grange, he had declared he would do so anyway, extralegally. Kleefisch had enthusiastically volunteered to help. But now that they were actually executing the plan, he felt more than a little trepidation. It was one thing to write scholarly essays on Professor Moriarty, the "Napoleon of crime," or on Colonel Sebastian Moran, the "second most dangerous man in London." It was quite another thing, he realized, to be actually out on the heath, with breaking and entering on the agenda.

"There's the Hampstead Heath constabulary, you know," he said.

"Indeed," came the response. "What's their complement?"

"Maybe a dozen or so. Some use police dogs."

To this there was no response.

They skirted South Meadow and passed into the heavy woods of the Dueling Ground. To the north, Kleefisch could make out the lights of Highgate.

"Then there's the National Trust groundskeepers to consider," he added. "There's always the chance one of them might be loitering about."

"In that case, I would suggest keeping that lantern well concealed."

They slowed as their objective came into sight over the lip of a small hill. Covington Grange was sited just at the far edge of the Dueling Ground, surrounded on three sides by woods. Stone Bridge and Wood Pond lay to the right. To the north, a green lawn ran away in the direction of sprawling Kenwood House. Beyond, late-night traffic hushed along Hampstead Lane.

Pendergast looked about him, then nodded to Kleefisch and made his way forward, keeping to the edge of the wood.

The Grange itself was an archaeological enigma, as if its builder could not decide which school, or even which era, he wished it to belong to. The low façade was half-timbered and Tudor, but a small addition to one side was a bizarre bit of neo-Romanesque. The long sloping wooden roof, bristling with exposed eaves, presaged the Craftsman era by a good half century. A greenhouse clung to the far side, its glass panels now cracked and covered with vines. The entire structure was enclosed by a hurricane fence, sagging and weathered, which appeared to have been erected as a security measure decades ago and long since forgotten.

Following Pendergast's lead, Kleefisch crept up to the front of the building, where a narrow gate in the fencing was held in place with a padlock. Beside it, a weather-beaten sign read: PROPERTY OF H. M. GOV'T. NO TRESPASSING.

"Shall we, Roger?" Pendergast asked, as calmly as if he were inviting Kleefisch in for cucumber sandwiches at the Ritz.

Kleefisch glanced uneasily around, clutched the dark lantern more closely to him. "But the lock—" he began. Even as he spoke, there was a faint clicking noise and the padlock sprang open in Pendergast's hand.

They stepped quickly past the gate, and Pendergast closed it behind them. Clouds had drifted over the moon; it was now very dark. Kleefisch waited in the forecourt while Pendergast made a quick reconnoiter. He was aware of a variety of sounds: distant laughter; a faint staccato honk from the motorway; and—or so he imagined—the nervous beating of his own heart.

Pendergast returned, then gestured them toward the front door. This, too, yielded almost immediately to the FBI agent's touch. The two passed inside, Pendergast shut the door, and Kleefisch found himself in utter darkness. He was aware of several additional things now: the smell of mildew and sawdust; the pattering of small feet; the low squeaking of disturbed vermin.

A voice came out of the darkness. "To aid us in our search, let us review again what we know. For over a decade, from about 1917 to 1929, Conan Doyle came here frequently, as a guest of Mary Wilkes, to further his study of spiritualism and to read his writings on the subject to like-minded friends. He died in 1930, bound for—in his words—'the greatest and most glorious adventure of all.' Mary Wilkes herself died in 1934. Her daughter, Leticia Wilkes, lived here—joined in the early years by her niece and nephew—until her own death in 1980, at which time she left the property to the government. It has not been lived in—indeed, it has apparently remained untouched—ever since."

Kleefisch could add little to this, so he said nothing.

A small glow of red appeared. Pendergast was holding up a flashlight, a filter fixed to its end. The faint beam swept here and there, revealing a hallway leading back into what was obviously a furnished and, at one time, well-lived-in house, circa 1980. There were piles of books set along the wall in disorganized ranks, and various tiny gnomes and glass figurines sat on a brace of side tables, heavy with dust. The far end of the hallway gave onto a kitchen: to the left and right were openings leading to a parlor and dining room, respectively. The first floor seemed to be covered in shag carpet of a detestable orange color.

Pendergast sniffed the air. "The odor of wood rot and decay is strong. My friend at the National Trust was correct: this house is in a state of dangerous decrepitude and may be structurally unsound. We must proceed with caution."

They moved into the parlor, pausing in the doorway while Pendergast swept his muted light around the room. It was a scene of confusion. An upright piano stood in one corner, sheet music spilling from its music stand and overturned bench onto the floor; several card tables, furry with mold, held abandoned jigsaw puzzles and half-finished games of Monopoly and Chinese checkers. Magazines were spread haphazardly across the chairs and sofas.

"It would appear Leticia Wilkes allowed her charges to run wild," Pendergast said with a disapproving sniff.

The rest of the first floor was the same. Toys,

bric-a-brac, discarded jackets, swimming trunks, and slippers—and everywhere that same odious orange carpet, lit a dreadful crimson by Pendergast's hooded light. No wonder the National Trust had let the place fall to wrack and ruin, Kleefisch thought to himself. He could imagine some poor functionary, poking his head into the place for a minute, taking an exploratory glance around, and then closing the door again, despairing of renovation. He stared at the paisley-papered walls, at the worn and stained furniture, looking for some ghostly evidence of the enchanted cottage in which, once upon a time, Conan Doyle had worked and entertained. He was unable to find any.

The basement yielded nothing more than empty storage rooms, a cold furnace, and dead beetles. Pendergast led the way up the dangerously creaking stairs to the second floor. Six doors led off the central hallway. The first was a linen closet, its contents ravaged by time and moths. The second was a common bathroom. The next three doors opened onto bedrooms. One, in somewhat decent order, had apparently been that of Leticia herself. The others had obviously been used by her niece and nephew, as attested to by the Dion and Frankie Valli posters in the first room and the numerous issues of the *Sun*, all opened to page three, in the other.

That left just the single, closed door at the far end of the hall. Kleefisch's heart sank. Only now did he realize how much he'd allowed himself to hope that, at long last, the missing Holmes story might actually be found. But he'd been a fool to believe he would succeed where so many of his fellows had already failed. And especially in this mess, which would take a week to search properly.

Pendergast grasped the knob, opened the final door—and as quickly as Kleefisch's heart had sunk, it leapt anew.

The room that lay beyond was as different from the rest of the house as day was from night. It was like a time capsule from a period that had vanished well over a hundred years before. The room was a study, sparsely but tastefully furnished. After the dreadful clutter of the rest of the house, it was to Kleefisch like a breath of fresh air. He stared, excitement overcoming his apprehension, as Pendergast moved his light around. There was a writing desk and a comfortable chair. Sporting prints and daguerreotypes hung on the walls in simple frames; nearby stood a bookcase, nearly empty. There was a single diamond-pane window, high up. Ornamental hangings, of austere design but nevertheless tasteful, were placed along the walls.

"I believe we might risk a little more light," Pendergast murmured. "Your lantern, please."

Kleefisch brought the lantern forward, grasped its sliding panel, and slid it open a crack. Immediately, the room leapt into sharper focus. He noticed with admiration the beautiful wood floor, composed of polished parquet, laid out in an old-fashioned design. A small square carpet, of the kind once known as a drugget, lay in the middle of the room. Against a far wall, between the hangings, was a chaise longue that appeared to have also served in the capacity of a daybed.

"Do you think—?" Kleefisch asked, turning to Pendergast, almost afraid to ask the question.

As if in answer, Pendergast pointed to one of the daguerreotypes on the wall beside them.

Kleefisch took a closer look. He realized, with some surprise, that it was not a daguerreotype after all, but a regular photograph, apparently from early in the twentieth century. It showed a young girl amid a pastoral, sylvan scene, chin supported by one hand, gazing out at the camera with a look of bemused seriousness. In the foreground before her, four small creatures with slender limbs and large butterfly wings danced, cavorted, or played tunes on wooden reeds. There was no obvious evidence of trickery or manipulation of the image: the sprites seemed to be an integral part of the photograph.

"The Cottingley Fairies," Kleefisch whispered.

"Indeed," Pendergast replied. "As you well know, Conan Doyle firmly believed in the existence of fairies and in the veracity of these pictures. He even devoted a book to the subject: *The Coming of the Fairies.* Two Yorkshire girls, Elsie Wright and her cousin Frances Griffiths, claimed to see fairies and to have photographed them. These are some of their photographs."

Kleefisch stepped back. He felt his heart accelerate. There could no longer be any doubt: this had been Conan Doyle's study away from home. And the Wilkes family had preserved it with loving care, even while allowing the rest of the house to go to wrack and ruin.

If the missing story was anywhere to be found, it would be in this room.

With sudden energy, Pendergast stepped forward, ignoring the fearful creaking of the floorboards, his flashlight arrowing here and there. He opened the desk and made an exhaustive search of its contents, removing drawers and tapping on the sides and back. Next he moved to the bookshelf, removing the few dusty tomes and looking carefully through each, going so far as to peer down the hinges of each spine. Then he took the pictures from the wall one at a time, looked behind each, and felt gently along the paper backings for anything that might be hidden within the frames.

Next, he approached each of the decorative hangings in turn, feeling carefully along their lengths.

He paused, his silvery eyes roaming the room. Taking a switchblade from one pocket, he stepped over to the chaise longue, made a small, surgical incision where the fabric met the wooden framing, inserted his light into it, and then his fingers, making a painstaking examination of the interior—obviously to no avail. Next, he applied himself to the walls, holding one ear to the plaster while knocking gently with his knuckles. In such a fashion, he circled the room with agonizing thoroughness: once, twice.

As he watched this careful search, done by an expert, Kleefisch felt the familiar sinking feeling return once again.

His eyes fell to the floor—and to the small rug that lay at its center. Something was familiar about it: very familiar. And then, quite abruptly, he realized what it was.

"Pendergast," he said, his voice little better than a croak.

The FBI agent turned to look at him.

Kleefisch pointed at the carpet. "'It was a small, square drugget in the center of the room,'" he quoted. "'Surrounded by a broad expanse of wood-flooring in square blocks, highly polished.'"

"I fear my knowledge of The Canon is not as nuanced as yours. What is that from? 'The Musgrave Ritual'? 'The Resident Patient'?"

Kleefisch shook his head. "'The Second Stain.'"

For a moment, Pendergast returned his gaze. Then, suddenly, his eyes glittered in comprehension. "Could it be so simple?"

"Why not recycle a good thing?"

In a moment, Pendergast was kneeling upon the floor. Pushing away the carpet, he began applying his fingertips as well as the blade of his knife to the floorboards, pushing here, probing gently there. Within a minute, there was the squeak of a long-disused hinge and one of the parquet squares flipped up, exposing a small, dark cavity beneath.

Pendergast gently reached into the hole. Kleefisch looked on, hardly daring to draw breath, as the agent withdrew his hand. When he did, it was clutching a rolled series of foolscap sheets, brittle, dusty, and yellowed with age, tied up with a ribbon. Rising to his feet, Pendergast undid the ribbon—which fell apart in his hands—and unrolled the quire, brushing off the topmost sheet with care.

Both men crowded around as Pendergast held his light up to the words scrawled in longhand across the top of the page:

*The Adventure of Aspern Hall*

Nothing more needed to be said. Quickly and silently, Pendergast closed the little trapdoor and pushed the rug back into place with his foot; then they stepped out of the room and made for the head of the stairs.

Suddenly there was a dreadful crash. A monumental billow of dust rose up to surround Kleefisch, blotting out his lantern and plunging the hallway into darkness. He waved the dust away, coughing and spluttering. As his vision cleared, he saw Pendergast, his head, shoulders, and outstretched arms down at the level of Kleefisch's feet. The floor had given way beneath him and he had saved himself from falling through at just the last minute.

"The manuscript, man!" Pendergast gasped, straining with the effort of holding himself in place. "Take the manuscript!"

Kleefisch knelt and plucked the manuscript carefully from Pendergast's hand. Snugging it into a pocket of his ulster, he grabbed Pendergast's collar and—with a great effort—managed to pull him back up onto the second-floor landing. Pendergast regained his breath, stood up and, with a grimace, dusted himself off. They maneuvered their way around the hole and had begun creeping down the stairs when a slurred voice sounded from outside:

"Oi! Who's that, then?"

The two froze.

"The groundskeeper," Kleefisch whispered.

Pendergast gestured for Kleefisch to shutter his lantern. Then, raising his hooded light to reveal his face, he put a finger to his lips and pointed to the front door.

They moved forward at a snail's pace.

"Who's there!" came the voice again.

Silently, Pendergast drew a large handgun out of his jacket, turned it butt-first.

"What are you doing?" Kleefisch said in alarm as he grasped Pendergast's hand.

"The man's intoxicated," came the whispered reply. "I should be able to, ah, render him harmless with little effort."

"Violence?" Kleefisch said. "Good Lord, not upon one of Her Majesty's own!"

"Do you have a better suggestion?"

"Make a dash for it."

"A dash?"

"You said it yourself—the man's drunk. We'll rush out of the gate and run south into the wood."

Pendergast looked dubious but put away the weapon nevertheless. He led the way across the carpeting to the front door, opened it a crack, and peered out. Hearing nothing further, he motioned Kleefisch to follow him down the narrow walkway to the hurricane fence. Just as he opened the gate, the moon emerged from behind the clouds and a shout of triumph came from a nearby stand of hemlock:

"You, there! Don't go no further!"

Pendergast burst through the gate and took off at high speed, Kleefisch at his heels. There was the shattering blast of a shotgun, but neither paused in their headlong run.

"You've been hit!" Kleefisch gasped as he struggled to keep up. He could see droplets of blackish red liquid fly up from Pendergast's shoulder with every stride the man took.

"A few superficial pellet strikes, I suspect; nothing more. I'll remove them with a tweezers back at the Connaught. What of the manuscript? Is it undamaged?"

"Yes, yes. It's fine!"

Kleefisch had not run like this since his Oxford days. Nevertheless, the thought of the drunken groundskeeper and his weapon brought vigor to his limbs, and he continued to follow Pendergast, past Springett's Wood to the Vale of Health, and from there—*Deo Gratias!*—to East Heath Road, a taxi, and freedom.

## 45

It was still snowing when Corrie awoke in her room at the Hotel Sebastian, after a night full of restless, fragmentary nightmares. She got up and looked out the window. The town lay under a blanket of white and the snowplows were working overtime, rumbling and scraping along the downtown streets, along with front-end loaders and dump trucks removing the piles of snow and trucking them out of town.

She glanced at her watch: eight o'clock.

Last night had been awful. The police had come up immediately, to their credit, with the chief himself leading the way. They took away Jack's corpse and the note, asked questions, collected evidence, and promised to investigate. The problem was, they were clearly overwhelmed by the serial arsonist. The chief looked like he was on the verge of a nervous breakdown, and his men were so sleep-deprived they could have been extras in a zombie flick. There was no way they were going to be able to conduct a thorough investigation on this, any more than they were on the shooting at her car—the target of which she was no longer in any doubt.

And so Corrie had driven back into town and booked a room at the Hotel Sebastian. Including the stint in the jail, she'd been in Roaring Fork for three weeks now, and she'd been burning through her four thousand dollars with depressing speed. Lodgings at the Sebastian would take up a good portion of the money she had left, but she was so frightened by the murder of her dog that there was no way she could spend the night in that mansion—or any night, ever again.

She had called Stacy, telling her what had happened and warning her it was too dangerous to return to the Fine house. Stacy said she would make arrangements to spend the night in town—Corrie had a horrible feeling it might have been at Ted's place—and they'd agreed to meet that morning at nine in the hotel's breakfast room. In one hour. It was a conversation she was not looking forward to.

Adding to her woes, the police had contacted the owner of the mansion, and he had then called Corrie on her cell, waking her up at six, screeching and hollering, saying it was all her fault, that she had broken every house rule, turning up the heat and letting in squatters. As he got more and more worked up, he called her a criminal, speculated that she might be a drug addict, and threatened to sue her and her dyke friend if they went back into the house.

Corrie had let the man vent, and then given the bastard a royal licking of her own, telling him what a despicable human being he was, that she hoped his wife took every penny he had, and concluding with a speculation on the relationship between the failure of his marriage and the inadequate size of his dick. The man had become inarticulate with rage, which gave Corrie a certain satisfaction as she hung up at the start of yet another foulmouthed rant. The satisfaction was short-lived once she considered the problem of where she was going to stay. She couldn't even go back to Basalt, because of the closed road, and one more night in the Hotel Sebastian—or any hotel in town, for that matter—would bankrupt her. What was she going to do?

The one thing she did know was that she was not leaving Roaring Fork. Was she afraid of the bastards who'd shot at her, who'd killed her dog? Of course she was. But nobody was going to drive her out of town. How could she live with herself if she allowed that to happen? And what kind of

law enforcement officer would she be if she backed
down in the face of these threats? No: one way or
another, she was going to stay right here and help
catch the people responsible.

Stacy Bowdree was already seated with a big mug
of coffee in front of her when Corrie entered the
breakfast room. Stacy looked awful, with dark circles under her eyes, her auburn hair unkempt. Corrie took a seat and picked up the menu. Three
dollars for an orange juice, ten for bacon and eggs,
eighteen for eggs Benedict. She put the menu
down: she couldn't even afford a cup of coffee.
When the waitress came over she ordered a glass
of tap water. Stacy, on the other hand, ordered the
Belgian waffles with a double side of bacon and
a fried egg. And then pushed her coffee mug forward. "Go ahead," she said.

With a grunt of thanks, Corrie took a sip, then
a big drink. God, she needed caffeine. She drained
the mug, pushed it back. She didn't quite know
where to start.

Luckily, Stacy started it for her. "We need to
talk, Corrie. About this scumbag threatening your
life."

*Okay. If you want to start there, fine.* "It makes me
sick what they did to Jack."

Stacy laid a hand on hers. "Which is why this

is no joke. The people who did this are bad, *bad* people, and they aren't fooling around. They see you as a huge threat. Do you have any idea why?"

"I can only assume I dug up a hornet's nest somewhere in my research. Came close to something somebody wants to keep hushed up. I wish I knew what."

"Maybe it's the Heights Association and that bitch Kermode," said Stacy. "She looks like she's capable of anything."

"I don't think so. All that's been resolved, the new location of the cemetery has been approved, they're busy tracking down various descendants and getting permission—and most important, you're not insisting any more on having your ancestor reburied in the original Boot Hill."

"Well then, do you think it might be the arsonist?"

"Not the same M.O. at all. The key is for me to figure out what information I have, or almost got, that spooked them so badly. Once I know that, maybe I'll be able to identify them. But I don't really think they're going to kill me—or they would've done it already."

"Corrie, don't be naive. Anyone who would decapitate a dog is totally capable of killing a person. Which is why, from now on, I'm not leaving your side. Not me or..." Stacy patted the place where she carried her .45.

Corrie looked away.

"What's wrong?" Stacy said, looking at her anxiously.

Now Corrie saw no reason to hold back. "I saw you with Ted last night. The least you could do was tell me you were going to date him. Friends don't do that to friends." She sat back.

Stacy sat back herself. An unreadable expression crossed her face. "Date him?"

"Well, yeah."

"*Date* him? Jesus Christ, how the hell could you even think such a thing?" Stacy had raised her voice.

"Well, what was I supposed to think, seeing you two go into that restaurant—"

"You know why we went into that restaurant? Because Ted asked me to dinner to talk about *you*."

Corrie looked at her, astonished. "Me?"

"Yes, you! He's totally smitten with you, says he might be in love with you, and he's worried he's doing something wrong, thinking that he rubbed you the wrong way. He wanted to ask me about it—we spent the whole damn evening talking about you and nothing else. Do you think I enjoyed getting out of bed and driving into town, with a pounding head, to listen to some man spend the night talking about another *woman*?"

"I'm sorry, Stacy. I guess I was jumping to conclusions."

"You're goddamn right!" Suddenly, Stacy was on her feet, her face a mixture of reproach and betrayal. "It's the same old bullshit! Here, I befriend you, protect you, look after your best interests at the expense of my own—and what's my reward? Fucking accusations of two-timing with your boyfriend!"

Stacy's sudden upwelling of anger was scaring Corrie. The few other diners in the room were turning their heads. "Look, Stacy," Corrie said in a calming voice. "I'm really, really sorry. I guess I'm kind of insecure about my relationships with guys, and you being so attractive and all, I just—"

But Stacy didn't let her finish. With a final, blazing glance, she turned on her heel and stalked out of the restaurant—leaving her breakfast unfinished and unpaid for.

# 46

The familiar, silken voice invited her in. Corrie took a deep breath. He'd agreed to see her; that was a good first step. She'd been telling herself that he hadn't contacted her since leaving Roaring Fork only because he was too busy; she'd fervently hoped that was the case. The last thing she wanted to do, she now realized, was allow her relationship with Pendergast to be damaged by her own impetuousness and shortsightedness.

And now he was back just as abruptly as he had left.

That afternoon, the basement was, if possible, even stuffier than the last time Corrie had visited Pendergast's temporary office. He sat behind the old metal desk, which was now swept clear of the chemistry apparatus that had cluttered it before. A thin manila file was the only thing that lay on the scarred surface. It must have been eighty-five degrees in the room, and yet the special agent still had his suit jacket on.

"Corrie. Please take a seat."

Obediently, Corrie sat. "How did you get back into town? I thought the road was closed."

"The chief kindly sent one of his men in a snow-cat to pick me up in Basalt. He was, it seems, rather anxious to have me back. And in any case there is talk of the road being reopened—temporarily, at any rate."

"How was your trip?"

"Fruitful."

Corrie shifted uncomfortably at the small talk and decided to get to the point right away. "Look. I wanted to apologize for the way I acted the other day. It was immature, and I'm embarrassed. The fact is, I'm incredibly grateful for all you've done for me. It's just that...you sort of overshadow everything you get involved in. I don't want my professors at John Jay saying, *Oh, her friend Pendergast did it all for her.*" She paused. "No doubt I'm overreacting, this being my first big research project and all."

Pendergast looked at her a moment. Then he simply nodded his understanding. "And how did things go while I was gone?"

"Pretty well," said Corrie, avoiding his direct gaze. "I'm just finishing up my research."

"Nothing untoward happened, I hope?"

"There was another awful fire, right up on the hill behind town, and a road-rage killing out on Highway 82—but I suppose the chief must've told you all about that."

"I meant untoward, directed at you."

"Oh, no," Corrie lied. "I couldn't make any headway solving the crimes, so I've decided to drop that. I did stumble over a few interesting tidbits in my research, but nothing that shed light on the killings."

"Such as?"

"Well, let's see…I learned that Mrs. Kermode is related to the Stafford family, which owned the old smelter back during the silver boom and is still the force behind the development of The Heights."

A brief pause. "Anything else?"

"Oh, yes, something that might intrigue you—given your interest in Doyle and Wilde."

Pendergast inclined his head, encouraging her to continue.

"While digging through some old files at the Griswell Archive, I came across a funny letter about a codger who buttonholed Wilde after his lecture and, it seems, told him a story that almost made him faint. I would bet you anything it was the man-eating grizzly tale."

Pendergast went very still for a moment. Then

he asked: "Did the letter mention the old fellow's name?"

Corrie thought back. "Only a surname. Swinton."

Another silence, and then Pendergast said: "You must be low on funds."

"No, no, doing fine," she lied again. Damn it, she was going to have to get a temporary job somewhere. And find another place to live. But no way was she going to take any more money from Pendergast after all he'd done for her already. "Really, there's no reason for you to worry about me."

Pendergast didn't respond, and it was hard to read his expression. Did he believe her? Had he heard anything from the chief about the shot through her windshield or the dead dog? Impossible to tell. Neither had been covered in the local paper—everything was still about the serial arsonist.

"You haven't told me anything about your trip," she said, changing the subject.

"I accomplished what I set out to do," he said, his thin fingers tapping the manila folder. "I found a lost Sherlock Holmes story, the last ever written by Conan Doyle and unpublished to this day. It is most interesting. I recommend it to you."

"When I have time," she said, "I'll be glad to read it."

Another pause. Pendergast's long fingers edged the file toward her. "I should read this now, if I were you."

"Thanks, but the fact is I've still got a lot on my plate, finishing things up and all." Why did Pendergast keep pushing this Doyle business? First *The Hound of the Baskervilles*, and now this.

The pale hand reached out, took the edge of the folder, and opened it. "There can be no delay, Corrie."

She looked up and saw his eyes, glittering in that peculiar way she knew so well. She hesitated. And then, with a sigh of acquiescence, she took out the sheaves of paper within and began to read.

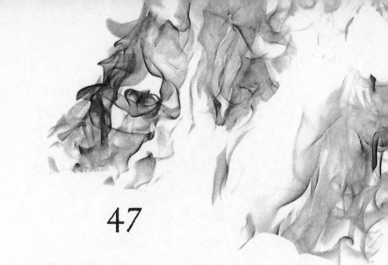

47

## The Adventure of Aspern Hall

Of the many cases of Sherlock Holmes for which I've had the privilege to act as his Boswell, there is one I have always hesitated to put to paper. It is not because the adventure itself presented any singularly grim or *outré* elements—no more so than Holmes's other investigations. Rather, I believe it due to the ominous, indeed baneful air that clung to every aspect of the case; an air that chilled and almost blighted my soul; and that even today has the power to vex my sleep. There are some experiences in life one might wish never to have had; for me, this was one. However, I will now commit the story to print, and leave it to others to judge whether or not my reluctance has merit.

It took place in March of '90, at the beginning of a drear and comfortless spring following hard on the heels of one of the coldest winters in living memory. At the time I was resident in Holmes's Baker Street lodgings. It was a dark evening, made more oppressive by a fog that hung in the narrow streets and turned the gaslights to mere pinpricks of yellow. I was lounging in an armchair before the fire, and Holmes—who had been striding restlessly about the room—had now placed himself before the bow window. He was describing to me a chemical experiment he had undertaken that afternoon: how the application of manganese dioxide as a catalyst accelerated the decomposition of potassium chlorate into potassium chloride and, much more importantly, oxygen.

As he spoke, I silently rejoiced at his enthusiasm. Bad weather had kept us very much shut in for weeks; no "little problems" had arisen to command his attention; and he had begun to exhibit the signs of *ennui* that all too frequently led him to indulge his habit of cocaine hydrochloride.

Just at that moment, I heard a knock at the front door.

"Are you expecting company, Holmes?" I asked.

His only reply was a curt shake of the head. Moving first to the decanter on the sideboard, then to the gasogene beside it, he mixed himself a brandy and soda, then sprawled into an armchair.

"Perhaps Mrs. Hudson is entertaining," I said, reaching for the pipe-rack.

But low voices on the stairs, followed by footfalls in the passage, put the lie to this assumption. A moment later there came a light rap on the door.

"Come in," cried Holmes.

The door opened and Mrs. Hudson appeared. "There's a young lady to see you, sir," she said. "I told her it was late, and that she should make an appointment for tomorrow, but she said it was most urgent."

"By all means, show her in," Holmes replied, rising once again to his feet.

A moment later, a young woman was in our sitting room. She was wearing a long travelling coat of fashionable cut, along with a veiled hat.

"Pray have a seat," Holmes said, ushering her towards the most comfortable chair with his usual courtesy.

The woman thanked him, undid her coat and removed her hat, and sat down. She was possessed of a pleasing figure and a refined carriage, and a decided air of self-possession. The only blemish of which I

was aware was that her features seemed rather severe, but that may have been the result of the anxiety
that was present in her face. As was my custom, I
tried to apply Holmes's methods of observation to
this stranger, but was unable to notice anything of
particular value, aside from the Wellington travelling
boots she wore.

I became aware that Holmes was regarding me with
some amusement. "Other than the fact that our guest
comes from Northumberland," he told me, "that she
is a devoted horsewoman, that she arrived here by hansom cab rather than the Underground—and that she is
engaged to be married—I can deduce little myself."

"I have heard of your famed methods, Mr.
Holmes," said the young woman before I could answer. "And I expected something like this. Allow me,
please, to deduce your deductions."

Holmes gave a slight nod, an expression of surprise
registering on his face.

The woman held up her hand. "First, you noted my
engagement ring but saw no wedding band."

An affirmative incline of the head.

She kept her hand raised. "And you perhaps remarked on the half-moon callus along the outer edge
of my right wrist, precisely where the reins cross when

held by someone of good seat, with riding crop in hand."

"A most handsome callus," said Holmes.

"As for the hansom cab, that should be obvious enough. You saw it pull to the kerb. For my part, I saw you standing in the window."

At this, I had to laugh. "It looks as if you've met your match, Holmes."

"As for Northumberland, I would guess you noted a trace of accent in my speech?"

"Your accent is not precisely of Northumberland," Holmes told her, "but rather contains a suggestion of Tyne and Wear, perhaps of the Sunderland area, with an overlay of Staffordshire."

At this the lady evinced surprise. "My mother's people were from Sunderland, and my father's from Staffordshire. I wasn't aware I had retained a hint of either accent."

"Our modes of speech are bred in the bone, madam. We cannot escape them any more than we can the colour of our eyes."

"In that case, how did you know I came from Northumberland?"

Holmes pointed at the woman's footwear. "Because of your Wellingtons. I would surmise you began your journey in snow. We have not had rain in the last four days; Northumberland is the coldest county in England; and it is the only one presently with snow still on the ground."

"And how would you know there is snow in Northumberland?" I asked Holmes.

Holmes gestured at a nearby copy of *The Times*, a pained expression on his face. "Now, madam, do me the kindness of telling us your name and how we may be of assistance."

"My name is Victoria Selkirk," the woman said. "And my impending marriage is, in large part, why I am here."

"Do go on," Holmes said, relapsing into his seat.

"Please forgive my calling on you without prior notice," Miss Selkirk said. "But the fact is I don't know who else to turn to."

Holmes took a sip of his brandy and waited for the young lady to continue.

"My fiancé's estate, Aspern Hall, is situated a few miles outside Hexham. My mother and I have taken a cottage on the grounds in preparation for the wedding. Over the last few months, the region has been plagued by a ferocious wolf."

"A wolf?" I remarked in surprise.

Miss Selkirk nodded. "To date it has killed two men."

"But wolves are extinct in Britain," I said.

"Not necessarily, Watson," Holmes told me. "Some believe they still exist in the most remote and inaccessible locales." He turned back to Miss Selkirk. "Tell me about these killings."

"They were savage, as would be expected of a wild beast." She hesitated. "And—increasingly—the creature seems to be developing a taste for its victims."

"A man-eating wolf?" I said. "Extraordinary."

"Perhaps," Holmes replied. "Yet it is not beyond the bounds of possibility. Consider the example of the man-eating lions of Tsavo. When other game is scarce—and you will recall the severity of last winter—carnivores will adapt in order to survive." He glanced at Miss Selkirk. "Have there been eyewitnesses?"

"Yes. Two."

"And what did they report having seen?"

"A huge wolf, retreating into the forest."

"What was the distance from which these observations were made?"

"Both were made across a blanket bog...I would say several hundred yards."

Holmes inclined his head. "By day or by night?"

"By night. With a moon."

"And were there any particular distinguishing characteristics of this wolf, besides its great size?"

"Yes. Its head was covered in white fur."

"White fur," Holmes repeated. He put his fingertips together and fell silent for a moment. Then he roused himself and addressed the young woman again. "And how, exactly, can we be of help?"

"My fiancé, Edwin, is the heir to the Aspern estate. The Aspern family is the most prominent in that vicinity. Given the fear that has gripped the countryside, he feels it necessary to take onto himself the task of destroying this beast before it kills yet again. He has been going out into the forest at night, often alone. Even though he is armed, I'm terrified for his safety and fear that some misfortune may befall him."

"I see. Miss Selkirk—" Holmes continued, now a little severely— "I fear that I am unable to assist you. What you need are the services of a game hunter, not a consulting detective."

The anxiety on Miss Selkirk's features deepened. "But I had heard of your successful close with that dreadful business at Baskerville Hall. That is why I came to you."

"That business, my dear woman, was the work of a man, not a beast."

"But..." Miss Selkirk hesitated. Her air of self-possession grew more tenuous. "My fiancé is most determined. He feels it an obligation because of his station in life. And his father, Sir Percival, hasn't seen fit to prevent him. Please, Mr. Holmes. There is no one else who can help me."

Holmes took a sip of his brandy; he sighed, rose, took a turn round the room, then sat down again. "You mentioned the wolf was seen retreating into a forest," he said. "May I assume you are speaking of Kielder Forest?"

Miss Selkirk nodded. "Aspern Hall abuts it."

"Did you know, Watson," Holmes said, turning to me, "that Northumberland's Kielder Forest is the largest remaining wooded area in England?"

"I did not," I replied.

"And that it is famed, in part, for housing the country's last large remaining population of the Eurasian red squirrel?"

Glancing over at Holmes, I saw that his look of cold disinterestedness had been replaced with one both sharp and keen. I of course knew of his great interest in *Sciurus vulgaris*. He was perhaps the world's foremost expert on the creature's behaviour and taxonomy, and had published several monographs on the subject. I also sensed in him an unusual admiration for this woman.

"In a population bed that large, there may well be opportunities to observe variances heretofore undiscovered," Holmes said, more to himself than to us. Then he glanced at our guest. "Do you have rooms in town?" he asked.

"I arranged to stay with relatives in Islington."

"Miss Selkirk," he replied, "I am inclined to take up this investigation—almost in spite of the case rather than because of it." He looked at me, and then—significantly—at the hat stand, upon which hung both my bowler and his cloth cap with its long ear-flaps.

"I'm your man," I replied instantly.

"In that case," Holmes told Miss Selkirk, "we will meet you tomorrow morning at Paddington Station, where—unless I am much mistaken—there is an 8:20 express departing for Northumberland."

And he saw the young woman to the door.

The following morning, as planned, we met Victoria Selkirk at Paddington Station and prepared to set off for Hexham. Holmes, normally a late riser, appeared to have regained his dubiousness concerning the case. He was restless and uncommunicative, and as the train puffed out it was left to me to make conversation with the young Miss Selkirk. To pass the time, I asked her about Aspern Hall and its tenants, both older and younger.

The Hall, she explained, had been rebuilt from the remains of an ancient priory, originally constructed around 1450 and partially razed during Henry VIII's dissolution of the monasteries. Its current owner, Sir Percival Aspern, had been a hatter by trade. In his youth he had patented a revolutionary method for making green felt.

Holmes paused in his perusal of the passing scenery. "Green felt, you say?"

Miss Selkirk nodded. "Beyond its use for gaming tables, the colour was most fashionable in millinery shops during the '50s. Sir Percival made his fortune with it."

Holmes waved a hand, as if swatting away an insect, and returned his attention to the compartment window.

Sir Percival's specialty hats, Miss Selkirk informed me, now held a royal warrant from Queen Victoria and formed the basis for his knighthood. His son Edwin—her fiancé—had gone into the army quite early, having held a commission in the light dragoons. He was now in temporary residence at the Hall, considering whether or not to make the military a lifelong career.

Although Miss Selkirk was the most tactful of her sex, I nevertheless sensed that, whilst Edwin's father wished him to take up the family trade, Edwin himself was of two minds on the subject.

As our journey lengthened, the rich grasses and hedgerows of the Home Counties began giving way to wilder vistas: moorlands, bogs, and skeletal trees, punctuated at intervals by rocky outcroppings and escarpments. At length we arrived at Hexham, an attractive country-town, consisting of a cluster of cottages fashioned of thatch and stone, huddled along a single High Street. A wagonette was waiting for us at the station, a dour-looking servant at the reins. Without a word, he loaded our valises and grips, then returned to his perch and directed his horses away from the station, along a rutted country lane in the direction of the Hall.

The road made its way down a gentle declivity, into an increasingly damp and dreary landscape. The snow—which Holmes had remarked on the day before—could still be seen in patches here and there. The sun, which had at last made its appearance during our train journey, once again slipped behind clouds, bestowing the vista round us with a sense of oppressive gloom.

After we had gone perhaps five miles, Holmes—who had not spoken since we alighted from the train—aroused himself. "What, pray, is that?" he enquired, pointing off in the distance with his walking-stick.

Looking in the indicated direction, I saw what appeared to be a low fen, or marsh, bordered on its fringe by swamp grass. Beyond it, in the late-afternoon mist, I could just make out an unbroken line of black.

"The bog I spoke of earlier," Miss Selkirk replied.

"And beyond it is the verge of Kielder Forest?"

"Yes."

"And am I to infer, from what you mentioned, that the wolf attacks occurred between the one and the other?"

"Yes, that is so."

Holmes nodded, as if satisfying himself on some point, but did not speak further.

The country lane ambled on, making a long, lazy bend in order to avoid the bog, and at length we could make out Aspern Hall in the distance. It was an old manor-house of a most unusual design, with unmatched wings and dependencies set seemingly at cross-angles to each other, and I attributed this architectural eccentricity to the fact that the manse had risen from the ruins of an ancient abbey. As we drew closer, I could make out additional details. The façade was rusticated and much dappled by lichen, and wisps of smoke rose from a profusion of brick chimneys. Sedge and stunted oaks surrounded the main structure as well as the various cottages and outbuildings. Perhaps it was the chill in the spring air, or the proximity of the bog and the dark forest, yet I could not help but form the distinct notion that the house had absorbed into itself the bleakness and foreboding of the very landscape in which it was situated.

The coachman pulled the wagonette up beneath the mansion's porte-cochère. He removed Miss Selkirk's travelling bag, then started for ours, when Holmes stopped him, asking him to wait instead. Following Miss Selkirk, we stepped inside and found ourselves in a long gallery, furnished in rather austere taste. A man, clearly the squire of Aspern Hall himself, was waiting for us in the entrance to what appeared to be a salon. He was gaunt and tall, some fifty-odd years of age, with fair thinning hair and a deep-lined face. He wore a black frock-coat, and held a newspaper in one hand and a dog-whip in the other. Evidently he had heard the wagonette draw up. Putting the newspaper and dog-whip aside, he approached.

"Sir Percival Aspern, I presume?" Holmes said.

"I am, sir; but I fear you have the advantage of me."

Holmes gave a short bow. "I am Sherlock Holmes, and this is my friend and associate, Doctor Watson."

"I see." Sir Percival turned to our female companion. "So this is the reason you went into town, Miss Selkirk?"

Miss Selkirk nodded. "Indeed it is, Sir Percival. If you'll excuse me, I must see to my mother." She departed the gallery rather abruptly, leaving us with the squire.

"I have heard of you, Mr. Holmes," Sir Percival said, "but I fear that you have made a long journey to no purpose. Your methods, brilliant as I understand them to be, will have little application against a beast such as the one that plagues us."

"That remains to be seen," Holmes said shortly.

"Well, come in and have a brandy, won't you?"

And Sir Percival led us into the salon, where a butler poured out our refreshment.

"It would appear," Holmes said once we were seated round the fire, "that you do not share your future daughter-in-law's concern for the safety of your son."

"I do not," Sir Percival replied. "He's lately returned from India, and knows what he's about."

"And yet, by all reports, this beast has already killed two men," I said.

"I have hunted with my son in the past, and can vouch for his skill as both tracker and marksman. The fact is, Mr.—Watson, was it?—Edwin takes his responsibilities as heir to Aspern Hall very seriously. And I might say that his courage and initiative have not gone unnoticed in the district."

"May we speak with him?" Holmes asked.

"Certainly—when he returns. He is out in the forest at present, hunting the beast." He paused. "If I were a younger man, I would be at his side."

This excuse seemed to me to betray a streak of cowardice, and I shot a covert glance at Holmes. However, his attention remained fixed on Sir Percival.

"Still, womanish fears or not, the fair sex must be humoured," the man went on. "I am certainly willing to give you free run of the place, Mr. Holmes, and offer you all the assistance you might need, including lodgings, if you so wish."

The invitation, generous as it was, was offered with a certain ill-grace.

"That won't be necessary," Holmes said. "We passed an inn back in Hexham—The Plough, I believe—which we will make our base of operations."

As he was speaking, Sir Percival spilt brandy on his shirtfront. He set the glass aside with a mild execration.

"I understand, sir, that you are in the hat-making trade," Holmes said.

"In years past, yes. Others look after the business for me now."

"I've always been fascinated by the process of making felt. Purely a scientific curiosity, you understand: chemistry is a hobby of mine."

"I see." Our host dabbed absently at his damp shirtfront.

"The basic problem, as I understand it, is in softening the stiff animal hairs to render them sufficiently pliable for shaping felt."

I glanced again at Holmes, wondering where in the devil this particular tack could be leading.

"I recall reading," Holmes continued, "that the Turks of old solved this problem by the application of camel urine."

"We have come a long way from those primitive methods," Sir Percival replied.

Miss Selkirk entered the salon. She looked in our direction, smiled a trifle wanly, and took a seat. She was evidently much worried about her fiancé, and seemed to be at pains to maintain her self-command.

"No doubt your own process is much more modern," Holmes said. "I should be curious to hear its application."

"I wish I could satisfy you on that score, Mr. Holmes, but it remains a trade secret."

"I see." Holmes shrugged. "Well, it is of no great consequence."

At this point there was a commotion in the hall. A moment later, a young man in full hunting dress appeared in the doorway. This was clearly Sir Percival's son, and—with his determined features, his military bearing, and the heavy rifle slung over one shoulder—he cut a fine figure indeed. Immediately, Miss Selkirk rose and, with a cry of relief, flew to him.

"Oh, Edwin," she said. "Edwin, I beg of you—let this time be the last."

"Vicky," the young man said, gently but firmly, "the beast must be found and destroyed. We cannot allow another outrage to occur."

Sir Percival rose as well and introduced Holmes and myself. My friend, however, interrupted these civilities with some impatience in order to question the new arrival.

"I take it," he said, "that this afternoon's foray was unsuccessful."

"It was," Edwin Aspern replied with a rueful smile.

"And where, may I ask, did you undertake your stalk?"

"In the western woods, beyond the bog."

"But was nothing discovered? Tracks? Scat? Perhaps a den?"

Young Aspern shook his head. "I saw no sign."

"This is a very devious, clever wolf," Sir Percival said. "Even dogs are hopeless to track it."

"A deep business," Holmes murmured. "A deep business indeed."

Holmes declined an invitation to supper, and after a brief survey of the grounds we rode the wagonette back into Hexham, where we took rooms at The Plough. After breakfast the following morning, we made application to the local police force, which, it turned out, comprised a single individual, one Constable Frazier. We found the constable at his desk, employed in jotting industriously into a small notebook. From my earlier adventures with Holmes, I had not formed a particularly high opinion of local constabulary. And at first sight, Constable Frazier—with his dark olive dustcoat and leather leggings—seemed to bear out my suspicions. He had heard of Holmes, however, and as he began to respond to the enquiries of my friend, I realized that we had before us—if not necessarily a personage of superior intellect—at the least a dedicated and competent officer with, it seemed, a laudable doggedness of approach.

The wolf's first victim, he explained, had been an odd, vaguely sinister individual, a shabbily-dressed and wild-haired man of advanced years. He had shown up abruptly in Hexham some weeks before his death, skulking about and frightening women and children with inarticulate ravings. He did not stay at the inn, seemingly being without ready funds, and after a day or two the constable was called in by concerned citizens to learn the nameless man's business. After a search, the constable discovered the man staying in an abandoned wood-cutter's hut within the borders of Kielder

Forest. The man refused to answer the constable's enquiries or to explain himself in any way.

"Inarticulate ravings?" Holmes repeated. "If you could be more precise?"

"He spoke to himself a great deal, gesturing frantically, quite a lot of nonsense, really. Something about all the wrongs that had been done him. Amongst other rot."

"Rot, you say. Such as?"

"Mere fragments. How he had been betrayed. Persecuted. How cold he was. How he would go to law and get a judgement."

"Anything else?" Holmes pressed.

"No," replied the constable. "Oh yes—one other very odd thing. He often mentioned carrots."

"Carrots?"

Constable Frazier nodded.

"Was he hungry? Did he mention any other foods?"

"No. Just carrots."

"And you say he mentioned carrots not once, but many times?"

"The word seemed to come up again and again. But as I said, Mr. Holmes, it was all a jumble. None of it meant anything."

This line of questioning struck me as a useless diversion. To dwell on the ravings of a madman seemed folly, and I could see no connection to his tragic end at the jaws of a wolf. I sensed that Constable Frazier felt as I did, for he took to looking at Holmes with a certain speculative expression.

"Tell me more about the man's appearance," Holmes said. "Everything that you can remember. Pray spare no details."

"He was singularly unkempt, his clothes mere rags, his hair uncombed. His eyes were bloodshot, and his teeth black."

"Black, you say?" Holmes interrupted with sudden eagerness. "You mean, black as in unsound? Decayed?"

"No. It was more a dark, uniform grey that in dim light almost looked black. And he seemed to be in a state of continual intoxication, though where he got the money for liquor I haven't the faintest idea."

"How do you know he was intoxicated?"

"The usual symptoms of dipsomania: slurred speech, shaking hands, unsteady gait."

"Did you come across any liquor bottles in the wood-cutter's hut?"

"No."

"When you spoke with him, did you smell spirits on his breath?"

"No. But I've had to deal with enough drunkards in my time to know the signs, Mr. Holmes. The matter is absolutely beyond question."

"Very well. Pray continue."

The constable took up again the thread of his narrative with evident relief. "Well, opinion in town was strong against him, so strong that I was about to run him off, when that wolf did the job for me. The morning after I questioned him, he was found on the edge of the forest, his body dreadfully torn and mangled, with tooth marks on the arms and legs."

"I see," said Holmes. "And the second victim?"

At this point, I confess I nearly objected to the line of enquiry. Holmes had questioned the constable closely on trivial matters, but was leaving the main points unbroached. Who, for example, had found the body? But I held my tongue, and Constable Frazier continued.

"That took place two weeks later," the constable said. "The victim was a visiting naturalist up from Oxford to study the red fox."

"Found in the same location as the first?"

"Not far away. Somewhat nearer the bog."

"And how do you know both killings were done by the same animal?"

"It was the look of the wounds, sir. If anything, the second attack was even more vicious. This time, the man was...partially eaten."

"How did the town react to this second killing?"

"There was a lot of talk. Talk—and fear. Sir Percival took an interest in the case. And his son, who was recently returned from the Indian campaign, began roaming the woods at night, armed with a rifle, intent on shooting the beast. I opened an investigation of my own."

"After the second killing, you mean."

"Beg pardon, Mr. Holmes, but there didn't seem to be any purpose to one before. You understand: good riddance to that ancient ruffian. But this time, the victim was a respectable citizen—and we clearly had a man-eater on our hands. If the wolf had killed twice, he would kill again...if he could."

"Did you interview the eyewitnesses?"

"Yes."

"And did their stories agree?"

The constable nodded. "After the second killing, they saw the beast skulking back into the forest, a fearsome creature."

"Seen from how far away?"

"At a distance, at night, but with a moon. Close enough to note the fur on its head having gone snow white."

Holmes thought for a moment. "What did the doctor who presided over the inquests have to say?"

"As I said, amongst other things he noted the fact that, whilst both victims were severely mauled, the second had been partially eaten."

"Yet the first merely had a few tentative bite marks." Holmes turned to me. "Do you know, Watson, that that is the usual pattern by which beasts become man-eaters? So it was with the Tsavo lions, as we spoke of previously."

I nodded. "Perhaps this wolf's hunting range is deep within the forest, and it has been driven closer to civilization because of the long, cold winter."

Holmes turned back to the constable. "And have you made any further observations?"

"Lack of observations is more like it, I'm afraid, Mr. Holmes."

"Pray explain."

"Well, it's strange." Constable Frazier's face assumed a look of perplexity. "My family farm is at the edge of the forest, and I've had opportunity to go out looking for traces of the animal half a dozen times, at least. You'd think a beast that large would be easy to track. But I only found a few tracks, just after the second killing. I'm no tracker, but I could swear there was something unusual in that beast's movements."

"Unusual?" Holmes asked. "In what way?"

"In the paucity of sign. It's as if the beast were a ghost, coming and going invisibly. That's why I've been out of an evening, searching for fresh track."

At this, Holmes leaned forwards in his chair. "Permit me to advise you right now, Constable, I want you to put a stop to that immediately. There are to be no more nocturnal ramblings in the forest."

The constable frowned. "But I have certain obligations, Mr. Holmes. Besides, the person in true danger is young Master Aspern. He is out half the night, every night, looking for the creature."

"Listen to me," Holmes said severely. "That is utter nonsense. Aspern is in no danger. But you, Constable, I warn you—look to yourself."

This brusque dismissal, and the notion that Miss Selkirk's fears for her fiancé were unfounded, amazed me. But Holmes said nothing more, and had no further questions—save to again warn the constable to stay out of the woods—and, for the time being at any rate, our interview had ended.

It being Sunday, we were forced to confine our investigations to interviews with various inhabitants of Hexham. Holmes first tracked down the two eyewitnesses, but they had little to add to what Mr. Frazier had already told us: they had both seen a large wolf, remarkably large in fact, loping off in the direction of the bog, the fur on the top of its head a brilliant white in the moonlight. Neither had investigated further, but instead had the good sense to return to their homes with all speed.

We then repaired to The Plough, where Holmes contented himself with asking the customers their opinion of the wolf and the killings. Everyone we spoke to was on edge about the situation. Some, as they lifted their pints, made brave statements about taking on the hunt themselves one day or another. The majority were content to let young Master Aspern track down the beast on his own and expressed much admiration for his courage.

There were only two dissenting opinions. One was a local grocer, who was of the firm belief that the killings were the result of a pack of feral dogs that lived deep within Kielder Forest. The other was the publican himself, who told us that the second victim—the unfortunate Oxford naturalist—had stated point-blank that the beast which committed these outrages was no wolf.

"No wolf?" Holmes said sharply. "And to what erudition, pray tell, do we owe this unequivocal statement?"

"Can't rightly say, sir. The man simply stated that, in his opinion, wolves were extinct in England."

"That's hardly what I would call an empirical argument," I said.

Holmes looked at the publican with a keen expression. "And what particular beast, then, did the good naturalist substitute for the wolf of Kielder Forest?"

"I couldn't tell you that, sir. He didn't offer anything else." And the man went back to polishing his glassware.

Save for the interview with the constable, it proved on the whole to be a day of rather fruitless enquiry. Holmes was uncommunicative over dinner, and he retired early, with a dissatisfied expression on his face.

Early the following morning, however, barely past dawn, I was awakened by a cacophony of voices from beneath my window. Glancing at my watch, I saw it was just past six. I dressed quickly and went downstairs. A cluster of people had gathered in the High Street, and were all talking and gesturing animatedly. Holmes was already there, and when he saw me emerge from the inn he quickly approached.

"We must hurry," he said. "There has been another wolf sighting."

"Where?"

"In just the same spot, between the bog and the edge of the forest. Come, Watson—it is imperative we be the first on the scene. Do you have your Webley's No. 2 on your person?"

I patted my right waistcoat pocket.

"Then let us be off with all speed. That pistol may not bring down a wolf, but at least it will drive him away."

Securing the same wagonette and ill-tempered driver we had employed before, we quickly left Hexham at a canter, Holmes urging the man on in strident tones. As we headed out into the desolate moorlands, my friend explained that he had already spoken to the eyewitness who had caused this fresh disturbance: an elderly woman, an apothecary's wife, who was out walking the road in search of herbs and medicinal flowers. She could add nothing of substance to the other two eyewitnesses, save to corroborate their ob-

servations about the beast's great size and the shock
of white fur atop of its head.

"Do you fear—?" I began.

"I fear the worst."

Reaching the spot, Holmes ordered the driver to
wait and—without wasting a second—jumped from the
wagonette and began making his way through the
sedge- and bramble-covered landscape. The bog lay to
our left; the dark line of Kielder Forest to our right.
The vegetation was damp with a chill morning dew,
and there were still patches of snow on the ground.
Before we had gone a hundred yards, my shoes and
trousers were soaked through. Holmes was far ahead
of me already, bounding on like one possessed. Even
as I watched, he stopped at the top of a small hillock
with a cry of dismay, and abruptly knelt. As I made
my way to him, my pistol at the ready, I was able to
discern what he had discovered. A body lay amidst the
swamp grass, not two hundred yards from the edge of
the forest. A military rifle, apparently a Martini-Henry
Mk IV, lay beside it. All too well I recognized the
dustcoat and leather leggings, now torn and shredded
in a most violent fashion. It was Constable Frazier—or, more precisely, what was left of him, poor
fellow.

"Watson," Holmes said in an imperious tone, "touch nothing. However, I would appreciate, via visual observation only, your medical opinion of this man's condition."

"He's obviously been savaged," I said, examining the lifeless body. "By some large and vicious creature."

"A wolf?"

"That would seem most likely."

Holmes questioned me closely. "Do you see any specific and identifiable marks? Of fangs, perhaps, or claw marks?"

"It's difficult to say. The ferocity of the attack, the ruined condition of the body, render specific observation difficult."

"And are any pieces of the body—missing?"

I took another look. Despite my medical background, I found this a most disagreeable undertaking. I had seen, more than once, native tribesmen of India who had been mauled by tigers, but nothing in my experience came close to the savagery under which Constable Frazier had fallen.

"Yes," I said at length. "Yes, I believe some few."

"Consistent with the description of the second victim? The naturalist?"

"No. No, I'd say this attack was more extensive in that regard."

Holmes nodded slowly. "You see, Watson. It is again as it was with the man-eating lions of Tsavo. With each victim, they grow more brazen—and more partial to their newfound diet."

With this, he removed a magnifying glass from his pocket. "The rifle has not been fired," he announced as he examined the Martini-Henry. "Apparently, the beast snuck up and struck our man from behind."

After a brief inspection of the corpse, he began moving about in an ever-increasing circle, until—with another cry—he bent low, then started slowly forwards, eyes to the ground, in the direction of a distant farmhouse surrounded by two enclosed fields: the residence, I assumed, of the unfortunate constable. At some point, Holmes stopped, turned round, and then—still employing the magnifying glass—returned to the body and moved slowly past it, until he had reached the very edge of the blanket bog.

"Wolf tracks," he said. "Without doubt. They lead from the forest, to a spot near that farmhouse, and thence to the site where the attack took place. No doubt it emerged from the woods, stalked its victim, and killed him on open ground." He applied his glass once more to the swamp grass along the verge of the marsh. "The tracks go directly into the bog, here."

Now Holmes undertook a circuit of the bog: a laborious activity, involving several halts, backtracks, and exceedingly close inspections of various points of interest. I stayed by the body, touching nothing as Holmes had instructed, watching him from a distance. The process took over an hour, by which time I was drenched to the skin and shivering uncontrollably. A small group of curious onlookers were by now standing back along the roadside, and the local doctor and the magistrate had come up—the latter being the titular authority, with the demise of Constable Frazier—just as Holmes completed his investigation. He said not a word of his discoveries, but simply stood there amongst the marsh grass, deep in thought, as the doctor, the magistrate, and myself wrapped up the body and carried it to the wagonette. As the vehicle rolled off in the direction of town, I made my way back out to where Holmes remained standing, quite still, apparently oblivious to his soaked trousers and waterlogged boots.

"Did you remark anything of further interest?" I asked him.

After a moment, he glanced at me. Instead of answering, he pulled a briar pipe from his pocket, lit it, and replied with a question of his own. "Don't you find it rather curious, Watson?"

"The entire affair is mysterious," I replied, "at least insofar as that blasted elusive wolf is concerned."

"I am not referring to the wolf. I am referring to the affectionate relationship between Sir Percival and his son."

This *non sequitur* stopped me in my tracks. "I'm afraid I don't see what you're driving at, Holmes. From my perspective, the relationship seems anything but affectionate—at least, with regard to the father's callous unconcern for his son's life and safety."

Holmes puffed at his pipe. "Yes," he replied enigmatically. "And *that* is the mystery."

Being now rather closer to Aspern Hall than to Hexham, and having had our transportation commandeered by the magistrate, we made our way down the road to the Hall, arriving there in just under an hour. We were met by Sir Percival and his son, who had just finished breakfasting. The news of the latest attack had not yet reached them, and almost immediately the estate was thrown into an uproar. Young Edwin stated his intention of setting out directly to track the beast, but Holmes counselled him against it: in the wake of this latest attack, the animal had no doubt retreated to his lair.

Next, Holmes asked Sir Percival if he could have the use of his brougham; it was his intention to ride into Hexham without delay and catch the first train to London.

Sir Percival expressed astonishment but gave his consent. Whilst the coach was being called for, Holmes glanced in my direction and suggested we take a stroll round the garden.

"I think you should ride into Hexham with me, Watson," he said. "Gather up your things from The Plough and then return here to Aspern Hall for the night."

"What on earth for?" I ejaculated.

"Unless I am much mistaken, I will be returning from London perhaps as soon as tomorrow," he said. "And when I do, I shall bring with me the confirmation I seek as to the riddle of this vicious beast."

"Why, Holmes!"

"But until then, Watson, your life remains at grave risk. You must promise me that you will not leave the Hall until I return—not even for a turn about the grounds."

"I say, Holmes—"

"I insist upon it. In this matter I shall not give way. Do not leave the main house—especially after dark."

Although this request seemed eccentric in the last degree—especially given the fact that Holmes believed the much more aggressive Edwin Aspern to be in no danger—I relented. "I must say, old man, that I don't see how you can be so certain of solving the case," I told him. "The wolf is here in Hexham—not in London. Unless you are planning to return with a brace of heavy-calibre rifles, I confess that in this matter I see nothing."

"Quite the contrary—you see everything," Holmes retorted. "You must be bolder in drawing your inferences, Watson." But just at that moment there was a clatter of horseshoes on the gravel drive and the brougham drew up.

I spent a dreary day at Aspern Hall. A wind came up, followed by rain: light at first, then rather heavier. There was little to do, so I occupied the hours with reading a day-old copy of *The Times*, jotting in my diary, and glancing through the books in Sir Percival's extensive library. I saw nobody but servants until dinner. During that meal, Edwin declared his intent of going out again that very evening in search of the wolf. Miss Selkirk, who was by now naturally even more concerned for her fiancé's well-being, protested violently. There was an ugly scene. Edwin, though not unmoved by Miss Selkirk's objections, remained determined. Sir Percival, for his part, was clearly proud of his son's courage and—when confronted by his daughter-in-law-to-be—defended himself with talk of the family honour and the high approval of the countryside. After Edwin had left, I took it upon myself to stay with Miss Selkirk and try to draw her into conversation. It was a difficult business, given her state of mind, and I was heartily glad when—at around half past eleven—I heard Edwin's footsteps echoing in the Hall. He had again been unsuccessful in the hunt, but at least he was safely returned.

It was very late the following afternoon when Sherlock Holmes reappeared. He had wired ahead to have Sir Percival's brougham meet him at the Hexham station, and he arrived at the Hall in high spirits. Holmes had brought the magistrate and the town doctor with him, and he wasted no time in assembling the family and servants of the Hall.

When all were settled, Holmes announced that he had solved the case. This caused no end of consternation and questioning, and Edwin demanded to know what he meant by "solving" the case when everyone knew the culprit was a wolf. Holmes refused to be sounded further on the matter. Despite the late hour, he explained, he would return to his rooms at The Plough, where he had certain critical notes on the case, in order to put his conclusions into order. He had made use of the carriage ride to confer with the magistrate and the doctor, and had only come out to the Hall in order to bring me back to town with him to assist with the final details. Tomorrow, he declared, he would make his conclusions public.

Towards the end of this little speech, a coachman came in to make known that the rear axle of Sir Percival's carriage had broken and could not be repaired until morning. There was no way that Holmes—or the magistrate or town doctor, for that matter—could return to Hexham until the following day. There was nothing for it; they would all have to spend the night at Aspern Hall.

Holmes was dreadfully put out by this development. During almost the entire dinner that followed he said not a word, a peevish expression on his face, morosely pushing the food on his plate idly about with his fork, one elbow lodged on the damask table-cloth in support of his narrow chin. Just as dessert was served, he announced his intention of walking back to Hexham.

"But that's out of the question," said Sir Percival in astonishment. "It's over ten miles."

"I shan't be taking the road," Holmes replied. "It's far too indirect. I shall make my way from Aspern Hall to Hexham in a direct line, as the crow flies."

"But that will take you right past the blanket bog," Miss Selkirk said. "Where..." She fell silent.

"I will accompany you, then," Edwin Aspern spoke up.

"You shall do nothing of the sort. The wolf's most recent attack occurred just the night before last, and I doubt its hunger will have returned so soon. No; I shall undertake the trip on my own. Watson, once I reach Hexham I will leave word for the wagonette to come for you and the others in the morning."

And so the matter was settled—or so I thought. Shortly after the men had passed into the library for brandy and cigars, however, Holmes took me aside.

"Look here," he told me *sotto voce*. "As soon as you are able to effect it successfully, you will contrive to sneak out of the house, making sure your departure is undetected. That point is most vital, Watson—you *must* leave undetected. Remember that, for the time being, you remain in grave danger."

Despite my surprise, I assured Holmes that I was his man.

"You are to make your way unobserved to the vicinity of that small hillock where we found Constable Frazier. Find a suitable hiding spot from which no approach can reveal your position—not the bog, not the forest, not the road. Be sure to be in position no later than ten o'clock. And there you are to wait for me to pass by."

I nodded my understanding.

"When I come into sight, however, under no circumstances are you to call out, or stand, or in any manner betray your presence."

"Then what am I to do, Holmes?"

"Depend upon it—when it comes time to act, you shall know. Now: do you still have your pistol about you?"

I patted my waistcoat pocket, where my Webley had been in residence ever since we had arrived at the Hall the previous day.

My friend nodded his satisfaction. "Excellent. Keep it close at hand."

"And you, Holmes?"

"I myself will spend some time here before I take my leave, engaging young Aspern in conversation, billiards, or whatever proves necessary to distract him. It is vital that he not indulge his penchant for wolf-hunting, tonight of all nights."

Accordingly, I bided my time, waiting until the gentlemen were engrossed in a game of whist. Then, retiring to my room, I retrieved my cap and travelling coat, and—making sure I was observed by neither family nor servants—I left the house by way of the French doors of the morning room, slipped across the lawn, and from there out onto the Hexham road. The rain had stopped, but the moon remained partially obscured by clouds. Heavy tendrils of mist lay across the bleak landscape.

I followed the muddy lane as it curved leisurely to the northeast, anticipating in its course the expanse of bog that lay ahead. It was a chill night, and here and there patches of snow could still be seen amidst the brambles and swamp grass. After several miles, at the bend where the road reached its northernmost point and angled eastwards towards town, I struck off south through the low undergrowth in the direction of the bog itself. The moon had by now emerged from behind the clouds and I could just make out the bog ahead, shimmering with a kind of ghastly glow. Beyond it, and barely discernible in the darkness, was the black border of Kielder Forest.

Reaching the hillock at last, I glanced round, then set about following Holmes's instructions: to find a blind in which I could remain unseen from all directions. It took some doing, but at last I found a depression on the eastwards side of the hillock, partially surrounded by gorse and furze, which afforded excellent opportunities for concealment, whilst at the same time commanding a view of all approaches. And here I settled down to wait.

Over the next hour I held a most gloomy vigil. My limbs grew stiff from inactivity, and my travelling coat did little to keep out the damp and chill. From time to time, I examined the various approaches; on other occasions, from sheer force of nervous habit, I checked the state of my weapon.

It was past eleven o'clock when I at last heard the sound of footsteps, coming through the marsh grass from the direction of Aspern Hall. Carefully, I peered out from my place of concealment. It was Holmes, unmistakable in his cloth cap and long coat, his thin frame emerging out of the mists with its characteristic loping stride. He was walking along the very edge of the blanket bog, headed in my direction. Slipping the

Webley out of my waistcoat pocket, I steeled myself for whatever action might now transpire.

I waited, motionless, as Holmes continued his approach, hands in his pockets, heading for Hexham with perfect equanimity, as if out for nothing more than an evening's stroll. Suddenly, from the direction of the forest, I saw another form appear. It was large and dark, almost black, and as I watched in horror it bounded directly towards Holmes on all fours. From his position on the far side of the hillock, my friend would not yet be able to catch sight of the creature. I tightened my grip on the Webley: it was beyond any doubt that here was the fearsome wolf itself, and that it was intent on bringing down a fourth victim.

I watched it draw near, ready with my pistol should the beast get too close to Holmes. But then—when the animal was some hundred yards from my friend, and just as it came into view of Holmes himself—the most peculiar thing happened. The beast stopped short, creeping forwards with savage menace.

"Good evening, Sir Percival," Holmes said matter-of-factly.

The beast greeted this sally with a vicious bark. I was by now out of my blind and approaching the wolf from the rear. The wolf abruptly reared up on its hind legs. Drawing closer, whilst trying my best to conceal the sound of my approach, I saw to my astonishment that the creature was, in fact, human: Sir Percival, dressed in what appeared to be a heavy bearskin coat. The soles of his leather boots had been fitted out with makeshift claws, and wolf pads dangled by large buttons from his gloves. One hand appeared holding a pistol; the other a large, claw-like implement with a heavy handle and long, wicked tines. His fair, thinning hair shone a pale, unnatural white in the light of the rising moon. I found myself almost paralysed by this bizarre and wholly unexpected turn of events.

Sir Percival laughed again—a maniacal laugh. "Good evening, Mister Holmes," he said. "You shall make an excellent repast." And with a raving torrent of words that I could not begin to follow or understand, he cocked his pistol and raised it at Holmes.

This extremity broke my paralysis. "Stand down, Sir Percival," I cried from his flank, my own weapon raised. "I have you in my sights."

Caught off guard, Sir Percival wheeled towards me, aiming in my direction. As he did so, I squeezed off a shot, catching him in the arm. With a cry of pain, the man clutched at his shoulder, then fell to his knees. In a moment, Holmes was at his side. He relieved Sir Percival of his weapon and the grotesque device—no doubt, I realized, used to simulate the lacerations of a wolf's claws—then turned to me.

"I should be glad, Watson, if you could head into town as quickly as you can," he said calmly. "Return with a dog-cart and several able-bodied men. I shall remain here with Sir Percival."

The rest of the particulars can be summed up in short order. After Sir Percival was taken up by the authorities and remanded to the police-court, we returned to Aspern Hall. Holmes spoke briefly, in turn, with the magistrate; young Edwin Aspern; and Miss Selkirk, and then insisted on our returning to London by the very next train.

"I must confess, Holmes," I told him as our carriage made its way along the road back towards Hexham just as dawn was breaking, "that whilst I have often been in the dark in past cases, this is your most singular surprise yet. Without doubt it will prove your *coup-de-mâitre*. How on earth did you know that a human, not a wolf, was behind these outrages—and how in particular did you know it was Sir Percival, if in fact you knew that at all?"

"My dear Watson, you do me a disservice," Holmes replied. "Naturally I knew it was Sir Percival."

"Then pray explain yourself."

"Several clues presented themselves, for anyone with the discernment to sift the important from the mere coincident. To begin with, we have the madman—the first victim. When there is more than one killing to reckon with, Watson, you must always pay particular attention to the *first*. Frequently the motive, and therefore the entire case, rests upon that particular crime."

"Yes, but the first victim was nothing but a mindless vagrant."

"He might have been so in recent years, but he was not always thus. Recall, Watson, that in his ravings, a single word stood out again and again: *carrot*."

I recalled this, and Holmes's fascination with it, all too well. How it could have any significance seemed to defy credibility. "Go on," I said.

"Carroting, you must understand, was a process by which animal fur is bathed in a solution of mercury nitrate, in order to render the hairs more supple, thus producing a superior *felt*." At this last word, he threw a significant glance in my direction.

"Felt," I repeated. "You mean, for the making of hats?"

"Precisely. The solution is of an orange colour,

hence the term *carroting*. However, this process had rather severe side effects on those who worked with it, which is why its use today is much reduced. When mercury vapours are inhaled over a long enough period of time—particularly, for our purposes, in the close quarters of a hat-making operation—toxic and irreversible effects almost inevitably follow. One develops tremors of the hands; blackened teeth; slurred speech. In severe cases, dementia or outright insanity can occur. Hence the term *mad as a hatter.*" Holmes waved a hand. "I know all this, of course, due to my long-abiding interest in chemistry."

"But what does all this have to do with Sir Percival?" I asked.

"Let us proceed in a linear fashion, if you please. You will recall that Constable Frazier believed our vagabond to be a drunkard, citing as evidence the man's slurred speech and impaired movement. And yet he detected no smell of alcohol on the man's breath. I immediately assumed that the real cause of the man's affliction was not drunkenness, but rather the effects of mercury poisoning. His mention of 'carrots' explained how this poisoning had come about: as an occupational hazard of making felt, from working as a hatter. I naturally realized that there could be no coincidence between Sir Percival's former occupation and the sudden arrival of this curious fellow upon the scene. No: this man had clearly once been in business with Sir Percival. Recall, if you will, two things. First, how this man had raved about betrayal, about getting a judgement from a court of law. Second, how Sir Percival made his fortune by a unique felt-making process—a process, you may recollect, he refused to discuss with me when I broached the topic at Aspern Hall."

The carriage continued its jostling way towards Hexham, and Holmes went on. "Remarking on these facts, I began to consider the possibility that this man, now sadly reduced, had once been Sir Percival's business partner—and, perhaps, the true author of that revolutionary felt-making process. Now, years later, he had returned to square accounts with his former partner, to expose and ruin him. In other words, this whole matter began as a mere business dispute; one that Sir Percival solved in a traditional manner—by murder. It seemed to me highly likely that when this fellow appeared in Hexham, Sir Percival had promised him amends, and had agreed to meet with him in a lonely spot at the edge of the bog. There, Sir Percival murdered his former partner, and—to keep any suspicion from ever redounding upon him—tore the body cruelly, even going so far as to leave some tentative bite marks, so as to make it appear the work of a large and savage beast, most likely a wolf."

"And in so doing, he seemed to have been entirely successful," I said. "Why, then, kill again?"

"The second person killed, you will recall, was a naturalist from Oxford. He was heard in the local inn debunking the rumours of a wolf, declaring that no wolves still survived in England. By killing this man, Sir Percival accomplished several goals. He silenced the man's insistence on the extinction of the English wolf—the very last thing Sir Percival would want was attention returning to the initial killing. Also, by this time he had of course heard the rumours in Hexham about a wolf being the culprit in his partner's murder. In case he was spotted, he had now had the opportunity to fit out a large bear coat, complete with wolf-paw gloves and boots that he—with his hatter's skill—could make entirely convincing. He used this disguise to run to and from the second murder scene on all fours. I believe, Watson, he was actually *hoping* for a witness this time, in order to inflame the rumours of a man-eating wolf. In this, at least, he was fortunate."

"Yes, I can see a cruel logic in such a course of action," I said. "But what, then, of the constable?"

"Constable Frazier was, if not the world's most accomplished investigator, a man of great doggedness and persistence. No doubt Sir Percival perceived him to be a threat. Recall how the constable hinted at certain suspicions about the wolf's behaviour. Those suspicions, I would hazard, had to do with why the wolf tracks entered the bog *but never came out again*. The constable would have remarked on this after the second murder, if not before. I myself found this curious phenomenon to be the case after the constable's own death, when I made a circuit of the bog. Wolf tracks entered the region from the east; only human tracks emerged from the west. Sir Percival, you see, would have entered the bog on all fours, as a wolf; he would have used the concealing vegetation to come out from the bog as merely himself, should anyone encounter him. The constable must have mentioned his suspicions to Sir Percival—remember, Watson, his remarking he'd been to the Hall just the day before, to warn young Aspern to cease his hunting of the wolf—and in so doing, signed his own death warrant."

Hearing these revelations, presented in Holmes's

complacent tone, was nothing less than astounding. I could only shake my head.

"What clinched the case for me was Sir Percival's cavalier, indeed encouraging, attitude towards his son's hunting of the beast. He seemed to evince total unconcern for young Edwin's well-being. Why? At this point in the game, the answer was obvious to me: he knew his son was in no danger from the wolf, *because the wolf was himself.* Then, of course, there was the manner in which Sir Percival spilt his brandy."

"What of it?"

"He was making great pains to hide his trembling hands. That incipient palsy demonstrated to my satisfaction that he himself was well on the road to madness brought on by mercury poisoning, and that he would soon be reduced to the same pitiable state as his former partner."

By this time we had arrived at the Hexham station; we descended with our valises and mounted the platform, just in time for the 8:20 to Paddington.

"Armed with these suspicions," Holmes went on, "I went to London. It did not take me long to uncover the facts I was looking for: that, many years before, Sir Percival did indeed have a business partner. At the time, he accused Sir Percival of stealing a valuable patent, claiming it as his own. He was adjudged a lunatic, however, and was committed to an asylum—through the offices of Sir Percival himself. This poor unfortunate was released just days before the initial appearance of the raving madman in Kielder Forest.

"I returned from London, secure in the knowledge that, not only was there no man-eating wolf, but Sir Percival himself was the murderer of three men. The only question remaining was how to catch him up. I couldn't very well reveal the truth—that there was no wolf. No; I had to find a reason to manoeuvre Sir Percival into making me his next target, and to arrange it, so to speak, on home ground. Hence my dramatic announcement of having solved the case—and my nocturnal shortcut across the open countryside, between the bog and the forest edge, site of the previous killings. Unless I had made a mistake in my calculations, I felt certain Sir Percival would take the opportunity to make me his fourth victim."

"But you undertook that walk only because Sir Percival's carriage broke an axle," I said. "How could you have anticipated such an eventuality?"

"I did not anticipate it, Watson. I precipitated it."

"You mean—?" I stopped.

"Yes. I fear I committed an act of sabotage against Sir Percival's brougham. Perhaps I should send down a cheque for its repair."

A faint whistle echoed out across the morning sky. A moment later, the express came into view. Within minutes we were boarding. "I confess myself astonished," I said as we entered our compartment. "You are like the artist that outdoes his best work. There remains only one particular I do not understand."

"In that case, my dear Watson, pray unburden yourself."

"It is one thing, Holmes, to make a killing look like the work of an animal; quite another to actually devour portions of a body. Why did Sir Percival continue to do so—and, in fact, to an increasing extent?"

"The answer is quite simple," Holmes replied. "It would seem Sir Percival, in his growing madness, had begun acquiring a taste for his, ah, *prey*."

The subject of the Hexham Wolf did not come up again until perhaps half a year later, when I came across a notice in *The Times* stating that the new owner of Aspern Hall and his fiancée were to be married in St. Paul's the following month. It appeared that—in local opinion, at least—the atrocities of the father were more than compensated for by the son's military success, and by the courage he had displayed in his hunt for the would-be wolf. As for myself, I would have wished to have spent more time, had the circumstances been more pleasant, in the company of one of the handsomest young ladies of my acquaintance: Miss Victoria Selkirk.

On the lone occasion Holmes himself later referred to the case, he merely expressed a passing regret that the excursion had not furnished him with an opportunity to further his study of *Sciurus vulgaris*—the Eurasian red squirrel.

# 48

Corrie finished the story and looked up to find Pendergast's silvery eyes upon her. She realized she had been holding her breath, and exhaled. "Holy crap," she said.

"One could say that."

"This story...I can hardly get my head around it." A thought struck her. "But how did you know it was key?"

"I didn't. Not at first. But consider: Doyle was a medical man. Before starting his private practice, he had been the doctor on a whaling ship and ship's surgeon on a voyage along the West African coast. Those are among the most difficult postings a medical man could experience. He had surely seen a great deal of unpleasantness, to put it mildly, on these voyages. A story that would send him fleeing from the dining table had to be far more re-pugnant than a mere man-eating grizzly."

"But the lost story? What led you to that in particular?"

"Doyle was so unsettled by the story he heard from Wilde that he did what many authors do to exorcise their demons: he incorporated it into his fiction. Almost immediately after the meeting in the Langham Hotel he wrote *The Hound of the Baskervilles*, which of course has a few parallels to Wilde's actual story. But *Hound*, while a marvelous story in its own right, was a mere ghost of the truth. Not much exorcism to be had there. One can surmise that Wilde's story continued to work on his mind for a long time. I began to wonder whether, in later years, Doyle finally felt compelled to write something closer to the bone, with much more of the truth in it, as a kind of catharsis. I made some inquiries. An English acquaintance of mine, an expert in Sherlockiana, confirmed to me a rumor of a missing Holmes story, which we surmised was titled 'The Adventure of Aspern Hall.' I put two and two together—and went to London."

"But how did you know it was *that* story?"

"By all accounts the Aspern Hall story was soundly rejected. Never published. Consider that: a fresh Sherlock Holmes story, from the master himself, the first one in ages—and it is rejected? One might surmise it contained something unusually objectionable to Victorian taste."

Corrie wrinkled her nose in chagrin. "You make it sound so simple."

"Most detection is simple. If I teach you nothing else, I hope you'll learn that."

She colored. "And I was so dismissive of this lead for so long. What an idiot I am. I'm sorry about that, really."

Pendergast waved a hand. "Let us focus on the matter before us. The famed *Hound of the Baskervilles* merely touched on the grizzly story. But this tale: this *incorporates* far more of what Doyle heard from Wilde, who had in turn heard it from this fellow you found, Swinton. A commendable discovery, that."

"An accident."

"An accident is only a puzzle piece that hasn't yet found its place in the picture. A good detective collects all 'accidents,' no matter how insignificant."

"But we need to figure out what connection the story has to the real killings," said Corrie. "Okay: you have a bunch of cannibalistic murderers who are behaving somewhat like this guy Percival. They're killing and eating miners up on the mountain, trying to disguise what they're doing as grizzly killings."

"No. If I may interrupt: the identification of the killings with a man-eating grizzly was originally made by chance, as you've probably learned for yourself. A grizzly bear passed by and masticated the remains of one of the early victims, and that clinched matters to the town's satisfaction. Later random sightings of grizzlies seem to confirm the connection. It is all about how human beings construct a narrative out of random events, baseless assumptions, and simple-minded prejudices. In my opinion, the gang of killers you mention *did not* set out to disguise their work as the result of a man-eating grizzly."

"All right, so the gang wasn't trying to disguise their killings. But still, the story doesn't explain *why* they're killing. What's the motivation? Sir Percival has a motivation: he kills his partner to cover up the fact that he cheated him and stuck him in an insane asylum. I can't see how that has anything to do with what prompted the killers in the Colorado mountains."

"It doesn't." Pendergast looked at Corrie a long time. "Not directly, at any rate. You're not focusing on the salient points. One should ask, first: why did Sir Percival *eat* portions of his victims?"

Corrie thought back to the story. "At first, to make it look like a wolf. And then later, because he was going crazy and thought he was developing a taste for it."

"Ah! And *why* was he going crazy?"

"Because he was suffering from mercury poisoning as a result of making felt." Corrie hesitated. "But what does hat making have to do with silver mining? I can't see it."

"On the contrary, Corrie—you see everything. *You must be bolder in drawing your inferences.*" Pendergast's eyes gleamed as he quoted the line.

Corrie frowned. What possible connection could there be? She wished Pendergast would just tell her, rather than pulling the Socratic method on her. "Can we dispense with the teachable moment? If it's obvious, why can't you just tell me?"

"This is not an intellectual game we are playing. This is deadly serious—particularly for you. I am surprised that you have not already been threatened."

He paused. In the silence, Corrie thought of the shot at her car, the dead dog, the note. She should tell him—clearly he would find out sooner or later. What if she confided in Pendergast? But that would only result in him putting more pressure on her to leave Roaring Fork.

"My first instinct," Pendergast went on, almost as if reading her thoughts, "was to spirit you away from town immediately, even if it meant commandeering one of the chief's snowcats. But I know you well enough to realize that would be futile."

"Thank you."

"The next best thing, therefore, is to get you thinking properly about this case—what it means, why you are in extreme danger, and from where. This is not, as you put it, a *teachable moment*."

The seriousness of his tone hit her hard. She swallowed. "Okay. Sorry. You've got my attention."

"Let's return to the question you just asked, which I will rephrase in more precise terms: what does nineteenth-century English hat making have in common with nineteenth-century silver refining?"

It came to her in a flash. It *was* obvious. "Both processes use mercury."

"*Precisely.*"

All of a sudden, everything started to fall into place. "According to the story, mercury nitrate was used to soften fur for the making of felt for hats. Carroting, they called it."

"Go on."

"And mercury was also used in smelting, to separate silver and gold from crushed ore."

"Excellent."

Now Corrie's mind was racing. "So the gang of killers was a group of miners who must've worked in the smelter. And gone crazy, in turn, from mercury poisoning."

Pendergast nodded.

"The smelter fired the crazy workers and hired

fresh ones. Perhaps a few of those who were fired banded together. Without work, totally nuts, unemployable, they took to the hills, angry and vengeful, where they went progressively crazier. And, of course...they needed to eat."

Another slow nod from Pendergast.

"So they preyed on isolated miners up at their claims, killing and eating them. And like the man-eating lions of Tsavo—and Sir Percival—they began to develop a taste for it."

This was followed by a long silence. *What else?* Corrie asked herself. Where did the present danger come from? "All this happened a hundred and fifty years ago," she finally said. "I don't see how this affects us now. Why am I in danger?"

"You have not put the last, crucial piece into place. Think of the 'accidental' information you told me you'd recently uncovered."

"Give me a hint."

"Very well, then: who owned the smelter?"

"The Stafford family."

"Go on."

"But the history of labor abuses and the use of mercury at the smelter are already well known. It's a matter of historical record. It would be stupid for them to take steps to cover that up now."

"Corrie." Pendergast shook his head. "Where *was* the smelter?"

"Um, well, it was somewhere in the area where The Heights is now. I mean, that's how the family came to own all that land to turn into the development."

"And...?"

"And what? The smelter's long gone. It was shut in the 1890s and they tore down the ruins decades ago. There's nothing left of...*Oh, my God.*" She clasped one hand to her mouth.

Pendergast remained silent, waiting.

Corrie stared at him. Now she understood. "Mercury. That's what's left of it. *The ground beneath the development is contaminated with mercury.*"

Pendergast folded his hands and sat back in his chair. "Now you are starting to think like a true detective. And I hope you will live long enough to become that detective. I fear for you: you have always been, and still remain, far too rash. But despite that shortcoming, even you must see what is at stake here—and the grave danger you have placed yourself in by continuing this most unwise investigation. I would not have revealed any of this to you—not the lost Holmes story, not the Stafford family connection, not the poisonous groundwater—were it not, given your, ah, impetuous nature, necessary to convince you to leave this ugly place, as directly as I can make arrangements."

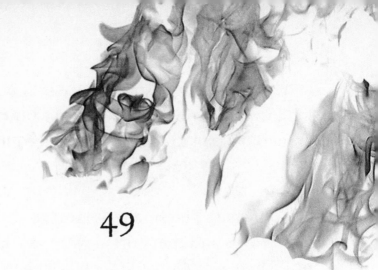

# 49

A. X. L. Pendergast surveyed the town of Leadville with tightly pursed lips. A sign announced its altitude, 10,150 feet, and stated it was the HIGHEST INCORPORATED TOWN IN THE UNITED STATES. It stood in stark contrast with Roaring Fork, across the Continental Divide. Its downtown strip was a single street bordered by Victorian buildings in various states of shabbiness and disrepair, with frozen heaps of snow along the verges. Beyond, forests of fir trees swept up to immense mountain peaks in almost all directions. The excessive Christmas decorations draped over every cornice, lamppost, streetlight, and parapet lent a sort of desperate air to the forlornness of the town, especially two days before Christmas. And yet despite the early-morning hour and the bitter cold, Pendergast was aware of a certain relief simply to be away from the oppressive wealth, entitlement, and smugness that hung like a miasma over Roaring Fork. Leadville, while impoverished, was a real place with real people—although it was nevertheless inconceivable why anyone would want to live in this white Gehenna, this algid Siberian wasteland, this desert of frost buried in the mountains, far from the delights of civilization.

He had had the devil of a time tracking down any progeny of the aged Swinton, first name unknown, who had buttonholed Oscar Wilde after the Roaring Fork lecture and told him the fateful story. With the help of Mime, he had finally identified one remaining descendant: a certain Kyle Swinton, born in Leadville thirty-one years previously. He was an only child whose parents had been killed in a car accident around the time he dropped out of Leadville High. After that, his digital trail had vanished. Even Mime, Pendergast's shadowy and reclusive computer genius and information gatherer, had been unable to track the man beyond establishing the crucial fact that there was no record of his death. Kyle Swinton, it seemed, was still alive, somewhere within the borders of the United States; that was all Pendergast knew.

As soon as the snow had stopped in Roaring Fork—or rather paused, as the main event was still to come—the road had been cleared and Pendergast had made his way to Leadville to see if he could pick up a trace of the man. Weighed down by a sweater vest, heavy black suit, down vest, overcoat, two scarves, thick gloves and boots, and a woolen hat under his trilby, he exited his vehicle and made his way into what appeared to be the only five-and-dime drugstore in the town. He glanced around the store and selected the oldest employee: the pharmacist manning the prescription counter.

Unwrapping his scarves so he could speak, Pendergast said, "I am trying to trace the whereabouts of a man named Kyle Swinton, who attended Leadville High School in the late '90s."

The pharmacist looked Pendergast up and down. "Kyle Swinton? What do you want with him?"

"I'm an attorney, and it's about an inheritance."

"Inheritance? His family didn't have two nickels to rub together."

"There was a great-uncle."

"Oh. Well, good for him, I suppose. Kyle, he doesn't come into town very often. Maybe not till spring."

This was excellent. "If you could direct me to his house, I should be grateful."

"Sure, but he's snowed in. Lives off the grid. You won't get up there except on a snowmobile. And..." The man hesitated.

"Yes?"

"He's one of those survivalist types. He's holed up in Elbert Canyon waiting for, I don't know, the end of civilization maybe."

"Indeed?"

"He's got a bunker up there, stockpiles of food—and a big-time arsenal, or so they say. So if you go up there, you'd better be damn careful or he's liable to blow a hole in you."

Pendergast was silent for a moment. "Where, pray tell, may I rent a snowmobile?"

"There's a couple of places, it's a big sport in these parts." He gave Pendergast another once-over, doubtfully. "You know how to operate one?"

"Naturally."

The druggist gave Pendergast the information and drew a map, showing him how to get to Kyle Swinton's place up in Elbert Canyon.

Pendergast exited the pharmacy and strolled down Harrison Avenue, as if shopping, despite the five-degree weather, the piles of snow, and the side-walks so icy that even the salt froze to them. Finally he went into a gun-and-ammo store that also doubled as a pawnshop.

A man with a tattoo of an octopus on the shaved dome of his head strolled over. "What can I do for you?"

"I would like to buy a small box of the Cor-Bon .45 ACP."

The man placed the box on the counter.

"Does a Mr. Kyle Swinton shop here?"

"Sure does, good customer. Crazy fucker, though."

Pendergast considered for a moment the kind of person a man like this might think of as crazy.

"I understand he has quite a collection of firearms."

"Spends every last penny on guns and ammo."

"In that case, there must be quite a variety of ammo he buys from you."

"Hell, yes. That's why we got all these rounds here. He's got a collection of heavy-caliber hand-guns you wouldn't believe."

"Revolvers?"

"Oh, yeah. Revolvers, pistols, all loads. Probably got a hundred K worth of firearms up there."

Pendergast pursed his lips. "Come to think of it, I'd like to also purchase a box of the .44 S&W Special, one of the .44 Remington Magnum, and another of .357 S&W Magnum."

The man placed the boxes on the counter. "Else?"

"That will suffice, thank you very much."

The man rang the purchase up.

"No bag, I'll put them in my pockets." Everything disappeared into his coat.

Business had not been good at the nearest snow-

mobile rental place. Pendergast was able to over-
come their initial difficulty about renting him a
machine for the day, despite his wildly inappropriate dress, southern accent, and lack of even mini-
mal familiarity with its operation. They put a helmet and visor on his head and gave him a quick
lesson in how to ride it, took him out for a five-
minute practice spin, had him sign multiple dis-
claimers, and wished him luck. In so doing, Pendergast learned more about Kyle Swinton. He appeared to be known to all Leadville as a "crazy
fucker." His parents had been alcoholics who finally went through the guardrail at Stockton
Creek, drunk as skunks, and rolled a thousand feet
down the ravine. Kyle had lived off the land ever
since, hunting, fishing, and panning for gold when
he needed ready cash to buy ammunition.

As Pendergast was leaving, the rental shop manager added: "Don't go rushing up to the cabin,
now, Kyle's liable to get excited. Approach real nice
and slow, and keep your hands in sight and a
friendly smile on your face."

# 50

The ride to Swinton's cabin was exceedingly unpleasant. The snowmobile was a coarse, deafening, stinking contraption, prone to jackrabbit starts and sudden stops, with none of the refinement of a high-performance motorcycle, and as Pendergast maneuvered it up the winding white road it threw up a steady wake of snow that plastered his expensive coat, building up layers. Pendergast soon looked like a helmeted snowman.

He followed the advice he'd been given and slowed down as soon as he saw the cabin, half buried in snow, with a trickle of smoke curling from a stovepipe on top. Sure enough, as he came within a hundred yards a man appeared on the porch, small and ferret-like, with a gap between his two front teeth visible even at this distance. He was holding a pump-action shotgun.

Pendergast halted the snowmobile, which jerked to a stop. Plates of snow broke off and fell from his coat. He fumbled awkwardly with the helmet and finally managed to raise the visor with his bulky gloves.

"Greetings, Kyle!"

The response was a conspicuous racking of the pump. "State your business, sir."

"I'm here to see you. I've heard a lot about your outfit up here. I'm a fellow survivalist and I'm touring the country looking at what other people are doing, for an article in *Survivalist* magazine."

"Where'd you hear about me?"

"Word gets around. You know how it is."

A hesitation. "So you're a journalist?"

"I'm a survivalist first, journalist second." A cold gust of wind swirled the snow about Pendergast's legs. "Mr. Swinton, do you think you might extend me the courtesy of your hospitality so that we could continue this conversation in the confines of your home?"

Swinton wavered. The word *hospitality* had not gone unnoticed. Pendergast pressed his advantage. "I wonder if keeping a man freezing in the cold at gunpoint is the kind of hospitality one should accord a kindred spirit."

Swinton squinted at him. "At least you're a white man," he said, putting down the gun. "All right, come on in. But see that you broom yourself off at the door; I don't want no snow tracked in my house." He waited as Pendergast struggled through the deep snow to the porch. A broken broom stood next to the door and Pendergast swept himself as clean as he could while Swinton watched, frowning.

He followed Swinton in the cabin. It was surprisingly large, extending into a warren of rooms in the back. The gleam of gunmetal could be seen everywhere: racks of assault rifles, AK-47s and M16s illegally altered to fire on full-auto; a set of Uzis and TAR-21 bullpup assault rifles; another set of Chinese Norinco QBZ-97 rifles and carbines, again altered for fully automatic action. A nearby case contained a huge array of revolvers and pistols, just as the man in Leadville had said. Beyond, in one of the rooms, Pendergast glimpsed a collection of RPGs, including a pair of Russian RPG-29s—all quite illegal.

Other than the walls being completely covered with weaponry, the cabin was surprisingly cozy, with a fire burning in a woodstove with an open door. All the furniture was handmade of peeled logs and branches, draped with cowhides. And everything was neat as a pin.

"Shed that coat and seat yourself, I'll get the coffee."

Pendergast removed the coat and draped it over a chair, straightened his suit, and sat down. Swinton fetched some mugs and a coffeepot off the woodstove and poured two cups. Without asking he heaped in a tablespoon of Cremora and two of sugar before handing it to Pendergast.

The agent took the mug and made a show of drinking. It tasted as if it had been boiling on the stove for days.

He found Swinton looking at him curiously. "What's with the black suit? Somebody die? You come up here by snowmobile in that getup?"

"It was functional."

"You sure as hell don't look like a survivalist to me."

"What do I look like?"

"Some pussy professor from Jew York City. Or with that accent, maybe Jew Orleans. So what're you packing?"

Pendergast removed his .45 Colt and laid it on the table. Swinton picked it up, immediately impressed. "Les Baer, huh? Nice. You know how to fire that?"

"I try," said Pendergast. "This is quite a collection you have. Do *you* know how to fire all those weapons?"

Swinton took offense, as Pendergast knew he would. "You think I hang shit like that on my wall if I don't know how to fire it?"

"Anyone can pull the trigger on a weapon," Pendergast said, sipping his coffee.

"I fire almost every weapon I own at least once a week."

Pendergast pointed to the handgun cabinet. "What about that Super Blackhawk?"

"That's a fine weapon. Updated Old West." He got up, took it down from the rack.

"May I see it?"

He handed it to Pendergast. He hefted it, sighted, then opened the barrel and dumped out the ammo.

"What you doing?"

Pendergast picked up one of the rounds, inserted it back in the barrel, gave it a spin, then laid the revolver down.

"You think you're tough, right? Let's play a little game."

"What the hell? What game?"

"Put the gun to your head and pull the trigger. And I'll give you a thousand dollars."

Swinton stared at him. "Are you stupid or something? I can see the fucking round isn't even in firing position."

"Then you've just won a thousand dollars. If you pick the gun up and pull the trigger."

Swinton picked the gun up, put it to his head, and pulled the trigger. There was a click. He laid it down.

Without a word, Pendergast reached into his suit-coat pocket, pulled out a brick of one-hundred-dollar bills, and peeled off ten of them. Swinton took the money. "You're crazy, you know that?"

"Yes, I am crazy."

"Now it's your own damn turn." Swinton picked up the revolver, spun the barrel, laid it down.

"What will you give me?"

"I don't got no money, and I ain't giving you back the thousand."

"Then perhaps you'll answer a question instead. Any question I choose to ask. Absolute truth."

Swinton shrugged. "Sure."

Pendergast removed another thousand and put it on the table. Then he picked up the gun, placed it at his temple, and pulled the trigger. Another click.

"And now for the question."

"Shoot."

"Your great-great-grandfather was a miner in Roaring Fork during the silver boom days. He knew quite a bit about a series of killings, allegedly done by a man-eating grizzly bear, but in actuality done by a group of crazy miners."

He paused. Swinton had risen from his chair. "You're no damn magazine writer! Who are you?"

"I am the one who is asking you a question.

Presuming that you're a man of honor, I will receive an answer. If you wish to know who I really am, that must await the next round of the game. Provided, of course, you have the fortitude to continue."

Swinton said nothing.

"Your ancestor knew more than most people about those killings. In fact, I think he knew the truth—the entire truth." Pendergast paused. "My question is: What *is* the truth?"

Swinton shifted in his chair. The expression on his face went through several rapid changes. He exposed his ferrety teeth several times, his lips twitching. This went on for a while, then at last he cleared his throat. "Why do you want to know?"

"Private curiosity."

"Who are you gonna tell?"

"Nobody."

Swinton stared hungrily at the thousand dollars sitting on the table. "You swear to that? It's been a secret in my family for a long, long time."

Pendergast nodded.

Another pause. "It started with the Committee of Seven," Swinton said at last. "My great-great-granddaddy, August Swinton, was one of them. At least, that's what was passed down." A tinge of pride edged into his voice. "As you said, those were no grizzly killings. They was done by four crazy bastards, former smelter workers, who were living wild in the mountains and had turned cannibal. A man named Shadrach Cropsey went up to track the bear and discovered it wasn't a bear at all, but these fellers living in an abandoned mine. He figured out where they were holed up and then pulled together this Committee of Seven."

"And then what happened?"

"That's a second question."

"So it is." Pendergast smiled. "Time for another round?" He picked up the revolver, spun the cylinder, and laid it down.

Swinton shook his head. "I can still see the round, and it ain't in the firing chamber. Another thousand bucks?"

Pendergast nodded.

Swinton picked up the gun and pulled the trigger again, put it down, held out his hand. "This is the dumbest damn game I ever saw."

Pendergast handed him a thousand dollars. Then he picked up the gun, spun the barrel, and without looking at it put it to his head and pulled the trigger. *Click.*

"You really are one crazy motherfucker."

"There appear to be a great many like me in this area," Pendergast replied. "And now for my question: What did Shadrach Cropsey and this Committee of Seven do then?"

"Back in those days, they handled problems the right way—they did it themselves. Fuck the law and all its bullshit. They went up there and smoked those cannibals. The way I heard it, old Shadrach got his ass killed in the fight. After that, there weren't no more 'grizzly' killings."

"And the place where they killed the miners?"

"Another question, friend."

Pendergast spun the barrel, placed it on the table. Swinton eyed it nervously. "I can't see the round."

"Then it is either in the firing chamber or in the opposite chamber, hidden by the frame. Which means there is a fifty–fifty chance you will live."

"I ain't playing."

"You just said you would. I didn't imagine you were a coward, Mr. Swinton." He reached in his pocket and pulled out the brick of hundreds. This time he peeled off twenty. "We'll double the stakes. You will receive two thousand—if you pull the trigger."

Swinton was sweating heavily. "I ain't gonna play."

"You mean, you pass on your turn? I won't insist."

"That's what I mean. I pass."

"But I do not pass on my turn."

"Go ahead. Be my fucking guest."

Pendergast spun the barrel, held the revolver up, pulled the trigger. *Click.* He put it down.

"My final question: Where did they kill the miners?"

"I don't know. But I do have the letter."

"What letter?"

"The one that got passed down to me. It sort of explains things." He rose from his creaking chair and shuffled off into the dim recesses of the cabin. He returned a moment later with a dusty old piece of yellow paper sandwiched in Mylar. He eased himself back down and handed the letter to Pendergast.

It was a handwritten note, undated, with no salutation or signature. It read:

*mete at the Ideal 11 oclock Sharp to Night they are Holt Up in the closed Christmas Mine up on smugglers wall there are 4 of them bring your best Guns and lantern burn this Letter afore you set out*

Pendergast lowered the letter. Swinton held out his hand, and Pendergast returned it. Swinton's brow was still beaded with sweat, but the look on his face was pure relief. "I can't believe you played that game without ever looking at the cylinder. That's just crazy-ass dangerous."

Pendergast dressed again in his coat, scarves, and hat, and then took up the revolver. He opened the cylinder and let the .44 magnum round drop into his hand. "There was never any danger. I brought this round with me and substituted it for one of yours after I unloaded the gun." He held it up. "It's been doctored."

Swinton rose. "Mother*fucker!*" He came at Pendergast, drawing his carry, but in a flash Pendergast had shoved the round back in and rotated it into firing position, pointing the Blackhawk at Swinton.

"Or maybe I *didn't* doctor it."

Swinton froze.

"You'll never know." Pendergast picked up his own Les Baer, and—while covering Swinton with it—removed the round from the Blackhawk and put it in his coat pocket. "And now I will answer your earlier question: I'm not a magazine writer. I'm a federal agent. And there's one thing I promise you: if you lied to me, I'll know it, sooner rather than later—and in that case, none of your weapons will save you."

# 51

That same day, at three o'clock in the afternoon, Corrie lounged in the room she had acquired at the Hotel Sebastian, wearing a terry-cloth bathrobe supplied by the hotel, first admiring the view, and then checking out the mini-bar (which she couldn't afford, but enjoyed rummaging through anyway) before moving into the marble bathroom. She turned on the shower, adjusted the water, and slipped out of the bathrobe, stepping in.

As she luxuriated in the hot shower, she considered that things were looking up. She felt badly about what happened at breakfast the day before, but even that paled in comparison with Pendergast's revelations. The Doyle story, the mercury-crazed miners—and the Stafford family connection—it was truly remarkable. *And* truly frightening. Pendergast was right: she had placed herself in grave danger.

Roaring Fork had now pretty much resumed the ghost-town status it once held, except it was all dressed up for Christmas with nowhere to go. Totally surreal. Even the press seemed to have packed up their cameras and microphones. The Hotel Sebastian had lost most of its guests and staff, but the restaurant was still going strong—stronger than ever, as those remaining in town, it seemed, all wanted to eat out. Corrie had managed to drive a hard bargain with the hotel manager, snagging room and breakfast free of charge in return for six hours of kitchen work every day. And although her arrangement with the hotel came with only one meal a day, Corrie had plenty of experience with all-you-can-eat deals and was confident she could scarf down enough food in one sitting to last twenty-four hours.

She got out of the shower, toweled off, and combed her hair. As she was drying it, she heard a knock at the door. Quickly donning the bathrobe again, she went to the door and peeked through the eyehole.

Pendergast.

She opened the door, but the agent hesitated. "I'd be glad to return later—"

"Don't be silly. Sit down, I'll only be a moment." She went back into the bathroom, finished blowing out her hair, wrapped the bathrobe a little tighter, and came back out, seating herself on the sofa.

Pendergast did not look well. His usual alabaster face was mottled with red and his hair looked like it had been in a wind tunnel.

"How did it go?" Corrie asked. She knew he had gone to Leadville to see if he could trace a Swinton descendant.

Instead of answering the question, he said, "I am delighted to find you safely ensconced in the hotel. As for the cost, I'd be happy to help—"

"Not necessary, thank you," Corrie said quickly. "I managed to finagle free room and board in return for a few hours of kitchen work."

"How enterprising of you." He paused, his face growing more serious. "I regret that you felt it necessary to deceive me. I understand from the chief that your car was shot at and your dog killed."

Corrie colored deeply. "I didn't want you to worry. I'm sorry. I was going to tell you eventually."

"You didn't want me to take you away from Roaring Fork."

"That, too. And I wanted to find the bastard who killed my dog."

"You must not attempt to find out who killed your dog. I hope you now understand you're dealing with dangerous and highly motivated people.

This is far bigger than a dead dog—and you're intelligent enough to realize that."

"Of course. I understand that clearly."

"There's a development worth two hundred million dollars at stake—but this isn't just about money. It will lead to heavy criminal indictments against those involved, some of whom happen to belong to one of the wealthiest and most powerful clans in this country, beginning with your Mrs. Kermode and quite likely ending with members of the Stafford family as well. Perhaps now you can understand why they will not hesitate to kill you."

"But I want them brought to justice—"

"And they will be. But not by you, and not while you're here. When you're safely back in New York, I will bring in the Bureau and all will be exposed. So you see, there's nothing left for you to do here except pack your bags and return to New York—as soon as the weather permits."

Corrie thought about the coming storm. It would close the road again. She supposed she could start writing things up, get an outline of her thesis nailed down, before she had to leave.

"All right," she said.

"In the meantime, I want you to stay within the confines of the hotel. I've spoken to the chief of security here, an excellent woman, and you'll be safe.

You may be stuck here for a few days, however. The weather forecast is dire."

"Fine with me. So...are you going to tell me about your trip to Leadville?"

"I am not."

"Why?"

"Because the knowledge would only put you in more unnecessary danger. Please allow me to handle this from now on."

Despite his kindly tone, Corrie felt irritated. She'd agreed to what he asked. She was going back to New York as soon as the weather cleared. Why couldn't he take her into his confidence? "If you insist," she said.

Pendergast rose. "I would invite you to dine with me, but I have to confer with the chief. They have made little progress on the arsonist case."

He left. Corrie thought for a moment, and then went over to the mini-bar. She was starving and had no money for food. Her breakfast deal didn't begin until the next morning. The can of Pringles was eight dollars.

*Screw it*, she thought as she tore off the lid.

# 52

Three o'clock in the morning, December twenty-fourth. After flitting like a specter past the worn shopfronts and dark windows of Old Town, Pendergast took just seconds to break into the Ideal Saloon, picking the picturesque but ineffectual nineteenth-century lock.

He stepped into the dim space of the bar-*cum*-museum, its interior illuminated only by several strips of emergency fluorescent lighting, which cast garish shadows about the room. The saloon consisted of a large, central room, with circular tables, chairs, and a plank floor. A long bar ran the entire length of the far end. The walls consisted of wainscoting of vertical beadboard, gleaming with varnish and darkened by time, below flocked velvet wallpaper in a flowery Victorian pattern. The wall was decorated with sconces of copper and cut glass. Behind the bar and to the right, a staircase led up to what had been a small whorehouse. And farther off to the right, in an alcove partly under the staircase, stood some gaming tables. Velvet ropes just inside two swinging doors created a viewing area, preventing visitors from proceeding into the restored saloon.

Moving without noise, Pendergast ducked under the ropes and took a long, thoughtful turn about the room. A whisky bottle and some shot glasses stood on the bar, and several tables were also arrayed with bottles and glasses. Behind the bar stood a large mirrored case of antique liquor bottles filled with colored water.

He moved through the bar and into the gaming area. A poker table stood in one corner, covered with green felt, with hands of five-card stud laid out: four aces against a straight flush. A blackjack table, also artfully arranged with cards, stood beside a splendid antique roulette wheel with ivory, red jasper, and ebony inlay.

Pendergast glided past the gaming area to a door under the stairs. He tried to open it, found it locked, and swiftly picked the lock.

It opened into a small, dusty room, which remained unrestored, with cracked plaster walls and peeling wallpaper, some old chairs, and a broken table. Graffiti, some bearing dates from the 1930s, when Roaring Fork was still a ghost town, were scratched into the wall. A pile of broken whisky bottles lay in one corner. At the back of this room stood a door that led, Pendergast knew, to a rear exit.

He took off his coat and scarf and carefully draped them over one of the chairs, and looked around, slowly and carefully, as if committing everything to memory. He stood, quite still, for a long time, and then finally he stirred. Choosing a vacant spot on the floor, he lay down on the dirty boards and folded his hands over his chest, like a corpse in a coffin. Slowly, very slowly, he closed his eyes. In the silence, he focused on the sounds of the snowstorm: the muffled wind shaking and moaning about the exterior walls, the creaking of the wood, the rattling of the tin roof. The air smelled of dust, dry rot, and mildew. He allowed his respiration and pulse to slow and his mind to relax.

It was in this back room, he felt certain, that the Committee of Seven would have met up. But before he went down that avenue, there was another place he wished to visit first—a visit that would take place entirely within his mind.

Pendergast had once spent time in a remote Tibetan monastery, studying an esoteric meditative discipline known as Chongg Ran. It was one of the least known of the Tibetan mind techniques. The teachings were never put down in writing, and they could only be transmitted directly teacher-to-pupil.

Pendergast had taken the heart of Chongg Ran and combined it with several other mental disciplines, including the concept of a memory palace as described in a sixteenth-century Italian manuscript by Giordano Bruno titled *Ars Memoria*, Art of Memory. The result was a unique and highly complex form of mental visualization. With training, careful preparation, and a fanatical degree of intellectual discipline, the exercise allowed him to take a complex problem with many thousands of facts and surmises, and mentally stitch them together into a coherent narrative, which could then be processed, analyzed—and, especially, *experienced*. Pendergast used the technique to help solve elusive problems; to visualize places, via the force of his intellect, that could not be reached physically—far distant places, or even places in the past. The technique was extremely draining, however, and he employed it sparingly.

He lay for many minutes, as still as a corpse, first arranging a hugely complex set of facts into careful order, then tuning his senses to the surrounding environment while simultaneously shutting down the voice in his mind, turning off that incessant running commentary all people carry in their heads. The voice had been especially voluble of late, and it took a great deal of effort to silence it; Pendergast was forced to move his meditative stance from the Third Level to the Fourth Level, doing complex equations in his head, playing four hands of bridge simultaneously. At last, the voice was silenced, and he then began the ancient steps of Chongg Ran itself. First, he blocked every sound, every sensation, one after another: the creaking of the building, the rustling of the wind, the scent of dust, the hard floor beneath him, the seeming infinitude of his own corporal awareness—until at length he arrived at the state of *stong pa nyid*: the condition of Pure Emptiness. For a moment, there was only nonexistence; even time itself seemed to fall away.

But then—slowly, very slowly—something began to materialize out of the nothingness. At first it was as miniaturized, as delicate, as beautiful as a Fabergé egg. With that same lack of hurry, it grew larger and clearer. Eyes still shut, Pendergast allowed it to take on form and definition around him. And then, at last, he opened his eyes to find himself within a brightly lit space: a splendid and elegant dining room, refulgent with light and crystal, the clinking of glasses, and the murmur of genteel conversation.

To the smell of cigar smoke and the learned discourse of a string quartet, Pendergast took in the

opulent room. His eyes traveled over the tables, finally stopping at one in a far corner. Seated at it
were four gentlemen. Two of the men were laugh-
ing together over some witticism or other—one
wearing a broadcloth frock coat, the other in
evening dress. Pendergast, however, was more interested in the other two diners. One was dressed
flamboyantly: white kid gloves, a vest and cutaway
coat of black velvet, a large frilled necktie, silk knee
breeches and stockings, slippers adorned with
grosgrain bows. An orchid drooped in his buttonhole. He was in deep descant, speaking animatedly,
one hand pressed against his breast, the other
pointing heavenward, index finger extended in a
travesty of John the Baptist. The man beside him,
who seemed to be hanging on his companion's
every word, presented an entirely different appearance, a contrast so strong as to almost be comical.
He was a stocky fellow in a somber, sensible
English suit, with big mustaches and an awkward
bearing.

They were Oscar Wilde and Arthur Conan
Doyle.

Slowly, in his mind, Pendergast approached the
table, listening intently, as the conversation—or,
more frequently, monologue—became audible.

"Indeed?" Wilde was saying, in a remarkably
deep and sonorous voice. "Did you think that—as

one who would happily sacrifice himself on the pyre of aestheticism—I do not recognize the face of horror when I stare into it?"

There was no empty seat. Pendergast turned, motioned to a waiter, indicated the table. Immediately, the man brought up a fifth chair, placing it between Conan Doyle and the man Pendergast realized must be Joseph Stoddart.

"I was once told a story so dreadful, so distressing in its particulars and in the extent of its evil, that now I truly believe nothing I hear could ever frighten me again."

"How interesting."

"Would you care to hear it? It is not for the faint of heart."

As he listened to the conversation taking place beside him, Pendergast reached forward, poured himself a glass of wine, found it excellent.

"It was told to me during my lecture tour of America a few years back. On my way to San Francisco, I stopped at a rather squalid yet picturesque mining camp known as Roaring Fork." Wilde pressed his hand to Doyle's knee for emphasis. "After my lecture, one of the miners approached me, an elderly chap somewhat the worse—or, perhaps, the better—for drink. He took me aside, said he'd enjoyed my story so much that he had one of his own to share with me." He paused for a sip of burgundy. "Here, lean in a little closer, that's a good fellow, and I'll tell it you exactly as it was told to me."

Doyle leaned in, as requested. Pendergast leaned in, as well.

"I tried to escape him, but he would have none of it, presuming to approach me in a most familiar way, breathing fumes of the local *ubriacant*. My first impulse was to push past, but there was something about the look in his eye that stopped me. I confess I was also intrigued—in an anthropological fashion, Doyle, don't you know—by this leathern specimen, this uncouth bard, this bibulous miner, and I found myself curious as to what he considered a 'good story.' And so I listened, and rather attentively, as his American drawl was nigh indecipherable. He spoke of events that had occurred some years earlier, not long after the silver strikes that established Roaring Fork. Over the course of one summer, a grizzled bear—or so it was believed—had taken to roaming the mountains above the town, attacking, killing...*and* eating...lone miners working their claims."

Doyle nodded vigorously, his face concentrated with the utmost interest.

"Naturally, the town fell into a state of perfect terror. But the killings went on, as there were many lone men upon the mountain. The bear was merciless, ambuscading the miners outside their cabins, killing and savagely dismembering them— and then feasting upon their flesh." Wilde paused. "I should have liked to have known whether the, ah, *consumption* commenced while consciousness was still present. Can you imagine what it would be like to be devoured alive by a savage beast? To watch it tear your flesh off, then chew and swallow, with evident satisfaction? That is a contemplation never even considered by Huysmans in his *À Rebours*. How sadly lacking the aesthete was, in hindsight!"

Wilde glanced over to see what effect his words were having on the country doctor. Doyle had grasped his glass of claret and taken a deep draught. Listening, Pendergast took a sip of his own glass, then signaled a waiter to bring him a menu.

"Many a fellow tried to track the grizzled bear," Wilde continued, "but none was successful—save for one miner, a man who had learned the fine art of tracking while living among Indians. He conceived a notion that the killings were not the work of a bear."

"Not the work of a bear, sir?"

"Not the work of a bear, sir. And so, waiting until the next killing, this chap—his name was Cropsey—went a-tracking, and soon discovered that the perpetrators of this outrage were a group of men."

At this, Doyle leaned back rather abruptly. "I beg your pardon, Mr. Wilde. Do you mean to say that these men were...cannibals?"

"Indeed I do. American cannibals."

Doyle shook his head. "Monstrous. Monstrous."

"Quite so," Wilde said. "They have none of the good manners of your English cannibals."

Doyle stared at his fellow guest in shock. "This is no matter for levity, Wilde."

"Perhaps not. We shall see. In any case, our Cropsey tracked these cannibals to their lair, an abandoned mine shaft somewhere on the mountain, at a place called Smuggler's Wall. There was no constabulary in the town, of course, and so this fellow organized a small group of local vigilantes. They cognominated themselves the Committee of Seven. They would scale the mountain in the dark of night, surprise the cannibals, and administer the rough justice of the American West." Wilde toyed with his *boutonnière*. "The very next night, at midnight, this group gathered at the local saloon to discuss strategy and no doubt fortify themselves for the coming ordeal. They then departed by a back door, heavily armed, and equipped with lanterns, rope, and a torch. This, my dear Doyle, is where the story turns...well, not to put too fine a point on it, rather ghastly. Do steady yourself, there's a good chap."

The waiter brought over a menu, and Pendergast turned his attention to it. Three or four minutes later, he was jarred from his perusal by Doyle's sudden violent rise from the table—knocking his chair over in his agitation—and subsequent flight from the dining room, his face a mixture of shock and disgust.

"Why, whatever's the matter?" Stoddart said, frowning, as Doyle disappeared in the direction of the gentlemen's lounge.

"I suspect it must be the prawns," Wilde replied, and he dabbed primly at his mouth with a napkin...

...As slowly as it had come, the voice began to fade from Pendergast's mind. The sumptuous interior of the Langham Hotel began to waver, as if dissolving into mist and darkness. Slowly, slowly, a new scene materialized—a very different scene. It was the smoke-filled, whisky-redolent back room of a busy saloon, the sounds of gambling, drinking, and argument penetrating the thin wooden walls. A back room, in fact, remarkably similar to the one in which Pendergast was—in the Roaring Fork of the present—currently situated. After a brief exchange of determined voices, a group of seven men rose from a large table: men carrying lanterns and guns. Following their leader, one Shadrach Cropsey, they made their way out the back door of the little room and into the night.

Pendergast followed them, his incorporeal presence hovering in the cool night air like a ghost.

# 53

The group of miners walked down the dirt main street of town, casually and without hurry, until they reached the far end, where settlement ceased and the forests mounted upward into the mountains. It was a moonless night. The scent of wood fires was in the air, and in the nearby corrals, horses were moving restlessly about. Silently, the group lit their lanterns and proceeded along a rough mining road, which made its way by switchbacks up, and then farther up, passing beneath the dark fir trees.

The night was cool and the sky was pricked with stars. A lone wolf howled somewhere in the great bowl of mountains, quickly answered by another. As the men gained altitude, the fir trees grew smaller, shorter, twisted into grotesque shapes by incessant winds and deep snows. Gradually the trees thinned out into matted thickets of krummholz, and then the cart path broached the tree line.

In his mind, Pendergast followed the group.

The line of yellow lanterns advanced up the barren, rock-strewn slopes approaching Smuggler's Cirque. They were now entering a recently abandoned mining zone, and around the men appeared ghostly tailings, like pyramids, spilling down the sides of the ridge, the gaping holes of the mines above, punctuated by rickety ore chutes, trestles, sluice boxes, and flumes.

Looming in the darkness to the right was an immense wooden structure, set into the flat declivity at the base of Smuggler's Cirque: the main entrance to the famed Sally Goodin Mine, still in operation now, in the early fall of 1876. The building housed the machines and pulley works used to raise and lower the cages and buckets; it also enclosed the two-hundred-ton Ireland Pump Engine, capable of pumping over a thousand gallons per minute, used to dewater the mine complex.

Now all the lanterns went out but one: a red-glass lamp that cast a bloody gleam in the murky night. The cart path divided into many winding tracks cut into the hillsides rising above the cirque. Their objective lay above, the highest of the abandoned tunnels high on the slope known as Smuggler's Wall, situated at an altitude close to thirteen thousand feet. A single track led in that direction, carved by hand out of the scree, switchbacking sharply as it climbed. It came over a ridge and skirted a small glacial tarn, the water black and still, its shore dotted with rusted pumping machinery and old flume gates.

Still the group of seven men climbed upward. Now the dark, square hole of the Christmas Mine became visible in the faint starlight against the upper scree slope. A trestle ran from the hole, and below it stood a tailings pile of lighter color. A jumble of wrecked machinery was strewn about the slope below.

The group paused, and Pendergast heard a low murmur of voices. And then they silently divided. One man made his way up, hiding among boulders above the entrance. A second took up a covered position among the scree just below the entrance.

Lookouts in place, the rest—four men led by Cropsey, now holding the lantern himself—entered the abandoned tunnel. Pendergast followed. The shutter on the red lamp was adjusted to produce only the faintest glow. Arms at the ready, the men walked single-file along the iron rails leading into the tunnel, making no noise. One carried a torch of pitch, ready to be lit.

As they proceeded, a smell came toward them,

a smell that became ever more awful in the hot, moist, stifling atmosphere.

The Christmas Mine tunnel opened into a crosscut: a horizontal tunnel driven at right angles to the main tunnel. The group paused before the crosscut and readied their weapons. The torch was lowered, a match was struck, and the pitch set afire. In that moment, the men rounded the corner, weapons aimed down the tunnel. The smell was now almost overwhelming.

Silence. The flickering flames disclosed something in the darkness at the end of the tunnel. The group cautiously moved forward. It was an irregular, lumpy shape. When they drew close, the men saw that it was a heap of soft things: rotting burlap, old gunnysacks, leaves and pine needles, chunks of moss. Mingled into the material were pieces of gnawed bone, broken skulls, and strips of what looked like dried rawhide.

Skin. Hairless skin.

All around the heap lay a broad ring of human feces.

One of the men spoke hoarsely. "What...*is* this?"

The question was initially answered with silence. Finally, one of the others replied. "It's an animal den."

"It ain't *animal*," said Cropsey.

"God Almighty."

"Where are they?"

Now their voices were rising, echoing, as fear and uncertainty began to set in.

"The bastards must be out. Killing."

The torch sputtered and burned as their voices rose, discussing what to do. The guns were put away. There was disagreement, conflict.

Suddenly Cropsey held up his hand. The others fell silent, listening. There were sounds of shuffling, along with guttural, animalistic breathing. The noises stopped. Quickly the man carrying the torch doused it in a puddle of water, while Cropsey shut the lantern down. But now all was deathly silent: it seemed likely the killers had seen the light or heard their voices—and knew they were here.

"Give us some light, for Jesus's sake," whispered one of the men, his voice tight with anxiety.

Cropsey opened the lantern a fraction. The others were crouching, rifles and pistols at the ready. The dim glow barely penetrated the gloom.

"*More* light," someone said.

The lantern now threw light to the edge of the cross tunnel. All was silent. They waited, but nothing came around the corner. Nor were there sounds of flight.

"We go get 'em," Cropsey announced. "Afore they get away."

No one moved. Finally Cropsey himself began stalking forward. The others followed. He crept to the crosscut. The rest waited behind. Holding up the lantern, he paused, crouched, then suddenly swung around the corner, wielding the rifle like a pistol in one hand, the lantern in the other. *"Now!"*

It happened with incredible speed. A flash of something darting forward; a gargling scream; and then Cropsey spun around, dropping his rifle and writhing in agony. A naked, filthy man was astride his back, tearing at his throat, more like a beast than a human being. None of the other four could fire; the combatants were too close together. Cropsey screamed again, staggering about, trying to shake off the man who tore at him with nails and teeth, ripping away anything he could reach: ears, lips, nose; there was a sudden spurt of arterial blood from the neck and Cropsey went down, the monster still on top of him, the lantern falling to the ground and shattering.

Simultaneously, as with a single mind, the other four began to shoot, aiming wildly into the darkness. From the muzzle flashes more figures could be seen, bellowing like bulls, running toward them from around the corner of the crosscut, a melee amid the wild eruption of gunfire. The two lookouts came charging down the tunnel, aroused by the din, and joined in with their own weapons. The guns roared again and again, the flashes of light blooming within clouds of ugly gray smoke—and then all went silent. For a moment, there was only darkness. Then came the sound of a match, scraping against rock; another lantern was lit—and its feeble light illuminated a splay of corpses, the four cannibals now just ruined bodies scattered about the tunnel, taken apart by heavy-caliber bullets, lying like so much ropy waste atop the sundered carcass of Shadrach Cropsey.

It was over.

Fifteen minutes later, Pendergast opened his eyes. The room was cool and quiet. He rose, brushed off his black suit, bundled himself up, and let himself out the back door of the saloon. The storm was in full blast, the fury of it thundering down Main Street and shaking the Christmas decorations like so many cobwebs. Bundling his coat around himself, wrapping his scarf tighter, and lowering his head against the wind, he made his way through the storm-shaken town back to his hotel.

# 54

At eleven o'clock that morning—Christmas Eve day—after buttering two hundred pieces of toast, washing twice that number of dishes, and mopping the kitchen from wall to wall—Corrie went back to her room, bundled up in her coat, and ventured out into the storm. The idea that Kermode or her thugs might be out in this weather, waiting for her, seemed far-fetched; nevertheless, she felt an electric tickle of fear. She consoled herself with the thought that she was on her way to the safest place in town—the police station.

She had decided to confront Pendergast. Not so much confront him, exactly, but rather to make another pitch about why he should share with her the information he'd apparently gotten on his trip to Leadville. The way she saw things, it was unfair of him to withhold it. She had, after all, discovered the Swinton connection and shared the name with him. If he'd found information about the old killings, the least he could do would be to let her include it in her thesis.

The wind and flying snow came buffeting down the street as she turned onto Main. She leaned into it, holding her cap. The business district of Roaring Fork was relatively compact, but even so it proved a damn long journey in a blizzard.

The police station loomed up through the blowing snow, its windows glowing with yellow light, perversely inviting. All were apparently at work despite the storm. She walked up the steps, stomped off the snow in the vestibule, shook out her woolen hat and scarf, and went in.

"Is Special Agent Pendergast in?" she asked Iris, the lady at the reception desk, with whom she had gotten friendly over the past ten days.

"Oh, dear," she sighed. "He doesn't sign in and out, and he keeps the oddest hours. I just can't keep track." She shook her head. "Feel free to check his office."

Corrie went down into the basement, grateful for once for the heat. His door was closed. She knocked; no answer.

Where could he be, in a storm like this? Not at the Hotel Sebastian, where he hadn't been answering his phone.

She turned the handle, but it was locked.

She paused for a moment, thoughtfully, still grasping the handle. Then she went back upstairs.

"Find him?" Iris asked.

"No luck," said Corrie. She hesitated. "Listen, I think I left something important in his office. Do you have a key?"

Iris considered this. "Well, I do, but I don't think I can let you in. What did you leave?"

"My cell phone."

"Oh." Iris thought some more. "I suppose I *could* let you in, so long as I stay with you."

"That would be great."

She followed Iris back down the stairs. In a moment the woman had opened the door and turned on the light. The room was hot and stuffy. Corrie looked around. The desk was covered with papers that had been carefully arranged. She scanned the surface with her eyes but it was all too neat, too squared away, to expose much information.

"I don't see it," said Iris, looking about.

"He might have put it away in a drawer."

"I don't think you should be opening up any drawers, Corrie."

"Right. Of course not."

She looked frantically around the desk, this way and that. "It's got to be here somewhere," she said.

And then Corrie caught a glimpse of something interesting. A page torn out of a small notebook, covered with Pendergast's distinctive copperplate handwriting, its top part sticking out of a sheaf of documents. Three underlined words jumped out: *Swinton* and *Christmas Mine.*

"Is it over here?" Corrie bent over the desk, as if looking behind a lamp, while "accidentally" pushing the notebooks with her elbow, exposing a few more lines of the torn page, on which Pendergast had printed:

*mete at the Ideal 11 oclock Sharp to Night they are Holt Up in the closed Christmas Mine up on smugglers wall there are 4 of*

"*Really*, Corrie, it's time to go," Iris said firmly, with a frown on her lips at noticing Corrie reading something on the desk.

"Okay. I'm sorry. Now, where *did* I leave that darn phone?"

Back at the hotel, Corrie quickly wrote out the lines from memory, then stared at them thoughtfully. It seemed obvious Pendergast had copied a note or old document that mentioned the place where the attack on the cannibals would take place: the Christmas Mine. In the Griswell Mansion, she had seen a number of maps of the mining district, with each mine and tunnel marked and identified. It would be simple to find the location, and maybe even the layout, of this Christmas Mine.

This was interesting. This changed everything. She'd suspected the mercury-crazed miners had been hiding in some abandoned mine. If they were killed in a tunnel or shaft, their remains could still be there somewhere.

*The Christmas Mine*...if she recovered a few bone and hair samples from the remains, she could have them tested for mercury poisoning. Such a test was cheap and easy; you could even send away for a home kit. And if the tests were positive, it would be the final feather in her cap. She would have definitely solved the old murders and established a most unusual motivation.

She thought about her promise to Pendergast—to stay in the hotel, to abandon any attempt to find the person who'd shot at her and decapitated her dog. Well, she *had* abandoned the attempt. Pendergast shouldn't have withheld information from her—especially information of such crucial importance to her thesis.

She glanced out the window. The blizzard was still going strong. Since it was getting on toward Christmas Eve, everything was closed, and the town was almost completely deserted. Right now would be a perfect time to pay a little visit to the archives in the Griswell Mansion.

Corrie paused for a moment, then pocketed her small set of lock picks. The Griswell place would most likely have a period lock—no challenge at all.

Once again she bundled up and ventured out into the storm. Encouragingly, nobody except the snowplows was out and about as she made her way through the deserted streets. Some of the Christmas decorations, evergreen garlands and ribbons, had blown loose in the wind and were flapping and swinging forlornly from lampposts and street banners. Strings of bulbs had also come loose and were sputtering erratically. She couldn't see the outline of the mountains, but she could still hear, muffled by the snow, the hum and rumble of the lifts, which had been kept running despite all that had happened and the almost complete absence of skiers. Perhaps skiing was such an ingrained part of Roaring Fork culture that the lifts and snow-grooming equipment simply never stopped operating.

As she turned the corner of East Haddam, she suddenly had the impression someone was behind her. She spun around and peered into the murk, but could see nothing except swirling snow. She hesitated. It might have been a passerby, or perhaps her imagination. Still, Pendergast's warning echoed in her mind.

There was one way to check. She retraced her steps—still quite visible in the snow. And indeed: there were additional footprints. The footprints had apparently been tracing hers, but they had suddenly veered away and gone off into a private alley—at just about the point where she had spun around.

Corrie suddenly found her heart beating hard. Okay, someone *was* following her. Maybe. Was it the thug who'd been trying to drive her out of town? Of course it might also be coincidence, paired with her justified sense of paranoia.

"Screw this," she said out loud, turned back, and hurried down the street. Another corner and she found herself in front of the Griswell Mansion. The lock, as she figured, was old. It would be a simple matter to get inside.

But was the place alarmed?

A gust of wind buffeted her as she peered inside the door panes for signs of an alarm system. She couldn't see anything obvious like infrared sensors or motion detectors mounted in the corners; nor was the building posted with an alarm warning. The place had an air about it of neglect and penny pinching. Maybe no one felt the piles of paper inside had any value or needed to be protected.

Even if the place *was* alarmed, and she set it off, were the police really going to respond? Right now they had bigger fish to fry. And in a storm like this, with high winds, falling branches, and ice, alarms were probably going off all over town.

Looking around, she removed her gloves and quickly picked the lock. She slipped inside, shut the door, took a deep breath. No alarm, no blinking lights, nothing. Just the shudder of the wind and snow outside.

She rubbed her hands together to warm them. This was going to be a piece of cake.

## 55

Half an hour later, hunched over a pile of papers in a dim back room, Corrie had found what she needed. An old map showed her the location and layout of the Christmas Mine. According to the information she had dug up, the mine was a bust, one of the first to become played out and be abandoned, way back in 1875, and as far as she could tell never again reopened. That was probably why the crazed miners had used it as a home base.

She took another, more careful, look at the map. While the mine was high up on Smuggler's Wall, at nearly thirteen thousand feet in altitude, it was readily accessible by the web of old mining roads on the mountain, now used by four-wheelers in the summer and snowmobilers in the winter. The mine stood above a well-known complex of old structures situated in a natural bowl known as Smuggler's Cirque, which was a popular tourist

destination in the summertime. One of the buildings, by far the tallest, was famous for holding the
remains of the Ireland Pump Engine, supposedly
the largest pump in the world when it was constructed, which had been used to dewater the
mines as the shafts were dug below the water table.

The Christmas Mine would surely be sealed—
all the old mines and tunnels in Roaring Fork, Corrie had learned, had been bricked up or, in some
cases, plated with iron. The mine might be difficult
or even impossible to break into, especially considering the snow. But it was worth a try. She had
every reason to believe the remains of the cannibals would still be there, perhaps secreted away
someplace by the vigilantes who killed them.

As she looked over the papers, maps, and dia-
grams, she realized that—quite subconsciously—a
plan had already formed in her mind. She'd go up
to the mine, locate the bodies, and take her samples. And she'd do it now—while the routes out of
town were still impassable, and before Pendergast
could force her to return to New York.

But how to get up there, way up the side of a
mountain in a furious storm? Even as she posed
the question, she realized the answer. There were
snowmobiles up at the ski shed. She would simply
go up to The Heights, borrow a snowmobile…and
pay a quick visit to the old Christmas Mine.

And now really was the perfect time: Christmas Eve day, when ninety percent of the town had left and everyone else was hunkered down at home. Even if somebody *was* tailing her, they'd never follow her to the mine—not in weather like this. Just a brief reconnaissance up to the mountain and back…and then she'd hole up in the hotel until she could make arrangements to leave town.

It occurred to her that it wasn't just Kermode's thugs she should be aware of, but the weather as well. If anybody else would be crazy going out in this storm, then wasn't she acting a little crazy, too? She told herself she'd take it one step at a time. If the storm got too bad, or if she felt she was getting into a situation she couldn't handle, she'd abandon the recon and head back.

Pocketing the old map of the mine and another map of the overall mining district showing all the connecting tunnels, she made her way back to the Hotel Sebastian, keeping an eye out for the suspected stalker but seeing no sign. In her room she began to prepare for the task ahead. She packed her backpack with a small water bottle, sampling bags, headlamp with extra batteries, extra gloves and socks, matches, canteen, Mars Bars and Reese's Pieces, her lock-picking tools, a knife, Mace (which she carried everywhere), and her cell phone. She took another look at the Christmas

Mine map she'd liberated from the archives, noting with satisfaction that the underground courses of the tunnels were clearly delineated.

The hotel concierge was able to provide—most useful of all—a snowmobile route map of the surrounding mountains. She also managed to "borrow" from hotel maintenance a claw hammer, bolt cutter, and wrecking bar.

She bundled up, loaded her car, and headed down Main Street in the storm, windshield wipers slapping. The snow was lightening a bit, the wind dropping. The snowplows were still out in force—snow clearing was amazingly efficient in this town—but even so the storm had gotten ahead of the clearing and there were three to four inches of snow on most of the roads. Nevertheless, the Ford Explorer handled well. As she approached The Heights, she rehearsed what she would say to the guard on duty; but when she actually arrived at the gate she found it open and the guardhouse empty. And why not? The workers would want to be home on Christmas Eve—and who in their right mind would be out in this storm anyway?

The heated road beyond was not bad, even though the snow was overwhelming the ability of the heating system to keep up. She almost got stuck a few times. But she shifted into 4L and managed to keep going. At least on the way out it would be mostly downhill.

The clubhouse came into view through the blowing snow, its lights on, the big plate-glass windows casting an inviting yellow glow. But the parking lot was empty, and Corrie pulled up close to the side of the building, got out of the car. In a storm like this, she doubted anyone would be inside. Nevertheless, she didn't want any prying eyes observing her taking one of the snowmobiles from the ski shed. After stamping and brushing the snow off herself, she walked around to the front and tried the door.

Locked.

She peered in the little row of panes to the right of the door. Inside, the place was lit up and festooned with decorations. A gas fire burned merrily in a fireplace. But nobody could be seen.

Just to be safe, she walked around the rest of the building, staring through windows, the wind, though abating, still crying in her ears. It was the work of five slow, careful minutes to satisfy herself that there was no one home.

She headed back to the side of the building, ready to continue up toward the ski shed. As she walked across the parking lot, she noticed that the snow had almost ceased. The unpaved road leading to the shed would still be passable. She got into the Explorer, started the engine. Everything was going her way. She'd have her pick of snowmobiles to choose from...and she still had the key to the shed padlock.

But then, as she was pulling around the circular driveway to the clubhouse and back toward the main, heated road, she noticed a second set of tire tracks in the snow, lying on top of hers.

# 56

Coincidence? It was certainly possible. Corrie told herself that the tracks might be from someone in the development—after all, there were dozens of houses up there. Perhaps it was just some resident, hurrying home before the storm got worse. On the other hand, she'd been followed earlier, back in town. And why had the car pulled in to the parking lot? She felt a surge of apprehension and looked around, but there were no other vehicles in sight. She glanced at her watch: two o'clock. Three hours of daylight left.

The Explorer fishtailed up the road, Corrie gunning its engine. She skidded around the last bend and pulled the car up to the fence surrounding the shed. The snow had slacked off even further, but looking up she could see thick gray clouds that promised more on the way.

Keeping the car running, she double-checked

her backpack—all was there, in good order. She didn't have a snowmobile suit, but had put on practically all her layers of winter clothes, along with two pairs of gloves, a balaclava, and heavy Sorel snow boots.

She got out of the car and hefted the heavy backpack, slinging it over one shoulder. It was strangely still. Everything was bathed in a cold, gray light; the air was frosty, her breath condensing. It smelled like evergreens. The tree boughs were laden with snow and drooping, the roofline of the shed piled deep, the rows of icicles dull and cold in the half light.

She unlocked the padlock with her key and entered the shed, turning on the light. The snowmobiles were all there, neatly lined up, keys in the ignitions, helmets hung on a nearby pegboard. She walked down the line, looking them over, checking the gas gauges. While she had never driven a snowmobile, as a teenager back in Kansas she had spent a fair amount of time on dirt bikes, and the snowmobiles seemed to work the same way, with the throttle on the right handlebar and the brake on the left. It looked straightforward enough. She picked out the cleanest-looking one, made sure it had a full tank of gas, selected a helmet, and stowed her backpack in the under-seat storage compartment.

Stepping over to the main door of the shed, she unlocked it from the inside and slid it open with difficulty. Snow piled up against the door avalanched inside. Starting the snowmobile, she sat on the seat and looked over the controls, throttle, brakes, and shift, then turned the lights on and off a few times.

Despite the fear and anxiety that gnawed at her, she couldn't help but feel a sense of excitement welling up. She should be looking at this as a sort of adventure. If someone was following her, would they follow her up the mountain? It seemed unlikely.

She put on the helmet and gave the machine a little gas, edging it cautiously through the doorway. Once outside she tried to shut the shed door, but the snow that had fallen inside prevented it from sliding.

It occurred to her that she was, in fact, stealing a snowmobile, which was probably a felony. But with the holiday, the snowstorm, and the police occupied with the arsonist, the chances of getting caught seemed nil. According to the map, the Christmas Mine entrance was about three miles away, up old mining roads that were now established snowmobile trails. If she proceeded cautiously, she could be there in, say, ten to fifteen minutes. Of course, a lot of things could go wrong.

Maybe she wouldn't be able to break into the tunnel, or would find it caved in; perhaps the remains would have been buried or hidden. Or—God forbid—she might find Pendergast there ahead of her. After all, she'd indirectly learned the location from him. But at least she'd feel she'd done her best. Regardless, she could be up and back in less than an hour.

She took a long look at her maps, trying to memorize the route, then tucked them into the glove box below the small windshield. She eased the machine farther into the snow, where it began to sink alarmingly. With a little more gas, however, it rode higher and more securely. Gingerly goosing the throttle, she accelerated up the service road that, according to her map, joined the network of snowmobile trails into the mountains, eventually leading to the old mining road that would take her to Smuggler's Cirque and the mine entrance above.

Pretty soon she had the feel of the controls and was moving at a good clip, twenty miles per hour, the machine throwing up a wake of snow behind. It was unexpectedly exhilarating, flashing through the spruce trees, the frosty air rushing by, magnificent mountain peaks all around. She was plenty warm in her many layers.

As she attained the ridge, she came to the main

snowmobile trail, conveniently marked with a sign. The heavy snow had obliterated any snowmobile tracks that might have been there, but the road cut itself was clearly visible as it went up Maroon Ridge, marked by tall posts with Day-Glo orange cards.

She continued on. As the altitude increased, the trees became smaller and stunted, some mere lumps of snow—and then, quite suddenly, she emerged above the tree line. She stopped to check her map—all good. The views were outstanding: Roaring Fork itself was spread out in the valley below, a miniature village, doll-like, cloaked in white. To her left, the ski area rose into the mountains in ribbons of white trails. The lifts were still running, but only the most hard-core skiers seemed to be out. Behind her stood the awe-inspiring peaks of the Continental Divide, fourteen thousand feet high.

According to the map, she was already halfway to the area of old mining buildings in the cirque.

She suddenly heard a distant buzzing sound coming up from below and halted to listen better. It was a snowmobile engine. Looking back down the route she had come up, she caught a glimpse of a black dot coming around one of the hairpin turns of the trail before vanishing into the trees.

She felt a wave of panic. Someone *was* following

her. Or could it be just another snowmobiler? No—coincidence was one thing, but this was the third time that day she'd had the feeling she was being followed. It *had* to be the stalker—Kermode's hired thug, she was certain, the person who had menaced her, killed her dog. At the thought a fresh surge of fear swept over her. This wasn't an adventure. This was sheer foolhardiness: she'd placed herself in a vulnerable position, alone on the mountain, far from help.

She immediately took out her cell phone. No service.

The sound of the engine grew rapidly. She didn't have much time.

Her mind raced. She couldn't turn around and go back—there was only one trail down, unless she went straight down the almost vertical ridge. She couldn't pull off the trail and hide—the machine made such obvious tracks. And the snow was too deep for her to abandon the snowmobile and go on foot.

It began to sink in that she had put herself in real trouble. The best thing, she decided, would be to continue on up to the mine, break in if she could, and get away from the stalker in there. She had a map of the Christmas Mine and he surely did not.

Even as she started up the trail again, she saw the snowmobile come around the final bend before the tree line, accelerating toward her.

Goosing the throttle, she tore up the trail, notching the snowmobile up to thirty miles an hour, then thirty-five, then forty. The machine practically flew, an almost sheer cliff to one side of the trail, on the other a steep wall of snow. In another five minutes the trail came over the lip of a hanging valley and she found herself in the old mining complex, nestled in the broad hollow marked on the map as Smuggler's Cirque: surrounded by high ridges, with derelict mining buildings scattered about, their sagging rooflines mantled with snow, some mere piles of broken boards. She paused briefly to orient herself with the map. The Christmas Mine was higher still, on a steep slope halfway up the mountainside, directly above the old buildings. Smuggler's Wall. Map in hand, she squinted upward in the gray light, locating the entrance. The official snowmobile trail ended here, but the map showed an old mining road, still extant, that led up to the mine. As she looked at the steep wall of the cirque she made out the road cut, switchbacking up in a series of terrifying hairpin turns, with heavy drifts of snow lying across it.

Again, she could hear the snowmobile closing in behind her.

Stuffing away the map, she gunned the engine, riding past the old buildings and heading for the far side of the bowl, where the slope climbed upward again. She was surprised to see fresh snowmobile tracks among the buildings, somewhat snowed over but clearly made earlier in the day.

She reached the base of the road cut. This was going to be scary. But even as she contemplated the almost vertical wall above her, the sound of the pursuing snowmobile grew louder and she turned to see it coming over the rim of the cirque, not half a mile away.

Revving the throttle, she started up the trail, keeping as much to the inside edge as she could, blasting through drifts and fins of snow. The first hairpin turn was so steep and narrow, it just about stopped her heart. As she crawled around it, decelerating sharply, she almost became stuck in a drift and her efforts to get loose sent snow cascading down in a plume, the snowmobile tipping. She gunned it hard, spewing snow, and just managed to get back on the track. She paused, breathing hard, terrified by the yawning white space below her. It occurred to her that the avalanche danger on this steep slope must be high. She could see her pursuer was now riding through the old mining complex, following in her tracks. He was close enough for her to see the rifle slung over his shoulder.

She realized she had allowed herself to become

cornered on the mountain. The road ended at the mine, and there was nothing but vertical cliffs above. And a killer below.

She made it past another half a dozen terrifying turns, driving recklessly through the deep snow, not letting the machine stop and settle. She finally reached the entrance to the Christmas Mine, marked by a rickety trestle and a square opening of massive, rotten timbers. She pulled the snowmobile right up to the opening, tore off her helmet, pulled up the seat, and hauled out her backpack. As soon as the engine was off she could hear the roar of the other snowmobile, much closer.

The door was set back into the tunnel about ten feet, which meant it was not drifted up with snow. The entrance had a rusted door set into a plate of riveted steel, deeply pitted by age, fixed with a heavy, ancient padlock.

The engine sound got louder. Corrie began to panic. She stripped off her gloves, grabbed her lock-pick tools, and tried to insert a bump key, but it was immediately apparent the lock was frozen with rust and unpickable. Even as she fumbled around she could hear the approaching roar of the snowmobile.

She grabbed the bolt cutters from her pack, but they were not heavy enough for the jaws to fit over the thick bar of the lock. They did, however, fit partway across the hasp. She jammed the jaws of the cutter over the hasp and drew down hard, the jaws closing with much effort. Taking the hammer, she gave the partially cut hasp a tremendous blow, then another, bending it enough for her to cut it the rest of the way through. Even so, everything was so solid with rust she had to pound the pieces with the hammer to shake them loose.

She threw herself against the iron door but it hardly budged, letting out a great screech of protesting metal.

The approaching snowmobile engine gave a sudden roar; she saw a flurry of snow; and then it appeared at the mouth of the mine, driven by a man in a black helmet and puffy snowsuit. He rose from the machine, undoing his helmet and unshipping his rifle at the same time.

With an involuntary cry she threw herself against the door, almost dislocating her shoulder in the process, and with a loud *scree* it budged open just enough for her to squeeze through. Grabbing her backpack she rammed herself through the opening, then turned and threw herself back against the iron, thrusting the door shut again—just as there came a deafening boom from the rifle, with a round clanging off the door and ricocheting into the mine, sending up sparks as it splintered on the rocks behind her.

A second push shut the door completely. Bracing against it, Corrie fumbled out her headlamp, pulled it on over her balaclava, and turned it on. A pair of rounds smacked into the door with a deafening noise, but it was made of thick iron and they left only dents. And now she felt a person slam into the door on the other side, pushing it open a few inches. Once more, she threw herself against it hard, slamming it shut again, and then she yanked the wrecking bar out of her pack and wedged it under the door edge, giving it a blow with a hammer, then another blow, until it held, even as she felt the man on the other side shouldering the door, trying to force it open.

He pounded furiously on the door, the bar sliding back just a little. It would hold only so long. She cast about. Broken rocks lay everywhere, along with old pieces of iron and ancient equipment.

*Wham!* The man was now throwing himself against the door, jarring the wrecking bar loose.

She hammered it back into place and began piling rocks and iron against the door. Down the tracks she could see an old ore cart, and with great difficulty she got it moving, levering it off the tracks so that it tipped over against the door. She rolled some larger rocks in place. Now the door would hold—at least for a while. She sagged against the rock wall, panting hard, trying to recover her breath and figure out what to do next.

More shots were fired against the door, producing a series of deafening clangs in the enclosed space and causing her to jump. Grabbing her pack, she turned and retreated down the tunnel. For the first time she could see the space she was in. The air was cold, but not so cold as outside, and it smelled of mold and iron. The tunnel ran straight ahead through solid rock, supported every ten feet or so by heavy wooden timbers. A set of ore tracks led into darkness.

She started down the tunnel at a jog. The sounds of the stalker trying to break in echoed down the passageway. Corrie came to a cross tunnel, turned in to it, and then, at a cul-de-sac, finally had to stop to rest. And think.

She had bought some time, but eventually the man would manage to wedge open the door. The old map she had indicated that a section of the Christmas Mine connected to other, lower mines, forming a maze of tunnels and shafts—assuming they were all still passable. If she could reach them, find her way out...but what good would that do? The snow outside was several feet deep, impossible to walk through. There was only one way off the mountain—via snowmobile.

And nobody knew she was up here. She hadn't

told anyone. *My God*, she thought, *what a mess I've gotten myself into*.

At that moment she heard a shriek of metal, then another. She looked around the corner of the passage, back toward the distant door, and saw a wedge of light. Another screech and the wedge grew wider.

The man was prying open the door. She made out a shoulder, a cruel-looking face—and an arm with a handgun.

She ran as the shot was fired.

## 57

The shots came screaming past her, sparking off the stone floor of the main tunnel ahead, the ricocheting fragments whining away like bees. She ran in terror, leaping the old car rails, expecting any moment to feel a round slam into her back and knock her to the ground. The tunnel ended in another cross tunnel, a wall of rock. Another fusillade of shots came booming down the tunnel, smacking the timbers above her with a burst of splinters and dust, flashing against the rock face before her.

She skidded around the corner and kept running. She desperately tried to remember the layout of tunnels she'd seen on the map, but her mind had shut down in panic. The shots had temporarily stopped after she turned the corner, and now she saw another, much narrower tunnel going off to the right, sloping steeply downward in a series of crude steps like a gigantic stone staircase. She flew down them, two steps at a time, to find herself in a lower tunnel, a trickle of water flowing along its bottom. It was warmer here, maybe even above freezing, and she was sweating in her bulky winter outfit.

"You can't escape," came a yell from behind. "It's all dead ends in here!"

*Bullshit*, she told herself with a bravado she didn't feel, *I've got a map.*

Another pair of shots came, but they struck to the rear and she felt the spray of rock pepper her jacket. She looked around. Another tunnel branched off to the left—also headed downward at an even steeper angle, the steps slick with water, with a rotting rope strung along as a kind of banister.

She took it, running at a reckless speed. Partway down she slipped and grasped frantically for the rope, which came apart like dust in her hands. She pitched forward, breaking her fall with her shoulder and rolling hard downhill, finally crashing into the bottom and sprawling on the wet stone. Her bulky winter clothes and woolen hat cushioned the fall—but not by much.

She staggered to her feet, her limbs aching, a burning cut on her forehead. She was in a broad, low seam, barely five feet high, with pillars of rock holding up the ceiling. It extended in two dimensions as far as the beam of her headlamp could penetrate. She ran at a crouch, zigzagging past the pillars, briefly shining the light ahead to see where she was going, and then turning it off again and running onward into the dark. She did this two more times, and then on the third time, while the light was off, she took a sharp right angle, slowing down and moving as silently as she could.

The flashlight beam of her pursuer lanced through the darkness behind her, wobbling as he ran, probing this way and that. She moved behind a pillar and pressed herself against it, waiting. He was now off course and heading past her. In a moment she could see him slow down and look around, a pistol in his right hand. Clearly, he realized he had lost her.

She slipped from behind the pillar and went back the way they had come, then veered off into a new passage, creeping ahead in the dark, not daring to turn on the headlight but rather feeling her way with her hands. She blinked, wiped her eyes—blood was running freely from the cut on her forehead. After a while she saw a flicker of light behind her and realized he, too, had turned around and was coming back. She hurried faster now, pulling the headlamp off her head and holding it down low, just flicking the beam on for a second to see ahead so she could move faster.

Bad move: a pair of shots boomed out and then she heard him running, his light beam flashing around, illuminating her. Another shot. But the idiot was firing while running, which only worked on TV, and she took the opportunity to sprint like mad.

She almost didn't see it in time—a vertical shaft yawning directly ahead. She stopped so fast that she slid on her side like a base runner. Even so, one leg went over the edge. She scrambled and clawed her way back from the gaping chasm with an involuntary yelp of fear. An iron catwalk crossed the chasm, but it looked rotten as hell. An iron ladder went down into the blackness—also corroded.

It was either one or the other.

She chose the ladder, grasped the rung, and swung around, her foot finding a rung below, then another. The thing groaned and shook under her weight. A stale draft of still-warmer air came up from below. No going back now: she started down as fast as she could, the entire ladder shuddering and swaying. There was a loud snapping sound, then a second, as bolts holding the ladder to the stone broke free, and the ladder jerked violently down. She clung to it, tensing for a horrible, fatal fall—but with a screech of metal it came to an uneasy stop.

A light shone down from above, along with the

gleam of a gun. Grabbing the edges of the ladder with her gloves, and taking her feet from the rungs and pressing them against the vertical sides of the ladder, she slid down—faster, faster, the rust coming off in a stream, until she hit the bottom hard, tumbling away, just as the shots came, gouging holes into the stone floor where she had just been.

Damn, she'd done something to her ankle.

Did he have the guts to descend the precarious ladder? Right at its base was a pile of rotting canvas and a stack of old planking. Limping over, she half dragged, half hauled the canvas underneath the ladder. The material was dry as dust and practically falling apart in her hands. The ladder was shaking now, groaning—her pursuer was descending.

Which meant he wouldn't be able to fire his weapon.

She shoved the heap of canvas against the base of the ladder and piled on the planks, pulled out her lighter, and lit the makeshift pyre. It was so desiccated, it went up like a bomb.

"Burn in hell!" she screamed as she dragged herself down the tunnel, trying to ignore the pain in her ankle. God, it felt like it was broken. Limping, the pain excruciating, she continued along another tunnel and then another, taking turns at random, now completely lost. Clearly, though, she was well out of the Christmas Mine and deep into the labyrinths of the Sally Goodin or one of the other, lower mines that honeycombed the mountain. She could hear sounds from behind, which seemed to indicate her pursuer had somehow gotten past the fire, or perhaps he'd just waited until it burned out.

Ahead, her headlight disclosed a cave-in, a bunch of jagged boulders strewn about on the floor of the tunnel, with some crossed beams lying atop. A narrow path, however, could be seen twisting through the rubble. Cold air streamed down from above. She climbed painfully over the piles of rock and broken timbers, then looked up. A crack disclosed a piece of dark, gray sky—but that was all. There was no way out, no way to reach it.

She continued picking her way through the rubble and came at last to a flat area on the far side. Suddenly, she heard a buzzing noise. She stopped, shone her light ahead, then gave a little cry and shrank back. Nestled among the fallen boulders, blocking the way, was a huge, ropy mass of hibernating rattlesnakes. They were half asleep in the cold air, but the twisted clump still moved in a kind of horrible slow motion, pulsing, rotating, almost like a single entity. Some were awake enough to be rattling in warning.

She shone the light around and saw that other rattlers were coiled up into the various small spa-

ces between the rocks. They were everywhere—
seemingly hundreds of them. Even—she realized
with a sickening sensation—behind her.

Suddenly the boom of the gun sounded, and she
felt one hand jerk in response to an impact. Instinctively, she leapt over the mass of snakes, scrambling
among the boulders, the pain in her ankle even
more excruciating. Another shot followed, then
another, and she took refuge behind a large boulder—right next to a fat, sleeping rattler. There
were some stones nearby—this was an opportunity she couldn't pass up. She picked up a heavy
stone in her right hand—something was wrong
with her left hand but she'd worry about that
later—and jumped onto the large boulder, letting
the rock fly with great violence at the main mass
of snakes.

The rock smacked into the bolus of reptiles,
and the reaction was immediate and terrifying—an
eruption of buzzing that filled the tunnel with a
sound like a thousand bees, accompanied by an explosive writhing of movement. The lazy mass of
snakes suddenly turned into a whirlwind, coiling,
striking, sliding off in all directions—several coming straight at her.

She scrambled backward. Another shot struck
the rocks around her, ricocheting about, and she
fell in between two boulders. The buzzing filled

the cave like a vast humming dynamo. She got up and ran, dragging her injured ankle. Half a dozen snakes struck at her and she jumped away. Two got hung up by their fangs on the thick fabric of her snow pants. With a scream she whacked them off, fairly dancing among the striking snakes, as another pair of shots whined among the rocks. A few moments later she was beyond the furious mass, limping away, until she could stand it no longer and finally collapsed in pain. She lay there, gasping, the tears running down her face. Her ankle was certainly broken. And then there was her hand: even in the dark she could see that her glove was soaked with warm liquid. She removed it gingerly, held her hand up to the light, and was amazed by what she saw: her pinkie finger was dangling by a mere thread of skin, blood welling out.

"Fuck!"

She shook off the useless finger, almost passing out from a combination of dizziness and disgust. Unwrapping her scarf, she cut a strip of it off with a knife and wrapped it around her hand and the stump of the finger, tightening it to stem the flow of blood.

*My finger. Jesus.* In a dream, almost in shock from disbelief, she pulled the glove back over the wadded scarf as best she could to hold it in place. As she did so, she heard a shout from behind, then a scream, and the wild firing of the gun. But this time the shots were not directed at her. A rattling noise filled the tunnel with an unholy sound of reptilian fury. More shots and yells.

She had to keep going—eventually he would get through the snakes, unless by great good luck he was bitten. She hauled herself to her feet, fighting the dizziness and, now, a growing nausea. Christ, she needed a crutch, but there was nothing at hand. Limping badly, she continued along the tunnel, which descended steadily for some distance, passing several crosscuts. In time she came to a small side alcove, blocked up with rocks that formed a makeshift wall, now half collapsed. A place to hide? She dragged herself to it, pulled out some more stones, and looked in.

The beam of light fell upon a horde of rats, which erupted in excitement and went scurrying every which way with a chorus of squeals—exposing the remains of several bodies.

She stared with something like stupefaction. There were four in all, laid out in a row of skeletons—or rather, partial mummies, as they still had dried flesh on their bones, rotten clothes, old boots, and hair. Their dried-up heads were tilted back, their jaws wide open as if screaming, exposing mummified mouths full of black, rotten teeth.

As she crawled in to look more closely, she

could see all the signs. They had been shot—she could see numerous holes in their skulls, many other bones broken by what looked like bullet impacts. A firing-squad attack far in excess of what would have been necessary to kill them—a display of violent, homicidal fury.

*The four mercury-crazed miners.* They'd been killed somewhere in this tunnel system, probably the Christmas Mine, and their bodies dragged down here and hidden.

Near the corpses lay a long, heavy stick—a cudgel, really, perhaps carried by one of the killers. It would do for an improvised crutch.

As quickly as she could without compromising the integrity of the evidence, Corrie took off her knapsack, removed the specimen bags, and laid them out. Removing the glove from her good hand and dropping to her knees, she crawled from body to body, taking from each a sample of hair, a fragment of papery dried flesh, and a small bone. She sealed them in the bags and put them back in her backpack. She photographed the bodies with her cell phone, then put the pack back on.

With a gasp of pain, she managed to get to her feet, leaning on the cudgel. Now she had to figure out where she was and find her way out—without getting shot in the process.

As if on cue, she could hear, way back near the

cave-in, additional firing. She almost imagined she could hear the buzzing of the rattlers, a soft hiss in the distance: pleasant, like the ocean.

She made her way farther down the tunnel, gasping with pain, trying to find some distinctive landmark that she could in turn locate on the map, and thus orient herself toward an exit. And to her great relief, ten minutes of slow wandering brought her to a junction of tunnels—three horizontal ones and a vertical shaft coming together. She collapsed, took out the map, and scrutinized it.

And there it was.

*Thank God. A break, at last.* According to the map, she was now in the Sally Goodin Mine, not far from a lower exit. A dewatering tunnel, containing a large pipe, lay a few hundred yards from where she was, and it led directly to the Ireland Pump Engine, in the cirque below the Christmas Mine. Folding up the map, she tucked it away and took the indicated tunnel.

Sure enough: after a few more minutes of excruciating travel she finally came to a low stream of water that covered the rock floor, and then to the opening of an ancient pipe, nearly three feet in diameter, that ran along one side of the tunnel. She stooped and crawled into its mouth, grateful to be off her feet, and began making her way down its length.

It was dark and close, and her bulky suit kept catching and tearing on rusted areas of the pipe. But the going was relatively clear, with no cave-ins or narrowings. Within ten minutes she could feel the flow of air growing colder and fresher, and she fancied she could smell snow. In another few minutes she made out the dimmest of lights ahead, and soon she emerged, first through a shunt, and then a partially open wooden door, into a dark, dingy space, thick with rusted pipes and giant valves. It was now very cold, and a dim gray light filtered in through gaps and cracks in the wooden ceiling. She figured she must be somewhere in the depths of the old Ireland Pump building.

Giving a sob of relief, she looked around and saw an old staircase leading upward. As she limped toward it, she saw, out of the corner of her eye, a dark, moving shape. A human shape—coming at her fast.

*He's gotten through the snakes. Somehow he's gotten through the snakes and flanked me...*

One arm wrapped around her waist; another around her neck, covering her mouth, stifling her scream and pulling her head back. Then a face appeared, in the dimness—a face that was just recognizable.

*...Ted.*

"You!" Ted cried, suddenly loosening his grip

and uncovering her mouth. "It's *you*! What on earth are you doing here—?"

"Oh, my God," she gasped, "Ted! There's a man. Back there...he tried to kill me..." She gasped, unable to continue, as he held her.

"You're bleeding!" he exclaimed.

She started to sob. "Thank God, Ted, thank God you're here. He's got a gun..."

Ted's grip tightened again as he held her up. "He's fucked if he comes here," he said quietly, in a dark voice.

She sobbed, gasped. "I'm so glad to see you...My finger's been shot off...I need to get to a hospital..."

He continued to hold her. "I'm going to take care of you."

# 58

At half past two o'clock in the afternoon, a man wearing an enormous greatcoat, bundled up in gloves, silk scarf, and a trilby hat, carrying a bottle of champagne, rang the doorbell of the large Italianate mansion at 16 Mountain Trail Road. A maid, dressed in a starched black uniform with a white apron and cap, answered the door.

"May I help—?" she began, but the man came striding in with a cheery Christmas greeting, overriding her voice. He handed her his hat, scarf, and coat, revealing himself to be dressed in a severe black suit.

"The storm seems to be letting up!" he said to no one in particular, his voice loud in the echoing marble foyer. "My goodness, it's cold out there!"

"The family is at Christmas Eve dinner—" the maid began again, but the man in black didn't seem to hear as he strode across the foyer and past the great curving staircase into the long hall leading to the dining room, the maid hurrying after him, burdened with his outerwear. "Your name, please, sir?"

But the man paid no attention.

"I'm supposed to announce you—"

She could hardly keep up with him. He arrived at the great double doors to the dining room, grasped the handles, and threw them open, to reveal the entire family, a dozen or more, seated around an elegant table gleaming with silver and crystal, the remains of a suckling pig on a giant platter in the center. The pig had been reduced to a rib cage surrounded by greasy gobbets and bones, the only thing remaining intact being its head, with its crispy curled ears and the requisite baked apple in its mouth.

Everyone at the table stared at the man in surprise.

"I tried to—" the maid began, but the gentleman in black interrupted her as he held up the bottle of champagne.

"A bottle of Perrier-Jouët Fleur de Champagne and a Merry Christmas to each and every one of you!" he announced.

A shocked silence. And then Henry Montebello, sitting at the head of the table, rose. "What is the meaning of this interruption?" His eyes narrowed. "You—you're that FBI agent."

"Indeed I am. Aloysius Pendergast, at your service! I'm making the rounds of all my friends, bringing season's greetings and gifts of cheer!" He sat down in the only empty chair at the table.

"Excuse me," Montebello said coldly. "That chair is reserved for Mrs. Kermode, who should be here momentarily."

"Well, Mrs. Kermode's not here yet, and I am." The man plunked the champagne down on the table. "Shall we open it?"

Montebello's patrician features hardened. "I don't know who you think you are, sir, bursting into a private family dinner like this. But I must ask you to leave this house at once."

The agent paused, swaying slightly in the chair, a hurt expression gathering on his face. "If you're not going to open the champagne, fine, but don't send me away without a little glass of *something*." He reached over the table and picked up a half-full bottle of wine, examining the label. "Hmmm. A 2000 Castle's Leap Cabernet."

"What are you doing?" Montebello snapped. "Put that down and leave at once, or I shall call the police!"

Ignoring this, the man plucked a nearby glass off the table, poured a measure of the wine, and made a huge production of swirling it about, sticking his nose in the glass, sipping, noisily drawing in air, puffing his cheeks, sipping again. He put the glass down. "Some good berry notes, but no body and a short finish. Dull, I'm afraid; very dull. What sort of wine is this to serve at a Christmas Eve dinner? Are we but barbarians, Squire Montebello? Philistines?"

"Lottie, call nine-one-one. Report a home invasion."

"Ah, but I was invited in," said Pendergast. He turned to the maid. "Wasn't I, dear?"

"But I just opened the door—"

"And what is more," Montebello said, his voice crackling with fury as the rest of the family looked on with blank consternation, "you are *drunk!*"

In that moment, as if on cue, a cook entered from the kitchen, flanked by attendants, carrying a huge flambé, the flames leaping up from the silver server.

"Cherries jubilee!" Pendergast cried, jumping to his feet. "How marvelous!" He surged forward. "It's too heavy for you—let me help. That fire could be dangerous—especially here, in Roaring Fork!"

The cook, alarmed at the drunken man coming at her, took a step backward, but she was too slow. The FBI agent seized the great flaming platter; there was a sudden moment of imbalance; and then it overturned, the platter, cherries, ice cream, and burning brandy all crashing to the table and splattering over the remains of the pig.

"Fire! Fire!" Pendergast cried, aghast as the flames leapt up, his face a mixture of dismay and panic. "This is dreadful! Run! Everyone outside!"

A chorus of cries and shrieks went up around the table as everyone scrambled backward, knocking over chairs, spilling wine.

"Out, quickly!" shouted Pendergast. "Pull the alarm! The house is burning down! We'll be burned alive *just like the others!*"

The sound of terror in his voice was infectious. There was instant pandemonium. A smoke alarm went off, which only increased the mindless panic to get out, to get away at all costs from the fire. In mere seconds the diners, cook, and wait staff had all cleared the room, some pushing others away in their panic, and stampeded down the hall and across the foyer. One after another, they burst out the front door and into the night. The man in black was left alone in the house.

With sudden calm, he reached out, picked up an enormous gravy boat, and poured it over the alcohol flames, which were largely sputtering out anyway due to the melting ice cream and juices of the roasted carcass. A dash of wine from the bottle of inferior Cabernet completed the fire suppression. And then, with great aplomb and rapid efficiency of movement, he strode through the dining room, into the living room, and through it to a series of formally decorated rooms in the back, where Henry Montebello maintained his home legal office. There, Pendergast went straight to a cluster of filing cabinets. Perusing the labels on the front of each, he chose one, jimmied it open with a swift, sure motion, flipped through the papers, removed a fat accordion file, shut the cabinet, and carried the file back through the house to the front hall, plucking his bottle of champagne from the dining table in the process. In the front hall, he retrieved his greatcoat, scarf, hat, and gloves from where the maid had dumped them on the floor in her panic, secreted the file in the bulk of his coat, and stepped outside.

"Ladies and gentlemen," he announced, "the fire is out. It's safe to return now."

He strode off into the snowy afternoon, to his waiting car, and drove away.

# 59

Corrie felt Ted's powerful arms around her, holding her tight. The tightness of it made her feel safe. Relief flooded through her. She relaxed and took the pressure off her broken ankle as he continued to hold her up. "I'm going to take care of you," he said again, a little louder.

"I can't believe you're here," she sobbed. "That guy in the mine—he's a goon, hired by Kermode to run me out of town. He's the one who killed my dog, shot up my car…and now he's trying to kill me."

"Kermode," Ted said, his voice taking on an edge. "Figures. That bitch. I'm going to take care of her as well. Oh, God, will I take care of *that* bitch."

She was a little taken aback by his vehemence. "It's okay," she said. "God, I'm so light-headed. I think I need to lie down."

He didn't seem to have heard. The arms tightened even more.

"Ted, help me sit down..." She twisted a little because he was gripping her so hard it was beginning to hurt.

"Fucking bitch," he said, louder.

"Forget Kermode...Please, Ted—you're hurting me."

"Not talking about Kermode," he said. "Talking about you."

Corrie was sure she hadn't heard right. She was so dizzy. His arms tightened even more, to the point where she could hardly breathe. "Ted...That hurts. Please!"

"Is that all you've got to say for yourself, *bitch*?"

His voice was different now. Rough, hoarse.

"Ted...*what*?"

"*What, Ted, what?*" He mimicked her in a high, squeaky voice. "What a piece of work you are."

"What are you talking about?"

He squeezed so hard she cried out. "You like that? 'Cause you *know* what I'm talking about. Don't play the innocent little girl."

She struggled, but had almost no strength left. It was like a nightmare. Maybe it *was* a nightmare—maybe all of this was. "What are you saying?"

"What are you *say*-ing?" he mimicked.

She twisted, trying to break free, and he roughly spun her around, his face almost touching hers. The red, sweaty, misshapen, furious look that disfigured his face frightened her terribly. Both his eyes were bloodshot and leaking water. "Look at you," he said, lowering his voice, his lips warped with anger. "Leading me on, always teasing, first promising and then saying no, making a fool of me."

He gave her a sudden, violent squeeze with his powerful arms and she felt a rib crack under the pressure, pain lancing through her chest. She screamed, gasped, tried to speak, but he squeezed her again, forcing the air from her lungs. "The cocktease stops right here, *right now*." Spittle splattered her face. His lips, covered with a white film, were now brushing hers, his strangely foul breath washing over her like fumes from a rotting carcass.

She tried to breathe but couldn't. The combined pain of her ankle, her hand, and now her ribs was so excruciating she was unable to think straight. Fear and shock sent her heart, already racing from the pursuit through the mines, into overdrive. She had never seen a face so twisted and so terrifying. He was completely mad.

*Mad. Mad*...She didn't want to think of the ramifications of that—she would not, *could* not, follow that thought to its natural conclusion.

"Please—" she managed to gasp.

"Isn't this perfect? You just running into my arms like this. It's karma. It saves me all the usual kinds of preparation. The universe wants to teach you a lesson, and I'll be the teacher."

With that he threw her to the ground. She fell sprawling, with a cry of pain. He followed up with a kick to her injured ribs. The pain was unbearable and she cried out again, gasping for air. She felt the world swirling around, a strange ethereal floating sensation, pain and fright and disbelief overpowering all rational thought. A mist passed before her eyes, and consciousness shut down.

A long, dark time seemed to pass before another searing lance of pain brought her back to herself. She was still in the dingy room. Mere moments must have ticked by. Ted stood over her, his face still grotesquely distorted, eyes watering, lips covered with a sticky bloom of white. He reached down, seized her leg, spun her around, and began dragging her over the rough floorboards. She tried to scream but couldn't. Her head banged roughly against the floor and once again she felt herself on the verge of passing out.

He dragged her from the back room into the main section of the structure. The vast pump rose above her, a monstrous juggernaut of giant pipes and cylinders. The tall building creaked in the wind. He pulled her alongside a horizontal pipe, yanked off her gloves, took notice of her damaged hand—lips curling into a malevolent smile at the sight—then lifted the other arm and roughly cuffed her wrist to the pipe.

She lay there, gasping, swimming in and out of consciousness.

"Look at you now," he said, and spat on her.

As she struggled weakly to sit up, gasping in pain, part of her mind seemed to sense that this was happening, not to her, but to somebody else, and that she was watching from someplace far, far away. But there was another part of her mind—cold and relentless—that kept telling her exactly the opposite. This was real. Not only that—Ted was going to kill her.

Having shackled her to the pipe, Ted stepped back, crossed his arms, and surveyed his handiwork. The dark mist that hovered around her seemed to clear slightly, and she grew more aware of her surroundings. Old pieces of lumber littered the floor. A couple of kerosene lanterns were hung nearby, casting a feeble yellow light. In one corner was a cot with a sleeping bag on it, a box of handcuffs, a couple of balaclavas, and several large cans of kerosene. A table held several hunting knives, coils of rope, duct tape, a glass-stoppered vial with some clear liquid within, wadded piles of wool socks and heavy sweaters, all black. There was a gun, too, that looked to Corrie like a 9mm Beretta. Why would Ted have a handgun? Pegs on the walls held a dark leather coat and—perversely—assorted clown masks.

This seemed to be a hideout of some sort. A lair—*Ted's* lair. But why should he need one? And what were all these things for?

An old woodstove was burning to one side, the light shining between the cracks in the cast iron, throwing out heat. And now she noticed an odor in the air—a vile odor.

Ted pulled up a chair, turned it around, and straddled it, balancing his arms on the chair back. "So here we are," he said.

Something was terribly wrong with him. And yet the furious, violent, half-demented Ted of the last few minutes had changed. Now he was calm, mocking. Corrie swallowed, unable to take all this in. Maybe if she talked to him, she could learn what was troubling him, bring him back from whatever dark place he was in. But when she tried, all that came out was a pathetic garble of sound.

"When you first arrived in town, I thought maybe you were different from the others around here," he said. His voice had changed again, as if his rage had buried itself deep in ice. It was re-mote, cold, detached, like someone speaking to himself—or, perhaps, to a corpse. "Roaring Fork. Back when I was young, it used to be a real town. Now the ultra-high-net-worth bastards have taken over, the assholes with their social-climbing bimbos, the movie stars and CEOs and Masters of the Universe. Raping the mountains, clear-cutting the forests. Oh, they talk a good line about the environment! About going organic, about reducing their carbon footprints by buying offsets for their Gulfstream jets, about how 'green' their ten-thousand-square-foot mansions are. Mother*fuckers*. That's just sick. They're parasites on our society. Roaring Fork is where they all gather, flattering each other, grooming each other of their lice like fucking chimpanzees. And they treat the rest of us—the real folk, the native-born residents—as scum fit only to sweep their palaces and stroke their egos. There's only one cure for all that: fire. This place should burn. It *needs* to burn. And it *is* burning." He grinned, another fleshy, demonic distortion, frighteningly close to the face he'd shown her before.

Kerosene. Handcuffs. Rope. *It needs to burn.* Now, through the fog in her head, Corrie understood: Ted was the arsonist. A huge shudder of fear coursed through her, and she struggled against the cuffs despite the pain that racked her body.

But then, as soon as she started to struggle, she

stopped again. He cared for her—she knew he did. Somehow, she had to reach him.

"Ted," she croaked, managing to speak. "Ted. You know I'm not one of them."

"*Oh, yes you are!*" he screamed, leaning toward her, the white scum flying off his lips in droplets. As quickly as it had come, the icy, methodical veneer fell away, replaced by a mad, bestial rage. "You faked it for a while, but no—you're just like them! You're here for the same reasons they are: *money.*"

His eyes were so bloodshot, they were almost red. His hands were trembling with rage. His whole body was trembling. And his voice was so strange, so different. Looking at him was like looking into the maw of hell. It was so awful, so inhuman an expression, Corrie had to avert her eyes.

"But I don't have any money," she said.

"Exactly! Why are you here? To find some rich asshole. *I* wasn't rich enough for you! That's why you *played* with me. Leading me on the way you did."

"No, no, that wasn't it at all…"

"*Shut* the *fuck* up!" he screamed at a larynx-shredding volume, so loud that Corrie felt her eardrums tremble at the pressure.

And then, just as abruptly as it had left, the icy control returned. The fluctuation—from homicidal, brutish, barely controlled rants to a cold and calculating distance—was unbearable. "You should be grateful," he said, turning away, sounding for a minute like the Ted of old. "I have conferred wisdom onto you. Now you understand. The others—the others that I've taught—they learned nothing."

Then, suddenly, he spun back, staring at her with a hideous, speculative grin. "You ever read Robert Frost?"

Corrie couldn't bring herself to speak.

He began to recite:

> *Some say the world will end in fire;*
> *Some say in ice.*
> *From what I've tasted of desire*
> *I hold with those who favor fire.*

He reached out, grasped a long, dry stick of old lumber from the many that littered the floor, and used the end of it to toggle the latch on the woodstove door open. The flames inside threw a flickering yellow light about the room. He shoved the stick into the fire and waited.

"Ted, *please.*" Corrie took a deep breath. "You don't have to do this."

He began to whistle a tuneless melody.

"We're friends. I didn't reject you." She sobbed

a moment, gathered her wits as best she could. "I just didn't want to rush things, that's all..."

"Good. That's very good. I haven't rejected you, either. And—I won't rush things. We'll just let nature take its course."

He withdrew the stick, the end burning brightly now, dropping sparks. His eyes, reflecting the dancing light of the fire, rolled slowly toward her, their bloodshot whites shockingly large. And Corrie, looking from him to the burning brand and back again, realized what was about to happen.

"Oh, my God!" she said, voice rising into a shriek. "Please don't. *Ted!*"

He took a step toward her, waving the burning stick before her face. Another step closer. Corrie could feel the heat of the flaming brand. "No," was all she could manage.

For a minute, he just stared at her, the stick sparking and glowing in his hand. And when he spoke, his voice was so quiet, so controlled, it nearly drove her mad.

"It's time to burn," he said simply.

# 60

Pendergast arrived in his office in the basement of the police station and placed the accordion file on his desk. It contained the documents he had earlier sought in the town's public records office but which had, according to the archivist, mysteriously disappeared some years back. As he expected, he found them—or copies of them—in the filing cabinet in the home office of Henry Montebello, the architect who had prepared them in the first place. The file contained all the records relating to the original development of The Heights—documents that, by law, were supposed to be a matter of public record: plats, surveys, permit applications, subdivision maps, and terrain management plans.

Delving into the accordion file, Pendergast removed several manila folders and laid them out in rows, their tabs lined up. He knew exactly what he was looking for. The first documents he perused involved the original survey of the land, done in the mid-1970s, with corresponding photographs. They included a detailed topographic survey of the terrain, along with a sheaf of photos depicting exactly how the valley and ridges looked before the development began.

It was most revealing.

The original valley had been much narrower and tighter, almost a ravine. Along its length, carved into a benchland a hundred feet above the stream known as Silver Queen Creek, stood the remains of an extensive ore-processing complex first built by the Staffords in the 1870s—the fountainhead of much of their wealth. The first building to be erected housed the "sampler" operation, to test the richness of the ore as it came from the mine; next came a much larger "concentrator" building, containing three steam-powered stamp mills, which crushed the ore and concentrated the silver tenfold; and finally, the smelter itself. All three operations generated tailings, or waste piles of rock, and those tailings were clearly visible on the survey as enormous piles and heaps of rubble and grit. The tailings from all of the operations contained toxic minerals and compounds that leached out into the water table. But it was the last set of tailings—from the smelter—that were truly deadly.

The Stafford smelter in Roaring Fork used the

Washoe amalgamation process. In the smelter, the crushed, concentrated ore was further ground up into a paste, and various chemicals were added... including sixty pounds of mercury for each ton of ore concentrate processed. The mercury dissolved the silver—amalgamated with it—and the resulting heavy paste settled to the bottom of the vat, with the waste slurry coming off the top to be dumped. The silver was recovered by heating the amalgam in a retort and driving off the mercury, which was recaptured through condensation, leaving behind crude silver.

The process was not efficient. About two percent of the mercury was lost in each run. That mercury had to end up somewhere, and that somewhere was in the vast tailings dumped into the valley. Pendergast did a quick mental calculation: a two percent loss equaled about a pound of mercury for each ton of concentrate processed. The smelter processed a hundred tons of concentrate a day. By inference, that meant a hundred pounds of mercury had been dumped into the environment on a daily basis—over the nearly two decades during which the smelter operated. Mercury was an exceedingly toxic, pernicious substance, which over time could cause severe and permanent brain damage in people who were exposed to it—especially in children and, to an even greater extent, to the unborn.

It all added up to one thing: The Heights—or at least, the portion of the development that had been erected in the valley—was essentially sitting atop a large Superfund site, with a toxic aquifer underneath.

As he replaced the initial documents, everything came together in Pendergast's mind. He understood everything with great clarity—everything—including the arson attacks.

Moving more rapidly now, Pendergast glanced through documents relating to the early development itself. The terrain management plan called for using the vast tailing piles to fill the narrow ravine and create the broad, attractive valley floor that existed today. The clubhouse was built just downstream from where the old smelter had been, and a dozen large homes were situated within the valley. Henry Montebello, the master architect, had been in charge of it all: the demolishment of the smelter ruins, the terrain alterations, the spreading of tailings into a nice broad, level area for the lower development and the clubhouse. And his sister-in-law, Mrs. Kermode, had also been an integral player.

Interesting, Pendergast thought, that Montebello's mansion was on the far side of town, and that Kermode's own home was built high up on the ridge, far from the zone of contamination.

They, and the other members of the Stafford family who were behind the development of The Heights, must have known about the mercury. It occurred to him that the real reason they were building a new clubhouse and spa—which had seemed the very essence of needless indulgence—and situating it on the old Boot Hill cemetery was, in fact, to get it out of the area of contamination.

Pendergast moved from one manila folder to the next, paging through documents relating to the original subdivisions and association planning. The lots were large—minimum two-acre zoning—and as a result there was no community water system: each property had its own well. Those houses situated in the valley floor, as well as the original clubhouse, would have obtained their water from wells sunk directly into the mercury-contaminated aquifer.

And, indeed, here was a file of the well permits. Pendergast looked through it. Each well required the testing of water quality—standard procedure. And every single well had passed: no mercury contamination noted.

Without question, falsified results.

Now came the sales contracts for the first houses built in The Heights. Pendergast selected those dozen properties in the contaminated zone in the valley for special scrutiny. He examined the names of the purchasers. Most appeared to be older, wealthy individuals in retirement. These houses had changed hands a number of times, especially as real estate values skyrocketed in the 1990s.

But Pendergast did recognize the name of one set of purchasers: a "Sarah and Arthur Roman, husband and wife." No doubt the future parents of Ted Roman. The date of purchase: 1982.

The Roman house was built directly on the site of the smelter, in the zone of greatest contamination. Pendergast thought back to what Corrie had told him about Ted. Assuming he was her age, or even a few years older, there was little doubt that Ted Roman had been exposed to toxic mercury in his mother's womb, and raised in a toxic house, drinking toxic water, taking toxic showers...

Pendergast put the records aside, a thoughtful expression on his face. After a moment, he picked up the phone and called Corrie's cell phone. It went directly over to her voice mail.

He then called the Hotel Sebastian and, after speaking to several people, learned that she had left the hotel shortly after her work shift ended at eleven. In her car, destination unknown. However, she had asked the concierge for a snowmobile map of the mountains surrounding Roaring Fork.

With somewhat more alacrity, Pendergast dialed the town library. No answer. He looked up the head librarian's home number. When she answered, she explained to him that December twenty-fourth was normally a half day at the library, but she had decided not to open at all because of the storm. In response to his next question, she replied that Ted had, in fact, told her he was going to take advantage of the free day by engaging in one of his favorite activities: snowmobiling in the mountains.

Again, Pendergast hung up the phone. He called Stacy Bowdree's cell, and it, too, went over to voice mail.

A furrow appeared on his pale brow. As he was hanging up, he noticed something he normally would have seen immediately had he not been preoccupied: the papers on his desk were disarranged.

He stared at the papers, his near-photographic mind reconstructing how he had left them. One sheet—the sheet on which he'd copied the message of the Committee of Seven—had been pulled partway out and the papers surrounding it displaced:

*mete at the Ideal 11 oclock Sharp to Night they are Holt Up in the closed Christmas Mine up on smugglers wall*

Pendergast quickly left his office and went upstairs, where Iris was still dutifully manning the desk.

"Has anyone been in my office?" he asked pleasantly.

"Oh, yes," the secretary said. "I brought Corrie down there for a few minutes, early this afternoon. She was looking for her cell phone."

# 61

The vile, rotting odor in the air seemed to intensify as Ted waved the burning stick about. The flames licking at its end began to die back into coals, and he pushed it back into the stove.

"Love is the Fire of Life; it either consumes or purifies," he quoted as he slowly twirled the stick among the flames, as if roasting a marshmallow. There was something awful—after his fierce and passionate ranting—about the calm deliberation with which he now moved. "Let us prepare for the purification." He pulled the stick from the stove and passed it again before Corrie's face, with a strangely delicate gesture, gingerly, tentative now—and yet it hovered so close that, although she twisted away, it singed her hair.

Corrie tried to gain control of her galloping panic. She had to reach him, talk him out of this. Her mouth was dry, and it was hard to articulate words through her haze of pain and fear. "Ted, I liked you. I mean I *like* you. I really do." She swallowed. "Look, let me go and I'll forget all about this. We'll go out. Have a beer. Just like before."

"Right. Sure. You'd say anything now." Ted began to laugh, a crazy, quiet laugh.

She pulled against the cuff, but it was tight around her wrist, securely fastened to the pipe. "You won't get in trouble. I won't tell anyone. We'll forget all about this."

Ted did not reply. He pulled the burning brand away, inspected it closely, as one would a tool prior to putting it to use.

"We had good times, Ted, and we can have more. You don't have to do this. I'm not like those others, I'm just a poor student, I have to wash dishes at the Hotel Sebastian just to pay for my room!" She sobbed, caught herself. "Please don't hurt me."

"You need to calm down, Corrie, and accept your fate. It will be by fire—purifying fire. It will cleanse you of your sins. You should thank me, Corrie. I'm giving you a chance to atone for what you did. You'll suffer, and for that I'm sorry—but it's for the best."

The horror of it, the certainty that Ted was telling the truth, closed her throat.

He stepped back, looked around. "I used to play

in all these tunnels as a kid." His voice was different now—it was sorrowful, like one about to perform a necessary but distasteful service. "I knew every inch of these mine buildings up here. I know all this like the back of my hand. This is my childhood, right here. This is where it began, and this is where it will end. That door you came out of? That was the entrance to my playground. Those mines—they were a *magical* playground."

His tone became freighted with nostalgia, and Corrie had a momentary hope. But then, with terrible rapidity, his demeanor changed utterly. "And *look what they did!*" This came out as a scream. "Look! This was a nice town once. Friendly. Everyone mingled. Now it's a fucking tourist trap for billionaires...billionaires and all their toadies, bootlickers, lackeys. People like you! *You...!*" His voice echoed in the dim space, temporarily drowning out the sound of the storm, the wind, the groaning timbers.

Corrie began to realize, with a kind of awful finality, that nothing she could say would have any effect.

As quickly as it had come, the fit passed again. Ted fell abruptly silent. A tear welled up in one eye, trickled slowly down his cheek. He picked up the gun from the table and snugged it into his waistband. Without looking at her, he turned sharply on his heel and strode away, out of her vision, into a dark area behind the pump engine. Now all she could see was the burning end of his stick, dancing and floating in the darkness, slowly dwindling, until it, too, disappeared.

She waited. All was silent. Had he left? She could hardly believe it. Hope came rushing back. Where had he gone? She looked around, straining to see in the darkness. Nothing.

But no—it was too good to be true. He hadn't really left. He had to be around somewhere.

And then she smelled a faint whiff of smoke. From the woodstove? No. She strained, peering this way and that into the darkness, the pain in her hand, ribs, and ankle suddenly forgotten. There was more smoke—and then, abruptly, a whole lot more. And now she could see a reddish glow from the far side of the pump engine.

"Ted!"

A gout of flame suddenly appeared out of the blackness, and then another, snaking up the far wall, spreading wildly.

Ted had set the old building on fire.

Corrie cried out, struggled afresh with the handcuffs. The flames mounted upward with terrible speed, great clouds of acrid smoke roiling up. A roar grew in intensity, until it was so ferocious it was a vibration in the air itself. She felt the sudden heat on her face.

It had all happened in mere seconds.

"No! *No!*" she screamed. And then, through her wild cries, she saw Ted's tall figure framed in the doorway to the dingy room from which she'd first emerged. She could see the open door to the Sally Goodin Mine, the dewatering tunnel running away into darkness. He was standing absolutely still, staring at the fire, waiting; and as it grew brighter and stronger she could see the expression on his face: one of pure, unmitigated excitement.

Corrie squeezed her eyes closed for a moment, prayed—prayed for the first time in her life—for a quick and merciful end.

And then, as the flames began to lick up all around, consuming the wooden building on all sides, bringing with them unbearable heat, Ted turned and vanished into the mountain.

The flames roared all around Corrie, so loudly that she couldn't even hear her own screams.

# 62

At three o'clock in the afternoon, Mike Kloster had pulled his VMC 1500 snowcat with its eight-way hydraulic grooming blade out of the equipment shed, getting it ready for the night ahead. Twenty inches of snow had fallen over the last forty-eight hours, and at least another eight were on the way. This was going to be a long night—and it was Christmas Eve, no less.

Turning up the heat in the cab, he let the machine warm up while he pulled over the tow frame and began bolting it on to the rear. As he bent over the hitch, he sensed a presence behind him. Straightening up again, he turned to see a bizarre figure approaching, bundled up in a black coat and trilby hat, wearing heavy boots. He looked almost clown-like.

He was about to make a wisecrack when his gaze fell on the man's face. It was as cold and pale as the surrounding landscape, with eyes like chips of ice, and the words died in Kloster's throat.

"Um, this is a restricted area—" he began, but the man was already removing something from his coat, a worn alligator wallet, which fell open to reveal a badge.

"Agent Pendergast. FBI."

Kloster stared at the badge. FBI? For real? But before he could even answer, the man went on.

"Your name, if you please?"

"Kloster. Mike Kloster."

"Mr. Kloster, unbolt that device immediately and get in the cab. You are going to take me up the mountain."

"Well, I've got to, you know, get some kind of authorization before—"

"You will do as I instruct, or you will be charged with impeding a federal officer."

The tone of voice was so absolute, and so convincing, that Mike Kloster decided he would do exactly as this man said. "Yes, sir." He unhitched the tow frame and climbed into the cab, sliding behind the wheel. The man got into the passenger side, his movements remarkably agile given the ungainly dress.

"Um, where are we going?"

"To the Christmas Mine."

"Where's that?"

"It is above the old Smuggler's Cirque mine complex where the Ireland Pump building is situated."

"Oh. Sure. I know where that is."

"Then proceed, if you please. Quickly."

Kloster engaged the gears, raised the front groomer blade, and started up the slopes. He thought of radioing his boss to tell him what was going on, but decided against it. The guy was a pain in the ass and he might just put up a fuss. Better to tell him after the fact. His passenger was FBI, after all, and what better excuse was there?

As they climbed, curiosity began to get the better of Kloster. "So, what's this all about?" he asked in a friendly way.

The pale-faced man did not answer. He didn't appear to have heard.

The VMC had an awesome sound system, and Kloster had his iPod all docked and ready to go. He reached out to turn it on.

"No," said the man.

Kloster snatched back his hand as if it had been bitten.

"Make this machine go faster, please."

"Well, we're not supposed to take it over three thousand rpms—"

"I'll thank you to do as I say."

"Yes, sir."

He throttled up, the groomer crawling a little faster up the mountain. The snow had started again and now the wind was blowing as well. The flakes were of the tiny, BB-pellet variety—from long experience, Kloster knew every variety of snowflake there was—and they bounced and ticked noisily off the windscreen. Kloster put on the wipers and flicked the lights to high. The cluster of beams stabbed into the grayness, the pellets of snow flashing through. At three thirty it was already starting to get dark.

"How long?" the man asked.

"Fifteen minutes, maybe twenty, to the mine buildings. I don't think this machine'll get any higher than that—the slopes are too steep above Smuggler's Cirque. The avalanche danger is pretty extreme, too. They're gonna be setting off avalanche charges all Christmas Day, I bet, with this new snow."

He realized he was babbling—this man sure made him nervous—but again the agent didn't even acknowledge having heard.

At the top of the ski slope, Kloster took the service road that led to the top of the ridge, where it joined the network of snowmobile trails. Arriving at the trails, he was surprised to see fresh snowmobile tracks. Whoever it was, they were hard-core, venturing out on a day like this. He continued on, wondering just what the heck his passenger was after...

And then, above the dark spruce trees, he saw something. A glow, up on the mountain. Instinctively he slowed, staring.

The FBI agent saw it, too. "What is that?" he asked sharply.

"I don't know." Kloster squinted upward. He could make out, beyond and above the trees, the upper part of Smuggler's Cirque. The steep slopes and peaks were bathed in a flickering yellow glow. "Looks like a fire."

The pale man leaned forward, gripping the dashboard, his eyes so bright and hard they unnerved Kloster. "Where?"

"Damn, I'd say it's in that old mine complex."

Even as they watched, the glow grew in intensity, and now Kloster could see dark smoke billowing upward into the snowstorm.

"Fast. *Now*."

"Right, sure." Kloster really gunned it this time, the VMC churning across the snow at top speed—only twenty miles an hour, but plenty fast for an unwieldy groomer.

"Faster."

"It's pegged, sorry."

Even as he made the last turn before the tree line, he could see that the fire in the cirque was big.

Huge, in fact. Flames were shooting up at least a hundred feet, sending up towering pillars of sparks and black smoke, as thick as a volcanic eruption. It had to be the Ireland Pump Engine building itself—nothing else up there was big enough to produce that kind of inferno. Even so, it couldn't be a natural fire—nothing natural could spread so fast and so fiercely. It occurred to Kloster that this must be the work of the arsonist, and he felt a stab of fear, which was not reassured by the strange intensity of the man next to him. He kept the pedal to the metal.

The last stubby trees slid past them and they were now on the bare ridge. The snow was shallower here, due to wind scouring, and Kloster was able to eke out a few more miles per hour. God, it was like a firestorm up there, mushroom clouds of smoke and flame pummeling the sky, and he fancied he could even hear the sound of it above the roar of the diesel engines.

They crossed the last part of the ridge and headed up the lip to the hanging valley above. The snow grew deeper again and the VMC churned its way forward. They cleared the lip and, instinctually, Kloster stopped. It was indeed the Ireland building, and it had burned so fast, so furiously, that all that remained was a burning skeleton of timbers—which even as they watched collapsed with a thunderous cracking noise, sending up a colossal cascade of sparks. It left the Ireland Pump itself standing alone, naked, the paint peeling and smoking. The fire began to die as quickly as it had exploded: when the building collapsed, huge piles of snow had fallen from the roof into the burning rubble, sending up volatile plumes of steam.

Kloster stared, stunned by the violence of the scene, the utter suddenness of the building's immolation.

"Move closer," the man ordered.

He eased the groomer forward. The wooden frame had been consumed with remarkable speed, and the cascade of snow from the collapsing roof and the continuing blizzard were damping down what remained of the fire. None of the other buildings had burned—their snow-laden roofs were protecting them from the incredible shower of sparks that rained downward all around them like the detritus of countless fireworks.

Kloster eased the cat among the old mining structures. "This is as far as I'd better go," he said. But instead of the argument he expected, the pale man simply opened the door and got out. Kloster watched, first in amazement, and then horror, as the man walked toward the smoking, fire-licked remains of the structure and circled it slowly, like a panther, close—way too close.

★ ★ ★

Pendergast stared into the hellish scene. The air around him was alive with falling sparks mingled with snowflakes, which dusted his hat and coat, hissing out in the dampness. The engine and all its pipework had survived intact, but the building was utterly gone. Plumes of smoke and steam billowed up from hundreds of little pockets of heat, and timbers lay scattered about, hissing and smoking, with tongues of fire flickering here and there. There was an acrid stench, along with the whiff of something else: singed hair and burnt meat. All that could be heard now was the low hiss of steam, the crackle and pop of isolated fires, and the sound of the wind moaning through the ruins. He made a circuit around the perimeter of the fire. There was enough light from the many dying fires to see everything.

At a certain point he paused abruptly.

Now, moving ever so slowly, he stepped deeper into the fire zone, raising the scarf to cover his mouth against the acrid smoke. Winding his way among pipes and valves, his feet crunching on the cracked cement floor littered with nails and glass, he approached the thing that had stopped him in his tracks. It resembled a long, black log, and it, too, was hissing and smoking. As he got closer he confirmed it was the remains of a human body, which had been handcuffed to a set of pipes. Even though the arm had burned off, and the body had dropped to the floor, a carbonized hand remained in the cuffs, the fingers curled up like the legs of a dead spider, blackened bones sticking out from where the wrist should have been.

Pendergast sank to his knees. It was an involuntary motion, as if all the strength was suddenly drained from his body, forcing him down against his will. His head fell forward and his hands clasped together. A sound came from his mouth—low, barely audible, but undeniably the by-product of a grief beyond words.

# 63

Pendergast did not linger long over the charred body. He rose, a tall figure among the smoking ruins, his cold gaze surveying the burnt remains of the pump building. For a moment, he remained as immobile as a statue, only his two pale eyes exploring the scene, pausing here and there to take in some invisible detail.

A minute passed. And then his eyes turned back to the corpse. He reached into his coat, slid out his custom Les Baer 1911 Colt, ejected the magazine, checked it, slid it back into place, and racked a round into the chamber. The firearm remained in his right hand.

Now he began to move forward, a small flashlight appearing in his other hand. The heat of the fire had melted much of the snow in the immediate vicinity of the area, leaving puddles of water and even, here and there, exposed brown grass, now quickly being reblanketed with snow. He made a circuit of the ruined building, peering through the falling snow, stepping over the innumerable piles of charred and smoking debris. Darkness was falling, and the snow thickened on his shoulders and hat, making him appear like a wandering ghost.

At the far side of the devastation, where the flanks of the mountainside began to rise up, he paused to examine a small, scorched wooden door, which covered what appeared to be a tunnel entrance. After a moment he knelt and examined the handle, the nearby ground, and then the door itself. He grasped the handle and tested the door, finding it locked from the inside—padlocked, apparently.

Pendergast rose and—with a sudden explosion of movement—stove in the door with a massive kick. He grasped the broken pieces and ripped them out by main force with his hands, throwing them aside. As quickly as it had come, the furious violence passed. He knelt, shining the light inside. The beam revealed an empty dewatering tunnel running straight into the mountain.

He turned the light to the ground. There were fresh scuffs and various confused marks in the dust, both coming and going. A moment of stasis...and then he was suddenly in motion, trotting alongside the pipe as smoothly as a cat, his coat billowing behind him, the Colt in his hand gleaming faintly in the dimness.

The pipe ended in a low stream of water that interrupted the tracks. Moving forward, Pendergast came to an intersection; continued on; reached another, and then—trying to think like his quarry—took a right, where the tunnel abruptly changed slope and ascended steeply to a higher level.

The tunnel continued for a quarter mile, deep into the mountain, until it struck what had once been a complex mineral seam, perhaps a dozen feet wide. This seam almost immediately divided the tunnel into a warren of shafts, crawl spaces, and alcoves, the spaces that remained after the ancient mining operation had cleared out every vein and pocket of a complex ore body that had once threaded this way and that through the heart of the mountain.

Pendergast paused. He understood that his quarry would have anticipated pursuit, and as a result had led his presumed pursuer to this very place: this maze of tunnels, where he, with his undoubtedly superior knowledge of the mine complex, would have the advantage. Pendergast sensed it was very likely his presence had already been noted. The prudent course of action would be to retreat and return with additional manpower.

But that would not do. Not at all. His quarry might use such a delay to escape. And besides, it would deprive Pendergast of what he needed to do so very badly that he could taste the bile of it in his mouth.

He doused the light and listened. His preternaturally acute sense of hearing picked up many sounds—the steady drip of water, the faint movement of air, the occasional *tick-tick* of settling rock and wooden cribbing.

But there was no light, no telltale sound or scent. And yet he sensed, he *knew*, that his quarry—Ted Roman—was near and well aware of his presence.

He turned the light back on and examined the surrounding area. Much of the rock in this section of the mine was rotten, shot through with cracks and seams, and extra cribbing had been placed to hold it up. He stepped over to a vertical member, removed a knife from his pocket, and pushed it into the wood. It sank into the cribbing like butter, all the way to the hilt. He pulled it out and pried away at the wood, pulling off big, dusty pieces.

The wood was thoroughly weakened by dry rot. It might not be hard to bring it down…but that would lead to unpredictable consequences.

He ceased moving and paused, frozen in place, listening. He heard a faint sound, the tiny drop of a pebble. It was impossible, in the echoing spaces, to tell whence it came. It almost seemed to him deliberate, a tease. He waited. Another ping of rock against rock. And now he knew for certain that Ted Roman was playing with him.

A fatal mistake.

With the light on, acting as if he had heard nothing, unsuspecting, Pendergast chose a tunnel at random and passed down it. After a few steps he halted to discard his bulky coat, gloves, and hat, and stuff them into an out-of-the-way alcove. It was much warmer here, deep in the mine—and the coat was too constricting for the work that lay ahead of him.

The tunnel twisted and turned, dipped and rose, dividing and redividing. Many small tunnels, stopes, and shafts branched off in odd directions. Old mining equipment, pulleys, cages, cables, buckets, carts, and rotting ropes were strewn about in various stages of decay. At several points, vertical shafts sank down into darkness. Pendergast examined each one of these carefully, shining his light on the descending walls and testing the depths with a dropped pebble.

At one shaft, he lingered somewhat longer. It took two seconds for the pebble to hit bottom; a quick mental calculation indicated the distance would be twenty meters, or about sixty feet. Sufficient. He examined the rock making up the wall of the shaft and found it rough, solid, with enough adequate footholds: suitable for the purpose he had in mind.

Now, making a detour around the shaft, he stumbled and fell hard, the flashlight dropping to the ground with a clatter and going out. With a curse, Pendergast lit a match and tried to edge around the shaft, but the match went out, burning his fingers, and he dropped it with another muttered deprecation. He got up and tried to light another match. It sputtered to life and he took several steps, but he was moving too fast now and the light went out again, right at the edge of the deep pit; he slipped and, in the process, swept a loose rock off the edge, giving a loud cry as he himself went over. His powerful fingers grasped a fissure just below the edge of the shaft, and he swung his body down so that he was dangling into the dark void, out of sight of the tunnel above. He abruptly cut off his cry when the rock he had dislodged crashed into the bottom.

Silence. Dangling, he found a purchase for his toes, his knees well flexed, giving him the leverage he needed. He waited, clinging to the edge of the shaft, listening intently.

Soon he could hear Roman cautiously making his way down the tunnel. The beam of a flashlight flickered over the lip of the shaft as the sound of movement paused. Then, ever so slowly, he heard the man advance toward the pit. Pendergast's muscles tensed as he sensed the man creeping toward the edge he hid beneath. A moment later, Roman's face appeared, bloodshot eyes wild, flashlight in one hand, handgun in the other.

Uncoiling like a snake, Pendergast leapt up and grabbed Roman's wrist, yanking him forward and pulling him toward the void. With a scream of surprise and dismay, Roman reared back, his gun and flashlight skittering off across the rocky ground as he used both hands to fend off the attack and counteract the pull. He was immensely strong and quick, surprisingly so, and he managed to correct the sudden imbalance and dig in his heels, striking at Pendergast's forearm with a bear-like roar of rage. But Pendergast was up and over the edge in a flash, Roman scrabbling backward. Pendergast raised his own gun to fire, but it was now black and Roman, anticipating the shot, threw himself sideways. The bullet ricocheted harmlessly off the rock floor, but the flash of the discharge betrayed Roman's position. Pendergast fired again, but now the muzzle flash revealed nothing: Roman had vanished.

Pendergast dug into his suit and pulled out his backup light: a handheld LED. Roman had apparently launched himself into a narrow, low-ceilinged seam that angled down steeply from the main tunnel. Dropping to his knees, Pendergast crawled into the seam and followed. Ahead, he could hear Roman in panicked flight, scrabbling along the low passage, gasping in fear. He, too, it seemed, had a second light: Pendergast could make out a jerky glow in the darkness of the seam ahead.

Relentlessly, Pendergast pursued his quarry. But as hard as he pushed, Roman stayed well ahead. The young man was in peak physical condition and had the advantage of knowing the tunnels, their fantastic complexity only adding to his edge. Pendergast was doing little more than moving blind, following the sound, the light, and—occasionally— the tracks.

Now Pendergast entered an area of large tunnels, cracks, and yawning, vertical chimneys. Still he pursued with monomaniacal intensity. Roman, Pendergast knew, had lost his weapon and was in a state of panic; Pendergast retained his weapon and his wits. To heighten Roman's terror and keep him off balance, now and then Pendergast would fire a round in the direction of the fleeing man, the bullet cracking and zinging as it tore through the tunnels ahead. There was little chance he would hit Roman, but that was not his intention: the deafening roar of the gun, and the terrifying ricochet of the rounds, was having the desired psychological effect.

Roman seemed to be going somewhere, and it soon became clear—as the air in the tunnels grew steadily fresher and colder—that he was heading outside. Into the storm...where Pendergast, having jettisoned his outerwear, would be at an additional disadvantage. Ted Roman might be beside himself with fear—but he was still able to think ahead and strategize.

A few minutes later, Pendergast's suspicions were confirmed: he rounded a corner and saw, directly ahead, a rusty steel wall with a door in it, open, swinging in the wind, the sound of the storm filling the entranceway. Rushing to the door, Pendergast shone his flashlight out into the murk. All was black; night had settled. The dim light disclosed a mine entrance, broken trestle, and the plunging slope of the cirque, falling away at a fifty-degree angle. The beam did not penetrate far, but nevertheless he could make out Roman's footprints in the deep snow, floundering off into the storm. Farther below, through the murk, he could see a cluster of glowing pinpoints—the smoldering remains of the pump building—and the lights of the idling snowcat nearby.

He turned off his light. He could just see the faint, bobbing glow of Roman's flashlight, descending the steep slope, about a hundred yards to one side. The man was moving slowly. Pendergast raised his weapon. It would be an exceptionally difficult shot, due to the high winds and the added complication of altitude. Nevertheless, Pendergast took a careful bead on the wavering light, mentally compensating for windage and drop. Very slowly, he squeezed the trigger. The firearm kicked with the shot, the report loud against the mountainside, the rolling echoes coming back from several directions.

A miss.

The figure kept moving, faster now, floundering downhill, getting ever farther out of range. Pendergast, without winter clothing, had no hope of catching him.

Ignoring the snow that stung his face and the vicious wind that penetrated his suit, Pendergast took another bead and fired, missing again. The chance for a hit was becoming nil. But then—as he took aim a third time—he heard something: a muffled *crack*, followed by a low-frequency rumble.

Above and ahead of Pendergast, the heavy snow surface was fracturing into large plates, the plates detaching and sliding downward, slowly at first, then faster and faster, breaking up and tumbling into chaos. It was an avalanche, triggered by the noise of his shots and, no doubt, Roman's own floundering about. With a growing roar the churning front of snow blasted past the mine entrance. The air was suddenly opaque, full of roiling, violent snow, and the gust of its passing knocked Pendergast backward as it thundered by him.

Within thirty seconds the roar had subsided. It had been a small slide. The slope before Pendergast was now swept clean of deep snow, the residual, trickling streams of it sliding down the mountain in rills. All was silent save for the cry of the wind.

Pendergast glanced downward to where Roman's bobbing flashlight had been. There was nothing now but a deep expanse of snow rubble. There were no signs of movement; no calls for help—nothing.

For a moment, Pendergast just stared down into the darkness. For the briefest of moments—as the blood rage that had taken possession of him still pulsed through his veins—he grimly contemplated the justice of the situation. But even as he stared, his fury ebbed. It was as if the avalanche had scoured his mind clear. He paused to consider what, subconsciously, he'd already understood until the sight of Corrie's burnt corpse swept all logic from his mind: that Ted Roman was as much a victim as Corrie herself. The true evil lay elsewhere.

With a muffled cry, he sprang from the mine entrance into the snow and struggled down the slope, coatless, sliding and floundering to where the avalanche had piled up along the top of the cirque. It took a few minutes to get there, and by the time he reached the spot he was half frozen.

"Roman!" he cried. "Ted Roman!"

No reply but the wind.

Now Pendergast jammed one ear into the snow to listen. Just barely, he could hear a strange, muffled, horrifying sound, almost like a cow bawling: *Мииииииии мииииии, мииии мииии.*

It seemed to be coming from the edge of the snow rubble. Moving toward it in the bitter cold, Pendergast began to dig frantically, with his bare hands. But the snow was compacted by the pressure of the avalanche, his hands inadequate to the task. Without jacket or hat, the cold had penetrated to his skin, and he weakened, his hands numbing to uselessness.

Where was Roman? He listened again, placing his ear against the hard-packed snow, trying to warm his hands.

*Мииии...мииии...*

It was rapidly growing fainter. The man was suffocating.

He dug and dug, and then paused to listen again. Nothing. And now he saw, out of the corner of his eye, a light coming up the slope. Ignoring it, he kept digging. A moment later a pair of strong hands grasped him and gently pulled him away. It was Kloster, the snowcat operator, with a shovel and a long rod in his hands.

"Hey," he said. "Hey, easy. You're going to kill yourself."

"There's a man down there," Pendergast gasped. "Buried."

"I saw it. You go down to the cat before you freeze to death. There's nothing you can do. I'll take care of it." The man began probing with the rod across the rubble of the avalanche, sliding it into the snow, working fast and expertly. He had done this kind of thing before. Pendergast did not go to the cat but stood nearby, watching and shivering. After a few moments Kloster paused, probing more gingerly in a tighter area, and then he began to dig with the shovel. He worked with energy and efficiency, and within minutes had exposed part of Roman's body. A few more minutes of extremely rapid work uncovered the face.

Pendergast approached as the man's light played over it. The snow was soaked with blood all around the head, the skull partly depressed, the mouth open as if in a scream but completely stoppered with snow, the eyes wide open and crazy.

"He's gone," said Kloster. He put an arm on Pendergast to steady him. "Listen, I'm going to take you back to the cat now so you can warm yourself up—otherwise, you're going to be following him."

Pendergast nodded wordlessly and allowed himself to be helped through the deep snow to the cab of the idling machine.

# 64

Half a mile away, on the lower, eastern slope of the cirque, a metal door opened at the entrance to a mine tunnel. Moments later a figure came staggering out, dragging one leg, leaning on a stick and coughing violently. The figure paused in the mine opening, swayed, leaned against a bracing timber, then doubled over with another coughing fit. Slowly, the figure slid down, unable to support itself, and ended up in the snow, propped against the vertical timber.

It was her. Just as he'd expected. He knew she had to come out sometime—and what a perfect target she made. She wasn't going anywhere, and he had all the time in the world to set up his shot.

The sniper, crouched in the doorway of an old mining shack, unshouldered his Winchester 94, worked the lever to insert a round into the chamber, then braced the weapon against his shoulder, sighting through the scope. While it was dark, there was still just enough ambient light in the sky to place the crosshairs on her dark, slumped form. The girl looked like she was in pretty bad shape already: hair singed, face and clothes black with smoke. He believed at least one of his earlier shots had hit home. As he'd pursued her through the tunnels, he had seen copious drops of blood. He wasn't sure where she'd been hit, but a .30-30 expanding round was no joke, wherever it connected.

The sniper did not understand why she was up here, why the snowcat had raced by on its way up the mountain, or why the pump building had burned. He didn't need to know. Whatever crazy shit she was involved in was none of his business. Montebello had given him an assignment and paid him well to do it—extremely well, in fact. His instructions had been simple: scare the girl named Corrie Swanson out of town. If she didn't leave, kill her. The architect hadn't told him anything more, and he didn't want to know anything more.

The shot through the car window hadn't done it. Decapitating the mutt hadn't done it—although he recalled the scene with a certain fondness. He was proud of the tableau he'd arranged, the note in the dead dog's mouth—and he was disappointed and surprised it hadn't scared her off. She had proven to be one feisty bitch. But she didn't look so feisty now, slumped against the timber, half dead.

The moment had come. He'd been following her almost continuously now for thirty-six hours, waiting for an opportunity. As an expert hunter, he knew the value of patience. He had not had a good shot either in town or at the hotel. But when she had gone to The Heights, stolen a snowmobile, and taken it up the mountain on whatever insane errand she was on, the opportunity was placed in his hands, like a gift. He had borrowed another snowmobile and followed her. True, she had proven unusually resourceful—that business with the rattlesnakes back in the tunnel had seriously put him out. But he had found another way out of the mine and—when he discovered her snowmobile was still there—decided to stick around: He positioned himself a little way down the mountain, in the darkness of a mining shack, a blind that commanded an excellent view of most of the old adits and tunnel entrances up on the cirque. If she was still inside the mountain, he'd reasoned, she would eventually come out one of those. Or, perhaps, from the Christmas Mine, where she'd left her snowmobile. In any case, she'd have to pass by him on the way down.

And now, here she was. And in a good location, away from the activity around and above, where the pump building had burned and where the snowcat was parked. Someone had fired shots, which, it seemed, had in turn triggered an avalanche. From his hiding place, through the magnification of the scope, he watched the frantic digging and the discovery of the body. Something crazy-big was going down—drugs, he figured. But it had nothing to do with him, and the sooner he killed the target and got his ass out of there, the better.

Easing out his breath, finger on the trigger, he aimed at the slumped girl. The crosshairs steadied, his finger tightened. Finally, the time had come. He'd take her out, climb on his snowmobile parked behind the shack, and go collect his pay. One shot, one kill...

Suddenly the rifle was knocked brutally from behind, and it went off, discharging the round into the snow.

"What the—?" The sniper grasped the rifle, tried to rise, and as he did so felt something cold and hard pressed against his temple. The muzzle of a pistol.

"So much as blink, motherfucker, and I'll make a snow angel with your brains."

A woman's voice—full of authority and seriousness.

A hand reached out, seized his rifle by the barrel. "Let go."

He let go the rifle and she flung it out into the deep snow.

"All your other weapons—toss them into the snow. *Now.*"

He hesitated. He still had a handgun and knife, and if he forced her to search him there might be an opportunity...

The blow against the side of his head was so hard it knocked him to the ground. He lay dazed on the wooden floor for a moment, wondering why the heck he was lying here and who this woman was standing over him. Then it all started to come back as she bent over him, searched him roughly, removed the knife and pistol, and threw them far out into the snow as well.

"Who...who the fuck are you?" he asked.

The answer came with another stunning blow to his face from the butt of her gun, leaving the inside of his lips torn and bloody and his mouth full of broken fragments of teeth.

"My name," she said crisply, "is Captain Stacy Bowdree, USAF, and I am the very worst thing that's happened to you in your entire shitty life."

# 65

Corrie Swanson saw the tall, handsome figure of Stacy Bowdree emerge out of the swirling snow, leading a man with his hands tied together and his shaggy head bowed. She dimly wondered if it was all a dream. Of course it was a dream. Stacy would never be up here.

As Stacy stopped before her, Corrie managed to say, "Hello, dream."

Stacy looked aghast. "My God. What happened to you?"

Corrie tried to think back on all that had happened, and couldn't quite bring it into focus. The more she tried to remember, the stranger everything became. "Are you for real?"

"You're damn right!" Stacy bent forward, examined Corrie closely, her blue eyes full of concern. "What are you doing with these handcuffs fastened to your wrist? And your hair is burned. Jesus, were you in that fire?"

Corrie tried to form the words. "A man...tried to kill me in the tunnels...but the rattlesnakes..."

"Yeah. This is him." Stacy shoved the man face-down into the snow before Corrie and put her booted foot on his neck. Corrie noticed the .45 in Stacy's hand. She tried to focus on the man lying on the ground but her eyes were swimming.

"This is the guy hired to kill you," Stacy went on. "I caught him just as he was about to pull the trigger. He won't tell me his name, so I'm calling him Dirtbag."

"How? How...?" It all seemed so confusing.

"Listen. We've got to get you to a hospital and Dirtbag to the police chief. There's a snowcat about half a mile away, near the burnt pump building."

*Pump building.* "Burn...He tried to burn me alive."

"Who? Dirtbag here?"

"No...Ted. I had my bump key...picked the cuffs...just in time..."

"You're not making much sense," Stacy said. "Let me help you up. Can you walk?"

"Ankle's broken. Lost...a finger."

"Shit. Let's take a look at you."

She could feel Stacy examining her, gently touching her ankle, asking questions and probing for injuries. She felt comforted. A few minutes later Stacy's face came back in focus, close to her own. "Okay, you've got a few second-degree burns. And you're right: your ankle's broken and a little finger's gone. That's bad enough, but luckily it seems to be all. Thank God you were bundled up in winter clothes, otherwise you'd be a lot more burned than you are."

Corrie nodded. She couldn't quite understand what Stacy was saying. But was it really Stacy, and not some vision? "You disappeared…"

"Sorry about that. When I cooled off I realized those assholes had hired some thug to drive you out of town, and so I shadowed you for a while and pretty soon saw Dirtbag, here, skulking after you like a dog sniffing for shit. So I followed him. In the end, I stole a snowmobile back there in the equipment shed—just as the two of you did—followed your tracks up here just in time to see Dirtbag vanish into the mine entrance. I lost you in the mines but figured he had, as well, and I managed to backtrack in time."

Corrie nodded. Nothing was making any sense to her. People had been trying to kill her—that much she knew. But Stacy had saved her. That's all she needed to know. Her head was spinning and she couldn't even seem to hold it up. Black clouds gathered in front of her eyes.

"Okay," Stacy continued, "you stay here, I'll take Dirtbag to the cat and then we'll drive back to get you." She felt Stacy's hand on her shoulder, giving it a squeeze. "Hang in there just a minute more, girl. You're dinged up, but you're going to be okay. Trust me, I know. I've seen…" She paused. "Much worse." She turned away.

"No." Corrie sobbed, reaching out for Stacy. "Don't go."

"Have to." She gently put Corrie's hand to her side. "I can't keep Dirtbag under control and help you, too. It's better if you don't walk. Give me ten minutes, tops."

It seemed a lot shorter than ten minutes. Corrie heard the roar of a diesel, then saw a cluster of moving headlamps stabbing through the murk, approaching fast, pulling up to the mine entrance in a swirling cloud of snow. A strange, pale figure emerged—Pendergast?—and she felt herself suddenly in his arms, lifted bodily as if she were a child again, her head cradled against his chest. She felt his shoulders began to convulse, faintly, regularly, almost as if he was weeping. But that was, of course, impossible, as Pendergast would never cry.

# EPILOGUE

The brilliant winter sun streamed in the window and lay in stripes across Corrie's bed at the Roaring Fork Hospital. She had been given the best room in the hospital, a corner single on a high floor, the large window overlooking most of the town and the mountains beyond, everything wreathed in a magical blanket of white. This was the view Corrie had awoken to after the operation on her hand, and the sight had cheered her considerably. That was three days ago, and she was set to be discharged in two more. The break in her foot had not been serious, but she had lost her little finger. Some of the burns she'd suffered might scar, but only slightly, and only, they had told her, on her chin.

Pendergast sat in a chair on one side of the bed and Stacy sat in another. The foot of the bed was covered in presents. Chief Morris had been in to pay his respects—he'd been a regular visitor since her operation—and after inquiring about how Corrie was feeling and thanking Pendergast profusely for his help in the investigation, he'd added his own gift (a CD of John Denver's greatest hits) to the pile.

"Well," said Stacy, "are we going to open them, or what?"

"Corrie shall go first," said Pendergast, handing her a slim envelope. "To mark the completion of her research."

Corrie tore it open, puzzled. A computer printout emerged, covered with columns of crabbed figures, graphs, and tables. She unfolded it. It was a report from an FBI forensic lab in Quantico—an analysis of mercury contamination in twelve samples of human remains—the crazed miners she'd found in the tunnels.

"My God," Corrie said. "The numbers are off the charts."

"The final detail you require for your thesis. I have little doubt you will be the first junior in the history of John Jay to win the Rosewell Prize."

"Thank you," Corrie said, and then hesitated. "Um, I owe you an apology. *Another* apology. A really big one this time. I messed up, well and truly. You've helped me so much, and I just never really appreciated it the way I should have. I was an ungrateful—" she almost said a bad word but amended it on the fly— "girl. I should have listened to you and never gone up there alone. What a stupid thing to do."

Pendergast inclined his head. "We can go into that some other time."

Corrie turned to Stacy. "I owe a big apology to you, too. I'm really ashamed that I suspected you and Ted. You saved my life. I really don't have the words to thank you..." She felt her throat close up with emotion.

Stacy smiled, squeezed her hand. "Don't be hard on yourself, Corrie. You're a true pal. And Ted...Jesus, I can hardly believe he was the arsonist. It gives me nightmares."

"On one level," Pendergast said, "Roman wasn't responsible for what he did. It was the mercury in his brain, which had been poisoning his neurons since he was in his mother's womb. He was no more a criminal than were those miners who went mad working in the smelter and ultimately became cannibals. They are all victims. The true criminals are certain others, a family whose malevolent deeds go back a century and a half. And now that the FBI is on it, that family will pay. Perhaps not as brutally as Mrs. Kermode did, but they will pay nonetheless."

Corrie shuddered. Until Pendergast had told

her, she hadn't any idea that, the whole time she'd been shackled to the pump, Mrs. Kermode had been in the building as well, out of sight, handcuffed to the far side of the engine—probably unconscious after being beaten up by Ted. *Oh, God, will I take care of that bitch*, he'd said...

"I was in such a hurry to escape the flames, I never even saw her," Corrie said. "I'm not sure anyone deserves to be burned alive like that."

The expression on Pendergast's face indicated he might disagree.

"But there's no way Ted could have known that Kermode and the Staffords were responsible for his own madness—was there?" Corrie asked.

Pendergast shook his head. "No. Her end at his hands was poetic justice, nothing more."

"I hope the rest of them rot in prison," said Stacy.

After a silence, Corrie asked, "And you really thought Kermode's burnt body was mine?"

"There was no question in my mind," Pendergast replied. "If I'd been thinking more clearly, I might have realized that Kermode was potentially Ted's next victim. She represented everything he despised. That entire *auto-da-fé* up on the mountain was arranged for her, not for you. You just fell into his lap, so to speak. But I do have a question, Corrie: how did you undo the handcuffs?"

"Aw, they were crappy old handcuffs. And I'd tucked my picks into the space between the inner and outer glove when I was trying to pick the lock into the mine—because, as you of all people know, you have to use several tools simultaneously."

Pendergast nodded. "Impressive."

"It took me a while to remember I even had the tools, I was so terrified. Ted was…I've never seen anything like it in my life. The way he shifted from screaming rage to cold, calculated precision…God, it was almost more frightening than the fire itself."

"A common effect of mercury-induced madness. And that perhaps explains the mystery of the bent pipes in the second fire—"

Stacy said hastily, "Um, let's open the rest of the presents and stop talking about this."

"I'm sorry I don't have anything for anyone," said Corrie.

"You were otherwise engaged," said Pendergast. "And while I'm on the subject, given what also happened to you in Kraus's Kaverns back in Medicine Creek, in the future I would advise you to avoid underground labyrinths, especially when they are tenanted by homicidal maniacs." He paused. "Incidentally, I'm very sorry about your finger."

"I suppose I'll get used to it. It's almost colorful, like wearing an eye patch or something."

Pendergast took up a small package and examined it. There was no card, just his name written on it. "This is from you, Captain?"

"Sure is."

Pendergast removed the paper, revealing a velvet box. He opened it. Inside, a Purple Heart rested on satin.

He stared at it for a long time. Finally he said: "How can I accept this?"

"Because I've got three more and I want you to have it. You deserve a medal—you saved my life."

"Captain Bowdree—"

"I mean it. I was lost, confused, drinking myself into oblivion every evening, until you called out of the blue. You got me here, explained about my ancestor, gave me purpose. And most of all...you respected me."

Pendergast hesitated. He held up the medal. "I will treasure this."

"Merry Christmas—three days late."

"And now you must open yours."

Stacy took up a small envelope. She opened it and extracted an official-looking document. She read it, her brow furrowing. "Oh, my God."

"It's nothing, really," said Pendergast. "Just an appointment for an interview. The rest is up to you. But with my recommendation, and your military record, I feel confident you will pass muster.

The FBI needs agents like you, Captain. I've rarely seen a finer candidate. Corrie here may rival you, one day—all she lacks is a certain seasoning of judgment."

"Thank you." It looked for a moment like Bowdree might hug Pendergast, but then she seemed to decide the gesture might not be welcome. Corrie smiled inwardly; this entire ceremony, with its attendant displays of affection and emotion, seemed to be making him a little uncomfortable.

There were two more presents for Corrie. She opened the first, to find within the wrapping a well-worn textbook: *Techniques for Crime Scene Analysis and Investigation: Third Edition.*

"I know this book," she said. "But I already have a copy—a much later edition, which we use at John Jay."

"I'm aware of that," Pendergast said.

She opened it, suddenly understanding. Inside, the text was heavily annotated with marginalia: comments, glosses, questions, insights into the topic being discussed. The handwriting was precise, and she recognized it immediately.

"This...this was your copy?"

Pendergast nodded.

"My God." She touched the cover, caressing it almost reverentially. "What a treasure trove. Maybe by reading this I'll be able to think like you someday."

"I had considered other, more frivolous gifts, but this one seemed—given your evident interest in a law enforcement career—perhaps the most useful."

There was one gift left. Corrie reached for it, carefully removed the expensive-looking wrapping paper.

"It's from Constance," Pendergast explained. "She just returned from India a few days ago, and asked me to give you this."

Inside was an antique Waterman fountain pen with a filigreed overlay of gold, and a small volume in ribbed leather, with cream-colored, deckle-edged pages. It was beautifully handmade. A small note fell out, which she picked up and read.

*Dear Miss Swanson,*

*I have read with interest some of your online "blogs" (hateful word). I thought that perhaps you might find indulging in a more permanent and private expression of your observations to be a useful occupation. I myself have kept a diary for many years. It has always been a source to me of interest, consolation, and personal insight. It is my hope this slight volume will help confer those same benefits on you.*

*Constance Greene*

Corrie looked at the presents scattered around her. Then she glanced at Stacy, seated on the edge of the bed, and Pendergast, relaxing in his chair, one leg thrown lightly over the other. All of a sudden, to her great surprise, she burst into tears.

"Corrie!" Stacy said, leaping to her feet. "What's wrong? Are you in pain?"

"No," Corrie said through her tears. "I'm not in pain. I'm just happy—so happy. I've never had a happier Christmas."

"Three days late," Pendergast murmured, with a twitch of his facial features that might have indicated a smile.

"And there's nobody on earth I'd rather share it with than you two." Corrie furiously brushed away the tears and, embarrassed, turned to look out the window, where the morning sun was gilding Roaring Fork, the low flanks of the mountains, and—farther up—the bowl-like shape of Smuggler's Cirque and the small, dark smudge against the snow where a fire had almost ended her life.

She tapped the journal. "I already know what my first entry will be," she said.

# Acknowledgments

We'd like to thank the following for their support and assistance: Mitch Hoffman, Eric Simonoff, Jamie Raab, Lindsey Rose, Claudia Rülke, Nadine Waddell, Jon Lellenberg, Saul Cohen, and the Estate of Sir Arthur Conan Doyle.

We salute the most excellent work of the Baker Street Irregulars.

And we apologize in advance for any liberties taken with Kielder Forest, *Queen's Quorum*, Hampstead Heath, and any other places or entities mentioned in *White Fire*.

# About the Authors

**DOUGLAS PRESTON** and **LINCOLN CHILD** are coauthors of many bestselling novels, including *Relic*, which was made into a number one box office hit movie, as well as *The Cabinet of Curiosities*, *Still Life with Crows*, *Brimstone*, *The Book of the Dead*, *Fever Dream*, and *Gideon's Sword*. Preston's bestselling nonfiction book, *The Monster of Florence*, is being made into a motion picture starring George Clooney. His interests include horses, scuba diving, skiing, and exploring the Maine coast in an old lobster boat. Lincoln Child is a former book editor who has published four bestselling novels of his own. He is passionate about motorcycles, exotic parrots, and nineteenth-century English literature. Readers can sign up for *The Pendergast File*, a monthly "strangely entertaining note" from the authors, at their website, www.prestonchild.com. The authors welcome visitors to their alarmingly active Facebook page, where they post regularly.